# FORSAKEN

D1566532

Every Shadow Lifted Series
Book Two

# FORSAKEN

## Ellie Maureen

ISBN 978-1-7379029-2-8

*To Deorc,*
*I know everyone is gonna hate you so much more than I do.*

# CONTENTS

# PRONUNCIATION GUIDE

Arokno– ah-roke-no

Bahram– ba-RAM

Berabo– BEAR-ah-boe

Cassabree– cass-SAW-bree

Dalmatia– dal-may-sha

Deorc– dee-ork

Gadferlin– gad-fur-lynn

Jaci– jay-see

Isi– iz-ee

Kyjar– key-yar

Py'aoka– pie-ah-OAK-ah

Mato– mah-toe

Mboi Tata– mm-boy tat-ah

Mbyja– mm-BY-ya

Tykaraijre– ta-car-ah-EE-ray

Wilu– will-oo

Ygary– ya-GAR-ee

# PART ONE

## THE EMERALD WILDERNESS

*For we do not struggle against flesh and blood, but against principalities, against powers, against the rulers of darkness of this age, against spiritual hosts of wickedness in the heavenly places.*

*–Ephesians 6:12*

Chapter — One

# SUNLIGHT

What an unbridled, strange place the jungle, running lawless and rampant, bereft of all rules, but doing so with such a perfect joy, like a carefree child with a wicked streak. Mystery and secrets awaited in each cast shadow, danger lurking like traps ready to spring under each tree, both colossal and willowy. But with tantamount (if not more) wonders to challenge these treacherous hazards, the canopied world would defy the beliefs of the most seasoned traveler. Imagine then, the senses so immeasurably overwhelmed of our two cave dwellers, crawling out of the darkness for the first time in their limited lives, their grey trained eyes blinking into a kaleidoscopic riot of colors, fettered lungs rising out of the musty stench into open spaces thick with wild things that made the nose tickle and the chest swell for more, ever more of this free air.

Kiara didn't believe that her eyes could ever grow tired of such sights nor her ears used to the way sound settled so much more restfully, finding its place in the world almost immediately after being heard. No more rattling off of walls, constantly begging for a second, if not third or fourth chance, like a needy child or a sore loser. Here there was contentment, peace in the enveloping warmth. Caught up in such wonder, absentmindedly, Kiara stroked each glossy leaf she drifted past as they continued their barrel ride down river. Ever since the rapids and the harrowing drop of the falls, the creek had been calm, unhurried after it reached the sun. She entwined her fingers in the splayed fronds of the low ferns, eyes roving over the great draping scenery she found so inexplicably easy to adore.

Starting out this next chapter of their journey with far too many questions neither could answer and countless thoughts of awestruck reverie, it was difficult for either Kiara or Hadyn to get their tongues to say anything at all. At length, however, their wandering eyes did happen to fall on each other. Matching grins crept onto their lips and an uncomfortable redness into their cheeks. Trance broken, they realized just how long they had been gaping without heed for anything but their own spellbound amazement. At once, they both attempted to break the silence, but only managed a jumbled jam of words, like sticks caught up in the creek. Kiara giggled and Hadyn's cheeks only grew redder.

"Go ahead," he said.

"Oh, it's just . . . Well, it's not really something I can put into words," she said, but with the way he smiled at her, she knew she didn't have to.

His left lid drooped more than usual, and she thought it no wonder that he was tired, not with the amount of times they had waved their hello's at death in the last twelve hours, especially him. His lips, still a little blue, reminded her of how desperate she had been to escape the cold dark of the tunnels, but not alone; together. She remembered the panic, not knowing what she would have done if his heart would have given up in that inky water. She didn't like it; she didn't like that she had even felt that way. It confused her and made her feel like she could shatter. Instead, she just tried to concentrate on how grateful she was to have him here, conscious and smiling.

She thought to hold his stare, gaze at that lopsided grin of his for more than the two seconds she allowed herself. Instead, she changed the subject. "Oh, but what were you going to say?"

"Somethin' similar."

She chuckled. "Oh . . ."

Turning her gaze back to the forest as they drifted along, she took in the quiet. "I wonder where all the animals are." Hadyn, just as perplexed, looked about, keeping his silence. "I thought it was supposed to be bursting with rambunctious life out here."

As if to reply in Hadyn's stead, something darted out of a covering of foliage and behind a tree, something dark and ill-defined. It looked large, but then Kiara had only seen it in a split second flash.

"Did you see that?"

Hadyn nodded, already scanning for another glimpse of it. "What do you think it was?"

"No idea . . ." She scrutinized the rows of trees, standing like fat columns in a great hall. The drifting of the river offered her new angles every few moments, but it seemed the shadowy thing had vaporized once caught in the light.

Kiara and Hadyn found each other's gazes each holding a deal of trepidation and uncertainty, and they did not speak for some time again, feeling somehow unwelcome in this new land. Time drifted as slowly as the river moseyed them along, and they began to notice a certain feeling of being watched, even though (besides the one flash of movement) they could spot for themselves no living thing. They felt alone yet under an ominous guard, as if by the forest itself. With eyes of its own and a great big held breath, it searched out and evaluated these intruders.

Kiara didn't like it in the slightest, like squirming under a scrutinizing gaze for an approval that will never come. Still you wait, even when you could free yourself, because something deep down inside so desperately needs to be loved and wanted, but when that something is broken and twisted, it rarely leads you to what you lack.

While the forest tested them, weighing them in encompassing, earthen hands, they meandered down the lazy river with far less direction than Kiara would have liked. The further they drifted, the further they traveled without any confirmation of whether they drifted to or away from her mother.

Something bumped her barrel, making Kiara jump and squeak. "Oh . . ." she sighed, turning to see a few more of the shipment barrels that had caught up with them.

Hadyn spun himself around and navigated himself over to the one that had bumped into her. Jamming his fingers around the lid, he heaved with all his might to pry it off.

"What are you doing?" Kiara asked. Hadyn didn't answer, face reddening from the strain, until the lid released and he flew back against the rim of his barrel. Kiara pursed her lips to stop from giggling.

"I could use a new paddle," he explained at last, beginning to untie the lid from its tether, "in case we run into any more treacherous waters."

"Ah, I see," she nodded unconvincingly. "I agree, this stream seems *very* dangerous."

Hadyn shook his head. "Think what you want. It didn't seem like we were heading for a waterfall before either."

While he worked on securing the new lid to his barrel, Kiara laid her hands on the one he took it from, peering inside to the shimmering stones. So many gems . . . and to be just tossed into a river. "Where do you think they're all going?" she voiced. "Just floating along like this, anyone could come by and pick them up."

Hadyn scanned both banks. "Except there isn't anyone. It's

empty out here."

"So why throw them out . . ?" Kiara's brow scrunched as she contemplated her father's mind. He did a lot of vexing, perplexing things, but this didn't make any sense.

Out of the quiet, a noise thumped in the distance, a heavy and continuous sound like metal hitting wood.

"You hearing that?" Hadyn asked.

Kiara cocked her head, eyes scrunching. ". . .Yeah."

They inclined their ears, straining to hear until they could make out muffled voices, shouts, and a great bustle. They exchanged wide-eyed looks.

"It's people . . ." Kiara said, almost breathlessly, because these weren't just any people, but people of the surface! And anything was better than directionless drifting. Hadyn, however, didn't appear as unquestionably giddy and scanned the overgrown banks for any sign of movement, his gaze piercing like a machete through the undergrowth. And just as they began rounding a bend in the river, his roving eyes found something.

"Get down!" he hissed.

"What? Why?"

"Just get down!" He motioned frantically for her to duck down into her barrel. "And put the lid on."

By the urgency in his voice, Kiara knew she should listen. Just before she shut herself in, she caught a split second glimpse of the bare back of a man with skin as dark as tanned leather. But then she knew only the shadowy space of the barrel and the musty smothering she would have preferred to never have breathed again. She sat uncomfortably in the water collected in the bottom of the barrel as the river carried them and wondered what could have happened to a person to make their skin turn that dark.

The voices outside grew louder and more frequent and yet, Kiara couldn't discern a single word. It all ran together, as understandable as gibberish. She jumped as she heard something hit her barrel, something heavy and pliable, like rope. But from underneath? It didn't make any sense. Her thoughts gave up on making sense of it rather quickly when she felt herself rising out of the water and into the air. She pressed her hands against the walls of the barrel and swallowed her squeals. She could hear the groans of wood and straining rope, but she didn't know why. She could feel herself swaying, suspended by something. Then she dropped, free falling for one sickening second, and slammed down hard on something solid.

She was out of the water.

She clenched her teeth to keep from groaning from the pain when she both heard and felt another mass slam onto . . . whatever kind of platform she must have been on. After more gibberish (which had never fully ceased) and unintelligible shouts, with a rough shove, her barrel was on its side. She slammed down onto the curved wall with a shock of pain to her right shoulder. Arching her back in agony, she began to think she'd rather not have to meet these people. Then, just when she thought it couldn't get much worse, the spinning started.

Unseen hands pushed her to some unknown destination, taking her little world and spinning it in a ruthless cycle, like clothes in a wash until she thought she would wretch. The rolling continued, mercilessly jostling her around inside the barrel. Kiara was certain every inch of her would be bruised by the end of it. She squeezed her eyes shut and made futile attempts to steady herself against the wall, which only resulted in more pain. She could actually feel the bile rising in her throat when, finally, everything stopped, even the strange voices sounded quieter.

She lay crumpled, unsure if every part of her was even in its right place anymore. She tried to listen and quiet the ever growing panic in her breaths. A loud crack split her ears as something jammed in between the lid and the barrel wall. Kiara flinched. The wood creaked and groaned as the lid was pried off. With a flash of light, Kiara could see out, but the world was upside down. She flicked the red strands of her own sopping hair out of her eyes and to her surprise she saw, through squinted lids, the sweet face of a small girl, maybe about five years old, holding a short, metal rod and looking down at her . . . or up it seemed.

Kiara craned her neck so she would be right side up.

The girl blinked a set of huge, doleful eyes, and Kiara had to give her head a small shake when she realized their earthy color. Brown eyes! She couldn't tear her gaze away from their beauty.

In her amazement, Kiara failed to notice that the little girl was just as shocked to see her (if not more so) until it was too late. Her brows furrowed together and her pouty lip began to tremble. Kiara braced herself for the inevitable.

"Wilu! Wilu!" the girl screamed and bolted from view, hysterically crying things Kiara didn't understand.

Kiara thought to crawl out, but every movement caused her pain. The voice of a young boy started to speak to the girl in a tone that told of his protectiveness and concern. The girl came back, tugging the hand of the boy, who wasn't much older than her, maybe eight. She kept crying and jabbing a pointing finger at Kiara.

The boy reared back when he saw her. Then, cocking his head, he asked, "English?"

Kiara nodded, thankful someone around here was understandable and reasonable.

The boy slowly, calmly knelt close to her. He picked up the lid of the barrel, watching her the whole time and with one quick shove, kicked it back into place, shutting her in the dark.

"Hey!" Kiara screamed.

The boy pressed his mouth close to the lid and whispered fiercely, "You value freedom? Don't make another sound."

# Chapter Two

# WORLDS COLLIDE

Another splintering crack and light shot inside the musty space, reaching piercing pin pricks. After being carried away on some kind of twisted ride yet again, at last everything but Kiara's head had stopped spinning. She feared it had been permanently set loose, her insides tangled up without hope of unknotting.

With one more heave from the outside, the lid flung off and Kiara was free again. The boy, the one who had shut her in before, backed away in a flash and braced himself for anything. The little girl was there too, peeking out from behind him, clutching a straw doll in place of the metal rod the boy now brandished.

"Why here?" the boy interrogated in broken English, watching her as if she might leap from the barrel at any moment, quick as a hungry jaguar. But Kiara lumbered out like a lazy, old dog with advanced arthritis, dripping and disheveled. Her cheeks filled with something terribly sour. She tried to swallow it down, burning the walls of her throat, but it was too late for that. She did her best to pull her hair back, turned away from them, and released what little she had in her stomach.

The shouts she heard before from inside the barrel had quieted with some unknown amount of distance. Kiara could still see the river, or at least some part of it a few yards away, but the kids had carried her off around some hedge, and there wasn't much to discern of her surroundings.

Gasping and wiping her mouth, she turned back to them and winced apologetically.

The boy seemed to relax, unclenching his fists and softening his expression. He stepped towards her. Instinctively, she pulled back, but to her surprise, the boy extended a hand. Her shock registered clear on her face, blinking at his fingers splayed not exactly in friendship, but undoubtedly in peace. Fear restricting her own movements, she reached back, timidly extending a dripping hand.

Without another moment of hesitation the boy took her pale hand with his dark one. Time froze. Kiara forgot to breathe or think at all. She had since seen life on the surface, but here was a new, incredible first in that she was actually meeting a part of that life, taking the hand of that world. The most jarring part? finding herself not unalike, finding the same fear, the same sorrow, the same worn out exhaustion of facing a cruel world that knew no bounds. Two kids from very different prisons, colliding in the sameness of their scars. It joined them (perfect strangers) like blood brothers.

The boy did his best to pull her to her feet. Both the children continued to inquire of her with their untrusting, searching, dark eyes.

"Why here?" The boy asked again.

Still a little shaky on her legs, Kiara lowered herself into a deliberate crouch this time, trying her best to just focus on one of them at a time. Unlike the sickly, pale creatures she knew as fellow humans, these two kids looked strong and capable, their tan skin seemingly thicker in appearance. Their individual facial features alone stood out to her as foreign and strange, but a beautiful strange. And she could not tear her gaze from their deep earthy eyes.

"Why here?" the boy asked yet again, growing impatient.

"I . . . I don't mean to be . . ." Kiara tried to speak, and the little girl cocked her head at her, now more curious than terrified. Her tangled and disheveled, black locks hung about her shoulders in clumps. "My friend and I . . ." Kiara tried again and her squinted eyes widened, horrified. "Oh no . . . Hadyn!" They cocked their heads at her in unison. "My companion, Hadyn," she explained, "he must still be in his barrel. Where are the other barrels?"

The boy considered her a moment, then nodded, beckoning her over to the hedge where he pushed aside some branches. Kiara realized he meant for her to look through. She bent low, squinting through the entanglement where she spotted the other barrels all lined up in immaculate rows, but her heart nearly stopped when she saw the two men going down either end of the rows. Both had a metal rod, much like her little friend, prying open the lids one by one, inspecting the barrels' contents. Any next one of them could be Hadyn's.

"Oh, dear god . . . Hadyn," she barely whispered, then turned to the children. "My friend is in one of those! We have to get him out of there!"

The boy didn't look worried, only contemplative. "We'll distract. You find friend."

"What? Really? What if I get caught?"

"You sneak," the boy said simply, assuming the posture of a stalking cat.

"And you two?" Kiara asked.

The boy crossed his arms and nodded his determination while the little girl at his side watched him, struggling to arrange her arms to match, until she crossed them just as stoutly.

A grin split Kiara's lips before worry took over again. ". . . Okay."

The boy took a step closer, touching her on the wrist. He met her gaze. "Must not let them see."

Breathless and eyes wide, Kiara nodded. "Right."

Without another word of a plan, the kids scampered off to their positions. Kiara watched behind the hedge as they started yelling in that language of theirs. She couldn't believe it. Whatever they said made both men stop what they were doing and immediately walk over to them. Kiara took a deep breath, knowing it was now or never. If they could be brave for someone they just met, then she could be brave for Hadyn. Shooting out of cover, she bolted for the barrels, never slowing until she was inside the rows. Skidding to a violent stop, she sat, back pressed up against a barrel and heart racing. She had done plenty of sneaking around in her life, but out here, in so much light, she felt terribly exposed.

She squeezed her eyes shut and took control of her breathing, gathering her thoughts for her next step, but it wasn't until she crouched within the actual rows of barrels that she realized just how many there were.

"One at a time, right?" she asked herself.

Curling her fingers into a fist, she grimaced reluctantly, thinking there had to be some better way to do this . . . Maybe not. She knocked lightly on the barrel closest to her. "Hadyn," she whispered. "You in there?" She waited before knocking a little louder. "*Hadyn.*"

Nothing.

As much as she wished to just check one and get him out of there, she moved on, tripping over her dress as she stumbled through the rows. She tapped out a soft rhythm on each barrel, calling his name as loud as she dared. Her foot caught on her dress once again and the trip landed her in the dirt. She could feel her frustrations rising. How was she ever going to find him in time?

She poked her head above the barrels to see how far she had gotten. The children still talked with the men, stalling beautifully. The boy caught sight of her out of his peripheral. Double-taking, his eyes popped open wide and he bounced his hand up and down to tell her to get back down. One of the men began to turn suspiciously, before the quick-thinking kid kicked up his volume, grabbing his attention back.

Kiara shot back into hiding as soon as she saw him turning, the boy's warning running through her head. Suddenly, she didn't want to move. What would they do if they *did* see?

She lifted the skirt of her dress as a stinging augmented into proper pain— fresh scuffs from tripping far too many times marked her knees and shins with an angry pink. She grimaced, but all pain was forgotten as she perked up her head at a new sound. A muffled pounding made her look left then right, trying to pinpoint the sound. It was Hadyn. It had to be.

She waited to hear it again and started crawling for it. She could hear his voice now too. "Hello?" he called. "Get me out of this thing!" He sounded so close, but the more she zeroed in the more he sounded like he could be in any one of the barrels.

"*Hadyn!*" she hissed back, unsure if he could hear her or not. She squinted in concentration.

Just as she thought she was almost sure which barrel he was in, the one to her left exploded with a violent shake, making her jump back and clutch her chest. Forcing air back into her lungs, a grin split her face. "Hadyn!" she nearly cheered then cupped a hand over her mouth. She scrambled to her feet, squatting at the barrel's side. "Shhh!" she hushed, patting the panels of its walls. "I'm gonna get you out of there."

Whether he heard her or just the taps on the outer walls, Hadyn fell silent. Kiara poked her head up over the height of the barrels, much more hesitantly this time. The kids had gathered a few more people, but none of them were looking her way. It seemed whatever they were telling them was causing quite the stir. Kiara dared to stand up a little taller. She flexed her fingers and jammed them under the lid, already regretting not grabbing one of those metal rods. As much stubborn will as she expended or how many slivers she endured, it wouldn't budge.

With a huff she stood back and smacked the lid, destroying whatever hopeless progress she had made. She wanted to smack herself for her foul temper, face blotching red. But, just then, a thought hit her. The barrel rows were generous, at least as wide as each barrel was tall. She glanced at the kids and the crowd they had gathered, then at the barrel.

"Sorry, Hadyn," she muttered.

Backing up as far as she could, she rammed the barrel throwing her shoulder into it and kept shoving until it toppled on its side. Muffled groans accompanied the drumming of the barrel bashing itself on the ground.

"Shh! Shh! Shhh!" She splayed her hands over the chaos, desperate for silence. She hardly dared to poke her head up again, but all seemed well; the others far enough and the kids animated enough to deem the ruckus unnoticeable.

Kiara got straight to work. Rolling the barrel, she navigated it through the rows to the quickest way out she could guess. She cringed, knowing first hand how it felt to be on the inside during such travel.

She paused when she came to the edge, peering out to check for anyone watching. The kids spotted her and waved their hands for her to get to their hiding spot. They straightened their spines in a flash, realizing the crowd still had their eyes on them. One of the men wondered what they were looking at, starting to turn. The boy grabbed him by the arms, raising his voice again. But locking eyes with Kiara, he jerked his head to the bushes, growing impatient.

"Alright, alright . . ." she muttered.

Having lost all momentum by stopping, she grunted and arched her back, stretching as far as she could to get the barrel moving again. She dug the toes of her boots into the earth, charging as fast as she could go, every thump inside the barrel another reason to cringe at the pain Hadyn must have been in. Then, with one last glance at her small accomplices, she vanished behind the bushes.

Finally safe, Kiara slumped to the ground, back against the barrel and arms limp at her side. But there was hardly time for rest. A crashing in the bushes made her shoot to her feet, limbs primed for anything.

Two smiling, young faces appeared from the bramble. "It's alright," the boy said. "Just us."

Kiara dropped her guard immediately. "Hey!" she smiled. "We did it!" Kiara clapped them on the back. "Well done you two. I couldn't have done that without you."

The children blushed, but even as she praised them, a muffled voice stole their attention and grins. "Hey! Let me out of here!" he bellowed, banging on the walls and lid.

"Hadyn!" Kiara rushed to swipe the metal rod from the boy, but he pulled back. "Hey, come on. We gotta let him out."

The boy's eyes flicked fearfully between her and the barrel.

"It's alright, he won't hurt you. Please . . . let him out."

The boy searched her eyes for a moment, desperate to know if he could trust her. With a nod he took up the metal rod and began prying the lid open.

"Thank you," Kiara said.

The boy had hardly even cracked the lid, when a pent up force from within shoved it the rest of the way. The boy jumped back, placing the little girl behind him again. Hadyn exploded from the barrel, sputtering sludge and water. He tried to stand and ended promptly back on his hands and knees.

Kiara placed a hand on his shoulder. "Careful! They're already scared. They helped me get you out."

At her words, he stopped struggling and focused on simply lifting his head. Water dripped from his curls and into his eyes as he stared at the frightened kids.

The young boy held the metal rod like a weapon and the girl, who had since relaxed, froze up like a statue.

"*He* your friend?" the boy almost accused.

"Yes." Kiara smiled disarmingly and patted his shoulder. "His name is Hadyn. I'm Kiara," she said, realizing she hadn't introduced herself.

"Sorry . . ." Hadyn said. "I didn't mean to scare you."

The boy remained stiff and uneasy, asking yet again, "Why here?"

"Well . . . because the barrels brought us here."

"No. Why here?"

Kiara spoke slowly, trying her best to match his fear with patience. "An accident. We didn't mean to."

"We've never been here before . . ." Hadyn added, slowly recovering once his world stopped spinning. "We didn't know where we were going."

"You from the city," the boy stated more than asked. "The city under the earth."

Kiara blinked at him. "Yes . . . how do you—"

"You have no orders?" he cut her short, confusion twisting his face.

Kiara shook her head, mirroring his puzzled expression. "No . . . no orders."

The boy lowered the rod and huffed a pent breath. "Then, what do you want?"

Kiara couldn't help the pity that filled her gaze. "Nothing. To tell you the truth, we are just as scared as you are." Both the children visibly relaxed. "What are your names?" Kiara asked.

"I 304 and she 312." The boy patted his chest and then the girl's head.

Kiara's face fell in a deep and sudden sorrow. "No, your names. I want to know your real names." Then, looking at them with such concern, she realized for the first time the scarring around their little wrists and the way their skin clung to their wiry, but bony frames. The exhausted, hope-depleted look in their eyes alone was enough to make her wonder how she didn't see any of the signs before.

She exchanged a sad look with Hadyn. He had begun to put the pieces together too. "You . . . you do have names, don't you?"

The slightest smile grew on the boy's face as if he didn't know if he was allowed to be happy. "Yes." He put a hand on his chest, this time in a proud gesture. "Wilu and this my sister, Isi."

Isi held her doll out. "Suni."

Kiara smiled. "She's very pretty."

Isi's smile exploded on her face and then she shrank away and hid behind her brother.

Wilu looked at them, his face shifting back to concern. "Why you 'fraid? What is wrong?"

"We're lost," Hadyn confessed, "and have no idea how not to be."

"Where you trying to go?"

". . . Some place the river is supposed to lead us to. Except we don't know what the river is."

"I can help!" Wilu said excitedly, thumping his chest.

"Really?"

"Is that it?" Kiara asked, pointing behind them to the water that had carried them here. "Is that the river?"

Wilu threw his head back with laughter, a wholesome sound like the sunshine they had caught through the trees, but just like the sun it was only a glimpse, a fraction of the joy he deserved.

"That?" He pointed. "That's a trickle! The River . . ." he fought for the words. ". . . You will know."

"But," Kiara pressed, "how can we find it?"

"The Great Road, point north . . . toward river. Follow that way," he pointed, "about four days walk."

*Head north until you find the river* . . . the vague instructions of her mother's letter strolled through Kiara's mind. When she still had no idea what north was, she had thought the river underneath Caverna might be what her mom meant. But realizing north must be a direction of the surface and that the river was still so far away, she grew dizzy again at the enormity of the world.

"But not by road," Wilu continued, voice darkening with warnings. "They see. You must go far away. You must not let them see."

Kiara fixed him with a grave look. "Who . . . are they?"

Wilu's eyes wandered to Hadyn and he swallowed hard. "The masters."

At that, Kiara thought she felt her heart crack. Not so much because of the words, but the way he said it; not like a problem that called for a remedy, but as if he feared it so much, he had succumbed to living with it.

Little Isi had snuck out again and caught Kiara's gaze as she stared so intently at her. So young and yet her hands bore the countless calluses and cuts of endless work. Innocence still had a place in her raindrop eyes, but there was already a knowledge of the cruelty of the world set deep within her gaze.

"Why is it this way?" Kiara asked and they both blinked their big eyes at her. "You're just kids . . . but your hands have seen more work than some of the oldest people I know. Why do you give numbers instead of your names?"

"We are slaves." Wilu shrugged. "It's what we deserve."

At his last words, that crack in her heart tore itself in half. Kiara knew right away, he was only repeating what he heard everyday, spoken into his soul until he breathed it as truth . . . because she had done the same.

"But you are people," she said. "Children . . . You're not any different from me or Hadyn. We're the same and we all deserve the same. Whatever anyone has told you, whatever the masters say, it is wrong. You are worth more than just your hands and labor, Wilu, don't you ever think otherwise."

"No one has ever said that . . ." He looked at his sister. "Not even *Ami* and *Abi* . . ." Wilu tried to be brave, but his hands trembled, and Isi's eyes welled with tears. "You truly believe that about us?"

Kiara took one of his small, trembling hands as he had done to her and stilled it with her own. "With all my heart."

Wilu said nothing. He just stood, broken like shattered glass. One tear dripped from Isi's eyes. Wilu turned to her, speaking softly in their own strange language and wiping her cheeks. Kiara felt like an intruder, eavesdropping on the tenderness of their bond. Then Isi rose to her tiptoes and whispered something to her brother.

Wilu gave Kiara a small grin. "She wants you to know, you very beautiful."

Kiara's cheeks flushed and she smiled. "Thank you, Isi, but it's *you* that is beautiful."

Isi pulled her shoulders up and swayed nervously.

"Truly," Wilu said, "we not seen any like you. We heard, ah—" his words caught in his throat and he cocked his head. "Unless . . . you are the Red Princess . . . the city under the earth."

"I–" Kiara shoved her hair behind her ear subconsciously, suddenly more ashamed of that title than she had ever been. ". . . Yes."

But instead of distancing himself, Wilu only grew more excited. "Have you come to free us?"

"Yes," she heard herself say and Hadyn shot her an uncertain look. "I mean, no . . . I–" Wilu's face fell and he seemed to stop breathing. "I want to . . . more than anything." She looked to Hadyn and her gaze stilled with a decision. "I will," she said turning back to the siblings. "But I have to do something first. Is that alright?"

Wilu gave her a brave smile and nodded his head.

Kiara searched both their faces, too many emotions tugging her features down. "If I had half your bravery, I know I'd be back even sooner, but I promise you," she placed a hand on one of both of their shoulders, "I will come back. I–"

The blast of a concussive horn ripped through the air and cut her promises short.

Isi shot behind her brother and Wilu's eyes widened. "You must go!" he said. "Before they see!"

"But . . ." Kiara couldn't bring herself to just leave them like that, so Wilu got behind her, pushing her forward around a bend.

"Go!" he cried, desperately trying to get them to save themselves. "Go, follow road! They must not see!"

It killed her to listen, but so adamant and upset as he was, it terrified her to think of what would happen if they stayed, what would happen to any of them.

"Use steps," he pointed to a stone stairway that led up a steep rise just a few yards away. "Safe passage."

"But what about you?" Hadyn asked. "Will you be alright?"

"If you stay . . . no. Now go! Before they see!"

"Thank you," Hadyn said, "for your help," but Wilu would not stop, even to receive the gratitude, and kept shoving them towards the rough stairway.

Only because they saw no other way, they began to climb; not to save themselves, but to save the kids. A fourth of the way up, Kiara turned back to see Wilu and Isi still watching them go, making sure they made it to the safety of the forest. With one hand, Isi clutched her brother's and with the other she held Suni close to her chest. There was such conflict in her face for one as small as hers. She was overjoyed that they were going to be safe and yet utterly crushed that they had to leave. She let go of Wilu's hand for a short moment to wave to them. Like the rest of the world just fell away and stopped living altogether, in that moment, Kiara saw only her. She could sense Hadyn behind her, waiting two steps up, but she could only see Isi and the space between them like her ever growing sea of guilt. Kiara opened her palm to wave, a tear leaking from her eye. Wrenching her gaze away, she forced herself to climb.

Further up, the integrity of the stairs degraded steadily, becoming little more than bits of stone crumbling and mingling with the dirt of the rise. Their feet began to slip as they scampered to safety so they used the plants and vines at their sides for handholds. Hadyn made Kiara go ahead of him and when she picked a plant with surprisingly weak roots and slid back ready to tumble down the steep rise, she was glad to have him there to stop her.

When they finally pulled themselves to the top, panting and gasping, they turned around to see the steep edge of the rise encircling nearly all the way around save for where it met the creek, the sheer walls dropping into a huge crater of a clearing.

"Whoa . . ." Kiara said. "I've never seen so much at once in my life."

But, of course, Wilu and Isi weren't the only people down there and as soon as they came to their senses, they ducked for cover in the thick plants and looked out over the vast valley. Hundreds of people worked and labored throughout, all strong and dark-skinned compared to the pale faces they knew so well. Because of the distance, Kiara couldn't be certain, but she thought their faces looked so sad and tired. Then she noticed the work pattern and how they all seemed to group, and with each group, loomed one man. He stood, watching, just idling. Each had a whip in their clenched fists and all had familiar, scowling, pale faces and black hair.

"*Slaves.*" Kiara half breathed in fear and half spat in disgust.

"And by the looks of it, Caverna's slaves," Hadyn said.

Kiara watched as they bustled about, never having time for a breath.

"Well, now we know where all our food and resources come from," she said.

"Oh, but, Kiara, Fleard supplies all our needs," Hadyn replied sarcastically, an indignant fire kindling in his eyes.

Kiara's gut betrayed her with a violent twist. "I think I liked it better when that's all I knew."

Grass and mud-roofed houses stood along the fringes of the valley, and an impressive towering contraption stood at the docks by the stream, draping a large net that must have been responsible for fishing them out of the water. A wide road running through the middle of the clearing hopped over the creek and disappeared into the distant forest.

"Look!" Kiara pointed. "That must be the road Wilu mentioned."

"Looks like we'll have to cross the river . . . or trickle," Hadyn added.

Just then, a troop of slaves, lead by a few whip-wielding white men, came trudging out of the jungle, over the bridge and into the valley. They carried food, wood and other resources on their backs and in their arms. A different group met them to relieve them of their burdens, and carry the resources to a storehouse for later use. The first group, like they had finally passed the baton of a year long race, collapsed and lay on the ground, exhausted from their trek.

One of the slave drivers pounced on them like a wild cat. "This will not be tolerated!" he shouted in blistering fury. "All of you, get up! There is no resting until your shift is complete!"

Kiara watched in horror as he started to lash out madly with his whip. Every one of them shot to their feet, some cowering in fear.

"He can't just do that!" Her indignation pushed her to her feet, but Hadyn pulled her back down.

"Hadyn, let go! They can't just treat people like that."

"Just . . ." he whispered. "Wait."

"Wait? I can't just let them do that."

Hadyn didn't answer, only pointed.

Throughout the vale, tall trees grew up in various places, reaching up some hundreds of feet, their boughs meeting and obscuring the blue sky. Wooden platforms wrapped around the trunk of each tree, where more pale-faced men watched over the workers from above. Instead of whips, these held something more suited for distance and far more deadly— crossbows, their arrows trained on their assigned group. They seemed ready to fire upon the slightest test of authority.

"If you think I like just sitting here, you're wrong. But what do you think you're gonna do?" He raised his eyebrows. "Hmm?"

She set her jaw and held his gaze with a fierce look, but she knew he was right. Kiara pounded her fist in frustration as she turned back to watch.

"Is your shift complete?" they heard the man scream. The slaves all bobbed their weary heads. "Then get to the houses, so you can be replaced!"

# FORSAKEN

They walked to the "houses" faster than their tired limbs wanted, fearing being whipped at a slower pace.

Kiara leaned forward on her hands, trying to see as the slaves filed out of sight behind a building. She placed her weight on a dry root that stuck out from the cliff.

"Kiara, careful!" Hadyn warned.

A brittle crack announced her impending doom and just as she pitched forward, Hadyn reached out with a last minute reflex and caught her by the collar of her dress. Yanking her back as fast as he could, they both fell onto their backs. There he went, saving her rash hide again . . . but Kiara didn't say anything. They had bigger problems. Though she might have been saved a painful, possibly fatal tumble through the dirt of the cliff wall, the same could not be said for the root she had snapped. It slid down the cliff, the catalyst for a minor landslide. Through the leaves and fronds of their hiding spot they could already see it had drawn the attention of at least one platform guard and the aim of his crossbow.

# Chapter Three

# SHIFTING SHADOWS

They held their breath as the guard followed the trail of dust up the slope and squinted into the forest, crossbow trained on their racing hearts. Laying paralyzed, the very breath in their lungs, growing staler by the seconds, they hoped he couldn't see them as well as they could see him. And only let out that breath when, finally, he shook his head and gave up. As if her respiratory system had sprung a leak, Kiara's chest deflated and her limbs grew mushy.

"We need to go," Hadyn said, and though she hated it, Kiara nodded. He helped her up, but they remained crouched until they put enough distance and foliage between them and the edge of the rise. Kiara winced as she finally straightened and rubbed her arm, starting to feel the effects of the nightmarishly rough barrel rides–all of them.

"Are you alright?" Hadyn asked.

"Of course not. Hadyn, I don't know if I'll ever be able to stop thinking about them."

"Right. I meant, are you hurt?"

"I'll be fine," she brushed him off. Though she could already feel a gnarly knot forming at the back of her head and could only imagine the number of bruises that would appear in a few hours, she couldn't think of her own body right now, not with the horrors she had just learned of.

She looked back towards where they had come from and bit her lip. "This is my fault. I was the princess. I should have known about this. They're just children, Hadyn. No child should have to suffer like that. Their very childhoods have been stolen from them. Maybe if I would have known . . . Maybe . . ." Words evaded her, not wanting to admit it. Her brow furrowed and hot angry tears filled her eyes. "Maybe if I wasn't so constantly busy wallowing in my own self pity. Maybe if the only thing I thought about wasn't, 'oh, poor Kiara. She's got it so rough,' maybe, just maybe I could've actually done something good for people in real pain!"

Hadyn stared quietly, not because he had nothing to say, but because this reply required some time to ponder. She swiped a yet to drip tear from her eyes and gave a bitter chuckle. "This is when you say, 'oh no, Kiara, you're not selfish. How could you have known?'"

Still, he didn't speak, fearing he missed his chance to say anything.

"You think I'm right."

"No, Kiara, of course not. Would you stop talking circles and just let me think?"

She blinked in surprise.

"Look, none of this is your fault. You were a child, same as them, when people started hurting you. Maybe you never questioned the way things were done, but did anyone else? That city, that dungeon, is a festering evil, and all of us, you and I, Wilu and Isi, your mom, *everyone* in Caverna, we're all victims of the same darkness.

"You may not know the pain of slavery, or to be unfairly used merely for your strength and labor, but the way we were living wasn't necessarily free. And you do know what it's like to feel worthless, what it's like to feel unlovable."

She listened, her mouth shut and her eyes flicking back and forth across his face, so Hadyn continued. "Feeling sorry for yourself gets you nowhere at all. I learned that the hard way. But you can't diminish your pain just because someone else seems to feel more. Because the moment you do that, the moment you decide there's no reason why your life should get any better just because others have it even worse, that's when you lose your hope, Kiara. And without hope, how are you ever going to help others in chains?

"Instead of separating yourself because of your differences, move closer to them, by using whatever ways you can relate to them to help them."

He stated it like it was somehow simple, so Kiara responded with a simple question. "How?"

He smiled at her. "I know you'll find a way. You already did. What you said meant more to their little hearts than anything you could have given them. I know I can't help them. If I did what I wanted . . ." he stopped. "Well, I won't tell you what I wanted to do." He looked away and Kiara saw an oddly familiar look of guilt creep into his gaze. "Let's just say I would have ended up just as enchained if not worse." He met her gaze once more with bright hope. "But you can. You're their princess."

"No," she said. "No, I'm not. They deserve to be free. I would not rule them for a moment, unless it was to tell them one thing, and with those words I would set them free."

He smiled at her. "And that is exactly why they would follow you," he said, turning to make his way through the waist high ferns and brush.

She could do nothing but stare at his back as he walked away. She had never thought of herself as a leader. She had no great or commanding presence about her. She had always felt powerless in a crowd and though she was the king's daughter, she had very little affinity for ruling or status, now less than ever. She couldn't have cared less about that city or what happened to its people after her mother released them, for that matter. Yet Hadyn believed she could lead them, and somehow, he made her believe it too.

Hadyn threw a look over his shoulder. "You comin'?"

Kiara shook her head and trotted to keep up. "Why do you do that?" she asked.

"Do what?"

"Take the time to care. You listen to my broken thoughts and then turn them around until I see it differently . . . until I'm better."

"You would do the same for me. You already have."

They walked the ridge around the valley towards the road and creek.

"Well, thank you, all the same."

He smiled. "Of course. Besides, someone has to do it. We both know your temper is simply out of control." His tone grew significantly sarcastic. "Who knows what you would do to yourself if left unchecked."

"Ha, ha . . ." Kiara feigned a laugh, even though *she* felt, for herself, his words held more truth then he meant them to.

Heeding Wilu's warning, they stopped, yet some distance from the road, and turned themselves northward. They could just barely see the creek down the slope and through the forest, running lazily under the road and off to the distant right. Fortunately, the back side of the rise harbored a significantly more gentle decline, than the gouging drop into the valley.

Before heading down, Hadyn made a mental note out loud. "The road points north, so north we go, down into the . . ."

With a cock of her head, Kiara asked, "Green?"

Hadyn matched her lopsided grin with one of his own. "Into the green," he said and they began their descent.

They shuffled down the hillside, using vines when they

could and slowing considerably when they couldn't. Whatever difficulties were spared them in the grade of the hill were certainly made up in length. And in their struggle to reach level ground at the bank of the creek, Kiara began to properly notice for the first time just how hot the air felt. Certainly more open than the caves and yet it still felt roofed, somehow thick and sticky . . . very sticky. She could feel it on everything she touched, even her own skin.

But she couldn't focus too much on the heat, as everything around her, every sight, captured her in a constant reverie that would neither pass nor dull. At long last, she wasn't just dreaming of this world but touching it, walking upon it, and experiencing every piece of it. The thick foliage surrounding her, she drank in their smells and continued to test the way each leaf danced, pliable and moved even by the wind. If all this beauty came with it, she'd take the heat, calling even her discomfort wonderful.

She wiped the back of her sleeve across her brow as they, at last, came up on the edge of the creek. Kiara felt like she could count on her hands the number of times she had broken a sweat in her life, though she had been steadily running out of fingers ever since she had committed to this . . . well, she didn't really know what to call it.

"Hadyn?" she said. "What is this? What is this we're doing?" He looked at her curiously. "I mean, is it a quest? Simply a journey?"

Finally, he understood. "Well, I suppose you could call it an adventure."

Kiara pondered that. "An adventure. Yeah!" She grinned wide. "You're right!"

She took her first steps into the creek. The cool water washed up her legs as she waded deeper and refreshed what weariness she had already acquired. She waded till the water was at her chest and dunked her head under, cooling her scalp and sweaty brow. When she surfaced again, the light refracting of the water made her blink and squint. Rays from a small skylight in the canopy shimmered on the surface in a way that made her feel at peace just watching it. Swimming to the other side, she watched the way it reflected on the shadowed parts of the bank. Her firelight had comforted, but this subtle shifting of a light show created peace, imparting her with a joy simply for the immediate breath in her lungs, no contingencies attached. Such a rare gift, she wished she could bottle it up and save it for whenever she slipped, whenever she was too full of fear to hold on to the present.

Safely away from the slave camp, Hadyn felt the need to

recall a certain decision. "That barrel lid sure came in handy . . ."

Kiara hesitated to acknowledge the comment. "Why do I get the feeling you want me to say something?"

"Hmmm," he pondered. "How about, 'Gee, Hadyn, that was pretty quick thinking.'"

Kiara chuckled. "You didn't even grab it for that; you got it for rapids."

"So? It still saved our lives. Someone would have recognized you for sure, and then where would we be?"

Kiara felt her chest seize up. Where would she be? Drug back to her father, under his dark gaze, so much worse off than she was before. That dreadful fear threatened to sweep back over her. Why did she feel like she hadn't yet escaped?

"You alright?" Hadyn asked.

She shook her head, giving him a playful shove. "Of course," she said, and he sent her a splash in return.

Together, they sloshed through to the other side of the creek, still relishing the welcome cool down from their ridge running. Then pulling themselves out onto the muddy northern bank, Kiara cast one last longing look over her shoulder at the peaceful creek and set her feet into the forest, where they came to a true understory. A felled emergent tree left a gap in the canopy. The light pouring in fed plants and foliage so they grew so thick, they couldn't see a foot past their noses. It took only one fat leaf swinging back and smacking her in the face to make Kiara reconsider her thought of loving *everything* about the forest. She gave a cry and blinked astonishingly at the thing as if questioning how it could be so rude. Hadyn chuckled, but tried his best to suppress his grins, realizing she was quite serious.

"Here let me help," he said, but with the density of the leaves and branches to hold back at once, too many would slip through their hands, slapping them like a boomerang on the way back. It wasn't long before frustrated sighs and growls were frequently escaping Kiara's mouth, absolutely certain she had had her fill of bushwhacking to last a lifetime. Her heavy dress, freshly soaked from the creek, kept catching on branches and sticks. But she would not dare tear it shorter, unyielding in her unwillingness to bear such a breach in propriety.

Eventually the thick flora ran out of light to support such rampaging growth, the sudden sparsity causing Kiara to trade in her grumbling for a gasp of amazement. Like bursting forth from a blind fog only to find yourself in an equally grey wasteland, they could find nothing of directional value, just green, endless, dizzying swaths of it, stretching around them on all sides.

Kiara didn't know what she thought they'd find. But this? This intimidating expanse of unwalked, uncharted . . . unknownness? An impassable wall would have been a more welcome sight. At least she had experience with obstacles in her way, but this mystery . . . It was beautiful. It beckoned her. It fascinated her. And most of all, it terrified her. She twirled around until her head spun even when she stood still. With this ability to see, there grew up yet another problem— they had no idea where they were in comparison to the road.

Kiara didn't know why, but some wild part of her just wanted to run, in what direction, it didn't matter. Each way echoed freedom back from their endlessness.

"What are you thinking?" Hadyn asked.

She threw her hands up and slapped them back to her sides. "Well, we're lost, aren't we? And we're probably going to end up walking in circles."

He narrowed his eyes. "That didn't really look like a 'were lost' face. And anyway, we're not," Hadyn said, his head as level as ever.

"Not what?" she asked.

He chuckled. "Where are you?" He waved a hand in front of her face. "Lost. We're not lost. The road is that way." He pointed to his left.

"How can you be so certain?" she asked, almost disappointed.

"Because, when we were facing north before, the light came from our right and made the shadows stretch out to the left. The shadows are the same way now."

She grinned, astonished. "Have I ever told you you're a genius!"

He shook his head. "Don't think so. But you can definitely say it again."

"Not gonna happen." She started walking in the direction he had indicated.

"Hey! Come on. But what was so incredible about it?"

"Well, I would've never thought to look at something as seemingly invisible as light to guide me." She smiled at him. "Genius!"

"So," she began to ask, "we can't get lost?"

"I don't think so . . ." That, he didn't sound so sure of.

Playfully shaking her head, Kiara took two more surefooted steps north only to halt dead in her tracks with a gasp and one giant grin stretching her face. "Listen!"

"What?"

"You don't hear it?" Kiara gazed up and all about her, for the sound wasn't just in one place. It hummed all around them, readily replacing the silence as the new constant.

Hadyn looked about. Now that she'd pointed it out, he did hear it. "What do you think it is?"

Kiara had her guesses, but at the moment her heart and consequently her tongue found themselves arrested by another sound, something so high and pure it rang like a spring dawn, the melody playing like young things in puddles. Bird song. It made her ache and want to run forever at the same time. She wanted to stretch her arms out and take flight, or at least bound through the forest as free as that sound, but something held her back. So she stood there and pictured the divine creature responsible, gliding through the forest on crystalline wings, its eyes full and glowing with stardust.

Kiara turned to Hadyn. "Music!" she cried and there were tears in her eyes.

Finally, like the last handhold to pull herself up to the cliff top, she had it, the fifth gift, and what a view it provided. The last thing kept from her, the last thing forbidden, now unlocked like treasure from a sealed chest.

"It's music!" she said again and followed the sound into the tangle of green.

As they picked up the pace, ever so gently the forest began to wake all about them, the secrets once held so tight unfurling like butterfly wings from a chrysalis. Every color and facet stretched with a bright-eyed yawn and smoothed out its once esoteric crinkles with new and overwhelming wonder. They fell dumbstruck once more when the awe they were only just grasping soared to new heights. The buzz of insect wings rose to a constant hum, and a few darted past too fast to see, though that didn't stop Kiara from trying to chase each one.

Hadyn scrambled after struggling to keep up as she beckoned him to the trunks and bases of certain trees where the strangest and most wonderful discoveries could be made in seconds— colorful insects with shapes and forms their imaginations could have never conjured. There were new plants at every stop and even bright amphibians, hopping away as soon as they got close. Most times Kiara was off before he was finished looking, her wonder sweeping her up on energetic wings. It reminded him of chasing her around the Styx, and Hadyn smiled to see her so happy again.

They ate up every bit of sky they could find, eyes always checking the treetops for a break big enough to see through to the wide open blue.

Bouncy critters, high above, cried giggly screeches as they scampered through the canopy and bird song drifted to their ears like ancient melodies calling them to a long lost homeland. If the forest had held its breath before, measuring the weight of their merit with precise, piercing eyes, then it must have found the travelers acceptable, exhaling now with a contented sigh.

Hadyn followed after Kiara until he felt like he fought for each breath. He doubled over, leaning on his knees. "Wait, wait," he called. "Let's take a break."

"Right." She turned, panting just about as hard. "This traveling stuff is harder than I would have thought," she said, leaning over now too.

Hadyn leaned against a thick tree. "And I could do without this heat. Who knew the surface would be so much hotter?"

Kiara lifted her head with a chuckle, her yet damp curls hanging in her eyes. "It's not so bad, but do you really think it will take us four days to get to the river?"

"At our pace? Who knows."

"Are you calling us slow?"

Hadyn gave her a tired grin, but it faded quickly. "No matter how long it takes us, sooner rather than later, we should start thinking about food and water . . ." he trailed off like he'd rather not be the one to talk of such necessary but unpleasant reason.

"I know," she agreed. "I'm hungry already. I wish we could have saved the food Cida packed for us. It feels like such a waste."

A foreign sound broke their silence and gloom, a muffled, low pitched hoot that they could not ignore. Kiara's eyes lit with a glowing grin as she met Hadyn's confused gaze. The hoot sounded again and she scanned the tree branches to find a curious little bird proudly perched on a skinny twig.

"Hadyn, look!" she gasped.

The bird didn't even open its beak to make its call. Sounding warmly from deep in its throat, the hoot gave it a peaceful and confiding nature. The bird lighted off the branch and glided to one closer to them, cocking its head to examine them. The very first bird Kiara's eyes beheld and noticed in full detail had burnt orange feathers that lined its neck, breast, and belly and a tapered, black beak. Light blue lit up its crown like electricity and lined a black mask around its eyes. Its long tail ended in just two, strange feathers that dangled from what looked like strings.

Of course, you and I, and the educated naturalist in Kiara know this bird as the exceptionally beautiful blue-crowned motmot, but too the sunlight-deprived cave dweller inside her, it was a creature of legend, one of the great lords of the sky, the very same creatures she had spent childhood hours running about her room, arms outstretched, just to feel a breeze on her face, her greatest hope, to one day join them in flight.

"Incredible . . ." Hadyn whispered.

"How majestic!" Kiara breathed in reverence and then said softly, "Hello there, girl."

The motmot seemed to puff out its feathers illustriously as her admirers gaped.

"How do you know it's a girl?" Hadyn whispered.

Kiara couldn't take her eyes off the motmot. "I just do."

"But, I thought with birds, males are the colorful ones and the females are duller so they can better protect the eggs."

"Someone was paying attention when studying," she praised. "You're right, but with the motmots they look the same."

While they watched, imaginations and hearts so raptly captured, another (slightly bigger) motmot gave a low hoot and swooped onto the branch right next to her.

Kiara gasped with delight. "There. You see?"

Hadyn smiled and they continued to watch the pair, following them with their eyes as they hopped and flapped from tree to tree. They could have observed them all day and not grown tired of it, but the birds decided that it was time to get on with their day, gave a last goodbye hoot, and flapped off.

Kiara sighed wistfully. "What a wonderful world this is." She turned to Hadyn, and put her fists on her hips. "So, which way is north?"

When Hadyn looked at her he had to suck in a sudden breath. Turning his mouth down, he did his best not to grin.

Her brows scrunched in alarm. "What is it?"

"Nothing," he said quickly.

Kiara's shoulders slumped in short-fused exasperation. "What!" she spat.

He bit his lip and shrugged. "Nothing! . . . Nothing at all."

Seething, she looked at him sideways and raised her hands to her head. Her eyes rounded in horror as she found the start of her mane at what felt like a whole foot from her scalp. She gasped. "Oh, curse this hideous hair. There was already much too much of it to begin with!"

Snickering, Hadyn just shook his head. She huffed a fuming breath and pointed a wagging finger at him. "Try looking in a mirror, mophead! Just because I've got more of it," she said, trying desperately to flatten her curls with her sweaty palms, "doesn't mean you're exempt from," she wrestled all her wild strands into one hand, yanked them down, and tied them with a blade of grass she plucked from the ground, "whatever this is." She finished with her fists on her hips.

"Oh, but I . . . I think it's-it's-it's . . ." he shrugged one shoulder, palms raised, ". . . nice?"

Kiara frowned and with one minuscule snap, the grass blade broke and every wild strand, like disobedient children, rushed back into place, bigger and even more chaotic than before.

Hadyn doubled over with laughter.

"Mmm. Nice, huh?" Kiara mocked and started walking without him.

"Kiara, wait! I'm sorry!" Kiara stuck her nose in the air and didn't slow. "Here," he said, catching her. "Take this." He tore for her a loose fabric strand already ripping from the bottom of his shirt.

She sighed and tied her curls into a fluffy side pony.

"Don't call it hideous," Hadyn said. "It's you. Without it, you wouldn't be the same."

"Maybe I don't want to be the same."

His eyes grew sad. He wanted to say something, but no words came out and Kiara resumed stomping off.

She whipped her head back and forth. "Which way is north?" she asked again.

Hadyn went rigid, his eyes wide as he hurriedly searched the ground. "Oh, no! They changed! The shadows changed!"

"What? Impossible!" Kiara protested. "How could that have happened!"

She felt the panic take a hold on her, starting as a shaking in her hands and a tightening in her chest, as she prematurely condemned them to living the last of their days in an interminable green void. Then came reason fighting for a place in her actions. "Wait a minute. Calm down," she told herself. "Do you remember where north was before everything turned around?"

"Yeah . . . towards that tree." Hadyn pointed. "But what keeps us walking straight now that we know we can't rely on the shadows?"

Kiara looked up at him, bereft of ideas and searching for answers. "I don't know," she shuttered. "I don't know. The only thing we can do is try to go as straight as we can."

Hadyn nodded. "You're right."

Steeling their nerves and straightening their spines, they

started off again, their slower pace full of hesitation. Something about the forest seemed darker all of a sudden. The plants grew thicker once more along with their fears and the shadows. They stretched out farther than Kiara and Hadyn had given them credit for before, showing their true colors, taunting the travelers with the rumors of darkness in exchange for following and trusting in them as long as they had.

So warmly welcomed and accepted by the little motmot pair, their fears had all but dissipated. All that had changed now. In a blink of an eye, their confidence had been stolen and trepidation had taken its place, like how a thief would steal a rare precious stone from where it had been affectionately displayed and replace it with a hollow, glass counterfeit. Everything loomed over them, congealing into one dark being with an intangible but all-consuming scowl of judgment, making them believe that this place was not for them, that they did not belong.

Kiara's eyes skittered about to all the heavily leafed areas, each shadow a hiding place for danger. "How dark do you think it will get?" she asked. "At night, I mean."

"Well, the moon sits in a black sky, right?"

Kiara nodded, glancing up at a breach in the canopy where the blue had already darkened and there were hints of other strange colors.

"So, it will be dark," Hadyn continued, "but how much light does the moon give?"

"I'm not sure. And from what I've read, the moon isn't always there at night either . . ."

They fell silent, every sound of the deepening evening raising questions and hairs on the backs of their necks. Kiara stepped on a stick that made a particularly loud snap and left the ground with a squeak.

"Hadyn," she whispered, involuntarily inching closer to him, "I'm scared."

Hadyn glanced at her and then returned to scanning the forest with round eyes. "Me too."

Darkness was falling fast and each step they took in the suffocating shadows reminded them they were, in fact, unmitigatedly and utterly alone in a world they knew naught about.

Chapter  Four

# REST FOR WEARY TRAVELERS

K iara watched the forest as if it were a twice starved beast with a taste for redheads. The evening had only grown darker and consequently more hostile. But her wary vigilance could only hold its fists up for so long. Her feet began to drag and her arms hung limply at her side, that is when she wasn't swatting herself after another painful pinch. Unfortunately, after the forest decided they weren't half bad, the bugs had gone one further and decided rather promptly that they were delicious.

"Ouch!" Kiara swatted her arm, too late to punish the assailant. "Blast these insects! How do they get through the sleeve? I can hardly see them!" She scratched at the red dots on her hands, having started to appear only a minute after she felt the first bite. She watched Hadyn as he walked along without a single smack to his own arm or face.

"And what's the deal? They only hungry for spindly, freckled, redheads?"

Hadyn smirked at her. "Not sure," he shrugged, "but, I haven't felt a single bite."

Kiara huffed and rolled her eyes. "My head hurts. If we don't stop soon I'm gonna faint from dizziness."

"You're dehydrated. I feel it too."

"Really? I feel like I've drank my fill of water today."

"More like inhaled it."

That got a snicker from Kiara.

"But I think we should keep going," Hadyn continued, "while we still have light."

"While we still have light? You think we won't have any?"

"No! I didn't say that!" He put his hands up in an attempt to defuse previous implications. "I just think . . ." he scrambled for the words that would disarm her fear. "We both agreed we don't know how dark it will get."

Kiara gave a small nod.

"I just think, for now, we should cover as much ground as we can while we have this much light. If it doesn't get any darker, great. We can still stop, but . . . just in case." He brightened. "And who knows! We might just find some water."

She looked at him carefully. "What makes you so hopeful?"

"Call it . . . call it a hunch."

"A hunch?" She searched his eyes, her first mistake if she had wanted to win, realizing even as she did so that she didn't have to trust whatever it was he thought he felt; she just had to trust him. And she did. He'd been by her side through too much and had saved her life far too many times for her not to trust him.

"Okay."

Hadyn blinked at her quick resignation, but only gave her a small smile in reply, before turning and leading the way back onto their wandering path, both unsure if they even walked in the right direction. But, that desultory manner of wandering would soon morph to a desperate preservation for their lives. With the falling night, the deepening darkness emboldened the fortitude and mettle of certain watching eyes, mysterious things in their own right, and perhaps unwilling to yet show themselves.

Something shook the undergrowth at Kiara's right, as it shot violently away. She jumped and swallowed a scream. A chittering and growling crawled out of the dark areas, as the creature lurked about, remaining close. Eyes wide with fear, Kiara edged closer to Hadyn just as another burst of movement exploded on his left. They jumped in unison, but then the foliage stilled.

"What are they?" He wondered out loud.

Kiara's mind ran with all the most fear-inciting possibilities— jaguars . . . large monkeys . . . maned wolves . . . but perhaps they were none of those things, and something worse still. She caught a glimpse of one, shadowy and vague, not unlike the first strange figure they saw when they had only just escaped, and she didn't need any more incentive to run. She took off at a dead sprint. Hadyn followed fast on her heels, but so did the creatures, pursuing with fearless hunger.

Hadyn and Kiara stumbled over sabotaging vines and roots, nearly blind in the low light, while their hunters crashed through the understory, trampling any and all in their path. This only heightened Kiara's fear. Clearly they were faster than them. Why did they stay just at their backs, breathing down their necks? Were they herding them as prey to more members of their pack so that they could surround them with no escape?

Movement at their side came pressing in at their right, as if trying to make them turn away to a different path when, all at once, Kiara and Hadyn burst from the heavy shadows and into a sparser area where light yet fought for control over the day. A thick vine snatched both their feet and took them down, destroying all chance of fleeing. Kiara gasped to force air back into her lungs. If she was going to die, it wouldn't be from suffocation. She flipped over, certain she'd be overtaken by some horrible creature of the twilight, but all was quiet. Her eyes darted about as her breaths came short and fast.

Hadyn rose to a crouch, making his own survey of their surroundings, then helped her to her feet. Nothing moved except a large toucan, fluttering higher in the branches to find a roost for the night, sending Kiara's nerves into a frenzy once again.

She squinted into the dense forest they had come out of. "This doesn't make sense," she said. "Why would they just leave? Just give up? Almost like . . ."

"Something scared them off," Hadyn finished.

"Yeah. But what?" She shivered, turning to take in the rest of the area.

Here they saw a sight and their very reason for safety too. It seemed their mad flight had led them straight to the foot of a ponderous rock formation, stranger yet, there in its own deep shadow an old door marked its face, as if they could knock and find someone living inside. The door had an odd shape, the top slanted at an angle so one side was taller than the other.

Moving closer, they fell onto an obscure path of sorts, overhung with encroaching plants, but still very clearly leading up to the door in the rock face.

"How strange." Kiara cocked her head curiously as they padded up the path. Liana vines that had grown unchecked for years now entangled about its surface, giving it the appearance that the door had always been there, that it was meant to be there. In the fading light, it looked menacing, but in the same glance it had the presence of a small stronghold for some unknown, perhaps forgotten thing.

They looked to each other, none of their thoughts substantial enough to speak aloud. Every detail suggested abandonment, still they cautioned to approach. Hadyn, scanning the area, spotted a soggy and insect-chewed, wooden sign, almost completely swallowed by the jungle, an easy miss for less keen eyes. "Kiara, look!" he said and slowly removed the entanglement of greenery.

"What is it?" she asked, but now they could both see the painted words, faint and chipped by many years of rain. She could only read part of it; the other half was in a strange language she'd never seen.

Kiara squinted in the low light and read what she could out loud. "Rest for weary travelers." She looked at the door again. "But this old place looks abandoned."

Hadyn tapped the sign with a knuckle and it all but fell over. "Hmm, I think, here *was* rest for weary travelers, suits it better."

Kiara smirked at his attempt at humor, but it fell quickly as she caught a faint whiff of something undeniably scrumptious. The sweet scent filled her soul with warmth and with a deep inhale, she closed her eyes with a sleepy smile.

"Do you smell that?" she asked.

Hadyn sampled the air as Kiara had and gave her a pleasantly surprised look. "It smells like freshly baked bread!" He sniffed again. "Even better!"

"Exactly," she grinned, and with that mischievous light in her eyes she started her trot towards the rock face.

"Kiara, wait!" Hadyn hissed. He reached an arm out to grab her, but got nothing but empty air.

Kiara did freeze half way there; not because of his warning, but because a window near the door she hadn't noticed before began to glow softly. Small and round, the panes flickered with a warm light of a fallow coloration, making the once cold looking rock structure seem hospitable and inviting. She crossed the remaining distance and gingerly brushed the vines aside.

Kiara peered through the dirt streaked glass into a cozy room.

A home.

As much as one as she had ever seen. Wood paneled the floor and walls to cover up the cold stone. A lit fireplace, burning with a cheery glow now, illuminated the small room and danced flickering shadows across a stuffed bookcase on the far wall. Many mismatched chairs (Kiara thought they looked wonderfully comfortable) characterized the little sitting room, and a big, round rug covered most of the floor. Besides her mother's tapestry, it was the most beautiful piece of woven art she had ever seen.

"Hadyn!" she whispered. "You have to see this!" She moved so he could see the beauty of a simple home.

"Whoa!" He gasped. "Someone must actually live here then."

"Well . . . there is a way to find out." Kiara said, the glint returning to her eyes, and zipped away to try the door.

"Kiara, wait! Maybe we shouldn't."

She pivoted slowly on her heels. "Why?"

He sighed. "I don't know . . . I mean, we've known nothing but a hole in the ground our entire lives, and now you want to barge into a home, in a world we know absolutely nothing about?"

"Not barge in. I was going to knock. What, do you think I was raised by thieves or something?" Kiara bit down on her own tongue, but if Hadyn took offense, he did well to hide it.

"I'm just saying, we don't know who or *what* even lives here. Anything could happen."

"Yeah, well, I'm not too keen on hiking back into the forest with those monsters out there. It's only getting darker," she said, shoulders slumping and looked away.

Hadyn gathered a deep breath. He couldn't argue with that. "I'm sorry. I just . . . I won't let anything happen to you."

Kiara softened at his concern, and crossed the distance she had put between them. "At this point, I'm sure of that." She placed a hand on his shoulder and looked him straight in the eyes. "But just like you had a hunch which led us here of all places, I just have a feeling." She paused in thought. "I think it will be alright." Then she added with a smile, "And remember, we're in this *together*. We're watching out for *each other.* Right?"

Hadyn nodded his head. Kiara nodded back, her messy curls flopping in her eyes, and they walked to the door together.

Facing the door, Kiara paused with last minute apprehension. She closed her eyes and hoped against all that had gone wrong in her life, against her own nature, she hoped for good. Then, raising a fist, she knocked softly. They waited, listening to the undisturbed quiet. Exchanging a questioning look with Hadyn, Kiara stood there one silent moment before she tried again, a little louder, but nobody and nothing came.

"Maybe they don't like visitors?" Hadyn suggested.

Kiara sighed and turned away, but the noise of a turning lock, froze her in her tracks. Their gazes met with widened eyes, then drifted simultaneously to the door. They both held their breath as the handle rattled and then slowly turned.

# Chapter Five

# BARTHOLOMEW EBENEZER

A shock of white, wild hair; glasses; and round, blue eyes peeked out the door. And only after a great deal of blinking and inspecting did he come fully out, giving Kiara and Hadyn a turn to inspect him. A strange, little old man, he stood not much taller than Kiara, and to their surprise he had white skin. Though with their expectations so limitlessly void, they didn't know what they expected. More people like Wilu and Isi? He wore wide britches that looked three inches too short and a white long-sleeve shirt under a well loved, brown vest.

As he looked at them with searching but kind eyes, the silence started to get painful. He noticed. "Ah! Where are my manners?" he said at last in a voice also familiar to them. "My name is Bartholomew Ebenezer." He took a bow. "But you can call me Bart. And this," he turned around, "is my home, a rest place for weary travelers!" With a flourish, he gestured toward the sign and almost toppled over from shock. "Good gracious! Seems my front yard needs a good hedge trimming."

Kiara giggled. Bartholomew's "front yard" was nothing more than another overgrown piece of jungle.

He gaped at the mayhem of plants as if he had not a clue in the world how it had come to this. He waved a hand to snap out of it. "Oh, never mind that." He steadied his gaze on them. "Now, may I ask your names and where you are from?"

"Oh, I, uh—" Kiara clammed up, so Hadyn stepped in.

"My name is Hadyn and this is Kiara. We're just two travelers on our way to the river."

She gave him a look of thanks, and he smiled back.

Bartholomew did not look pleased. "Just travelers . . ." he muttered under his breath, putting his hand to his chin. He looked at them once more and sighed. "Not good. The King will know what to do."

"Sorry, the king?" Kiara blinked.

"But come along." Bartholomew didn't skip a beat. "You are weary travelers, all the same. Follow me!" he sang as he disappeared back inside.

Kiara and Hadyn exchanged quizzical looks as the strange, little man left them standing outside, the door nearly swinging closed again behind him. Kiara shrugged a shoulder, only now growing a little uncertain, but still wondering what the harm could be. Her desperate longing to see the inside of a real home fanned her curiosity until it got the best of her. She cautiously grasped the side of the door. Despite its old and heavy appearance, it glided with ease upon the hinges. She peered in, squinting with little blinks as she waited for her eyes to adjust to the dim, ruddy light. Pushing further, in her eyes rounded with delight and her breath caught in her throat.

"It's marvelous!" she gasped.

Hadyn followed her in and they stood awestruck just inside the doorway. Bartholomew was nowhere in sight, but they didn't need to go anywhere else at the moment, happy to take in the room from a distance.

The sweet smell, they had noticed yet outside the house, stuffed the space with a cozy, merry mood. The fire in the hearth cracked and popped contentedly, beckoning them with no conditions to come, drop their road weary limbs down, and just rest.

"It's so . . ." Kiara struggled to find a word.

"Peaceful," Hadyn finished.

Kiara smiled as she looked at him. "Yeah, peaceful."

From inside, Kiara could now see that the master architect of this home had found a place for not just one window, but many, so the entire room could be merrily lit with natural light, at least at some point in the day.

"It's so different from anything we've known," she muttered, "and yet it feels like the way it always should have been." She looked at him sadly, the blithesome smiles and wonder washed from her face. "We really were living a lie."

Hadyn's eyes welled with sadness. He didn't know why, but somehow she gathered up all the weight of the world and placed it on her own small shoulders. He opened his mouth to speak, but was cut off when Bartholomew, reappearing from another room, came in with some kind of small, flat cakes on two plates.

"Oh, there you are! Come, come! Please sit down. And you can take off those boots. You won't be needing them. I haven't had a snake in here for a while."

"Snakes!" Kiara asked, frantically checking the ground. She hadn't had much time to think about snakes, but hearing their name alone made her stomach twist into a knot of fear in no time at all. Suddenly, all she wanted to do was run and hide.

"Oh, yes." Bartholomew waved a hand. "Those vile, slithering beasts have gotten in here before, but I think I've boarded up most their entrances."

"Most?" Kiara squeaked.

Bartholomew cocked his head at Kiara, perceiving her fear all too late, and realized that in trying to make them feel at ease he had simply done the contrary. "Oh! But don't be frightened. It's quite safe."

Hadyn nodded to her, and reluctantly she began slipping off her boots. She hovered her first foot over the ground before placing it down on the wood floor. Completely strange to her, it's touch wasn't cold like stone floors, nor smooth. Instead, its rugged charm imbued it with imperfect character and beauty. With her bare feet, she sunk her toes into the soft, hearth-warmed rug and all but sighed. In Caverna, there wasn't a day when her feet weren't cold and clammy. Walking barefoot was the one thing worse than her tight princess shoes. But, she thought, if Caverna had rugs like these, she wouldn't have been caught dead in shoes.

"Your home is lovely, Mr. Ebenezer," she said politely, though in her mind she called it simply perfect.

She cast a glance at Hadyn. He too appeared caught up in the wonder of it. They sat down in the "wonderfully comfortable" chairs, which most definitely lived up to Kiara's expectations and breathed a sigh.

Bartholomew gave a small chuckle. "Yes, thank you. I think so, but it really isn't much. Did you not live your life in a mole's hole?"

Kiara fought a smile and caught Hadyn doing the same out of the corner of her eye.

"That's fine," Bartholomew grumbled. "Keep your secrets. Doesn't bother me . . . Oh!" he cried, remembering something. "These are freshly baked." He handed them the pastries. "Please eat. I must talk to the King about what is to be done with you."

Kiara shot to her feet. "Must something be done with us? And who is this king?" But Bartholomew had already gone. Kiara sat down with an exasperated sigh. "Argh!" Her eyes wandered about the room, then down to her plate suspiciously, and finally she met Hadyn's eyes.

Knowing what she was thinking, he drooped his head at her. "Kiara."

"Oh, I know it's silly, but I can't help but feel a little foolish, like I've made a mistake. He's a little . . ." She tilted her head back and forth.

"Crazy?" Hadyn raised his eyebrows.

"Shhh!" She grinned. "I mean, I don't know. What was I thinking? Can we really expect to trust anyone? I'm always getting myself into these things."

"But that's just it. You weren't thinking, Kiara," he said and she frowned. "You were listening to your heart. Your heart told you that it was going to be okay. You trusted that and I chose to trust you. But if you don't feel safe . . ."

Kiara bit her lip in thought, eyes straying to the window and the ever darkening forest. Going back out there wasn't much of an alternative choice.

Time for indecision ran out, when Bartholomew popped back in, his own decision clear on his face. "You are welcome here," he said confidently, "and if you wish, you may stay as long as you would like."

They stared at him wondering who on earth waited in the other room that would tell him to let perfect strangers stay in his home.

Bartholomew sat down in a chair across from them, with a tired but contented huff. Seeing that they had not taken a nibble from their cakes and the uncertainty in their eyes, he blinked at them, suddenly seeing them plainly for what they were— frightened, mere teens, the King's sheep, however lost they may be.

"I mean you no harm," he said evenly. "You need not fear, not me or outside things. You are safe here. I give you my word."

Kiara didn't want to believe him, but the sincerity in his eyes made her think otherwise. His gaze and words were too kind, too gentle, to be of malintent.

"Why would you trust us?" Kiara asked, trying to wrestle her own mind out of its conflicted turmoil.

"Because the King told me to. And He does not deceive."

"Well, who's this king? May we meet him."

Bartholomew laughed softly. "That, my dear girl, is entirely your decision." He gave an almost mischievous smile, but the profound wisdom in his eyes shone out like a light at the bottom of a deep well.

Kiara scrunched her nose. "What do you mean?"

"It is late, you must be hungry. If you will stay I will make you a hot meal. Then you need your rest. If you like, we can chat in the morning."

"Just one question. You may have your reasons," Hadyn raised an eyebrow, "but how do we know if we can trust *you*?"

"What a puzzle you two are. Well," Bartholomew said, "I gave you my word. And if that's not enough, trust the King's Word. 'He shall cover you with His feathers, and under His wings you shall take refuge; His truth shall be your shield and buckler,' " he triumphantly recited.

Kiara leaned toward Hadyn. "He has wings?" she whispered.

"You want us to trust someone we haven't met?" Hadyn asked.

"I told you, He does not deceive." Bartholomew said with a knowing smile. "In Him there is no variation or shifting shadow."

Kiara, arms crossed, tapped a thumb thoughtfully on her bicep. For some reason a smile wanted to grow on her face. "We will stay, but on one condition, Mr. Ebenezer, our business is ours and ours alone." She said with a sharp look in her eyes.

"Very well." He raised a finger with a shake of his head. "But I am not responsible if your mind changes before your visit is over." Again, now in the tone of his voice, Bartholomew seemed to know something that they didn't. "And if I may add a condition of my own?" They waited. "You may stay, so long as we drop such formalities, as Mr. and such and such, and you call me Bart, simple as that."

"Fair enough," Kiara said, just beginning to grin, ". . .Bart."

"Wonderful!" With a smile on his face he vigorously shook both of Kiara's hands, making their arms cross unnecessarily. Turning to do the same to Hadyn, he said, "Good, now we can eat! But first you must clean up a bit." He wiped his hands on his pant legs. "You two are filthy. Come along!" he sang.

# Chapter Six

# SOUPS AND STORIES

**B**artholomew led them through a bending, tunnel-like hall that rounded just over their heads. He showed them to the dining room, so that they could find their own way, and then off to where they could wash the grime from their hands and faces. After they had cleaned up (not nearly as much as Kiara would have liked) they both found their way back to the dining room, now empty and nearly solely lit by candles. The small, round room had a cramped, north-facing window, but with no real view, its purpose seemed solely to provide light. Filling almost the entirety of the little room, was a simple but well made table, built of a rich, dark red wood with four chairs of the same craft and color. Kiara ran her hand along its surface as she stepped into the room. A separate archway led off to another room where a great bunch of clanging sounds barged up the hall to them. *The Kitchen,* Kiara presumed with a smirk.

On the table, Bartholomew had left the flat pastries their own unease couldn't stomach before. The faintest whiff of the pastry prompted a quiet grumble from Kiara's stomach. Pulling out a chair, she gave in to her hunger and tried a nibble. Her eyes rounded as she pulled her head back. Even long cold and rather dense as it was, she had yet to try anything that tasted better. Hadyn tried it too. They grinned at each other like a pair of children finally left alone with a cookie jar. Before long they were both eating it by the mouthfuls. Kiara especially enjoyed the bites of chewy fruit throughout, little pieces bursting with tart sweetness. Finished, Kiara leaned back in her chair with a content smile, her hunger stalled by the delicious treat. The room was quiet, save for the ruckus of clanging from the kitchen, but quiet enough to notice another noise, too subtle to pick out before. She listened closer.

*Tick . . . tock . . . tick . . . tock . . .* it continued.

She craned back in her chair and looked up. There, on the

wall, hung the most bizarre, little contraption she had ever seen. The boxy, wood body had a cream disc set in its middle with Roman numeral symbols. Two spindles of arms stretched out from the center of the disc, one a little shorter than the other.

"Hadyn?" she asked inquisitively. "What do you suppose that is?"

Hadyn followed her gaze, and she turned to him to find a curious expression as his only reply.

Bartholomew returned, humming to himself and carrying a tray of three steaming bowls, but the tune caught in his throat as he stopped just in the arch way. He watched them, all but cocking their heads and scratching their chins, their brows furrowed with questions. Finally, he followed their dumbfounded puzzlement to the wall.

"Oh!" His eyes fluttered. "Have you never seen a clock before?"

"A what?" Kiara asked.

Bartholomew skipped twice and plopped the tray down. "A clock," he explained. "They keep time."

"Tick . . . tock . . ." Kiara whispered to herself.

He chuckled. "Why, yes!"

But Kiara wasn't thinking about clocks, she was thinking of her dear friend, a friend, she realized now, Bartholomew reminded her a bit of.

"Clocks were invented so we don't have to use the sun anymore," he said. "You're sure you've never seen one?"

"Yes. Yes, I'm sure, but I'm certain we've never used the sun to tell time either."

Hadyn, eyes wide, looked at her sideways and Kiara bit her lip. Bartholomew didn't seem to notice, much too aghast, but yet good natured. "Good gracious! How do you keep track of time?" he asked.

"Uh . . ." Kiara stammered.

"An hourglass," Hadyn said. "We use hourglasses to keep time." His tone and stern look left no room for questions.

"Oh," Bartholomew blinked, "that method is rather primeval. Clocks are the way now. I'm surprised you don't know . . . um . . ." His smile faded and he cleared his throat.

Kiara shot Hadyn a look and regret washed his face.

"Oh but enough of that," Bartholomew continued. "The stew is done and like my old papa used to say, 'eat while it's hot, 'cause you'll sure regret it if it's not.' "

Kiara chuckled. "Good advice."

Bartholomew smiled as he joined them at the table. "I'm sorry. I didn't mean to pry."

Hadyn cut in. "Don't be. To be honest, we're both just a little unsure of . . . well, just about everything. And almost anything becomes a touchy subject when you're not sure who you can trust."

"Yes!" Bartholomew said, like he nailed it right on the head. "Yes, I understand. But that is exactly why I'm apologizing. Your stay here is meant to be restful and peaceful. I don't want you to feel unsafe just because an old, nosy man can't mind his own business." He blinked at them under his glasses.

Kiara couldn't think of a time when someone had gone to such measures as to apologize for their behavior just for her comfort, and the sad sort of bittersweet smile it pulled out of her came straight from her heart. "Thank you," she said.

A small laugh escaped Bartholomew's throat and a warm smile started in his eyes and stretched across his face. "You know, there is something about you. Both of you. Like a word I just can't pin down." He shook his head. "Perhaps it will come to me."

Kiara eyed the three bowls at the table. "Doesn't the king need to eat?"

Bartholomew had to laugh. "Oh dear! I have confused you! I live here alone. And when I say I talk to the King, it's mostly me talking and Him listening."

She looked at him blankly.

"Haven't you ever prayed?"

Kiara shook her head.

Bartholomew thought for a moment. Nodding, he said, "In time. Shall we eat?"

Kiara drank in a deep inhale of the delicious smell steaming out of the bowl, and dipped her spoon in just when Bartholomew closed his eyes and started to talk again.

"Mighty King," he said, keeping his eyes shut, "thank You for bringing these two young travelers here, and for this food we have to share together. I ask that You give them peace while they remain with me and that You would sweep away their fears what-ever they may be. Amen."

Kiara didn't know who he thought he was talking to, though his words did seem to warm her heart.

Bartholomew smiled as he opened his eyes again and scooped up a mouthful of stew. Kiara and Hadyn took that as their cue to do the same. Kiara munched on her mouthful of the hearty stew and felt a new wave of comfort settle itself down inside her. The bold flavor, or so it was to her, hit her like a right hook to the jaw in the best way possible. Chewing faster, she turned her wide eyes on Hadyn to make sure she wasn't alone in this. His expression mirrored hers almost exactly.

Bartholomew watched them. "You don't like my stew?"

"No, it's very good." Kiara said. "It's just . . . I've never tasted anything like it."

Bartholomew's eyes filled with sadness as they wandered down to the table, thinking he was beginning to understand. "I see." But Kiara didn't care that there were so many things she hadn't seen, heard, or tasted; she only cared to know and learn about them now.

"What's in it?" she asked.

"Well, mostly beans, maze . . . a few tubers. My special seasoning, of course, venison—"

"Venison?" Kiara cocked her head. "Do you mean to say red meal?"

He blinked at her. "I'm not sure where you're from, but ask anyone, at least English speaking, and they'll tell you deer meat is called venison."

Hadyn's spoon clunked into his bowl. He held a half chewed mouthful behind tight lips, frozen in horror.

"Did I say something upsetting?" Bartholomew asked.

"Deer meat?" Kiara could only repeat.

"Why, yes." He looked them over again. "Good gracious! You're not vegetarians, are you?"

"Vegetarians?"

"You don't eat meat?"

"I . . . I'm not sure."

Kiara used her spoon to push around a chunk of meat. It was hard not to picture it once living or at least a part of a living creature, but the "venison" tasted just like red meal and she had learned and upheld the way of proper table manners far too long ago to deviate now. Hadyn watched her take up her spoon like a hero brandishing a great sword and reluctantly followed suit.

Bartholomew tried his very best not to watch them too closely, so they fell into an uncomfortable silence Kiara wanted more than anything to squirm out of. She cleared her throat. "It seems silly, because we've told you so little about ourselves, but I wonder . . . have you any tales or stories worth telling?"

"Oh, of course, many," he said, wiping his mouth with the back of his hand. Then with a raise of a white brow he said, "But only true ones."

"I've found those are the very best," Kiara said, intrigued.

"Good. Then I'd be happy to recall for you the tale of how I got here, that is, if I do not bore you to sleep before the end." They stared at him expectantly, making him chuckle. "Alright. Well, I was not always an old hermit, living out here by myself. I was young like you once. And had a thirst for adventure deep in my bones." At the word adventure, Kiara was all ears. "I grew up on a farm in Wales. A safe and good home, but I didn't have a lot of friends. Though that didn't keep me from play. As a boy I used to get my chores done early, just so that I could spend the rest of my day trouncing about in the old forest just beyond my father's wheat field." He laughed at the memories of his childhood. "And when I wasn't in the forest, I could be found harassing the animals around the farm. Oh, did those chickens get such a look in their eyes when they saw me coming, still a yard away. I would chase them all over the farm, pretending I was some valiant hero protecting my ocean-side town from pirates. Then I met my best friend. Her name was Priscilla. Her family had moved into the house on the other side of the forest, the same forest where we met. I never felt lonely another day in my life." he smiled, but contrary to what he said, even his smile looked lonely.

"What happened to her? Where is she now?" Hadyn asked.

"She . . . she died."

They both fell painfully quiet. "Oh, I'm sorry."

Bartholomew snapped out of it first. "It's quite alright, lad. It was a long time ago." He shook his thoughts away and continued the story. "As Priscilla and I grew older we longed for more than just our old woods and little streams. We dreamed of one day sailing the seas and exploring new lands. But our families were simple farmers and did not believe in it.

"Time went on, and we married. And with every winter that passed, our dreams became a little smaller. We thought of maybe having a family and farm of our own. But when we found out Priscilla couldn't have children, farm life didn't seem quite right either. We felt lost for a very long time. But that all changed one day when I met one special man. Aaron was his name. I was in town at the grocer's, picking up a few things for Priscilla, when in strode this young man with a natural confidence that seemed to not know of troubles. The smell of the sea clinging to his clothes, salt stains blotched his coat, and all the joy of life seemed to be found in his humble eyes. He came from a well-off family in England, the son of a popular preacher. He said he and his brother were only there for last minute supplies for their voyage they were setting out on very soon. They had charted a course for the vastly unknown land of the west, farther than Africa." He spoke with the same amount of wonder he had the day it happened as if not a spark of it had faded. "The land of foretold mystery and gold. But they weren't going for the gold, he had said. They were going for souls, not to possess riches, but to liberate people. He said they had heard of people living in the new lands that had never heard of the King. That he had been called by the King to bring the Word to them."

"And the Word," Kiara asked, "what is that?"

"Well, it's only the Bible, the living Word of the King Himself. Haven't you ever heard of the Bible?" Kiara and Hadyn shook their heads in unison, their skin prickling as if from the whispers of a hidden treasure. "Good gracious. Let's see . . . it is a gift, a written book filled with the tales and struggles of incredible people that did extraordinary things because of their great faith in their extraordinary God. It tells us of the ways of the King and His love for us. And, of course, there are the Gospels, Mathew, Mark, Luke, and John, that tell the story of Jesus."

"Jesus?"

"Yes, Jesus." Bartholomew smiled. "The best thing that has ever happened to our broken world, our only rescue. You see, the King loves us so much that He gave His Son, Jesus, to die for us so that our sins may be washed away. And rising from the grave, He conquered sin and death!"

Kiara had to get something straight. "The king is the creator?"

"Precisely!"

"And those who have turned from Him? Did His son die for them too?"

"Of course!"

"What about the guilty?" Hadyn asked and Kiara looked at him out of the corner of her eye, having yet to grasp why he always reverted to such a poor image of himself.

Bartholomew chuckled. "We're all guilty, lad. It's His love for our dirty souls that made Him come, to set us free from condemnation and give us a chance to live with Him in Heaven for eternity.

Kiara swallowed down a spoonful of stew, lost in thought. "Is that like the Place Always?"

A smile bloomed on his face. "I suppose you could call it that. Yes."

"I'm sorry," Kiara said. "Please continue your story."

"Oh, right!" He tapped his chin. "So! As I fell into conversation with this young man, nearly glowing with the journey ahead of him, I told him of how well I thought of what he was doing, so much so, I wished I could join him! But he didn't see why I couldn't. He said he could use a few more crew members and that I had that certain 'spirit' he was looking for, he could see it in my eyes.

"Well over forty years old, I had already succumbed long ago that I was never going to be a part of a great adventure. You can imagine the way my heart pounded then when he asked me that. My hopes flew to the sky. I told him, I wouldn't have to think twice if it wasn't for my wife. But he didn't mind if she came, in fact he implored it, said it would be a blessing from God if she came because his wife, Jane, was worried she was going to get lonely!

"So excited to tell Priscilla, I ran home faster than my legs had ever carried me even as a child. Of course, the news delighted her just as much as me, if not more, and we didn't waste another moment before packing and saying a goodby to our families. We set out with Aaron within the week." He burst with laughter. "Oh, it makes me laugh now, to think of how rash we were . . ."

"You were brave," Kiara said.

"Yes." He smiled contemplatively. "I suppose we were." He wiped his eye, whether from mirth, or sadness, or both, they couldn't tell.

He saw their empty bowls. "Ah, finished with dinner at last. Shall we continue this tale in a more comfortable room?" He stood, pushing his chair out behind him. "You two go wait in the sitting room while I take care of the dishes."

Kiara and Hadyn thanked him for the stew and walked back to the sitting room, finding it much altered. Even the dim light from before had seemed to crawl away to some other place. The light left leaking from the windows was a wash of pale blue, hardly differentiating silhouettes from shadows, and the fire had burnt itself down to embers.

Kiara crossed the room and settled her hands as gently as a leaf on the windowsill. "It's so dark," she whispered.

Hadyn joined her at the window. "I don't know what I expected, but . . ."

"Me either. It's so much like Caverna."

"Except, by morning it will already be bright again."

She smiled, part of her just knowing he'd say that. Then, gravitating to the brightest light in sight, they settled down close to the blush of the fire.

# ELLIE MAUREEN

Hadyn watched her silently, wanting to hear her thoughts before he said anything.

"He reminds me a little of Tick, in his curious ways," Kiara said, the embers glowing on her face, "but more clear minded and less unpredictable. He even calls the Creator the King."

Hadyn nodded. "You're right. I think it's safe to say, however strange he may be, he has a kind heart."

"Yes," she smiled. "It feels good to know that." Kiara thought for a moment, her smile fading at an even pace. She tore her gaze away from the marbling coals.

"What is it?" Hadyn asked.

She held his gaze. "I think we should tell him."

"Everything?"

She shrugged. "Our secrets do us no favors." She caught the start of a grin on his face. "What?"

"Nothing. It's just that he knew. Somehow. He knew we'd change our minds."

"So you agree?"

He nodded. "I do."

# Chapter Seven

# THE LEGEND OF THE KYJAR

**B**artholomew found them sitting close to the dying hearth. He hummed to himself, carrying a tray with three cups and a teapot. "Tea?"

Glued to the fire, Kiara broke out of her trance at the offer. "Oh, yes please," she said, tea, in fact, being very familiar to them and a staple in the diet of Caverna.

Bartholomew poured them each a cup, threw a couple logs on the fire, and dissolved into one of the chairs close to the hearth, singing a content sigh.

"Now," he rubbed his hands together, "where was I? Ah, the maiden voyage!" He gave a wistful, reminiscent smile at the memory. "Oh! The open ocean. Is there any place like it?"

Kiara giggled. "I wouldn't know."

His face scrunched with sad confusion a moment, but he returned to the delightful tale spinner yet again. "And so I wouldn't know how to describe it to someone who has yet to see it. Free, maybe?" He sighed, at a loss for words. "It is wonderful."

"It was a two and a half months voyage and I didn't meet Aaron's brother, Luekas until a week in. When he finally emerged from the bowels of the ship, he begrudgingly shook hands with me. He was much akin in looks with his brother, but his eyes lacked the brightness that was in Aaron's. I never really liked Luekas, he always had a strange look in his eyes when he thought no one was watching, like he was listening to something . . . that he shouldn't." Bartholomew's words faded as if burned up in the fire he stared into. The light flickered on his face and stretched the shadows to make his expression very grave indeed.

"You mean someone?" Kiara asked.

Bartholomew looked through her at first, but then he smiled. "Oh, yes, someone. Of course." He blinked the thoughts away. "But alas, the voyage was quite uneventful." He scrunched his brows. "Besides the storms, mind you, which I have to say were both terrifying and exhilarating. If you think you've experienced a thunderstorm, try riding one out in an eighty-ton, wooden bathtub! Every gale straining the timbers until they moaned for relief and every wave tossing us like a half mad horse bent on freedom. I've yet to find anything that compares to that feeling, that gut-twisting dread as you hold onto the riggings and whatever else for dear life, constantly wondering if the next wave will grow big enough to capsize her or if her masts will hold through the next onslaught of wild gusts."

Kiara and Hadyn listened, eyes wide in rapt attention, hanging on his every word. Little did Bartholomew know, they had never experienced a thunderstorm on land or at sea and his accounts sounded like something of legend.

"I saw a whale once," Bartholomew continued, "on a much calmer day, when the sun finally decided to rescue us from the storms. It got me thinking as I watched its graceful poise, gliding along . . . Huge! And yet it just cut through the water as silent as a mouse. I thought, if God can care and provide for a creature as vast as this, how much more can He care and provide for me?" He didn't look at them but stared off, as if he had traveled right back to that moment, feeling comforting arms surrounding him. "I didn't fear the storms after that.

" 'Are not five sparrows sold for two copper coins?' " he recited with a smile. " 'And not one of them is forgotten by God. But the very hairs of your head are all numbered. Do not fear therefore; you are of more value than many sparrows.' "

Kiara felt an unidentified spark of wonder inside her, just like when Hadyn read the scripture Maddie had copied down into her journal. She sipped her tea. "That's beautiful."

"I think so too." Bartholomew smiled. "When we finally arrived in the new world, we found it a strange and intimidating place. Overcoming the challenges of different languages with the native people was both the most difficult and most crucial task. Without them, most of us wouldn't have lasted a week in this complex and all too often savage jungle. It was a true joy and an honor watching Aaron work with them and teach them about the love of Jesus. And though that in itself came with its own dangers and hostilities, most we found were hungry for this love and had been searching for it already. Luekas constantly worked in the shadow of his brother. He just didn't have the heart for it as Aaron did.

"Then we met the Kyjar people." He paused, overcome with a moment of powerful memories. "It was like meeting a people you hear about in legends, but they were real! Speaking and interacting with us! Just humble travelers from a distant land seemingly far less fantastic than theirs." Bartholomew spoke like a child seeing his fantasies come to life before his eyes.

"The Arokno are their protectors, fierce and formidable warriors raised up from childhood to defend. They are a sight to see, but even with these great protectors, we found the Kyjar in a state of fleeing, as they told us they had been for some time. A nomadic tribe, but all they wanted was a place to call their home. Aaron helped them put down roots and showed them how they could protect their people without always having to run, and, in turn, they became like family to us. We built a village with them, but what was never planned was that it would become our home too. Not one of us expected how quickly and irreversibly they found a way into our hearts. We fell in love with their color, their life, their rich connection to all living things. One thing to know about the Kyjar, they know how to celebrate. If I miss anything most about the village of Py'aoka, it's the parties. They would fill the Berabo Glade with so many lights, too many to count. And, ah! The dancing and music! Such wild and spirited music." Kiara's heart skipped and a noise of delight escaped her. Bartholomew turned to her. "Something you want to say?"

"No, sorry. They sound wonderful." She could picture the glowing glade, full of so much cheer and twinkling brilliance.

"They are. They are." Bartholomew nodded. "Some of the members of our crew thought this so much, marriages were in order and so were more celebrations. I lived there until my dear Priscilla passed away. I still visit, but not as much as I'd like. We've had our share of both adventures and hardships with the Kyjar that are tales and stories of their own, but I think I've talked quite enough for one evening, don't you?"

Kiara smiled. "Not at all. I love hearing it. And . . . well, it's not like there's not much for us to say."

"I see."

"No, it's not like that, it's just, well," Kiara looked at Hadyn, "our lives aren't normal. At least I don't think they are."

"Oh. You know, I think I understand."

"You do?"

"Well, considering the things that you have not seen or do not know about, I would say you have escaped from a very dark and controlling cult."

# ELLIE MAUREEN

When they were silent he continued, "I mean, I've seen my fair share of them and just thought . . ."

"What–" Hadyn squinted. "What's a cult?"

"Good gracious! I'll stop making assumptions and you can tell me what you want on your time."

"But, you see, I think we'd like to tell you now." Again Kiara looked to Hadyn and he nodded.

"Of course. Whatever you need to tell me, I'll listen."

"I appreciate it, and we wouldn't burden you with this if it wasn't for our need of help."

"Nonsense! You are the farthest thing from a burden."

Kiara took in a heavy breath. "This is difficult . . . and I understand if you don't believe it, but until today, we have lived in an underground city where, for generations, our kings have led us all to believe that nothing, and I mean nothing else, existed outside of our cave."

She fell silent to let Bartholomew process. Then Hadyn continued for her. Eventually they both took turns feeding him bites of information, careful to let him swallow before the next. It was a lot to take in at once. When he had the gist of it, they paused again, half expecting him to burst with, "good gracious!" But he only stared, a listless hand moving to his head. For the first time that night, Bartholomew was at a loss for words. "Why did you not tell me before?"

"We didn't know what you would think." Kiara said.

Hadyn's mouth twisted with a crooked grin. "Though you weren't terribly far off when you mentioned the mole hole."

Bartholomew gave a small laugh, his brow quickly scrunching back down.

But Kiara had had her whole life to process it and her whole life, one question rattling around in her brain had managed to remain unanswered. Her voice was fragile, like a frightened child, when she asked it now. "Why would The King . . . why would God allow that?"

"I . . ." Bartholomew's voice broke. "I don't know." He thought for a moment. "You have to know it is *because* of God's love for us that we have free will. We have the choice to choose. To choose Him or evil. One of the most unavoidable facts is that evil is in the world, Kiara, and God is most certainly not the one who inflicts it. From our own darkness inside us, we choose. He's always cheering us on. Calling us home . . . but it is our job while we tarry here to fight the darkness and run the race. We must not stray into the Enemy's clutches."

Kiara turned from the fire and looked at him with a heavy gaze. "But all of the innocent people trapped there . . . If He is so powerful why can't He just break down the walls and save them?"

"I . . ." he faltered once more. "I'm afraid I don't have an answer." Little did he know his raw honesty meant more to her than any number of half baked excuses ever could. "All I can say is, I'm sorry. I'm so sorry."

They listened to the crack of the fire for sometime before a light slowly dawned in Bartholomew's eyes. "But think about this. What if He has raised *you* up to save them."

Kiara could only stare, as if caught in the way of some bombarding thing she had no power to stop. "Me?"

"Yes, Kiara. You. Both of you! You've freed yourselves, why not set the others free as well?"

She felt her insides grow trembly at the weight of those words.

"Perhaps there have been others all this time, but none strong enough, none obedient enough to answer His call."

She remembered clearly her promises of return and more than anything her heart longed to help free everyone, but she always supposed her mother would be the one to save them. *She* was their queen. And if she was fully honest with herself, she knew the further she got from Caverna, the more she feared going back and the less she felt she could do to help.

"And what makes you think I am? Sorry, but no. I can't."

"Why is it that you can not do these things?" Bartholomew asked in all seriousness.

Kiara fumbled for words and blinked at him, as though there was nothing that she could say that would be better than the obvious. "Well, because I'm me. And there's no great . . . well, anything in me. I'm fearful, and impatient, and far too quick-tempered for my own good! I give up when things get hard and if I didn't have people to stop me, I would have destroyed myself long ago."

"Well, you haven't given up thus far."

Kiara chuckled. "That's because no one let me!"

Hadyn noticed straight away as the lilt she kept under wraps most often came out in her voice. As far as he knew, that only happened when she was upset or excited, but right now she seemed somewhere in the middle.

"We need each other, lass," Bartholomew countered, "there's no way around that. And you may not believe it, but oh, there is something fierce in your heart. You have been called to great things, mark my words, to bring good news to the poor, to bind up the broken hearted, and to proclaim liberty to the captives, to swing wide the prison doors of those who are bound."

"You don't even know me."

"Perhaps. But you don't need eyes to see the sort of spark I see in you."

Kiara bit her lip and shook her head. "I just . . . I just want to save my mother."

"And so you shall! I believe that!"

"Well, bringing her back was always part of the plan, but she'll take care of the rest. I'm not strong enough. Not to face my—" she swallowed down the word, "King Nnyric!"

"You're right," Bartholomew said, almost jumping up from his chair, his eyes bright with passion and excitement, "but He is able to do exceedingly abundantly more than we ask or imagine! Moses was just one man, but him and his brother, Aaron, led a whole nation out of captivity!"

"Was he in the Bible too?" Kiara inquired.

Bartholomew nodded. "In the book of Exodus, and much like you, he thought he couldn't do it. But the King had called him and He does not make mistakes."

"Yes, you said that," Kiara muttered.

"Once Moses obeyed," Bartholomew continued, "God gave him the strength to succeed and Aaron to help him. All he had to do was follow! And look!" he shouted, throwing his hands out to Hadyn. "Your very own Aaron!"

Hadyn's eyes darted left and right at the sudden turn of attention. "Me?"

"Yes! You! Look at you two. It's incredible how clear it is!"

Kiara smiled at her friend as his cheeks began to redden.

Bartholomew raised his face to the ceiling with a wide grin. "Oh, it's so good to feel that again! I knew You wouldn't be silent forever. I just knew you weren't finished with this old fool yet!"

Kiara and Hadyn exchanged uncertain glances, then looked at him as if he just might be crazy.

"Feel . . . what exactly?" Kiara ventured.

He smiled at her. "Why, my dear, the voice of the Lord!"

"He spoke to you? Just now?"

"It's funny you should ask, seeing as though we're on the subject of callings and such. I've never been particularly good at much. Woodworking is a wee hobby of mine, but I'm not going to change the world with stools and kitchen tables now, am I?"

"It might change the world of the person who sits on that stool," Kiara opposed.

# FORSAKEN

"You're right there, lass, and that's awfully kind of you to say. But what I mean to say is, when I really feel useful is when I hear God speak to me. Now, it's been this way since I was a wee lad, so it's the normal way to me, but folks say I hear him more than most. I just say they don't listen close enough. It's been a long time, but just now I heard Him speak, and it was for you."

Out of nowhere, Kiara felt shivers run up her arms. "What did He say?"

Bartholomew frowned. "It's hard to explain. It's not to say I heard actual, audible words, but it's more like a guiding hand placed gently on my shoulder. In this particular instance, I heard Him say, 'her,'" he pointed at Kiara. "'For this task, I choose her.'" he tossed his head back and forth. "More or less."

The silence enveloped them. None of them dared to break it. Then Kiara cracked a grin.

"Rubbish!"

"No. It's true!" Bartholomew laughed. "I've lived long enough and let my judgments get clouded by personal and outside things too many times, to know by now when my God speaks. And let me tell you, it's a dangerous thing to ignore the voice of God. Believe me, I've tried."

Kiara pondered hard on his words, chewing them up in her mind even as the three of them continued to talk for long hours that felt short. They talked more about God until Kiara became frustrated again. They talked of happy things and the wonders of the world until they were so excited to learn that they wished it was day already. But finally, every one of them started nodding, their eyes growing heavy with sleep.

Presently, Bartholomew yawned, stretching like a bear emerging from hibernation and finally had the mind to call it a night. "We can talk more in the morning, but right now I need to go to bed before I fall asleep right here. And believe me, you don't want to see the ornery, cantankerous man that wakes up after a night in this armchair. It's ugly." He winked. "Come along. I will show you your rooms."

Bartholomew tipped his cup back, finishing his tea, and led them to a hallway along the front of the house, with a row of rooms only on the left side, so they might all have at least one window.

"Pick any of them. I must go to sleep. I never stay up this late. Help yourselves to anything you like. So long as you stay here, this is your home." He gave them candles to light their way.

Kiara's eyes strayed to the pitch window at the start of the hall, reflecting her frightened glance.

# ELLIE MAUREEN

"You needn't be afraid," Bartholomew reassured. "As intimidating a place the forest is, with the proper knowledge, it is not a thing to live in fear of."

"I assure you our fear is not without reason," Hadyn remarked.

Bartholomew's brow scrunched. "What do you mean?"

"We were chased by a pack of creatures from the forest, not a moment before we stumbled across your home," he answered.

A grin split his face. "Nonsense! Animals don't hunt people. Especially not a healthy pair of them. What species?"

"It was already dark," Hadyn said. "We didn't get a good look at them."

"Well, whatever they were, I'm sure it was just curiosity." Kiara didn't look all that convinced. "And hunted or not," he continued, giving Kiara's shoulder one last squeeze. "You are safe here. And inside these walls you can sleep soundly. I pray for sweet dreams for you both. Goodnight!" he sang cheerily. His words swept out all unease, like a stiff spring breeze blowing out the rot of winter and heralding the growth of new things.

Once he left, Kiara walked to the first room, but paused with her hand on the knob. "I'm glad we told him."

"Me too," Hadyn said. "What do you think about all the things he said?"

She sighed. "I don't know. You can't believe everything everyone says. Nothing Nnyric used to say was true."

"Yeah . . . How come you didn't tell him that Nnyric is your father?"

She shrugged. "I guess I'm just ashamed of it. You know how it is."

"Well, yes, but it's not quite the same, though."

"How can you say that?" Firelight illuminated the offense in her eyes and darkened her scowl. Immediately he regretted it. But how to take it back?

"Well . . . it's different, isn't it?"

"I didn't think so."

Silence drifted a wedge between them, before he tried again. "I'm sorry. I didn't mean to say that your pain is less than mine."

"Didn't you?"

"No, Kiara. I would never. I shouldn't have said anything. I'm sorry."

"Just forget it. I don't want to talk about it." She huffed and dropped it, but in that moment, a shadow had fallen on a piece of their friendship that would not be easily lifted.

She gazed down the black corridor, everything beyond the few feet of candle light dissolving to inky nothing.

"It's so dark," she whispered. "Bartholomew says there's nothing to be afraid of, but I'm still frightened."

"Hey. Don't be. I'll be right in the next room and it's different when you know dawn is coming to burn away the darkness and that there will be no heavy shadows when you wake up."

"Yeah, I guess you're right." A small smile betrayed her pout. "Goodnight."

"Goodnight, Kiara."

Kiara took in her room by the dim light of the candle. Just big enough to comfortably house a bed, a compact nightstand and a lanky dresser, she found it cozy and protective.

She dug through the drawers until she found something she could wear. She changed, glad to finally get out of her river-soaked, dried, then sweat-soaked, thorn-tattered, dirt-stained dress.

Kiara settled awkwardly into the bed, not so luxurious as her bed in the palace, but much better than anything she had in the Forbiddens, and the blanket was soft.

A cracked open window over the bed let in the sweet smell of the night, and the sounds of nocturnal life. A bird calling in the distance sounded close for its volume— a shrill, high pitched whistle, continuing persistently.

Kiara closed her eyes and listened. Her mind drifted into a memory, made more vivid by the coming sleep. What felt like ages ago, she had asked her mother if she could try to explain what music sounded like. Her mother's words came to her mind. "Hhmm," she mused. "My, what a fantastic question you've come up with, my curious girl. I think you might have me stumped this time. But let's see . . . Well, it would certainly be the most colorful sound you would ever hear."

Kiara remembered giggling at her mother for saying something so silly, and wholly disagreeing that sounds had colors. "Oh, sure they do," Eleanor insisted. "Here, close your eyes and tell me, what color do you picture when you listen to my voice?"

"Mmmm . . . blue!" she had said. "But not dark. Really light blue."

Eleanor laughed softly, a sweet and singsong noise Kiara only remembered hearing when no one else was around. She could hear it now as if she was there and it made her heart full and ache at the same time. "And why is that?" Eleanor had asked.

"Because blue is like a blanket, soft, comforting, and protecting."

She could see her mother's smile, crinkling the corners of

# ELLIE MAUREEN

57

her eyes. "I see." Then pulling her daughter onto her lap, she continued. "And if you ever get the chance to hear a bird, and I so hope you do, you'll know the sound because they like to sing all the time. I think they're praising the Creator for their wings, for He dearly loves to hear their voices."

As the memory faded back to only that, Kiara smiled. Back then, she had only thought of birds as a fantasy a mother made up for the delight of her daughter, but so did a lot of things, and now they sang as real as ever, one after the other joining in the chorus and giving her enough peace to puff out the candle on the nightstand.

Kiara closed her eyes with a content sigh, trying to imagine more of what the colorful people of the Kyjar were like, and listening to the equally as colorful voices of the night.

Of course, the screaming piha doesn't have the most pleasant call, but it has its own beauty, and to Kiara it was the closest thing to a lullaby she'd ever heard. The pihas sang her to sleep and then some, praising the Creator for their wings.

# Chapter Eight

# BURNT POTATOES

Hadyn awoke to the distant sound of bright laughter. Kiara's sweet giggle drifted through Bartholomew's tunneling home. He opened his eyes to light. Bright rays poured in through the window. Swinging his leg over the bed, he had to remember to breathe as he looked out on the world he wasn't so used to yet, not even close. A hush lay on the forest save for the clear chirps, trills, and whistles of the early birds. The breath of the waking earth hung in the air, only adding to the peace of the view, while shafts of light descending through a gap in the canopy transformed the mist into a fine, gold dust.

"Morning," he spoke, and the word had never sounded so sublime.

Once he had dressed and stepped out into the hall, he followed the sounds of mirth to the room they had sat in the night before.

He found Kiara with Bartholomew, sitting and chatting happily. Bartholomew spotted him as soon as he entered the room. "Good morning, lad!" he greeted cheerily.

Kiara turned around and smiled warmly. She wore a simple but elegant dress that must have belonged to Priscilla. With quarter-length sleeves the dress was a muted jade color like green smoke. He'd never seen her in anything but neutrals and with the sudden splash of color, he found it hard not to stare at the way it paired so perfectly with her hair, now pulled loosely back off her face.

"Come, sit down," Bartholomew said. "And don't worry. You haven't missed breakfast!" Hadyn settled into the chair next to Kiara. Bartholomew, having already made tea, poured Hadyn a cup. "I was just about to tell Kiara about one of the times I had a run in with a jaguar."

"Jaguars . . . Those are that kind of spotted . . ." Hadyn

paused, "cats, right?" He took the cup. "Thanks."

"Yes," he answered. "*BIG* cats and not something you would fancy bumping into."

Hadyn listened, scratching the back of his hand where a marble-size welt had grown overnight.

"Oh, my word! Hadyn!" Kiara snatched up his hand.

He chuckled. "I know. So much for them only having a taste for red heads."

"Nasty little buggers, aren't they?" Bartholomew remarked. "You're lucky it's the dry season."

Kiara whipped her head back and forth between them, sure it was as clear as she saw it. "These are bug bites," she said, raising her hand to show the many red but already fading dots peppering it. "That is . . . something else."

"Afraid not, my dear. They affect everyone a little differently."

Kiara didn't think it accurate to use the word little for this situation. "But I got these right away. And Hadyn didn't even feel any bites!"

"Like I said, it's different for everyone. Mine can last for weeks!"

"Weeks!" she cried, seeing that alone as a need for medical attention.

"Kiara, I'm sure it's nothing to worry about," Hadyn reassured.

"There. You see?" Bartholomew rubbed his chin. "Now where was I?"

" . . . Jaguars," she said reluctantly.

"Oh, right! So there I was, having a little bumble through the jungle, as I always liked to say." He chuckled to himself. "I was whistling along on my way, not a care in my head. I didn't fear the talons of the harpy eagles nor the jaws of the giant river otter, which, by the way, you can smell before you see. Those dastardly creatures have the courage of a warrior, and with no fear, they were found in camp making all sorts of panic numerous times. One time–" Bartholomew started to snicker. "One time when we found one in the village, we heard the cries of its victim before we even smelt it! It was the most, oh, how should I describe it? The most pathetic, high-pitched scream." Bartholomew had a good belly laugh now, where Kiara and Hadyn had yet to see the humor in the tale. "It was awful!" he continued. "But the best part was finding Luekas up a tree, shaking in his boots and staring down at the otter. It sat at the foot of the tree, waiting patiently, not even a fully grown adult. It

# FORSAKEN

took Luekas nearly an hour to come down after we shooed it away! Once he did get his feet back on the ground, he—" Bartholomew roared with a sudden burst of a laugh. "He fell right over, his legs too weak to hold him up! Oh, if you would have known the old tyrant you would be laughing as hard as me. He never lost his fear of otters too, and we never let him forget that day." Bartholomew stared at nothing with a smile on his face, dreaming of the past. "Good gracious! Where did the main road go? I saw a path to the otter story and I walked down it for far too long! Where was I?"

Kiara giggled. "You weren't afraid of anything?"

"Oh, right! Not even jaguars, but," he raised a grizzled brow, "I had never seen one. Then I found tracks." He paused on the word for emphasis. "I knew they were a jaguar's because of the large size, but I decided to try my hand at tracking anyway. A word of advice to you, if you think you're clever enough to track a jaguar, you're probably not. Don't underestimate the cats in their own world. They will always outfox you . . . always." Kiara and Hadyn just stared at him without a word, absolutely hooked and dying to know how the story ended.

"So, here I was attempting to track an adult jaguar, my head down, scanning every track." Bartholomew looked at them blankly. "My first mistake. To track properly, you have to be aware of *all* your surroundings. What an amateur I must have looked like! When the hairs on the back of my neck stood on end, I realized that what I thought to be fresh tracks, were *extremely* fresh tracks. Chills ran down my spine as my perception of a monitoring presence grew. When I finally looked up, I saw her, but she had seen me long ago, watching me the whole time as I fumbled around like an incompetent halfwit. Through the thick leaves, I could see her crouched body. I stared into her amber eyes, glowing like the embers in a dying fire. She was completely in control of the situation I had just gotten myself into. She knew what she was doing, which posed the question, why? She could have slunk off into the unknown without a trace or sound, but she had chosen to show herself. Why? I think the question might plague me till the day I die, and I'll never forget what I saw in those eyes."

"What did you see?" Hadyn asked.

"Well, first of all I saw power. Secondly, I saw beauty, such beauty . . . strength, and a fierceness beyond measure. Then, as I gazed even longer, I thought I saw a sadness deep within." His own eyes turned very sad as he spoke. Kiara and Hadyn hung on the somber silence, but Bartholomew shook it away. "Though my head might have made all that up. It does tend to create the wildest of things. Anyway, as I—"

"What is that smell?" Kiara caught a bitter scent in the air.

Bartholomew's eyes widened. "Good gracious! I forgot about the potatoes!"

He shot up and abandoned them at the edge of their seats. Before long, clangs, bangs, and a few shouts, tumbled out from the kitchen.

"He is a rather clumsy cook." Kiara giggled.

"Come on, let's go see if he needs any help," Hadyn said as he stood.

Nearing the kitchen, the stench of charred starch grew more and more potent and the ruckus of noise carried on. Kiara and Hadyn stood in the doorway as Bartholomew frantically paced around his kitchen. No windows lit this room of utter disarray. A wooden plate sat precariously on the edge of the table in the middle of the room, destined to fall. Pots and pans were strewn about. Corn flour spotted the walls and floor. The small stone oven burned red hot and the griddle that had once been over the fire now sat on the table, still popping and sizzling with blackened bits of potato.

Hadyn cleared his throat and Bartholomew jumped, almost dropping a knife he had been cutting with.

"We thought you could use some help," Hadyn said.

"No, no! I'm fine. Guests should not even have to lay their eyes on the kitchen, especially one like this!" Just then the wooden plate fell. He sighed. "This is truly my least favorite room in the house!"

"But, really," Kiara said emphatically, picking up the plate, "we don't mind."

"Well . . . if you insist. I do suppose I could use two more pairs of hands."

Bartholomew went over to the potatoes with a rag so that he could pick up the hot iron handle. "What am I going to do with these?" He rubbed his forehead. "I'm afraid I haven't had many house guests in the last couple years."

"It will be alright," Kiara encouraged. "May I?" Bartholomew handed her the knife and Kiara used it to scrape some of the black off the potatoes. "See, these are still edible."

"Yes, I suppose I was being a bit dramatic." Bartholomew said. He put Hadyn to work preparing some fresh fruit from the forest, and busied himself once more.

"Cida used to let me cook with her sometimes. Which I always thoroughly enjoyed." Kiara said to Hadyn. "I do miss her already."

"Me too."

"Who's Cida?" Bartholomew asked.

"Just a dear friend," she said solemnly. "But how does the story end, Bart? What happened with you and the Jaguar?"

"Right! Let's see. I blinked, there was a rustle of leaves, and she was gone. Without a trace." Bartholomew paused. "I'll never forget that."

"That's it?" Hadyn asked, "What did you do?"

"Well, I can tell you what I didn't do, lad! I didn't stick around to see if she would change her mind on the state of her stomach and come back for a late afternoon snack! I ran home as if the beasts of hell were behind me!"

After more stories over a fine breakfast, Kiara and Hadyn again praised Bartholomew's ingenious cooking while he told them it wouldn't have been as good without their help.

"So," Bartholomew began, "I was thinking . . . and I know you two are in a hurry to get on your way, but what if you stayed another day? I could teach you a few things about the jungle and show you my favorite places."

Kiara and Hadyn looked to each other for an answer.

"Well . . ." Kiara said, realizing just how much she had enjoyed their time with him "I suppose one more day would be okay."

Bartholomew clapped his hands together. "Wonderful! Oh, we're going to have such great fun!"

Kiara smiled and took a sip of her tea, "What should we do first?"

"What to do first, indeed. Would you like to see my favorite pond?"

Kiara said, "Oh, yes, please," and Hadyn nodded.

"Then it's settled! But I'm sure you've realized what Priscilla did the first day we arrived in this wild land. Those nice dresses she wore back in Aberporth just wouldn't do here in the jungle."

Kiara cocked her head. She had realized the difficulties, yes, the tears in her dress proved it, but she didn't see another option.

"Come along, I will show you what Priscilla used to wear. She made them herself."

Kiara stood alone in the room she had stayed in, staring in disbelief at the clothes Bartholomew had laid out for her.

"Trousers?" she exclaimed, gaping at the tan legs hanging over the bed and the white long-sleeve shirt paired with them.

She didn't mean to say it out loud, but this was too much! Certainly not the raiment of a princess. Back in Caverna she'd be frowned upon for less! She could feel her face growing red just looking at them. She'd rather break both her hands than wrestle herself into these atrocities, but she couldn't bear to offend Bartholomew. These *were* his wife's after all.

"Trousers . . ." she mumbled again before growling and giving in.

Kiara looked herself over, pulling at every inch of fabric. The shirt and trousers were never meant to be tight, and since Priscilla had not been quite as slight as Kiara, the clothes hung even looser on her. For that she was thankful. Craning her neck, she tried to see behind herself, searching for any breach in modesty. She felt wrong and debased, awkward and embarrassed. Besides the whole entire outfit, she found nothing wrong with it.

When she at length worked up the stubborn will to reenter the sitting room, Bartholomew and Hadyn sat talking casually, but she couldn't say what about, the blood pumping in her ears too loud to hear anything. It didn't matter. The conversation evaporated when Hadyn caught a glimpse of her out of the corner of his eye and shot to his feet. He wouldn't have said anything, if only to save his own skin, but especially not after seeing the redness of her face and the dangerous look in her eyes. Bartholomew, too, seemed to know better and decided to pretend that nothing had changed,

"I packed us lunch!" he said, holding up a straw basket, "I thought we may want to be out longer than our stomachs would allow." Silence took its turn for two seconds too long, as neither commented. Bartholomew tottered back and forth on his heels. "Well, if you two are ready, we can be on our way."

Once out the door, a breeze swept through the trees and brushed their faces. The ease of stepping back into the outdoors struck Kiara. No fighting through shadows, rapids, and treacherous falls; it was as easy as stepping one's feet over the threshold of a door. The wild air defused all uncomfortable feelings like a puff of smoke. The joy they had felt when they had first escaped filled Kiara and Hadyn again, overflowing in laughter. Kiara started it, but all three laughed together, faces growing red for much more wholesome reasons.

"Oh, I'm sorry, my dear," Bartholomew spoke first. "It was

# FORSAKEN

never my intention to make you uncomfortable."

"It's alright. I think I'm already getting used to it."

"Yes. I'm afraid I haven't been the best of hosts."

"No, you haven't," Kiara said, grinning. "You've been exceedingly more than."

A smile burst across his face at the sweet words.

"It's not as if we've been ideal guests," Hadyn added.

"Meeting new friends is a puzzling ordeal, full of obstacles and uncomfortable things," Bartholomew said, "especially when you haven't had any in a long, long time."

He gave them a smile etched with an ancient sorrow, but taught by an even older joy. "Come along. We have an adventure ahead of us!"

# Chapter Nine

# FOREST STARS

They followed a well-trodden path single file, Bartholomew leading the way and Hadyn at the back. He was more than happy to take in the jungle now with the comfort of a guide with them, but Kiara's curiosity was kind of an around-the-clock thing and she had had plenty of time to cook up a new question.

"Bart," she inquired, "may I ask why you live out here? Alone?"

"Well, after Priscilla was gone, I distanced myself from almost everyone."

"Oh, I'm sorry. You need not say more."

"No, it's quite alright," Bartholomew continued. "Though I'm afraid this tale is rather sad. I thought if I didn't have to see the happiness of others, I wouldn't feel my own sadness so terribly."

"And did it help?"

He turned to look at her. "No, my dear. It did not." He resumed his walk. "Aaron tried to help me, I can see that now. But when you go into as dark a place as I was, only the Maker of the light can bring you out to the sun. I questioned everything," he glanced at her, "just like you, Kiara. Why would He allow her to get sick? Why didn't He stop it? Why not me instead of her? Thousands of questions whipped around my head like the darkest, most treacherous tempest. I questioned what I believed. So I retreated to a solitary life, thinking I might do some good for those lost in the middle of the wild, but what guidance can someone who is lost themselves give? Far away from others, I was tossed like a wave in the storm. I was angry with God, with everything I could find to blame, when there was no one to blame at all. Jesus says, 'In Me you may have peace. In the world you will have tribulation; but be of good cheer, I have overcome the world.' Isn't that the truth? This world is full of hardship, it's ripe with it like a terrible stench, but does that mean He's not here with us, even through the bad?" He shook his head. "No. And I wish I knew that then. But in my defiance, I let the Enemy toy with my mind and once I was broken down to the point of not knowing if I loved God at all, I started to blame myself and I wished I had died instead. I had no love left for anything, not even the birds. All my love died with her."

He paused and Kiara asked, "What ever happened? What changed? You are so full of joy now."

"I was rescued," Bartholomew smiled. "Time dragged and I felt sorry for myself that no one came even though I told them not to. Then Aaron showed up at my door. He said he had found my Bible and thought I might want it." Bartholomew paused, realizing something. "He brought me my Bible and I didn't even thank him."

"Can't you thank him now?"

"Yes, I suppose I could . . ." He smiled. "After he left that day, I picked up that Bible, the same one I had read since I was a wee lad. The leather bound pages sat comfortably in my hands and yet my own fingers trembled with uncertainty. Every bend, every tear was familiar to me, but still it felt foreign, like I was no longer a part of this story, like I had never cared for the good news in my hands.

"Though my soul railed against the notion and would rather hurl it across the room, I began to read. The tears that had long rusted on my face, poured from my eyes and could not be stopped. Light touched the darkest part of me. Warmth thawed my dead heart like a fireside. And Love, True Love dried my tears. My King had not forsaken me like I had Him. In that moment, all I wanted was forgiveness, to drink from that never ending river, and when I allowed love back into my heart, slowly my broken soul mended and my scars healed.

"The joy that had found its way back to me . . . or that I had found my way back to, didn't let me stay away for long and I returned to the village. Then when I came back out here, it was for the right reasons, to remain a standing fortress for the King, to share His love with those who had lost their way.

"I visit the village now, maybe not as much as I'd like. But some things are just never the same. You can only hope that life would go back to the way it was, remembering all the good memories and laughs as if new ones can't be made. But without change where would we grow? How would we meet new people and spread our love, hope?" Bartholomew sighed, a mixture of bittersweet contentment. "So, Old Bart the Hermit lives on, asking the King everyday to give me purpose, to use me for something great and I think . . . He's finally given me a little bit of that purpose." He smiled at them over his shoulder, a light in his kind eyes. "The glades just ahead. I do hope you will like it!"

"Just ahead" took what felt like another hour to the steadily tiring troglodytes stumbling behind him. Kiara couldn't stop thinking about what Bartholomew had told them. She marveled at the way he had simply let go of his pain. He had experienced great hardship, great loss not so very long ago, something she didn't know if you could just get rid of, or get over. Not that she hadn't given it thought. She just thought something happened over time that would make it go away. But Bartholomew had seemed to set it down, like a heavy bag of rocks he realized he didn't need to carry. He made it look so easy. But the strangest part, even now that she knew she could drop hers, Kiara didn't know if she wanted to.

At last Bartholomew stopped and turned to his out of shape companions. They panted like they'd just hiked up a mountainside with no breaks. He chuckled. "Yes, catch your breath. We're finally here."

He pulled aside a handful of branches and revealed a perfect glade. A pond half blanketed in a green, duckweed carpet, glistened in the streams of light falling like gold waterfalls from the gaps in the canopy, its mossy banks sliding gently into the water. Kiara and Hadyn stepped into the clearing while Bartholomew held the branches, their smiles bright with awe.

"It's beautiful!" Kiara expressed.

A family of about twenty, stout, russet-colored rodents grazed placidly on the grass around the water's edge, standing about two feet tall at the withers, with stoic, blunt-snouted faces. The majestic Hydrochoerus hydrochaeris.

"See those beauties over there?" Bartholomew pointed to the capybaras, "I call them water pigs," he said with glee.

"They're extraordinary!" Kiara exclaimed. "I read about them in my books, but I never dreamed they'd be so huge! Tell me about them. What are they like? What do they do? I just want to know more and more about this wonderful world!"

Bartholomew laughed at her. "Well, they are gentle giants really. They are strictly herbivorous, which means . . ." Bartholomew paused for them to fill in the blank.

"They only eat plants." Hadyn said.

"Ah, see? You two know more about this world than you

think."

Kiara smiled, "What else?"

"Well, em, this is pretty much what they do." He gestured toward them eating, then grinned. "You know, it took them some time to get used to me, but it's plain to see, they liked you right away." Kiara beamed, feeling she had never been given a greater compliment.

Bartholomew sat down with his back against a tree. "But there's much to be learned from the beasts and wonders of nature, if you've got the eye to see it. These stout fellows will teach you a lesson in family with the way they protect each other from danger forming a pack in the water with the youngest at the very middle."

Kiara and Hadyn sat down next to him. Kiara couldn't wipe the smile off her face as she watched the young pups play and scamper about, free to run carelessly because of the loving protection of their family. Butterflies flitted in and out of the tall grass, and as they fluttered high up into the canopy their wings caught the sunlight and lit up like fireworks. Birds with striking colors and markings darted out of the trees for just enough time for them to steal a glimpse, before zooming back in, catching insects on their way.

Kiara felt her heart heave an unexpected sigh and her soul settle more restfully than it ever did while even asleep. "This really is a very special place," she said.

"Yes." Bartholomew sighed. "A sort of sacred sanctuary to me, it's where I do most of my talking with the King. I owe a great deal of my healing to the peace I found in this fine glade."

Healing . . . that's what it was. The whole glade seemed to radiate with it, sliding the tension of her shoulders and begging her to drop her pain. She wanted to or at least her body did, so why did she find her heart clinging to it like the only thing she had?

Bartholomew closed his eyes and began to hum one of his favorite songs. It fell upon Kiara's ears as the most foreign, but oh so delightful sound.

Kiara whipped her head to look at him. "What is that?"

The tune caught in his throat. "What is what?" he asked, bemused.

"That noise you were just making."

Bartholomew began to hum again.

She pointed, beaming a grin. "Yes, that!"

Bartholomew chuckled. "Well, I'm just humming. Do you mean to ask what song I'm humming?"

"A song . . . So it is music?"

"Yes." Bartholomew's brow scrunched and then he realized

with great empathy. "You've never heard music before, have you?"

Kiara shook her head.

"I have," Hadyn admitted.

Kiara turned her gaze on him and waited for an explanation, refraining from exploding the way she wanted to.

"Your grandfather used to visit the orphanage from time to time."

"Yes," Kiara said. "I know."

"He used to tell us stories. Some were silly while some were more serious, but whatever he had for us, I used to eat up every tale."

Kiara smiled, remembering. "He did tell the best stories."

"Yeah. Some were quite long, and as the other boys lost interest, nodding off one by one, I was always the last one awake or still sitting there. He told me, I had a great deal of patience, and if it was allowed, I'd probably be quite good at music. And . . . he gave me this."

Hadyn fished a small, but long, bronze whistle out of his pocket, that same one with the six holes bored down the length of it.

"That's a penny whistle!" Bartholomew grinned.

Hadyn nodded. "That's right."

Kiara's eyes flared wide. "I knew it!" She flew to her feet, snatching it from his hand and holding it like a precious artifact. "You said it was the headmasters! You lied to me. Straight to my face!"

"Kiara, what are you talking about?"

"Don't play dumb with me, Hadyn Stone. Back in Caverna, when I came to the orphanage, you talked as though you'd never seen this before in your life.

He sighed. "Yes, my apologies that I didn't know I could trust you after the, oh, what was it, second time we met?"

Kiara rolled her eyes. "And when I told you about music and said it was the one Forbidden gift I couldn't figure out? You just left me to my ignorance! You didn't say a word!"

"Maybe I knew if I told you, you wouldn't give up for nothing until I played it or let you. Kiara, it wasn't safe."

"Psh!"

"Your own grandfather told me never to play unless I was sure no one would hear, because music was against the rules. I only ever played deep in the caverns of the Forbiddens, deeper than you probably ever went."

Kiara crossed her arms, whistle still clenched in her fist.

# FORSAKEN

"Gareth used to show me the fingerings and then I would remember them and play the songs later. I also made stuff up, but I could play one of the songs he taught me now. I-if you want."

"Yes, please! Do that!" Bartholomew said, anxious to see an end to their fighting.

Kiara held to her pout a moment longer, finally huffed, and slapped the whistle in Hadyn's open palm. Suppressing a grin Hadyn lifted the whistle to his mouth. He began a playful and spirited lilt full of trills and slides. Without the fear of being caught or punished, the notes poured from his heart freer than they ever had.

Kiara's face fell in utter fascination, every clear, high note speaking to her like a word in a story. She sat in rapt silence, struggling to comprehend this new sound. The song was like a smile, so far from sorrows, she had yet to see it on someone's face; or like a feeling, so free from darkness, no mortal could possess it. She could hear her Grandfather Gareth in every phrase, the melody capturing his once buoyant and cheerful soul perfectly. Kiara could remember his laugh as if she heard it now. She loved the way he laughed, just like a child, throwing his head back in roaring, hearty laughter. But he was gone and Kiara felt the pain of his absence all over again, Hadyn's song making the hurt feel close at hand. When he died and no one wanted to say how or why, Kiara was left with no closure and feeling like some terrible wrong needed to be righted. Just like Betsie. Just like her mother . . . and that's why she couldn't let the pain go, because if she stopped hurting, how would there ever be justice? If she stopped hurting, what would she have left of them?

When Hadyn finished the song, he could see the pain on her face. "I'm sorry. I didn't mean to—"

"No," she said, brushing a tear away. She tried to fumble her feelings into words. "That was the most . . . Beautiful . . ." She stopped, at a loss. Then her brows scrunched and she bit her cheek. "Why didn't he show me? Why didn't he teach *me*? Why didn't my mother . . ."

"It was too dangerous, Kiara," Hadyn said. "They loved you too much to do that. But here, why don't you try it? It should belong to you now anyway." He held the whistle out to her. She looked at him, uncertain, before taking it. Holding it stiffly in her hands, Kiara waited for his guidance. Hadyn showed her the basics and when she couldn't stall any longer, she raised the whistle to her lips. A harsh shriek came from the instrument and Bartholomew tried not to grimace. Kiara cringed and pulled away.

"Try again," Hadyn said gently, "and this time with a little more— what's that word you say? Gumption."

Kiara chuckled at his misuse of the word. Reluctantly, she complied. With this attempt, slowly and mechanically changing the pitch. They sounded more like notes this time and less like a dying bird, but still nothing like the effortless, elegant sounds Hadyn had played. They blew out forced and strained, just notes, not music. She felt nothing more than awkward as her fingers fumbled about for the note holes. Finally, she gave up with a frustrated sigh.

"Did you sound like this when you started?"

"Well . . ." he began.

Kiara raised an eyebrow.

"No, I didn't," he admitted. "But I didn't sound like how I do now either."

Kiara handed the whistle back to him. "You keep it. You were meant to have it."

"No, Kiara, I—"

She forced his hand closed. "Hadyn, really. I mean that."

Kiara sat back not wanting to be mad, but yet unable to understand why he hadn't just told her sooner. Why he had kept it from her? It made her think of the other things he still refused to tell her. Things she had always assumed were nothing, but maybe they weren't, maybe he did have reason for the guilt he felt. She fingered the silver charm of her necklace, an involuntary attempt to comfort herself. Bartholomew seemed to notice the charm for the first time.

"That's a pretty pendant."

Kiara looked at him. "Oh, this? My mother gave it to me."

He nodded and held a hand out. "May I?"

"Oh, um . . . of course." Kiara struggled to take it off as it tangled in her curls.

Taking it, he handled it with care, holding it at arms length and then bringing it close to examine it. A smile slowly grew on Bartholomew's face. "Why, I haven't seen one of these in quite some time."

"Haven't seen one of what?"

He looked at her. "These wings, they're made of triquetras."

Kiara stared blankly.

"Celtic knots," Bartholomew explained. "And that song you played," Bartholomew said, turning to Hadyn. "If I'm not mistaken, it's an old Scottish tune."

With a jolt of remembrance, she was back to that day, shaking with fear. She could hear the horrible voice that had spoken through her father rattling around in her head. *Your first daft mistake was capturing that Scottish woman . . .*

She shuttered. "What does Scottish mean?"

"Well, Scotland is a country close to Wales, well, closer than we are right now. But for something or someone to be Scottish, it must have originated from there." Bartholomew explained and Kiara kept her thoughts to herself. "But yes," he continued, "a young boy I knew used to play that song. He had red hair like you, Kiara. He used to play his fiddle in the streets of Aberporth every Sunday. He was very good. Em, Fin, I think his name was." His face turned thoughtful. "Kiara, last night you said you learned from an old journal that the people of your city are of English descent?"

"Yes," Kiara answered. "Whatever that means."

"While I'm sure that's true for most of them," he said with a glint in his eye, "it's almost undoubtedly not so for your mother and her father for that matter."

Kiara stared at him. "What do you mean?"

"I'm not sure . . . and I don't know how or why, but I don't think your mother lived in Caverna her whole life."

He gently placed the necklace back in her small hands and Kiara looked at it as if she had never seen it before. She hung it back around her neck, an uncertain feeling stirring in her gut. But given time, even the smallest amount of tension could do little else but flee in that cheery glade. They spent the rest of their time there, sharing many laughs and stories. When they ate their picnic meal, Kiara noticed a few empty, glass jars in the basket.

"What are those for?"

"A surprise," Bartholomew said and shut the lid suspiciously.

Kiara just shrugged and let him have his secrets.

Bartholomew taught them of different plants and their uses. He told them of both the dangers and the joys of the various animals, every bit the perfect teacher and Kiara and Hadyn his fast studies. Time seemed to slow in that shaded clearing. They savored and soaked in each minute of conversation, lying quietly in the grass. Hadyn smiled as he watched Kiara get up to chase butterflies or scoot her way as close as she could to the capybaras. The darkness had crushed them to a point further than they even perceived and here in the light, they felt like they could finally breathe. The shadows eventually began to grow longer again, but this time it didn't frighten them.

Kiara sighed blissfully. "Bartholomew, please tell me you never get tired of this place."

He grunted. "Are you kidding? It's a piece of Heaven, brought down for us to see."

"If this is only a piece, then Heaven must be a truly wonderful place indeed."

He settled back against a thick tree, closing his eyes. "My dear, wonderful does not begin to describe it."

When at last they made their reluctant decision to head back, the sun was well on its last stretch to close its distance from the horizon, the capybaras had already snuggled in for the night and the butterflies had at last retired their dance, ready to wait for the sun to warm them once more in the morning light.

Dusk had fallen when they finally made it back to Bartholomew's home. Kiara and Hadyn, dragging their exhausted limbs, would have trudged right inside without him.

Bartholomew cleared his throat. "You haven't gone and forgotten all about the surprise, have you?"

They looked at him with sleepy confusion.

He waved a hand and, spry as ever, sang a bright, "Come along!"

He led them around to the back of the stone home, all the while a chirping, croaking chorus of frogs grew ever louder. The symphony apexed at a vast swamp dotted with trees growing on little grassy islands. A fine mist encircled the islands and curled up around the banks.

"Welcome to the opera house!"

Kiara didn't know what that meant, but she adored the way it sounded, and already found herself enthralled with the energy the frogs infused into the place. Without another word Bartholomew sat down on a half rotten log.

Hadyn yawned as he took a seat beside him. "I can hardly see a thing. What are we doing?"

"Wait and watch."

"For what?" Kiara asked.

"The surprise."

"Hrmph." Kiara crossed her arms and plopped down on the other side of Bartholomew.

The frogs kept on singing their little hearts out and the bugs didn't waste a moment taking advantage of a few stationary targets, but other than that, absolutely nothing happened. They just stared at the swamp as darkness stocked closer and closer. Kiara used a stick to gently stir up the water and propped her chin lazily in her hand.

Then she saw it, about ten feet away, a flicker of light, a tiny jolt of energy, electrifying the night air. She sat up straighter, thinking her eyes had played a trick on her from staring into the dark too long. But before long, hundreds, thousands even, joined in. Little lights blinked on and off, illuminating the fen in bursts. Kiara stood and let them surround her, eyes twinkling as she attempted to take in the dazzling sight.

"What are they?" she asked, whisked away in wonder.

"Back home we called them fireflies," Bartholomew answered. "I've heard them called fire dancers here, but I simply prefer to call them forest stars."

"I like that," Hadyn said, standing now too.

"I thought you might. They are actually insects. Beetles to be exact."

"So there *is* light, even in the darkest night," Kiara said.

"And don't you forget it." Bartholomew dug in the basket and pulled the jars out one by one, a giddy smile on his face. "Oh, I haven't done this in years!"

"Haven't done what in years?" Hadyn asked.

"Caught forest stars in a jar, silly."

"Oh, my apologies," Hadyn said and Kiara suppressed a snicker.

A playful light glowed behind Bartholomew's eyes. "Now, let's chase some stars!" he said and went running, jumping, and laughing like a kid.

"That does look like fun." Kiara smiled softly.

"Then why're you still standing there?" Hadyn jabbed her in the arm.

Kiara couldn't contain her excitement, all but squealing with delight, as she snatched up her jar and ran into the thick of the fireflies. Soon she and Hadyn were, like Bartholomew, jumping and laughing like the kids they never got to be.

Now filled with tiny, living lights, Kiara peered into her jar, eyes brimming with delight, her heart struck by the beauty of their glow.

"They're so small," Kiara said. "I would have thought them bigger . . . because of their light."

"Sometimes things seem small and significantly insignificant," Bartholomew winked, "but it is the Light inside that makes the difference, and carries them through each day."

Bartholomew set his jar aside and lit a lantern he had brought.

"Where did they go?" Kiara asked, feeling their departure like the sun's warmth when she used to sit at the Aperture of the

Void before the gates.

"They're still there. You just have to look a little harder."

Then, as she squinted her eyes, she could see them, just faint blinks outside the lantern's radius. In that moment, Kiara realized something. The fireflies weren't supposed to shine in the day, but rather, they had been created to shine in the darkness, to bring light where there was none, and the thought of it warmed her from the inside out.

She walked toward the water's edge and wrapped her arm around a thin tree. Leaning against it, there she rested in a firmly established peace. She turned her head and could see Hadyn and Bartholomew examining their captive fireflies and smiled. On turning back to the swamp, quick movement caught her eye as a frog hopped into the water, and floated on the surface. Not giving a thought to the water's depth, Kiara jumped in and reached out for the frog. The unsuspecting victim chirped in alarm, and the frog snatching champion stood knee deep in mucky water *she* had not suspected. Delighted anyway, she proclaimed, "I caught it! I caught a frog!"

"Good gracious . . ." Bartholomew said in disbelief. "You what?" he asked as he walked towards her.

She climbed out onto the bank, pant legs soaked and frog in hands.

"Well, I–" Bartholomew was at a loss while Hadyn laughed, not the slightest bit surprised. "My! You are a brave one."

"That was brave?" She asked.

"I'd say so!"

Kiara smiled. The frog's size sat comfortably in her two cupped hands. It had dark spots and blotches on its back and legs, like paint blobs on an abstract painter's canvas, and four gold stripes running the length of its body.

"I call those ones jaguar frogs," Bartholomew pointed out. "You're lucky it isn't one of the poisonous ones." Kiara and Hadyn just stared at him. "Oh, yes, with some of these little amphibians, their skin alone has enough toxins to stop a grown man's heart. But those are the little colorful ones anyway. They cause a sort of paralysis of the skeletal muscles. The natives use them as weapons, dipping their darts in the poison, though the bark of curare vines do just about the same thing and the toxin is much easier to procure. Oh, look. There's one right there." He grabbed the vine. "Yep," he grunted, "the jungle is quite the lethal place if you don't know your stuff. Luckily you two have me." He turned back to them and their wide eyes of horror and mortification.

Kiara held the frog awkwardly in her outstretched hands, even though he had told her it was safe, bent down, and set it free in the marsh.

"Oh, but enough of that," Bartholomew chuckled, waving a hand. "Let's go release our little lights. Shall we?"

When they opened their jars, away from the light of the lantern, the fireflies flew like sparks up into the night. Hadyn turned away first, content to rather watch the delight on Kiara's face. He wished for life to be kind enough for her to smile like that everyday. Reaching out, he gently grabbed a firefly from where it had tangled itself in her curls, igniting the spirals like a match now and again.

As if wondering why a bothersome fly was buzzing her ear, Kiara turned, but when he flattened his palm, revealing the little beetle, heat rushed into her cheeks.

"Look who doesn't think red is such a bad color," he said just as the firefly took flight to catch up with the rest. Kiara smiled, shoving him playfully.

Bartholomew retrieved the lantern and they trotted back to the door. They had gone out in laughter that day and tonight, they brought the joy back to the house, already laughing about Kiara's soaked pant legs and how she jumped into a bog without hesitation after a frog. The air had chilled with a wet mist, but once Bartholomew got the bright hearth roaring to life, they warmed up in a minute. They talked well into the night, Bartholomew waving them off when they told him they didn't want to see his ornery side, and finally trundled to their rooms to find some sleep.

Falling asleep was easy that night, but in the middle of the night, while darkness still lay thick on the jungle, Kiara awoke bolt upright from the sound of a great and powerful crack. She flew out of bed as a second one sounded in quick succession. Heart pounding, she hardly had a single coherent thought before her legs raced her out into the hall. Her mind had only begun to think to find Hadyn when she smacked straight into him. He steadied the candle in his hand as another frightfully loud boom shook their spines. They held each other's fearful gazes, replete with all the same questions. Quaking with fear, Kiara woke up enough to make observations. The great crashes sounded and felt like the rumbles and cave-ins of Caverna, but bigger, much bigger, and with a temper that seemed bent on destroying the planet.

Then the pitter-patter started. Soft, little taps on the rockface above their head drummed out a sporadic rhythm that grew harder and steadier by the beats. To their own surprise the louder the drumming became, the more effectively their fears melted down their backs. As if the rage-filled destroyer had suddenly calmed and decided to apologize, the taps came to them like a peace offering of steaming tea. Without warning, another crack shook their cores and Kiara jumped with a hiccup of a squeak, but the looks they shared from thereafter were much more filled with awe than fear.

Without a word, they walked out to where they could open a window and listened. The world beyond the glass yawned into a sightless pitch black, but they could still listen, listen to the endless, continuous peppering of the thick, latex-filled leaves, to the drenched plopping of drops joining with already gathered puddles, and to the silence in the midst of the noise. They breathed deep the sweet moist air as the ground released its answer to the sky, simply existing some place in between reverence and peace, somehow already deeply connected to something they had never experienced in their lives. The longer they listened, the more they came to antic-ipate the thunder and relish the way it rattled something deep in their chests. They stood amazed as the forest lit up for a split second before each crack, almost as bright as day, but somehow leached of most the color.

What a way to end their stay that they had indeed enjoyed more than they could have ever expected. No one could change their minds on what they had to do in the morning, but right now they could sit in an unbroken silence, listen to the sky cry its heart out . . . Daylight would come soon enough. Then, they would do what they had to do . . . then, they would say goodbye.

# Chapter Ten

# DISEASE OR DECISION

I n the morning, Kiara awoke with a fierce determination set deep inside. Despite how much she had grown to cherish the joy and time of peace they had shared with Bartholomew, it would never last knowing that her mother remained imprisoned. And with that, she wondered if she could really fool herself into thinking she'd be able to rest with even one soul left fettered in the dark of Caverna. Maybe not. She just hoped she didn't have to be the one to free them.

The three shared one last meal together just as the forest flushed blue with early light and Bartholomew gave them new packs filled with carefully selected provisions. Outside, his mouth ran with every last minute word of guidance he could think of.

"Now remember, you never drink water unless you boil it first and then let it cool. Don't eat anything particularly colorful that I haven't already told you you can eat . . . On second thought, don't eat anything I haven't told you is edible. And the giant grey birds I told you about? Stay away from their nests! I don't care how hungry you are for an omelet, or shall I mention their five inch talons once more?" They chuckled their replies. "Always stay wary of the giant otter," he continued, "which, like I said before, you can smell before you see. Very musty . . . They also make a strange clicking noise. Emm, the jaguars should leave you alone but never rule them out. Oh, yes! And snakes!" Kiara flinched at the word. "If you can, stay far away from them. No picking them up." He fixed Kiara with a look.

"Believe me, you have my word," she said.

"Oh, I feel like there is so much more to tell you, like I'm missing so much."

He started to fuss over little details of minor relevance, and Kiara's gut twisted, knowing that only meant his stalling had come to an end. She turned her face to the ground, immediately feeling stupid for the sorrow she felt, but it wasn't like they met souls as kind as Bartholomew Ebenezer's everyday.

Bartholomew stopped abruptly. "Oh, come now. Don't be sad. For this is not a bitter parting. Keep your chin up. You could be leaving in anger as so many broken hearts do. But today you should be joyful and go on your way dancing, because you are carrying on in the journey that has been set before you."

She bravely met his gaze. "But goodbyes are so hard."

"That they are, lass. But this pain is temporary. Stick with the King, and one day you will never have to say another goodbye or cry another tear. As pain itself will be, once and for all, put to death." She forced a smile and Bartholomew picked up their packs to help slide them over their backs.

"Oh! I almost forgot," Bartholomew said and fished something out of his pocket. In his palm he held a small brass compass. "It was my great grandfather's," he said, proudly, "while he captained the great ship *Atoll*. If you keep the needle pointing north you'll be sure to reach the river." He put the compass in Hadyn's hands, who held it like it was worth its weight in diamonds.

"Thank you," Hadyn said.

"You're very welcome," he said. "Try to go on your way as straight as you can and you might just make it to Aaron's village. There you will receive the most warm welcome!"

"We'll try our best," Kiara said. "I would love to meet the faces of your stories."

"Oh! Just one more thing. Despite all the survival tips I've given you, it'd be a shame to forget the best one."

"And what's that?"

Bartholomew smiled. "Pray. As much as you can. He will always listen. May I . . . may I pray for you now?"

"You may," Kiara said.

Gathering together Bartholomew placed a hand on either of their shoulders and asked the King to protect, strengthen and guide them on their journey, however long it may be or wherever it may take them.

When he finished, Kiara blinked back tears she didn't understand. "Thank you, Bartholomew, for everything."

He hugged them both. "It was my joy." And smiling brightly, he said, "Now may the God of peace who brought up our Lord Jesus from the dead, that great Shepherd of the sheep, through the blood of the everlasting covenant, protect you and keep you safe on your long journey north." Bartholomew watched them go, waving the whole time. "Grace be with you, my new friends."

They walked for quite some time in silence, just pondering on the words Bartholomew had imparted to them. For Kiara, most of his words brought a torrent of feelings, good and bad. It confused her, but not in such a horrible way that made her not want to figure it out.

Hadyn walked beside her, yet soaking in all of it, the information, the wisdom, the laughter. He had never met a man he wanted to trust so readily. After conversations with Bartholomew he felt stronger and more confident in a way he had never experienced.

"Do you think we will ever see him again?" Kiara finally said.

"I hope so," Hadyn said, checking the compass for the umpteenth time, to make sure they weren't going in circles.

Kiara smiled. "Me too."

When Kiara caught Hadyn checking the compass yet again, she placed a hand over its face. He looked at her, confused. But she only smiled, placing her other hand under his chin to tilt his face back to the forest.

"Look around you. North isn't going anywhere, nor will we stray so far off path in just a few steps."

He contemplated her advice hesitantly. Kiara closed her eyes as a mild breeze weaved through the forest to them. "And feel that? I don't care if it's only a soft breath; I don't think I'll ever get used to the way the air dances out here!" she said, spinning into its embrace.

Hadyn smiled, pocketing the compass at last. "Me neither."

The rainforest woke up and came to life before them, not hesitantly as before, but revealing in living color its beating, vibrant heart. Its frightening side hadn't ceased to exist entirely. The mysterious, even dark visage with its secrets and dangers remained, living intertwined with every tangled strand. The only thing that had changed was that now, equipped with life saving knowledge, they could see past their own fear, to the life and the beauty.

And what strange beauty they saw! Just from the insects alone, Kiara felt she could crash to her knees in awe. Elegant butterflies fluttered by flapping their stunning wings with movements both playful and graceful. Kiara's heart heaved a sigh, thinking that if there was a Creator, He had utterly lavished them with beauty!

# ELLIE MAUREEN

They saw tiny but brightly colored treehoppers and iridescent shield bugs, shining like little gems set into the trunks of trees instead of in stone walls. The grasshoppers, with their neon colors, looked ready for a midnight race, speeding and jumping through the undergrowth, lighting it up in streaks. Kiara and Hadyn found themselves now able to pick out more individual sounds too (thanks to Bartholomew's teaching) and mentally paired with their owners, even if they couldn't see them.

Life was so different here. Instead of having to scour the darkness for a single spark of beauty as deliberately as a bloodhound on a scent, here it only took stopping and really just opening one's eyes to find something beautiful. And with an overwhelming adoration for everything she saw, Kiara felt like she had to put everything but breathing on pause to successfully comprehend any of it.

But the falling of evenings had a sobering effect on Kiara's mood, visible enough for Hadyn to see, dimming her bright eyes, and hunching her shoulders with more than just fatigue. They focused simply on placing one foot in front of the other, staying on their northward course, and refraining from scratching at the many bug bites they had acquired. Every time one went away, there seemed to be four more to replace it. And some of Hadyn's larger welts had already scabbed over from relentless scratching. So much for the bugs leaving him alone. "Don't scratch," Kiara would tell him. "You'll only make yourself bleed," and he'd stop for a whole minute before returning to scraping in a fury.

As wonder was leached out and more fear was pumped into her veins, Kiara went from striding along in the grandeur and newness of it all, to allowing a deep sadness to settle into her heart. Her thoughts turned to Wilu and Isi again and how even though they saw the world every day, they were just as much captives as any soul in Caverna. She couldn't understand how someone could just decide they were greater than another. What makes a person think that they could possess or own another's soul? Their own ego? Evil itself? What is evil? What does it mean or how much power does it have? Does it need an invitation for it to change us or do its advances come upon us unwittingly, never realizing it until we're too far gone? Is it like a disease that spreads from one to another with no decision on our part? No, that couldn't be right. Bartholomew had told her we have a choice. But then how? How does anyone become so evil? These questions and thoughts plagued Kiara as her feet went into auto drive and her mind strayed from the here and now.

# FORSAKEN

Why are some people, like Bartholomew, so good? And when she decided to think of God as existing, it begged the question, was it only because of God that he was good? But that only made her angry, because if God was so good, why did innocent people and children suffer everyday? Why did Wilu and Isi suffer?

*In this world you will have tribulation; but be of good cheer, I have overcome the world . . .* Bartholomew's words drifted through her mind, like the gentle breezes of this colorful world. *The Place Always . . .* she thought. *Heaven. Then is the pain in this life meaningless? No, Bartholomew never said that.*

But maybe evil is like a disease, infecting us, even contagious in some ways, but instead of having a terminal fate, there's a Healer and He says we have a choice, a choice to fight the sickness that is in all of us. Like the perfect remedy to a snake's venom, He saves us from what's inside. But then, where was He when Betsie was murdered? Where was He when her mother was taken away? Why hadn't He saved them? Kiara felt lost in her head and instead of the black of Caverna, her mind had its own dark tunnels she kept stumbling around in, blind.

Hadyn leaned into her field of vision. "Are you okay?"

Kiara realized, as she felt her expression change, just how deep her frown had become. She sighed. "I'm not sure. I just feel . . . lost." She bit down hard on her lip. "I try to work it out in my head, but then it's all so confusing. Light, darkness, God, evil . . . What does it all mean? I thought on this search for light, I was looking for a way out of the darkness, to be rid of it."

"I . . . I don't follow."

"Well, have I really done that? How much darkness is inside of me?" She let her questions rest there. "Bartholomew talks of this inexhaustible, unconditional love that can ignite the coldest hearts and set the most enchained free, but does that kind of love really exist? And then, of all the conclusions I draw, if any, how can they be right? What do I know?" Kiara sighed, a heavy and helpless sigh.

"I've been thinking about it too," Hadyn began. "And, well, I've struggled, because when Bartholomew said that not everyone will have eternal life, that God will even turn some away . . . I didn't know what to feel. I think of my mother–" His words were caught in his throat. "And little Viviana. They never did anything wrong. How could He just . . ."

Kiara cocked her head sadly. "But you said it yourself, your mother believed in God."

"Well, she always talked like she did. She'd call Him Creator and say He was out there watching over us, even in the dark. I wanted so badly for it to be true, and she believed it as just that. But . . . was it enough?"

"Hadyn, if there is a heaven and if anyone is there, it's your mother and sister."

"You really think so?"

She made sure he looked her in the eyes before she replied. "I do."

"But what does that mean for the rest? How many others will be turned away? I hated my father more than I've ever hated anyone, but not that much. I don't know . . ."

"What?" she pressed.

"I don't know if I can trust a God that does that to people." He finally said and whether he trailed off or ended his sentence, silence took over until Kiara gave a cold laugh.

"Now where have we gotten?"

"Absolutely nowhere." Hadyn thought for a moment. "And then to make it all the worse, there's another part of me that wants so badly for this all to be true."

"Me too," she said quietly.

"Kiara, every good thing that we've ever seen or heard has something to do with God. So if He's real, somehow He's good, right?"

She knew that and agreed. "Okay. But . . . so what if God is good? What's evil?"

Hadyn shrugged. "It was evil when my father came home in his abusive rages. I knew it was because of evil . . . Well, when my sister was four year old, she got so sick. Nothing my mother did to help mattered; she only got worse. And on one of those many sleepless nights, my mother watched the life slowly drain from her only daughter. She could have died that night too and nothing would have changed, except I wouldn't have had to watch her soul agonizingly die before her body did. She never got sick, but she didn't last two months longer than Viviana." Hadyn stopped for a moment, pain etched on his face. "I was left alone with a monster for a father.

"I used to hide in this secret storage spot in the closet when he came home. I wouldn't dare come out until I heard him pass out in a drunken stupor. But one day he just never came back." His words choked with emotion. "I don't know how long I stayed in that cramped room before someone found me lying there, unconscious. But I know that it's because of evil that things like that happen. And . . . it's only because of the things that my mother talked about, that I made it through. She never really talked much,

# FORSAKEN

but the things she did say have never left me. There were nights when I dreaded closing my eyes. Even though he was asleep, I was afraid, afraid of what I used to call, the monsters in my head." He gave her a crooked smile. Kiara realized how intently she was watching him when their eyes met, something about that grin making her cheeks flush. "But my mom would simply hold my hands till they stilled," he said. "She'd tell me, 'just light your room a little brighter. Don't give the shadows a place to hide.' She said that the Creator didn't like the shadows either," Hadyn smiled, "but He wasn't afraid of them and He would protect us from them.

"When I woke up at the orphanage, they said my father had died of overuse of alcohol. I felt no sadness for this death, I only wished it could have happened sooner, preventing the monster from killing my mother and sister. I thought he should have died and they should have lived. And it's because of evil that it was the other way around." He stopped and looked at Kiara expectantly. "What about you?"

Kiara's eyes flared in shock, unsure how he had mustered the strength to do it himself, but he just nodded. "Okay . . ." she said, uncertainly. "I know it was evil that I saw in my father's eyes everyday. I heard it in the vile lies and words that came out of his mouth. It was the evil in Salin that allowed him to lead so many people into a dark captivity. It–" she stopped, not wanting to list another awful thing. "Hadyn, how is this helping?"

He chucked a stick he had picked off the forest floor. "I don't know . . . One thing's for certain, we know what it looks like. We have no problem with that."

"Yes, but why is it allowed? How does it grow in some people until it's all you see when you look at them? My mother would always talk about our real enemy. She'd say his greatest wish is for us to fail, to give in to evil, and he's trying to accomplish this at every moment. But if that's true, does he try harder with others, or are others just stronger?" Her face scrunched up and her fingers squeezed into fists. "I just wish I could understand!"

"Well . . . what if we just try?" Hadyn said, suddenly.

"Try what?"

"Try to understand."

Kiara blinked at him. "Did you not just hear a word I just said? Because I was pretty sure you were listening."

"No, I mean what if we just . . ." Hadyn couldn't find the word, "not pretend, but I don't know, say we believe and then just try to trust. Trust the Creator."

Kiara looked away.

"For-for now," Hadyn added, "and see what happens."

She squinted. "Like an experiment?"

"Yeah!" He brightened. "Like an experiment."

"I guess we could do that," Kiara said, but she still felt a lacking.

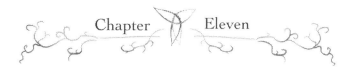

# Chapter Eleven

# LULLABY

**B**y the time they decided on a place to stop for the night, a dark cloud loomed over Kiara, though the storm once raging in her mind had died down to a drizzling, depressing rain. She was spent.

While they munched from the provisions Bartholomew had packed them, they talked about starting a fire, but the light had already faded to near twilight and they'd be lost in the dark before they could scrounge up enough dry firewood. Unrolling the blanket Bartholomew had given her, Kiara flattened it out, having no want for it except as a barrier (however thin) to separate her and the wild ground. Hot, sticky, and exhausted, Kiara sat on the blanket with her back against a tree and her arms held away from her body, trying in vain to cool down. The mosquitoes were relentless in their search for blood and they kept buzzing past her ears with a high pitched whine that made insanity look like a welcome hug.

She tried to stop thinking about things that confused or made her angry and sad, but those thoughts seemed like the only ones in her head. She wished she could just see happiness and become light-hearted or hear joy and be ready to laugh. Was that possible? Of course it was. She'd experienced it the day before with Hadyn's song. If joy had a sound, that would be it.

"Hadyn?"

"Yeah?" he said, just as he laid out his own blanket near a fallen tree he could use as a back rest.

"Could you maybe . . . Would you mind terribly playing another song, like you did yesterday?"

"Of course not. What do you want to hear?"

"Well, I've only ever heard the one song."

"Right." Hadyn remembered with a reddening of his cheeks.

"But, I'm sure I'd love anything you played," she reassured.

Hadyn pulled the whistle from his pocket and held it for a

moment while he tried to think of what to play. From his heart, he might have played something sorrowful, but they didn't need nor want anymore sadness. Then he remembered a contrasting, little tune he had composed one day when he was trying to cheer himself up. He brought the whistle to his mouth, paused to make sure he remembered the notes, inhaled, and began to play.

The jungle fell silent. Every bird, every buzz of insect wings seemed to stop in that moment. Kiara pulled her knees up and propped her chin on her arms. The song started out rather somber and slow as if some invisible force lethargically pulled the notes from the instrument. A simple melody to say the least, but Kiara could feel the sadness it expressed, beautiful, but terribly melancholy. The notes slowed to a halt and the song paused. Kiara waited. And when the song started again, it did so with a burst of joy. A smile pushed its way onto Kiara's face like a swift sunrise rolling over the horizon. Instead of the lower slow notes of the beginning, the song now moved along energetically, high and free. It reminded her a little bit of Hadyn himself, with its simple but beautiful hope. Kiara watched as his fingers looked as though they would tie in knots, and yet he never skipped a beat. The melody danced on as if nothing in the world could make it end, but then Hadyn went down the scale and it sounded like they were descending into the dark. Tragic tones started again, not slow as before, but urgent and pain drenched.

*It's a conversation!* Kiara thought.

The joyful side started persistently again as if to say, *Come on, my downtrodden friend, cheer up! The sun is only on the other side of the world right now.*

The cheerful one must have gotten through because when the song changed once more, it was bittersweet, like the moment a drought finally breaks and the heavens open to pour out their healing rains, the first tear one cries after holding on to a cold stone heart for so long, the hope a soldier keeps that he will one day return home to his family, or the first bud of spring that erupts through the snow, something brave and undeniably beautiful. The two voices of the song seemed to come together and there was victory in the symphony, celebration for healing and simply for feeling happiness again! And with triumphant finality, one last note announced the end.

Hadyn beamed a smile from ear to ear when he at last lowered his hands. Not because he was proud of himself, though he very well should have been, but because he was happy, because the song had done its perfect work, crept down into the deepest part of him, and taught him a joy, beautifully wrought despite the sadness. And when he looked, Kiara was smiling too. She smiled so big, great tears welled in her eyes as she gazed at him.

"That was . . . Incredible," she tried to scrounge up any words for this feeling swirling inside.

"Thank you." A subtle blush crept into his cheeks.

"You made that song, didn't you?"

"Yeah, I did."

She blinked in amazement. "Hadyn, do you understand how beautiful that is? I heard the story!"

Hadyn just kept smiling.

Kiara pondered back on the song, replaying it in her mind, wishing she could grasp it on a deeper level, one that would allow her to play too. Little did she know, she had gone the deepest one could and learned the reason for why the song was even formed.

"You should get some sleep," Hadyn said. "I'll stop playing now."

"No. You can . . . keep playing." The request felt clunky and awkward to say aloud, but she couldn't think of anything she wanted more. "If . . . if you want."

He smiled. "Okay."

Playing quieter, Hadyn started a new song, a very sweet and comforting melody with a steady, rain-like or waltzy pulse. The song took the fears and questions, wrapped them up tight in its melodies and notes, and made sure they went to sleep. Kiara leaned her head back against the tree and closed her eyes.

*It is the most colorful sound you'll ever hear,* the words came to her mind.

*Mom* . . . She thought and cherished the memory. She remembered her own skepticism in the notion that a sound could have colors, but, oh, how she was proved wrong! Music not only told stories, it painted elaborate pictures! The many colors sometimes splashed upon the canvas in wild creative bursts and other times delicately painted with deliberate and precise strokes of the brush. She smiled at the thought.

*I'm coming, Mom.*

Someone shook her shoulder. She could barely feel it, pulling her out of some dark place, a place she couldn't recall, a place that, more than anything, she wanted to get away from.

"Kiara, wake up." A voice in her ear.

All at once she came fully awake with a jolt. Instinctively, she jerked away from the touch and sat up.

"It's just me. It's Hadyn."

Kiara panted. Black surrounded her, threatening to choke her. She couldn't make out even the simplest form. She could feel her sanity slipping from her as her pulse raced. She wanted to scream.

"Hey, it's okay," the voice said. "There's nothing to be afraid of."

"Hadyn?" She felt her muscles loosen their tension.

"Yeah, that's right. You were talking in your sleep. You sounded so upset."

Kiara felt her head spinning in disoriented circles, even though she had no way to tell for sure. Sweat had beaded up on her forehead, and she felt so hot, but maybe that was because of the strange fear that had come over her.

"I can't see anything either," Hadyn said, knowing that she would wonder why she was blind.

Kiara gathered all her rapid breaths in an attempt to calm them and let them out in one heavy puff. "We should have started a fire."

"I know. Not only is it pitch black, but a warm fire would be nice about now! I didn't even think we would need the blankets Bartholomew gave us until now."

"You're *cold?*" Kiara asked. "I suppose the air does feel cooler than earlier."

"Well, I'm certainly not warm." Hadyn wrapped his blanket tighter around himself. "Are you alright?"

Kiara felt her hand tightly gripped around something, and realized she must have grabbed his hand sometime in her frightened delirium. Letting go, she said. "Yeah . . . I am now."

Kiara lay back down as she heard him scoot a few inches away. Her eyes wandered about the disturbingly complete darkness, the immaterial, discombobulating swirling just tricks of the eye. As she lay there her dream started to come back to her like an unwelcome guest. Kiara shut her eyes tightly.

"What did I say? . . . while I was asleep."

Silence worked its way between them as Hadyn wondered if he should say.

" 'It's not my fault,' " he finally said. "I didn't know if you were sleeping, so I responded to you. I said, 'I know,' but you continued as though I had said the opposite." Kiara cringed. "You kept crying that it's not your responsibility, that you hadn't asked for any

# FORSAKEN

of this. It seemed like you could use a hand to pull you out of those thoughts, so I woke you up."

Silence and then Kiara whispered, "Thanks . . ."

More silence, but Hadyn broke it this time. "You didn't have them at Bartholomew's, did you?"

"What?"

"Nightmares. You didn't have nightmares there."

Kiara tried to think back on both the nights spent in that cozy, little room. Had she actually slept through the night? She wouldn't think so, but to her surprise and confusion, she couldn't recall waking up once, besides when the storm got them both up.

"Not that I can think of, but . . . I'm certain I must have."

"Why?"

Kiara hesitated to answer. ". . . Because they're always there."

Hadyn remained silent, which she supposed was his version of a reply.

Soon, she did begin to feel quite cold, even to the point of shivering. A clammy chill, like mist out of a graveyard, crept up her spine and made her feel sick to her stomach. She wrapped her blanket around her, for more reasons than one. Not knowing what surrounded her, every unidentifiable noise made her muscles more and more tense. The trees creaked and then the branches rustled. A squeak sounded close by and something skittered across the debris of the forest floor.

*What sort of creatures prowled about in the night?* she thought. *More like the monsters that chased us through the dusk?*

Not good thoughts.

Kiara tried to shake them away, tried to think of brighter things. She thought about the stars and tried to imagine what they really looked like, but with the darkness so thick, it was hard to believe they were really out there.

"Hadyn?" she whispered, wondering if he was still awake.

"Yeah?" he whispered back.

"Do you think the stars are really above us right now?"

Hadyn didn't need long to think. "Of course I do."

Kiara smiled. Most of her knew it too, but to hear Hadyn say it was a comforting thing. He had surety that could be gentle and fierce at the same time and with it, it was easy for her to know they were still shining, even when they couldn't see them.

She snuggled deeper into her blanket. "Do you remember their names?" she whispered.

Hadyn left a gap of quiet for only a moment. "Vega . . .

Canopus . . . Arcturus . . ."

Kiara took up a turn. "Deneb . . . Sirius . . ."

Then they went back and forth.

"Altair."

"Rigel."

"Acrux."

"Capella."

"Achernar."

Kiara yawned. ". . . Pollux." And by her next turn she had drifted into an uneasy sleep.

Chapter Twelve

# THE SNAKE

The morning broke grey, the rainforest blanketed in a somber lull. Kiara had yet to open her eyes, but already her first thought was to make sure her lantern had stayed burning though the night. Then, for the first time, she struggled to pry open her lids, her eyes not ready for or even understanding the light already surrounding her. She propped herself on her elbows and, bit by bit, she opened her lids a little further, focusing on individual pieces of the forest, a twig, a bright, splayed fern. It all flooded back to her, making her head spin. She realized inside Bartholomew's little tunneling home, mornings were still dim enough to be gentle, but out here in the open, the early light took her breath away.

"Gonna take some getting used to, isn't it?" Hadyn rummaged through his pack, throwing together a simple breakfast for the two of them.

Kiara chuckled, noticing him for the first time. "Ya' think?"

Hadyn rubbed his eye and yawned as she sat all the way up. "You look terrible. Did you stay up all night?" Kiara asked.

He shook his head. "Of course not. Not . . . all night."

"Well, that's not going to work. Why didn't you wake me up?"

Hadyn didn't answer and continued rummaging through the packs for breakfast.

She laughed in disbelief. "Hadyn, you can't not sleep! Tomorrow night, you wake me up if you can't sleep without some-one on watch. We'll take it in shifts." He kept his silence. "You hear me?"

Hadyn raised a hand without turning around. "Yeah, yeah."

Kiara could only smirk and shake her head.

After their breakfast, they set off north again. With hardly a breeze in the day, the hours lumbered on like a lethargic sloth through the branches. The thick canopy seemed to let the hot air in and then trap it, creating a sort of suffocating, wet oven, ready to cook everything inside. At times they had to wade or even swim across minor rivers, smaller tributaries of the greats, all crossing and twisting over one another like the tunnels of the Forbiddens. And not all streams were as clear and inviting as the crystal underground spring they entered the jungle on. The murky dark waters gave the travelers pause as they pondered on all that could be swimming beneath, but thankfully none of the currents had proven very strong.

Their northward path took them once again through dense understories of unchallenged growth, especially around the streams and rivers creating yet another obstacle to slow their way. Half the time, Kiara felt the jungle itself was against them, bent on impeding them and pushing them to the brink of their patience. It seemed the farther they traveled the more difficult it became to keep going. The prison of Caverna was torture, but something about it looked comfortable compared to this struggle. Where was the momentum on a road that kept forcing barriers in your path?

With each leaf that swung back, whacking Kiara in the face and each branch that caught her curls and tangled them up in abominable knots, her anger rose and so did her temperature.

She followed behind Hadyn, huffing and puffing in her exasperation, about ready to blow a gasket when with a painful yank to her scalp, she was forced to a violent stop. Kiara whipped around with a growl and muttered to herself as she pulled at the caught hair. "Stupid, good for nothing atrocity."

Hadyn turned and jumped to action. "Hey! Careful! Let me help you."

She dropped her arms like heavy sacks of flour, face red and covered in sweat. "It's no use. Better off just chopping it."

Hadyn stayed quiet, concentrated as he detangled the copper strands, careful not to pull them the wrong way. Kiara tensed, watching him warily. His apparent insistence on touching her ugly mess continued to perplex her.

"It's always something new with this hair. And it's always something terrible. Mum didn't get it. Her hair's beautifully straight and ebony black. But it found me."

Hadyn gave a soft laugh, but despite her assumptions, it wasn't at her words. Finished with freeing her hair from the branch, he plucked something from close to the top of her head. "This little guy sure likes it." He lowered his palm so she could see the tiny, slug-like caterpillar now inching along his hand. Lilac and violet in color it looked like a cluster of living amethyst druzy, its gelatinous, semi-translucent body like a perfect cluster of crystals.

The corner of Kiara's mouth ticked up in a smile. "How incredible! It's like a little jewel."

"Exactly. And he liked your hair."

She knew what he was trying to do, always trying to downplay how awful it really was. She rolled her eyes. "How flattering. Insects and forest critters find it a cozy place to nest in."

Hadyn didn't comment and when he released the jewel caterpillar, he suggested they take a break. Kiara readily agreed.

While they sat against a rotting log, throats already parched with a thirst that could drink a river dry, their minds naturally turned to water and the definite limit of their current supply.

"We're going to have to collect some more from the rivers," Hadyn said.

"Drink that disgusting water?" Kiara's eyes flared. "No way."

"Either that or collect it from the leaves after it rains like Bartholomew said. We'll certainly need more before we reach Aaron's village."

Kiara breathed a tired laugh. "You say that like it's a when not an if," she said, wiping her sleeve across her forehead.

"Well, I thought—" Hadyn scrunched his brow.

"Yes, I know. But at some point, you'll agree, we have to start thinking realistically."

". . . Okay, but—"

"Like, what are our chances even?" She cut him off. "Look at this place!"

"You're just overwhelmed. Bartholomew said we just have to go as straight as we can."

"Yeah . . ." Kiara scoffed, "real informative."

Hadyn wasn't about to argue. He turned his face away.

Kiara blinked, shocked at how much her words had upset him. She sighed. She didn't know why she always had to say stuff like that, always bringing the shadow to snuff out the light. She didn't want to be a shadow. She loved the way he looked at life, so why would she ever attempt to poison it? It was destructive and wholly against her better judgment. His words just then were a gift, like the sunshine is to the earth, all she had to do was accept it.

While they rested, who else but the sun decided to show his

cheery face, not directly to them, shrouded by the tree tops, but they could still see its effects on the forest. As the rays stretched out from behind the clouds, the leaves slowly transformed and resumed their jewel-like shine. While still very green, the whole jungle seemed to glow with something golden.

*Just like the sunshine is to the earth* . . . Kiara mused.

They watched it in wonder, knowing if they happened to have been standing, they would have fallen to their knees in awe, and when their gazes found each other again, they wore smiles once more. They both clammed up at the sight of each other's goofy grins and laughed it off awkwardly.

Kiara's smile sobered first. "I'm sorry I say things like that. You're right. We *should* hope to find the village." She stood and looked at him with a new determination. "Hope is all we can do. But that's not such a terrible thing, now is it?" She stuck a hand out to him.

He considered her a good moment, a grin growing on his face. Shaking his head, he accepted her hand and popped to his feet. He shouldered his pack and consulted the compass to find exact north.

"Lead the way," she smirked, "Captain."

As they started going again, Kiara walked along, almost lightheartedly, trying to forget about the difficulties of getting anywhere in the thick foliage. Instead she took to admiring the trees once more. Strange formations, they seemed to grow slowly over long years, sort of like stalactites, but in a much more wholesome way, life giving and ever reaching for the sunshine. It struck her that even the least of these great trees must have been here for some time, the largest having withstood the test of time, floods, and harsh weather. They had earned their place on the earth establishing their roots deep into the ground, the same ground she walked on. The thought changed the way she put her feet down for a moment, taking deliberate, thinking steps. She raised her face at all their reaching branches and smiled at their strength, their silent grandeur.

"Hadyn, what did you think it would be like out here?" she asked. "What did you think the trees would be like, or the creatures? Before we saw them, of course." She waited a moment. "Can you even remember?"

Hadyn thought hard on that. "Not really."

She whipped her head, throwing him an astonished grin.

"Isn't that strange?"

"Maybe it's because it's all so much better than even our greatest expectations."

"So, our minds just decided we didn't need them?"

He snickered. "Well, I can tell you one thing, there wasn't much of an expectation to begin with. The sketches in the journals helped and all, but it was still hard. Never would I have even dreamed of all this."

"And to think, there's still so much more. There's the wide, open ocean just like in Bart's story. There's meadows, and deserts, and frozen places covered in snow! There's mountains, and valleys, and—"

"Kiara, stop!"

She threw a silly grin over her shoulder. "Stop what?" she said, taking another step, just as Hadyn leaped up beside her and shot his arm out in front of her.

"Watch out!" he warned.

When she turned back, Kiara stood face to face with black eyes and a forked tongue. The snake hung down from a limb, its neck coiled back, ready to strike. Kiara's muscles went as rigid as petrified wood. She didn't dare to blink. She didn't breathe. She tried to will her heart to stop beating so hard, fearing even the slightest sound or movement would provoke a strike. But it just stared at her, its lifeless eyes contradicting the fact that it even had a working heart, more like black holes where life was absorbed and promptly destroyed.

Kiara felt stuck. A desperate need to move raked at her soul, but she couldn't. The black eyes locked hers and the snake didn't stir, perturbing her all the more. Sweat dripped down the sides of her face. She thought she might faint. The question was, from which first— holding her breath or simply her own fear?

Kiara barely recognized the gentle hands carefully placed on either of her shoulders or the distance steadily growing between her and that flicking, searching tongue, as Hadyn, practicing the slowest, snail-like movements, pulled her backwards and away from the snake. He took passive, but deliberate steps, never deviating from that same, almost painful pace. Kiara never once took her eyes off the glaring serpent, scarcely breathing until distance and encroaching brush at last blocked it from view.

Finally something broke and Kiara breathed a huff, the air leaving her lungs taking with it the rest of the strength in her legs. She stumbled to the ground and let her pack slide off her back. Every inch of her trembled with the aftershock.

Hadyn knelt beside her. "Are you alright?"

"I'll be fine," she said, trying to calm down.

Her heart hammered in her chest and her tremors even shook her breaths. She grabbed her water from her pack and took a parched gulp. "It just stared at me, Hadyn. Why did it do that? Those eyes . . ."

He shook his head at a loss for words. She didn't like the amount of concern his eyes were placing on her, like she was some fragile piece of pottery. Shaking out of it like a bad dream, Kiara smashed a fist into her palm. "Out of all the countless creatures to nearly walk straight into, did it have to be a snake? Did it have to be me?"

Hadyn wrestled a grin, her angry lilt a welcome surprise compared to crushing fear.

"Well, we're far away from it now."

"Ha! Not far enough," she said, "I want to keep going."

"If you say so. But are you sure you can stand on those jelly legs?"

"Yes. I'm sure," she said definitively.

While they cut a wide detour around the snake, Hadyn kept the compass out to make sure they got back on track. Kiara couldn't shake her thoughts of those black eyes. Any strength she had mustered to fend off the gloomier feelings had been eaten up in those pits in a moment. Her shaky legs only just sufficed for traveling, and new waves of nausea came with a sick clamminess in the bottom of her stomach. Once she reached the crashing side of her adrenalin high, she could hardly take another step.

She fought to speak in between labored breaths. "Can we stop for the day? I can't go any further."

Outside the forest, the sun had only just begun to set. Hadyn noted this with a scan of their surroundings. "Of course. But is something wrong?"

"I'm fine," was her terse reply. "I just . . . don't feel very good."

He eyed her warily as she sat down against a tree. Not wanting to make the same mistake twice, Hadyn considered getting started on gathering the firewood.

"Look, I'm going to get some sticks and . . . whatever for a fire. But you just rest, okay?" He could see by her face alone that wasn't going to work. "I won't go far," he reassured. "Just yell if you need anything and I'll yell if I need you." Reluctantly, mostly because she was too tired to follow, she let him go.

True to his word, Hadyn did stay close, so close, Kiara could hear him crashing about in the leaves and branches the whole time. She heaved a sigh as she settled between the ridges of a fluted trunk. Her muscles twitched with exhaustion. She felt like she could fall asleep right there if it weren't for the sickening churning in her gut and the fact that every time she closed her eyes she saw the glossy, black pits of the snake. She wouldn't admit it to Hadyn, but it wasn't just the snake alone that terrified her, but the deep hatred she saw in its gaze and how it reminded her of something else she feared. She wouldn't believe it was just her imagination. Just like everything else, it seemed to be glaring at her, telling her to leave and not come back.

"Why?" she cried quietly, asking no one but the hot, thick air around her.

She got the feeling she didn't belong here, maybe neither of them did, but especially her. She didn't know anything about this world and everything was just so hard. How was she ever going to make it long enough to reach her mother? Maybe she didn't deserve this world. Maybe she had spent the extent of her life in the dark because she didn't deserve any better. It was how it was meant to be.

When Hadyn returned, he had a bundle of sticks and broken branches in his arms and a bright smile on his face. "Kiara, you have to see this!" He found her with her eyes closed, but he knew she wasn't asleep, her brow knit with the frustration of countless thoughts. "What's wrong?"

Her eyes fluttered open and she considered him for a moment as his face fell. "Nothing." She smiled. "What have you got there? What did you want to show me?"

Hadyn didn't think she'd appreciate it in her state of mind, but maybe, just maybe it would cheer her up. "You're not gonna believe this," he said, shoving the armful of sticks in her face.

She raised a copper brow. "I see sticks, Hadyn."

He ignored her lack of enthusiasm. "But that's what's so fascinating about it! Here, look at this." He held the pile with one arm and used his free hand to gently nudge one of the most delicate sticks on the top of the bundle.

Kiara gasped. The stick had moved!

"See!" Hadyn said and then tried to coax the curious little creature onto his hand.

Patient and gentle enough, Hadyn had the amiable critter

standing on his palm in no time. He let the wood tumble out of his arm and he and Kiara leaned in to examine the stick insect. Kiara could see now that what she once ignored as a simple stick, had six legs, two antennae, as well as two, little, round eyes.

"But it's beyond belief!" Kiara marveled, once again smiling.

"Told you."

"It was completely hidden before it moved. I would have never seen it!"

"I don't think there was anything about these in your books," Hadyn added.

"No. I don't suppose many people have ever seen them."

"Here, you hold it."

Kiara couldn't have been more delighted. Step by step, its delicate legs moved in an untroubled manner as he guided it onto her hands. Light as a feather, Kiara could barely feel it on her hand.

"Do you . . . do you think God hid it because it's defenseless otherwise?" she asked.

He smiled at her thoughtfully, just glad she was happy again. "Maybe."

While Kiara spent more time examining their phasmid friend, Hadyn got started on the fire. He prepared a spot, moving the brush aside and piled the sticks up in an orderly manner. With new strikers from Bartholomew, Hadyn splashed an explosion of sparks over the wood, but they died on impact with a pathetic sizzle.

Hadyn sat back on his haunches. "Hmm."

"What is it?" Kiara asked.

He put a hand to his chin. "I think the wood is too damp."

Kiara set the walking stick free on the ground. "Maybe if we can get some leaves to burn, the fire will get the wood hot enough to start a fire?"

"Worth a try." Hadyn shrugged.

Gathering some leaves, they stuffed them in and around the wood pile. The sparks hit the leaves and they ignited.

"Yes!" Kiara exclaimed.

They watched with anticipation, but despite the constant presence of fire back in Caverna, it was a different world out here with a whole new set of rules and they didn't get much more than smoke in their eyes. They gathered even more leaves and tried again. Each time the burst of sparks ended in a disappointing death, Hadyn's hands grew more and more raw, but Kiara wasn't about to spend another night in the pitch black.

"Let me try," she demanded, igniting the leaves. "Come on,

come on . . ." she said through her teeth as the fire dwindled once more. She threw more on top. "Come on!" More leaves, more sparks. She spewed out a desperate barrage, but all that remained when she finally paused to swipe the smoke out of the way was ash from the leaves and some very unscathed, uncharred sticks.

"No, no, no!" she protested.

"It's no use, Kiara. It's just too wet."

"But . . ." she began to tremble, her body knowing even better than her head of the dark to come and how much she feared it.

"It'll be alright. We'll take watches, remember? And maybe tomorrow we'll make it to Aaron's. Besides, we spent our whole life in the dark, another night isn't going to break us," he said defiantly.

Kiara just stayed silent. She didn't care whether or not it would break her. No matter its survival rate, she didn't want to bear another night of uncertainty and blindness.

While they munched on dinner, Kiara never found it in her to fully settle down, her hands having developed a dreaded shake that flared up whenever she dwelled on the steadily falling night. In another attempt to relax, she lay back in the nook she had found in the fluted tree, but every time she let her lids fall shut, the snake was back, eyes somehow glowing with a black light. She huffed before she could hyperventilate and laced her fingers tightly together to stop the shaking. She watched Hadyn as he finished tidying up their packs, seemingly calm. Maybe he was just trying to be strong.

"Hadyn, would you . . ." she trailed off.

"Sure," he said, fishing out his whistle.

She gave him a careful grin, wondering how he just knew things like that.

Hadyn played something wholly different from the previous night, but just like before the music tucked itself into her heart like a wooly blanket and surrounded her in a soft and unrelenting hug. One by one, she released her fingers from each other's grasps, the shake in her hands stilling with a sudden and steady peace.

Hadyn closed his eyes or looked out into the forest as he played. The music seemed to help him too. Kiara wondered if there was some kind of protection in it. If not, why did it make them feel so safe?

Her eyes drooped. She didn't want to sleep. She didn't want to drop her guard. She had planned to take the first watch, seeing how last night went. *Yes . . . the first watch, so Hadyn can sleep . . .* But by the next note, her lids had shut and her chin dropped to her chest.

# Chapter Thirteen

# DALMATIA

Running. Mad with fear and running into darkness, endless darkness. She didn't think the forest had made its way into her dreams yet, but it must have, because here she was and she knew it wasn't the first time.

A cold light shone behind her, like nothing she had ever seen, not warm and rutty like fire or sunlight, but clean and pale, yet it was so dim and all she could do was run as things she couldn't see grabbed and scraped her legs, arms, and face. Their noises filled the night with crazed cackles and howls of bloodlust. A clearing up ahead revealed the shadowed shape of a tall figure. She ran towards it like her only hope, loping in a panicked fury. Sharp features began to take shape and she knew this stranger.

"Father?" she could hear herself say.

He stood in the middle of the clearing, arms wide open as if for a hug. She slowed to a walk. The creatures had eerily vanished, hanging a mysterious silence around the black neck of the night. When she came near him, his eyes looked straight through her like she wasn't even there. She looked up at his almost pleasant expression.

"Father?"

His eyes settled on her then and he seemed to actually see her. For a moment her heart swelled to see his face again. Tears sprang to her eyes. "Oh, Father!" she cried. "It's been so dark! I don't know what to do! I'm just so tired and frightened!"

She thought she heard someone call her name, but her own words poured from her mouth like rain and drowned it out. With her arms wide she went to bury herself in his chest. Two firm hands on her shoulders jerked her to a stop at arms length.

They rejected her.

Tears rolled down her cheeks as she struggled to understand.

"But . . ." She looked into his eyes, but they were cold and already turning black. Kiara recognized the eyes of the snake before the black had even finished enveloping them and he was about to strike. She jerked back, horrified. With only a second more of hesitation, she bolted from him and fled back into the thick of the forest. The monsters were back on her heels, scratching, pulling and tripping her, their cries once again filling the night with bedlam. She fell on her face. Someone was screaming, and as she was at last ripped from the nightmare, she realized it was herself.

She thrashed and she sobbed, but someone held her tightly until she stopped.

She heard Hadyn's voice in her ear. "Kiara, it's okay! I'm right here. It was just another dream."

Struggling to take in each breath, Kiara strained to see, forgetting once again why it was so dark.

"Hey! You're alright. You're safe." His words chased out the fear, gentle and calm, and finally, slowly he began to let her go.

Kiara took one, big, shaky breath to try to calm down. Then the screaming started again, but this time the cries were not her own. They bellowed through the forest, inhuman and guttural, deep and loud, extremely, ear-shatteringly loud. Anger rode on the echoes of the cacophony.

Kiara and Hadyn slammed their hands over their ears, wincing at the ruckus and the pain it caused. Then as soon as the screams started, each one of them departed, leaving a ringing buzzing in the thick silence like a swarm of gnats. They hesitated to lower their hands from their ears, like they didn't know if they'd have to clamp them back on in an instant.

In between quaking breaths Kiara whispered, "What . . . was that?" Neither had an answer and silence wormed its way between them.

"We should move," Hadyn whispered. "We can't just sit here and wait for whatever's out there to find us."

"Where would you like to go, Hadyn?" Her clipped words shot out faster and harsher than she wanted, and when he didn't answer, she sighed. "It's pitch black and there's some unknown pack of beasts out there that can probably see better than we can. I don't want to stay here either, but I think it's safer than stumbling about in the jungle and leading it straight to us."

Fresh tears wet her face and she realized she didn't remember when the first ones had sprung. "What we need is light. It might scare it away . . ." she sniffed back a sob, "whatever it is."

As if triggered by her show of weakness, something moved

in the undergrowth, snuffling around.

Searching.

Hunting.

Kiara's thoughts were devoured by the creatures that had pursued them. Bartholomew said no creatures of the forest would hunt people, but she knew in her heart these were the very same, tracking them, smelling them out, intent on making this endeavor just like every other piece of her life— destined to fail.

She and Hadyn edged a bit closer to each other. Somewhere in front of them a low growling rumbled in the dark.

"Kiara," Hadyn ventured, his voice quivering as he spoke, "remember what Bartholomew said about God helping us when we ask?"

"Y-yes?" she squeaked.

"Well, maybe we should ask him for light."

"Alright. Go ahead."

"Oh . . . okay." *How does Bart say it?* he thought. "Mighty King . . . we could use some light right now . . . any kind really. So that we can . . . not die." He thought he should end it the way Bartholomew always did, but couldn't remember the word, so he settled on, "please."

Would it still work?

There was a huff and then the sound of crunching leaves and sticks as beating, angry feet, started a charge. Their hands found each other's, their eyes wide in their sightless panic. They tensed their muscles. Maybe if they held still enough it would run straight past them. Leaves crunched closer and closer. Probably not.

This was it. All their struggles, tears and pain . . . and they might die of exploding hearts before the creature even got to them. Kiara squeezed her eyes shut even though the darkness already rendered her blind.

Then, as the beating feet became more of a hopping prance, the sounds grew quieter as the charger suddenly became the absconder. They held their breath, unable to believe they were safe just yet. Why did it run? There was no light. They couldn't even see their own noses.

Kiara felt a hand on her shoulder and heard Hadyn say, "Stay here," as he wrestled his shaky legs into a stand. Kiara popped up at his side anyway. They peered about the total and complete darkness. Kiara felt hollow, the nightmare's claws yet firmly sunk into her shoulders. She squinted about, wondering if she was beginning to make out vague shapes or if her eyes were only playing tricks on her.

"There!" Kiara whispered.

Just a jaunt away, through the brush, firelight leaped to their eyes with wide open, welcoming arms. The wholesome scent of a bonfire lifted off the ashes and danced through the trees to their noses. A small, narrow path before them, most likely a tapir run, looked to traipse its way towards it.

"No way . . ." Hadyn breathed. "Do you think someone's over there?" The murmur of subtle laughter answered his question.

"Do you think the Creator sent them?" Kiara wondered out loud, but neither had to say another word, both shouldering their packs and taking a step toward the inviting fire.

One step was all Kiara managed, before a flicker out of the corner of her eye begged for some attention. A glossy leaf by her hand reflected a faint, blue glow. She cocked her head as she turned around to see the cause of it.

"Hadyn." Her voice sounded far away in his ears like only half of her still remained on earth.

"Yeah?"

"Look at this." She pulled on his arm without prying her eyes off the sight for a moment. He turned around but said nothing, both mesmerized as they stared at a set of flames only a few paces away.

Blue flames.

On a stone pillar, about three feet high, sat a bed of blue fire that washed every surrounding surface and leaf in a shade of indigo.

Kiara scrunched her nose. "Where did it come from?"

Allured by the blue flames, Kiara drifted ever closer without a single conscious thought, drawn by an unseen pull. The fire emitted no heat. Her wide eyes reflected the blue light, a strange desire and fascination falling upon her that she hardly even cared to place.

Her face split with a rapturous grin. "It's beautiful."

Hadyn didn't say a word, not because he didn't agree, but more because he did and was simply at a loss for words.

Just as two moths drawn to something they didn't even know why they loved, they felt content to stare forever. Then, like a strike of a match, two more pillars lit ablaze, one on each side of what looked like a wide path, and still not another soul could be spotted.

Because of their dark glow, nothing could be seen past the small area they illuminated, but as they watched, one after the other, the little blue fires revealed another piece of the path as it wound away and through the trees. They blinked in disbelief. Already, the path was much too long for them to see an end to, all new flames lost in the distance. Kiara turned to Hadyn, that child-like glint of mischief in her eyes. With nothing but excitement and wonder holding the reins of her heart, she led the waltz through the strange lights, without another thought of the first, humble campfire.

Happily, they lost track of time along this enchanted path. The lights led them like silent will-o'-the-wisps, only whispering with their wavering dance. They beckoned them to keep following. And follow is all they wanted to do because here they had direction and it didn't matter to where.

Kiara blinked and spun around, laughing in wide-eyed amazement. "It's like something out of a dream!" she said. For a fleeting moment she felt a contrasting pang of conflicted questioning, as if she didn't know what kind of dream she was implying. She pushed the thought away. Nothing this wonderful ever happened in nightmares. She didn't even think nightmares could exist here. The blue light washed away the world they were only just beginning to know, and painted them into a new land, a mysterious land, maybe even one better than this one and all its struggles.

Kiara danced a content circle to see all the lights winding through the jungle. "Simply magic!" she said.

She caught Hadyn smiling at her, and felt her cheeks grow warm. There was that look, that sweet grin, the first thing about him that found a place in her heart. Something about the enveloping light and the air so thick with enchantment made her feel like she could take a step closer to him and stroll hand-in-hand the rest of the way.

But the trail was already coming to an end and when they both turned back to the road ahead, they stopped frozen in their tracks. A man stood at the end of the trail. He seemed to be waiting, posture straight as a pin, hands behind his back. He held his head cocked to the side, a crooked smile on his face. He had fair, pale skin washed in the blue light, and dark, neatly cut wavy hair.

"Two little lambs lost in the woods . . ." he muttered, but then his smile broadened and it was clear he spoke to them. "Hello and welcome." His words carried authority, but the pleasant kind, the kind you wouldn't mind following. "We've been expecting you."

# PART TWO

## THE VILLAGE

*I will bring the blind by a way they did not know; I will lead them in paths they have not known. I will make darkness light before them, and crooked places straight. These things I will do for them, and not forsake them.*

−Isaiah 42:16

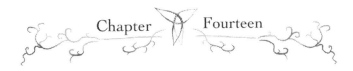

# Chapter Fourteen

# THE INTRODUCTION

Y ou might be wondering with some skepticism about this decision to follow the blue path if you do, in fact, remember a certain dream of Kiara's. I imagine you're thinking that at the very moment they rid themselves of their eternal night, they have walked straight back into shadows. And I can't avoid it, the strangeness that ensued from that one decision is hard to put in so many words, but I have tried my best to weather these absurdities and write them as they transpired.

Yes, it seems like a paradox to choose the dark when all you've ever wanted was light. But if all paths have a chance to be righted, can any be all that wrong, at least indefinitely? Light rises out of darkness everyday, like hope springs from tears. And as flowers bloom from the thawing ground of a frozen winter, all redemptions come from some story of corruption.

Kiara and Hadyn hesitated, gawking like buffoons as if this dark sprite of a man, standing out in the middle of the wilderness, could be talking to anyone else. When he only stared back, the crooked smile never once wavering, Kiara finally broke the silence with a bemused, "Expecting?"

"We?" Hadyn added.

The man's smile took on a warmer, more amused look. "My name is Deorc," he introduced. "Come, you must meet the others." Without another word wasted on pleasantries, he turned and started to walk away.

Kiara looked to Hadyn, hoping for some bit of sanity in this strangeness. He shrugged his shoulders. "We asked for light, didn't we?"

# FORSAKEN

"Yeah . . . you're right." She eyed Deorc as he walked further away, her curiosity tugging at her like a lead tied to his ankle. "Come on," she said, and they trotted to catch up with the man who had appeared from seemingly nowhere at all.

As they came up behind him, he addressed them once more, "I'm glad you decided to tag along. Now, I will introduce you to the rest. Until then, you mustn't speak a word. It's tradition!" he added merrily.

When they didn't make a sound of reply, Deorc glanced over his shoulder. "Ah, very good."

Kiara and Hadyn exchanged wary looks. Kiara had a million questions coursing through her mind, but they walked in silence because they were asked to, and because Deorc himself chose only a precise amount of words.

The blue flame pillars lit their path the entire way. Just when they thought the fires were done appearing, two more would bloom to life on either side of the path just where Deorc had last stepped, as if he somehow controlled them. Kiara's questions about the fires and how they worked burned the most wildly in her mind, but she thought better than to break the requested silence. So they plodded along, following this tall man through the sleeping jungle until, at last, Deorc came to an abrupt halt. Darkness lay before them.

"Come beside me so you can see it better." Deorc's voice was breathless with reverie, as he pulled them up, one on each side of him. "Welcome," he said, "to Tykaraijre!" With a lift of his hands, blue light sprang up everywhere, illuminating an entire town in its glow! Roads, houses, and gated gardens leapt out of the shadows of the night as quick as a spark. Kiara gasped at the sight. Never once expecting such a shock.

"Yes, you like it? It's my favorite part too." Deorc said, which had Kiara wondering how often new visitors came along.

"I am Deorc Tykara and this is *my* town," he formally introduced and strode forward, leading the way.

They walked past wooden houses and buildings with grass and leaf roofs, but in the eerie blue light and unbroken quiet something about the town seemed abandoned, and Kiara half wondered if it was.

As if reading her thoughts, Deorc explained, "The village is out right now, attending a gathering, not far from here. They will be back soon. Come, I'll bring you to the place where I will introduce you. You can wait there."

They followed him through the little blue town to an open area with a raised, wooden stage. Deorc led them behind the stage where two doors hung on tired, rusted hinges. Deorc fished a key ring out of a pocket and unlocked the corroded keyhole. He made a gesture with his hands for them to go in. A blue lantern on a small table weakly lit a low-ceilinged space under the stage. All of a sudden Kiara wasn't too sure she wanted to listen to everything he told them to do. She looked at Hadyn who also seemed uneasy, then at Deorc. He wore the same smile as before and seeing it closer, Kiara thought there was maybe something she didn't like about it, something slippery or uncertain. Deorc kept his hand outstretched until, at last, they filed inside. Kiara and Hadyn whipped around at the sound of creaking hinges, just in time to see the doors swinging shut.

"Wait here," he called from the other side of the doors. "Everyone will be back soon." His voice had seemed to change, colder, more calculating than before or perhaps that was just the muffled effect of the wood and Kiara's imagination. They heard his footsteps as he walked away.

Kiara stared at the closed door. "What . . . what did we just walk into?"

Struggling to decide if the roof was high enough for him to stand up fully, Hadyn took the lantern off the table and shed some more light on the cramped corners of the space where dusty crates and barrels awaited further use.

"I don't know," he shrugged. "Looks like some kind of storage area."

"Or a prison."

Hadyn froze in mid attempt to pry one of the lids off the crates and shot her a skeptical look.

"Well," Kiara said, "why do we have to 'wait in here for them to come?' Who's them anyway? It's question-raising to say the least."

With a sniff, Hadyn resumed his snooping. "At least he didn't lock the door."

Kiara stomped to the door to make sure. "Locked or unlocked there's something strange going on."

"Yep," Hadyn said, rummaging in the three foot tall crate.

She chuckled. "I don't get it. How are you so calm, Mister Untrusting?"

"Trust? Oh, no. I don't trust this Deorc, not a lick. But that's just it, don't trust anyone and you never have to deal with this struggle of deciding whether or not someone deserves it."

"Hmm . . . Do you trust me?"

Hadyn paused in his rummaging. "What? I didn't— Why

would you ask that?"

Kiara didn't want to acknowledge the sting that gave her. "Well, you said—"

Suddenly Hadyn's eyes lit up. "Kiara, you have to come look at this!"

Kiara abandoned her pacing and the conversation to rush to the crate. "Whoa!" she exclaimed, reaching in and pulling out an extravagant outfit made entirely of bright, flashy feathers. "This is incredible!" She put it down and searched the rest of the crate. "I wonder what these are used for. Deorc wasn't dressed like that."

Hadyn popped on a giant, feather headdress, crossed his eyes, and stuck his tongue out. Kiara laughed and shook her head, like he was the silliest fool she had ever seen. She reached in for a new item. Something rattled, clunking together as she pulled it out. One glimpse of dry, sun-bleached bones, strung strangely together by vines and she threw it back down. A sudden pang of fear dizzied her and set her hands shaking.

"We . . . we should put these away." She steadied herself with the wall of the crate.

"Sure." Hadyn's smile faded as he removed the feather hat and replaced the lid. "Are you alright?"

"I-I don't know. It was like . . . well, do you remember the first time we opened the trapdoor in the library? And we felt that . . . that awful dread?"

"Yeah," he said with grave recollection.

She wrung her hands to work out the quakes. "It was like that."

He searched her face. "Do you think—"

The doors swung open and there stood Deorc, a great smile plastered on his face. "Everyone is eager to meet you two!" he said with a bounce of his dark brows.

Kiara and Hadyn exchanged identical questions with their eyes. When they turned back, Deorc zoomed away with the energy of a child, ready to parade them on stage.

On the flip side of the stage, Kiara and Hadyn stood stiffly at Deorc's right hand side. A wordless greeting awaited them in the form of a silent and sizable crowd that seemed to have materialized out of thin air. They could pick out a few pale faces in all the heads, but most had the darker, not so thin-looking skin, they had seen with Wilu and Isi and the slaves. Each member held a blue flame candle in the palms of their hands creating an eerie glow, seemingly emanating from the crowd itself. Hundreds of faces, illuminated from below, stared up at them in a silence unbroken by even a sniff, and they didn't look particularly happy.

Kiara shifted her weight from one foot to the other and offered an awkward wave.

Finally Deorc spoke. "Ladies and Gentlemen, I introduce to you Hadyn and Kiara."

Kiara whispered to Hadyn out of the side of her pained smile, "I didn't think we told him our names."

He had an edge in his voice as he replied, "No, I know we didn't."

"They have come to us while you were away," Deorc continued. "I want you to welcome them with all warmth and hospitality. They will sojourn here with us tonight and however long they like." He bounced on his heels and beamed as if he had just had a glorious thought. "Or, I suppose, if they decide to make our humble town their home, they can do just that!"

The blue faces were silent. Kiara decided Deorc had introduced them and that she would break the silence. "Why don't they say anything?"

"Oh, don't take offense." Deorc said. "It is our way of showing respect. Their hearts are welcoming you already."

Even as they spoke the crowd began to break into groups, cordial conversations murmuring to life.

"Right," Kiara said dubiously.

Deorc left no time for thought, well onto the next task as if he had a checklist in his mind that he knew better than his own name. "Come, I want you to meet my daughter!" he said and didn't wait for their answer before striding down the steps of the stage.

He led them into the crowd to a group of young people, all carrying on various conversations at once.

"Darcy!" he called. "Darcy, come here. There's something I would like you to do."

A girl with chocolate brown hair reaching the base of her back turned around and peeled off from the group. She had big, sleepy, brown eyes and skin the color of creamed coffee.

Kiara tried to focus on her face because even glancing at whatever she wore made her squirmy. The top half of the outfit seemed to cut too low at the neckline and too short on the bottom; the skirt was made of just enough material to even be called a skirt; and a weighty amount of jewelry adorned her neck, wrists, ankles, and fingers. From her ears dangle earrings of bright feathers, orange and yellow, layered and full. With the lack of clothing and excess of jewelry, Kiara felt uncomfortable just looking at her.

"Yes, Father?" she asked, her voice high and smooth with a facade of innocence plastered over it, but she wasn't looking at her father. First, she looked at Kiara from the very top of her frizzy hair all the way down to her feet, seemingly amused at the way her clothes hung on her and Kiara felt the embarrassment of the trousers all over again. But when the girl's eyes came to Hadyn, they lingered. She blinked with the speed of a falling leaf.

"Sweet Darcy," Deorc said, "tomorrow I want you to give Kiara and Hadyn a tour of the town."

"It would be my pleasure, Father." But again she wasn't looking at her father.

Kiara thought she was going to be sick. Snapping out of it, she realized what had just been planned. "A tour?" she asked, and Deorc gave a giddy nod. "Oh . . . that sounds lovely and I'm sure it would be, but we really shouldn't stay long."

"Nonsense! You've only just arrived and Tykaraijre has been eagerly awaiting you. What could be so important that you have to leave in such a hurry?"

Kiara looked to Hadyn, not wanting to say.

"There, you see? You're just shy, but it's going to be great fun! Come now," he begged, "it's not often we get new visitors."

"Well . . ." Kiara couldn't avoid his eyes, expectant, like a small child asking another to play. "I suppose one day's delay won't hurt."

Deorc clapped his hands together. "Wonderful! Now, Darcy, make sure you take them everywhere. Don't forget a thing! And they'll be having dinner with us. Now, let's see . . . It is late. I suppose you can stay with us for now. Come! You must meet my wife."

Deorc didn't wait for a response, trotting off with a bounce in his step. Something about his innocent joy wouldn't allow Kiara to even be irritated.

Darcy watched them hesitate. "I know." She rolled her eyes. "He can be so annoying and bossy, but really, he's just excited. Come on." She gestured with her hand for them to follow her. "We have to catch up with him."

They started off at a brisk pace through the crowds. Darcy weaved in and out of groups of people, making it difficult to keep sight of her, suddenly seeming not to care a whole lot if they followed or not. As they made their way through the crowd, Kiara caught warm smiles from every gaze she met. She gave a small wave here and there and they just kept on smiling.

"Well, *now* they smile," Kiara said, quiet enough for only Hadyn to hear.

"They must be done showing respect," Hadyn answered with a wry grin.

Kiara's cheeks flushed with heat. She thought it was from all the eyes on her or the bodies all close together, but a fire blazed to life in her chest like a wave of panic. She began to think it was something to do with her; not the town, that maybe there was something wrong with *her*. And I'm sorry to confirm, but there was. There most certainly was.

She stumbled, though her feet met no obstruction, and her legs didn't feel like they could hold her up anymore.

Hadyn moved to catch her. "Whoa! You okay?"

She put her hand on his shoulder to steady herself, not sure if the nausea she felt was from the fear or something else . . . "I'm not sure. I don't feel so good. I just feel really dizzy all of a sudden."

"Here, put your arm around me," he said and looked around, but Darcy was nowhere in sight.

They pushed forward until they reached the edge of the crowd, where they found her waiting for them and not exactly pleased to see Hadyn helping "a not so good looking" Kiara walk.

She put a hand on her hip. "What took you so long?"

Hadyn turned from Kiara to her. "Well, you were so fast and we lost you."

"Yeah? You've got to be quick to keep up with me." Darcy flashed a smile, but returned to her initial point of annoyance. "What's wrong with her?"

Hadyn looked back to Kiara. "I don't think she's feeling very good."

"Well, then we should get her to the house. Let's get there already!" She started walking again.

"Wait, could you slow down!"

"No. It's alright. I'm okay," Kiara said, standing on her own. "I can keep up."

Darcy turned around and called back. "Come on!"

"She's about every bit as bossy as her father," Hadyn said, wide-eyed and Kiara snickered.

Darcy slowed to a pace that allowed them to catch up without running.

"What's the big hurry for?" Hadyn asked as they came to her side.

"Oh, no reason. I just don't like wasting time. You two need your sleep so we can start bright and early tomorrow! And anyway,

Father wouldn't want us to dawdle. Come on!" she said with energy, as if she could run for miles.

She led them through the now not so abandoned town as people all moseyed home for the night. As they came around a bend in the road, Darcy turned onto a path leading to the biggest (not to mention most impressive) structure in the whole town— a towering building all washed in the blue light of the village's strange fire.

"Here we are!" Darcy proclaimed, stopping so they could admire it. "Our home."

# Chapter Fifteen

# THE BLUE MANSION

**K**iara gaped in silence.

Small blue lights speckled the meticulously landscaped yard and front gardens, lighting it up like stars in the night sky. Three stories with an expansive porch wrapping around and out of sight on one side, the building stood like an imposing and great authority. A chill glow emanated from the windows of the wooden mansion. Kiara couldn't help but think, it didn't look too inviting. Instead it seemed hauntingly cold and to a point untouchable, a distant and high beauty she felt unworthy of.

Finally, she jumbled a string of words together. "This is your house?"

"Yes," Darcy replied matter of factly.

"It's incredible . . ."

Darcy started toward home at a skipping pace, shouting and calling out, "Father! Mother! We're here!"

Muffled voices poured from the once empty looking building, and Deorc popped out onto the porch. "Ah, Darcy, I was wondering when you were going to catch up!"

Kiara and Hadyn found each other's faces with the same scrunched brows. By the time Deorc made it back, there was no way he would have had to wait for them long.

"We just got a little held up in the crowd, is all, Father." Darcy fluttered her eyes playfully.

Beaming, Deorc waved a hand. "Well, come in. Come in!"

Kiara wondered where his emotions came from. They seemed to spring up for no reason or cause. What changed the quiet man, so strangely aloof, to this giddy, almost child-like person they saw now? Darcy seemed happy all of a sudden too.

"Come on!" She grinned and took the porch steps two at a time.

As Kiara and Hadyn ascended the steps much slower than Darcy, yet struggling to take in the grandeur of it all, Deorc watched with a proud smile.

"Welcome to our home," he said, and sticking his head back inside the door, he called, "Lyra, there's someone I want you to meet!"

They waited on the porch until a tall, striking beauty appeared in the doorway. Her skin was a shade darker than Darcy's, but Kiara could see their resemblance right away and now she also knew where Darcy had learned how to dress.

"Lyra, this is Kiara. Kiara, this is my wife, Lyra," he said, and Kiara had to wonder if she hadn't been at the gathering.

Lyra stretched out a thin, limp hand. "A pleasure," she said.

Hadyn stood behind Kiara, so Lyra leaned to see around her. "And who might this young man be?" she glanced at Darcy.

"Mother, this is Hadyn."

Kiara fought the urge to roll her eyes.

"Well, it's very nice to meet you, Hadyn."

"Thank you for taking us in," Kiara said to both of them. "Truthfully, we have our lives to thank you for."

"Oh?" Deorc's brows scrunched questioningly.

"Well, before we came upon the . . . The . . ." Kiara's eyes strayed to all the blue flames lighting up the space.

"The Dalmatia," Deorc said.

"Yes. We-well, are there any animals in the forest that would hunt a pair of people?"

He blinked, utterly perplexed. "Not that I know of . . . though, this is the jungle. Stranger things have happened."

Not the kind of answer she wanted to hear. She struggled to suppress the shiver crawling up her spine.

"Let us come in out of the night," Lyra suggested. "We can talk inside."

"Yes, come in, come in!" Deorc agreed.

Kiara and Hadyn followed the strange family through the door, where they were besieged with another bout of awe. Servants slipped their packs off their shoulders without a word and carried them off. A wide and grand staircase curved up to the second level in one smooth flourish. Blue candles lined its railings and sat just about everywhere else in the room. Mysterious, golden and carved artifacts sat on shelves and small tables; and a golden chandelier hung from the high ceiling.

Though, despite all its beauty and grandeur, it really couldn't even begin to rival Bartholomew's house for feeling like a true home, one that you come back to after a long day for comfort and rest, one that you share with the people you love best. Rather, this blue mansion more dazzled like an extravagant museum than a humble place of living. Of course Kiara and Hadyn didn't have time to compare these wonders to wholesome down to earth values, their minds thoroughly swept away in the delight that they could even be welcome here.

A piercing squawk ripped them from any and all observation as something swooped Kiara's head, grabbing a chunk of her curls in the process, and pulling hard before letting go. Kiara screeched and instinctively protected her head with her arms.

"Oh, Gadferlin!" Deorc chuckled affectionately. "Greeting our new guests are we?"

*"Greeting?"* Kiara said, petrified, just beginning to let her arms down.

There on Deorc's shoulder perched what you might suppose as someone's idea of a joke, if they had a sense of humor as black as the devil. A hideous version of an overgrown nightjar, it cocked its head at them blinking huge, bulging, yellow eyes and hanging its wide, curved beak agape. It reminded Kiara of Nnyric's scribe, Shrike and made her shiver.

"Of course! I'm sure Gadferlin didn't mean to frighten you. He just came to see the new people in his house. I hope you won't harbor any hard feelings toward him?" He waited for a reply, concern slanting his eyes.

Still shaken, Kiara didn't know if she agreed with what came out of her mouth. "No, of course not."

"Wonderful!" he said, once again ecstatic. "Shall we adjourn to the drawing room?"

As Deorc turned his back to lead them there, Gadferlin turned his head almost completely around, keeping his gaze locked on Kiara the entire time. She couldn't be certain in the strange light, but it seemed the bird narrowed his bulbous eyes at her. A small gasp escaped her agape mouth.

"Something wrong?" Darcy asked with a smirk and walked away before Kiara could answer. Kiara didn't know what she had done to deserve that. She looked at Hadyn wondering if he had heard it, but if he had, he made no indication of it, yet caught up in the wonder of every new area of the mansion as they all followed Deorc into another blue room. This one had chairs, all fancifully embroidered and ornately carved, but not one looked anything like the next, an eccentric and quirky assortment. More artifacts filled this room along with pieces of the jungle— potted orchids and jars full of feathers, boards pinned with an assortment of colored insects hung on the walls, along with painted masks, each with their own unique expression. Kiara roved her eyes about the room's treasures, at once taken by everything she saw. She gravitated to the nearest wonders.

"I see you have an eye for the remarkables of nature," Deorc said.

Kiara blushed, realizing how unpolished she must have looked, in all her wide-eyed, mouth-gaping wonder. "I've never heard it put that way."

"Well, you do. I should know, as I always have myself," he said, coming to walk with her along the displays.

For the first time, Kiara felt a personal warmth in his words, like he had found something pleasantly kindred in her and wanted her to know it.

"Did you collect all of it?"

"Most of it. Some were gifts from the surrounding tribes." He plucked a mask off the wall for example and held it to his face. Exquisitely painted, his own blue eyes sparkled in the firelight as he blinked behind the flowery false eyes of the mask. Kiara grinned and he hung it back up with a smile of his own.

"Which, I am always humbled to accept," he said.

Deorc settled into a high-backed chair, Gadferlin still perched on his shoulder, his chest feathers puffed out pridefully.

Yet taking in the room, Kiara went to take a seat.

"Excuse me?" Deorc asked. "Did I ask you to sit?"

"Oh. Sorry. No, I—" the rest of Kiara's words did not come, stopped by a lump of embarrassment in her throat. She and Hadyn both froze up.

Deorc smiled. "Tradition," he seemed to explain and as Lyra and Darcy sat down in the chairs on either side of him, he said pleasantly, "Now, will you not take a seat?"

They didn't question; they just did as told and sat down. Kiara didn't know what to make of it. She couldn't exactly call the behavior rude, but the silence that followed was intolerable, not knowing at any one moment just where to look. All the while, she felt Gadferlin's constant, unnerving gaze upon her, pinning her in a painful paralysis.

"This is a lovely home," Kiara blurted her attempt at cordiality, quickly before her heart exploded.

"Thank you." Lyra smiled. "But tell me, what brings you two here, to our humble village?"

"We came by accident, really," Hadyn said. "We're on our

way north. Do you, by chance, know of a man named Aaron? We've been trying to reach his village."

"Can't say I do," Deorc said. "Can't be near our neck of the woods, so to speak." He grinned at his own words, but then raised a questioning brow. "Are you sure you've been going the right way?"

Kiara looked down. ". . . No. Not entirely."

"Fear not. Though immensely large, this forest has a living beating heart. All things tend to work together in one way or another. Word and news travels in ways you won't expect. I'll see if I can't find out any information through the liana vines."

Kiara smiled. "Thank you."

"About how we came here . . ." Hadyn trailed off and his face scrunched with suspicion. "*You* found *us*." He looked at Deorc. "You said you were expecting us, how can that be?"

"So you came by the trails?" Darcy asked. "Oh, aren't they just the most romantic thing?"

Hadyn blinked, waiting for Deorc to answer.

Deorc's eyes remained ever steady. "The Beast told me you were coming," he stated, like it would clear everything up.

"What?" Kiara asked, shaking a shiver.

"The Beast told me you were coming," he said again, as if it were perfectly normal.

"How did *it* know we were coming? What is it?" Hadyn pressed further.

"He is our Lord."

"Oh!" Kiara said, thinking that she understood. "Why do you call him the Beast? Don't you mean the King?"

"The King? Yes, he is our king, but we call him the Beast because that is his name and because he is more powerful than all the beasts of the earth."

"And . . . he knew about our coming, how exactly?" Hadyn got the sense his question was being avoided.

"Well, the natives have a colorful way of explaining it. You see the Beast is said to have fiery bright eyes, rendering him nearly blind during the day, but at night . . . he can see all. The Dalmatia, the fires you came here by, are a representation of all those seeing eyes."

"Oh." Kiara fell silent, becoming more and more certain that whatever this thing was, it couldn't be the same as Bartholomew's King, but she thought she'd see for sure. "So, did he write the Bible?"

"The Bible!" Deorc scoffed, his eyes flaring. "Please do not speak of such a pathetic pretense of power, not while you reside in my household. The Beast could never write something so trifle and controlling." He huffed and said, "The Bible!" one more time, his face contorting like he had just taken a bite of some vile and rotting fruit.

Once again the silence throbbed as painful as an open wound. But, Deorc recovered, his eyes softening a great deal, and he sighed. "I do hope you do not believe in the so-called *holy scriptures*," he pressed, concern drenching this voice.

Truth be told, Kiara didn't know if she believed or not, but the way he acted made her want to say she did.

"There are other books written of the Beast," Deorc continued. "I'm sure if you read them you would see the flaws in the Bible."

Kiara and Hadyn didn't know how to answer him. What was there to say?

Deorc drew a breath, backing down for the moment. "You three should get your rest. You have a big day ahead of you tomorrow. Darcy, will you show them to where they'll be staying?"

"Yes, Father," she said. "Come on, it's this way."

"Forgive me for my outburst," Deorc said, stopping them on their way out. "I hope you won't think too horribly of us after that conversation." His voice was expectant, fragile, like what he had just done could ruin every good thing about their meeting. "You have to know, I'm very passionate about these things."

Kiara gave him her polite smile and nodded.

He returned hers with a genuine one. "Good. Sleep well."

Darcy led them to the guest bedrooms. "You can have these two." She pointed out the entrances to the rooms. "Unless," she smirked, "you'd rather have one."

The red creeping into Hadyn's cheeks didn't seem like something he could help, but Kiara met the comment with all seriousness. "No, no," she waved her off, "two rooms is just perfect, thank you."

"Good," Darcy said, turning and picking a blue candle up off the wall to light a lantern in each room. "You'll find your packs already inside. If you need anything in the night, the servants sleep just down the hall." She waited a moment. "Goodnight."

"I look forward to the tour tomorrow," Kiara tried to be cordial.

"Oh." Darcy's lips thinned in a smile. "Oh, right . . . the tour," she said, but that was it.

"Well . . . goodnight," Kiara said.

"Goodnight!" Darcy started to walk away, but turned around with one last thought. "Oh, yeah. And if you hear anything in the middle of the night . . . don't get up," she warned, and with a smirk, left them for real.

"What does that mean?" Kiara asked, eyes round with fear.

Hadyn's wary eyes were locked on Darcy as she disappeared around the corner. "I wouldn't worry about it, Kiara. She's just trying to mess with your head."

"Well, it worked," she huffed. "Great! I'm exhausted and now I'm not going to be able to sleep."

"Yeah, well, I don't think I'll be sleeping much either. But with what happened in the crowd and all, you need your rest."

Kiara's eyes slanted with concern. "You think I should be worried?"

"No! I didn't— You know . . . just in case. How do you feel now?"

"Alright, I guess. A little strange still, but I thought it had more to do with everything else. I promise though, I'll try hard not to think about what Darcy said or anything else for that matter. I know I would rest easier, if I knew that ugly bird was locked in a cage at night."

"You and me both."

"Well, goodnight," she said, but Hadyn didn't seem to be planning to go. ". . . Aren't you tired?"

"Oh, sure." He nodded. "Exhausted."

She squinted. "Yes . . ?"

"I just think I oughta keep watch. You know, at least for a little while."

"Hadyn. Look who's worried now."

"I know, but I'm not so sure about this place."

"Of course you're not. You don't trust people. It's what you do."

He frowned. "Not true. I trusted Bartholomew."

Kiara ignored the sting when he didn't use his trust in her as an example. "Not at first, you didn't."

"Neither did you." He sighed. "Look, all I'm saying is . . . he doesn't remind you of anyone?"

"Who? Deorc?" Hadyn waited expectantly. She gave him a sideways look of doubt. "You can't seriously be insinuating my—" she stopped herself, "Nnyric?" He just gave a quick raise of his eyebrows. "What?" She cracked a grin. "But that's ridiculous! You give Nnyric too much credit. Deorc's kinder than him to be sure, and if nothing else, he is much more interesting."

"If you say so. I'd still feel better keeping a watch."

"No. Absolutely not. You need your rest too. You are not my personal guard."

"But I—"

"No. Now, I won't hear it."

He shut his mouth, but the look he fixed her with said he could still argue.

"Hadyn . . ."

He sighed. "Alright."

"Good." She smiled. "Now, goodnight."

"Goodnight," he said begrudgingly.

Kiara shook her head, and walked into her room, closing the door behind her.

The lone lantern sat on the nightstand, dimly bathing the room in blue. A chill crawled up her arms. She wanted to blame it on the open window, claiming it was only the night breeze's tickling fingers, but there was just something about the light and the empty room. It frightened her now to think of the flame as an eye of the Beast, to think some being of unknown nature was watching her. Suddenly Hadyn's offer to keep watch looked more like a comfort than an annoyance. But not all fear is devoid of intrigue. And seized once again by questions she was only brave enough to whisper, she wondered how they made the blue fire. Maybe something in the wicks?

Kiara dug through her pack until she found the strikers. Being as careful as she could, she lit another candle in the room. The flame caught and burned with a warm red light. She reared back, shocked, as if the blue stuff was the normality and this the oddity.

*So it is the wicks*, she thought, coming to her senses. *And they only light the ones that burn blue.*

But with a creeping feeling, she thought she should be sure. Blowing the red flame out, she carried the candle to the lantern with the blue flame. She opened the glass and tilted the still smoking wick into the flame. To Kiara's astonishment the blue fire carried over to the candle and stayed burning with no heat. The candle trembled in her hand. She had no answers, no way to explain this. Feeling like she had just played with some strange magic that she shouldn't have, she blew on both the flames, but neither would go out, seemingly more persistent than regular fire. With the lantern she could shorten the wick until it went out, but as hard as she blew on the candle, (though the flame flickered and danced wildly) it demanded more effort to extinguish. Growing impatient, Kiara licked her thumb and index finger and squashed the wick between them.

"Ouch!" She jumped back and stuck her fingers in her mouth.

That sting! Not hot, but so cold it burned. Like dry ice, it seared into the pads of her fingers in minutes. She had never felt anything like it in her life, and yet a small part of her wasn't even surprised, like somehow she had expected it. An eerie familiarity tingled in her fingertips, similar to how the tunnels of the labyrinth beneath Caverna felt. It begged her to wonder if she had dreamed of this blue fire before she ever saw it, but no memory would oblige, fantastic or real.

She felt a clammy chill crawling up her spine and now, in the dark, the smell of the smoke hanging in the air, a shiver took hold of her body. Kiara jumped under the covers of the bed and didn't dare come back out until dawn came to get her.

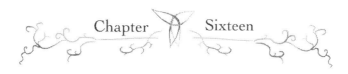

# Chapter Sixteen

# Harsh Awakenings

K iara squinted, straining to see through the shadows. Her senses felt muffled as if by some smothering smoke. Sight, hearing . . . Nothing felt clear. The shadows lifted ever so slightly. She could see prison bars, but what side of them she was on, she couldn't tell. She drew closer to them. There, beyond the bars, against a far wall of cold stone, sat a lost form, limp with some kind of awful defeat. She called out and the person, the man, barely began to lift his head. Terrible, sad eyes cried out from a discolored and swollen face. The bruises made it hard to tell, but despite the pain and abuse, she recognized this man. And in all her horror, her mind could only whisper his name.

*Deorc.*

But why? Why was he here? Who had done this to him?

Weak as he was, his mouth began to slowly open as if he would speak. But the shadows grew heavy again, and now they had forms, horrible, frightful forms, with wicked grins and searching, hungry claws.

Deorc's tired, surrendered eyes widened with seizing fear. Kiara saw him scrambling even as the shadows phased through the prison bars. She felt the fear as if it were her own, as if she was the prisoner the shadows were after, pressing in on her.

*"We're watching you . . . We always see you . . ."* She heard the voice as a crashing, seething wave all around. *"You really think you escaped? We always see."*

The words seemed to terrify Deorc all the more. He clawed at his chest as if his body, not the bars, was the prison and he longed desperately to set his soul free.

Kiara didn't know whether the message was for him or herself . . . or both. She wanted to rail against the bars or at the very least turn away from the sight, but she could do nothing; only watch.

*"We always see . . ."*

# ELLIE MAUREEN

Kiara gasped, bolting upright, fighting for each breath. A certain feeling of being watched gripped her like a tightening noose around her chest. The grey light of morning feebly reached its young hands through the window and dimly illuminated the room. She had thought she was awake before. The dream was just so real, but they almost always were. More often than not Kiara was plagued with nothing less than the kind of dreams that paralyzes one with fear, the kind that until you completely wake, you can't even begin to distinguish between what's real and what's just the lingering claws of the nightmare.

Kiara ran the back of her hand across her forehead, swiping away the beads of sweat and felt her sanity crawling back to her. And yet, she couldn't shake that chilling sensation of some secret thing watching her.

*What horrors . . .* she thought, scanning the still deep shadows of the room. What things to dream of a man she had only just met.

Every corner and dark space looked suspicious, like hiding spots, and something had taken advantage of the one atop the dresser. There, a hulking, impish form stared down at her. Kiara drew in a sharp breath, nearly jerking straight off the side of the bed, heart racing into her throat. Because it didn't move, she forced herself to take a closer look. Her eyes interrogated the shadowed thing until feathers and a beak came into view. It was Gadferlin, his pupils so big his eyes appeared black and his mouth propped open in what looked like an evil grin.

Kiara sighed with relief. "Oh, it's just you." Then she said in her head, *just you?* as a chill down her spine reminded her how disquieting this still was.

Gadferlin closed his mouth and cocked his head, watching Kiara as she pushed the covers off her legs and got out of bed.

"How did you get in here, you creepy bird?" Kiara looked at the open door she knew for certain she had shut the night before and steadily oscillated her head back to the bird, growing more perturbed by the seconds. He answered by cocking his head back to the other side. "Well, you can't stay in *here*." She reached up to grab him down, but Gadferlin wouldn't go so easily. He flapped his wings in an erratic spasm, squawking like his feathers were on fire.

"Shhhh!" she hissed. "You're going to wake up the entire house!" Gadferlin obliged. Instead of squawking, he simply pressed himself into the corner of the wall that met the dresser top. "Ugh!" She put a fist on her hip. "Not leaving, huh?"

A quiet knock on the door frame made her jump.

"Kiara?" came Hadyn's sleepy voice.

She sighed. "Did I wake you up?"

"Course not," he lied. "But what are you doing in here?"

She turned to point at Gadferlin. "Well, Gadferlin . . ." But Gadferlin was not there. She stared at the vacant dresser top, unable to do much else.

"Kiara, what are you saying? Did you have a nightmare?"

"No. Yes." She huffed. "That's not the point." Looking back to where Gadferlin had been, she shook her head, mystified. "I woke up and I felt like something was watching me. I swear to you, Hadyn, when I opened my eyes, there was Gadferlin. I tried to get him to leave, but he backed into the corner up there. You have to believe me. He was just there before you came."

"I believe you," he said, scratching the back of his head. "Not sure if anyone else would . . ."

"Hadyn," Kiara eyed the open door. "I shut that door last night."

"Well that's . . . unnerving."

"I thought so," she said, chewing on her lip. "I'm sorry. You should really try and get some more rest. I'm sure Darcy will get us up soon enough. I shouldn't have told you. There's nothing we can do about it."

"No, it's okay. I wouldn't have wanted to be alone with thoughts of a disturbing, demon bird flapping around in my head." Kiara couldn't help but laugh at the way that sounded. "You want me to help you look for him? You know, to make sure he's gone?"

"Sure."

They searched every potential hiding spot for a medium-sized bird— under the bed, in the dresser and the chest at the foot of the bed, only to find nothing but feathers. Somehow, someway, he had left without a sound.

"You sure you'll be alright?" Hadyn asked, preparing to return to his room.

"Yeah, I'll be fine. See you in the morning when there's less shadows and more light."

He smiled. "See you when there's less shadows."

Kiara shut the door and immediately checked the room over once more, but finding no sign of the potoo or his yellow eyes, she crawled back into bed and sat there hugging her knees. She stared at the door, knowing now that closing it did nothing to keep him

# ELLIE MAUREEN

out. She sprung back to her feet and cocked her head at the chest.

"You wouldn't mind if I moved you over there by the door, right? I bet that bird scares you as much as it scares me." She paused, mentally smacking herself. "Why am I talking to a chest? It's going over there whether it likes it or not."

Heavy, but not unmovable, Kiara heaved her shoulder into it, trying her best not to make too much of a racket. Satisfied she had it pressed tight against the door, she stood up and brushed her hands together, quite pleased with herself. She checked under the bed one more time for good measure and hopped under the sheets.

Sleep wasn't easy, but daylight was coming and the thought of it allowed her to fall into a strange and uneasy rest.

A fist on the door rapped out a mildly concussive rhythm.

"Kiara! Can I come in?"

"Huh, what?" Kiara sat up, groggy as a sloth waking from its eleventh nap. She squinted through watery, blurry eyes, utterly bemused.

"Where . . ? Oh, just come in, Cida . . ." she yawned and smacked her lips. "I hope you brought tea."

Kiara's head pounded with splitting aches and her stomach twisted with unwelcome instability. *Yes, tea would be good,* she thought.

"What?" The voice said. "Oh, would you just open the door!"

That wasn't Cida's voice. Cida would never sound so impatient. With recognition, Kiara sat bolt upright. *Darcy!* She threw her sheets off, just as the handle started jiggling violently, the chest keeping the door in a stubborn, unbudging state.

"Just a minute, Darcy!"

The handle stopped. With a grunt, Kiara hastily moved the chest back in place, her wild bedhead falling like a mop over her face. She jumped back to her feet, flipped her curls back over her head, and pinned them there with one arm as she wrenched open the door with her free hand. Darcy stood there, one eyebrow raised and arms crossed. However, her impatient annoyance lifted inch by inch into wide-eyed shock at the sight of the unruly mess on Kiara's head.

"Well, these doors don't lock, so . . . I would ask, but I really don't care. The only reason I'm here is because breakfast is ready."

"Oh, thank you." Kiara said, but Darcy wasn't finished.

"Apparently," she said, "my father cares that you don't miss it."

"Oh . . ."

Darcy started to go, but she turned around to look at her once more and shaking her head, she snickered. "You're a mess."

Kiara watched her go, long smooth locks swaying behind, falling like a waterfall from her head. All her air left her lungs. Her arm went limp at her side and her hair floofed out to the sides. She stepped to a mirror hanging on the wall and looked at her cheeks, blotchy with the heat of embarrassment. She grabbed a piece of her hair and twisted it in her fingers. Compared to Darcy's silky bay locks, she looked like a monster, but not even a fierce one, just a silly, ridiculously, fuzzy monster. Always she was surrounded by beautiful, *normal* people. And here it was happening again. Was this just her fate?

Kiara narrowed her eyes in disgust at the image she saw in the mirror. Just a freckled, skinny, big-eyed, fluffy, red beast. She tried desperately to smooth the curls down, licking her palms and sliding them down her scalp, but with no avail, she reluctantly resorted to pulling the mess back into a long, thick braid.

While plaiting, she drew her hand back at a sharp sting. She blinked at the pads of her thumb and index finger, blackened as if from frostbite. Where any other fire would have blistered or reddened the skin, the blue fire seemed to have froze the flesh in an instant. Sticking her fingers in her mouth, she searched her pockets for something to cover them. She fished out the fabric strip Hadyn had given her to tie her hair back and felt the tips of her ears grow warm. Unsure why she even still had it, she was glad it could at least come in handy. She ripped it into two smaller strips and wrapped them both around her fingers, using her teeth to tie them tight.

Kiara wandered out into the rest of the sweeping house, trying her very best not to get lost and noticing just how different it all looked with the daylight streaming through the windows, deeming the mysterious blue fire unnecessary. She had gone to sleep in an eclectic, blue mansion and woke up in a different place entirely, a more earthly or "human" one, still grand, but without the otherworldly eminence.

She followed any sounds of life until she found the dining room where she learned soon enough, she was the very last one up, even Hadyn already sat at the table, on Deorc's left and across from Lyra. Darcy however, was nowhere in sight, just as that potoo, Gadferlin, thankfully.

"Good morning, Kiara!" Deorc said warmly. "Come and sit down, you're not too late. How did you sleep?"

"Um, alright. Thanks you."

She couldn't tell if it was because of the dream or if, like the house, the daylight had changed him, but he seemed different, more human. Natural light poured in on his face, complimenting his charming smiles. She noticed his hair wasn't as dark as she first thought it, more of a deep brown with even some red tints at its very lightest.

Hadyn stood and pulled out the chair beside him. "How do you feel?" he asked, and Kiara realized she was staring.

"Thanks," she said, pulling her gaze away from Deorc and taking the seat. "Not the best," she answered.

"Oh?" Deorc said. "Are you unwell? I hope it won't affect you enjoying the tour with Darcy."

"Of course not. It's probably nothing." Pulling a smile onto her face she looked over the plates of colorful fruit, steaming hot potatoes, and sausage-like meat already spanning the table. "This looks delicious!" Kiara said.

"I'm glad you think so," Darcy said, suddenly appearing with one more plate of fruit. Much more casual today, gone was most the shine and jewelry she wore the night before, actually sporting a pair of loose-fitting, light pants instead. Of course paired with an animal skin half-shirt that left her entire waist exposed.

"You made it?" Kiara asked.

Darcy put the plate down. "Most of it. I like to cook. Oh, and I just absolutely love your braid, Kiara." She said, giving her frizzy plait a small tug as she walked behind her.

Hadyn watched the exchange closely, seeing when Kiara just stared at her empty plate that there was more to it than just a kind compliment.

"Also, I was sitting there," Darcy simpered, "but it's okay, I'll let you."

"Oh, I'm sorry. I can move."

"No, it's fine, really." She dropped another dose of sugar in her smile and took the seat next to her mother.

Passing around the plates, they dished themselves a breakfast fit for royalty. Kiara waited for Deorc to pray, but he carried on and began to eat without a word.

Kiara took her first bite, finding the smells delicious enough to elicit some form of an appetite. "So . . ." She hesitated to ask, though considering Kiara's curiosity, she had already waited a great deal of time. "I was wondering about the blue fire. How it's possible."

Deorc gave her a fleeting glance, but kept his silence.

"I mean, I thought it was a trick at first—"

"A trick?" he scoffed, clearly offended. "The Dalmatia is no trick."

"I mean no offense!" Kiara blurted. "It seemed too wonderful to be real."

Deorc softened, his tense neck muscles visibly relaxing.

"Course, now I know that it is very much real," Kiara said and continued to tell him of her experiment.

Deorc's eyes flared with fire once more. "You created red fire? Here? How dare you?"

Unconsciously, Kiara slipped her burned fingertips under the table. She felt caught, like a scolded child who didn't even know what she had done, but Hadyn eyed Deorc carefully, his grip tightening around his knife and fork.

"I'm sorry," Kiara said. "I didn't know."

"Red fire is forbidden!" His harshness did not abate, and the word surfaced wounds that, until now, only things related to Caverna agitated.

Darcy watched her father, but she didn't look the least bit shocked. "Dad . . ." She tried to calm him. "She didn't know and you couldn't have expected her to."

"It's a rule, Darcy," Lyra chastised.

"A rule she didn't know. Now she does."

Deorc sighed and rubbed his face. When he lowered his hand, his eyes almost looked sad, but about the fire or his own temper, Kiara couldn't tell. "Yes, I suppose so," he agreed. "And I'm sorry I yelled. But, Kiara, I tell you now, you are to never light red fire here again. The Dalmatia is sacred and we respect it as our only light."

"I understand," Kiara said, with a meek nod, and noticed for the first time how tense Hadyn had become, as he breathed out a subtle sigh.

They continued their meal, for a moment the only sounds coming from the scritch of the silverware on their plates.

Lyra cleared her throat. "Darcy, what are your plans for the day?"

"If you must know, Mother, I *want* to take them everywhere, as Father said, but we'll see. And I plan to end the tour with the enchanted trails tonight."

"Oh, sounds like a whole lot of fun. I remember when each day was a new opportunity for fun and excitement."

Darcy groaned like she knew what was coming, just as her mother dove into an elaborate story that took much longer than needed, about when she was young. Darcy ate her food with her head down too embarrassed, or annoyed, or both to look up. But as the story drug on, she couldn't hang her head forever, and Kiara caught her and her father passing irritated looks and smirking over their shared boredom. She liked to watch it, the way they communicated without any words.

Kiara tried to listen to Lyra, she really did, but the women rambled all over the place, making it difficult to follow her many "trains" of thought. She munched on her potatoes, cooked to near perfection and found herself preferring Bartholomew's burnt ones. As Lyra ate up the rest of the time it took them to finish breakfast, Kiara didn't know whether to secretly hate her or thank her.

Lyra sighed, her mouth, at last, seeming to run out of words. "Believe it or not, it was a very different place here, before my dear husband came and showed us the refined ways of the Beast." She gave him a pat smile, but Deorc's return grin seemed even faker than hers.

"Yes, Mother. Fascinating!" Darcy said. "But we have to go now. Be back for dinner, okay?"

"Oh, alright. See you later, Darcy. I hope you have a good time!"

Darcy made ready to lead them out when Deorc, deciding he was finished with his previous mood, cheerily called, "Stay out of trouble, Darce! And don't go on the unlit paths!"

"Oh, Father, you know trouble finds me wherever I go."

He shook his head. "And, Hadyn!" Deorc said, recalling something. "A word please?"

Darcy sighed. "Come on, Kiara, let's wait outside."

Hadyn threw Kiara a bemused look as Darcy pulled her out of the room.

"What was that about?" Kiara asked.

"Ugh! My father. Both of my parents just don't know when to stop. He probably just wants to give him some talk on respecting me. Thinks I'm some kind of royalty, or fragile possession that needs to be handled with care. That's why I came out here, I would have been way too embarrassed." She fluttered her eyes, eyes that, in the daylight, looked even bigger than before. Kiara realized that though she thought them brown, they were actually a deep blue in the right light, with vivid flecks like ice shards.

"Isn't that nice though?" Kiara asked. "That he cares so much?"

Darcy snorted. "Trust me, when the care is as fickle as the weather, it tends to lose its meaning." Darcy cut the conversation short, walking out into the yard.

Kiara couldn't decide if the wooden mansion looked more magnificent in the night or day. "This place is so incredible!" she said.

"Thanks. I think so too." Darcy actually sounded sincere. "My cousins think that because they are men, they should inherit it and not me. My father told them that he would leave it to whom he wished. That made me happy," she said, without a smile, "until I realized I don't know who he would wish to give it to."

For the first time Kiara felt something other than annoyance for her, not sorrow or even pity, but a great empathy, because she could relate. But, unwilling to bare her own heart, she tried to cheer her up instead. "Well, I say, stick it to those greedy cousins of yours! What right have they? This is your family, your house! They have just as much a right to rule another country as they do to take your home. They deserve no more than a, 'Away and bile on yer head!' from you."

Darcy laughed, a real laugh, a contagious, bubbly sound that just made you want to laugh with her, and for a moment Kiara thought she could actually get along with her, if it weren't for her issues.

"What's that mean?" she asked

Kiara grinned. "Don't rightly know. It's just somethin' my mum used to say when she got especially furious."

Darcy's smile faded to a solemness once again. "You know, I had a brother once. He came early and . . . died early. So small and crippled, yet so precious. He was gone before he could smile and I don't think I've smiled for true joy since." The corner of her mouth twitched up. "I always used to say he skipped out on us . . . and maybe he was right to." She sighed. "Sometimes I think of how it would have been if he would've grown up and lived his life, how he would inherit this place and ensure that I could live here forever. All I ever wanted was a sibling. Someone to laugh with and talk about how ridiculous Mother and Father are." She sighed. "Oh, but what do you care?"

Kiara opened her mouth to say she *did* care, but the slam of the front door swinging shut made her jump. Hadyn stood at the top of the porch steps, befuddled and looking at nothing at all as if half his mind remained inside in another conversation.

"What's happened?" Kiara asked.

He turned his gaze on her. ". . . I don't even know."

Darcy laughed again, but it was different this time, a pathetic and high-pitched giggle. Compared to her once hearty laughter, it was so fake it made Kiara want to gag. And with the instability of her stomach right now, she thought she just might throw up.

"Shall we get started?" Darcy asked, and even her voice had raised a pitch.

Kiara rolled her eyes.

Issues.

# Chapter Seventeen

# DELSIN

**D**arcy started the tour off with the town circle, the same place at which Deorc had introduced them to the village the night before, except this time, not a soul walked its cobbled ground. Set with colored stones, without all the traffic, they could now clearly see they made a perfectly symmetrical pattern of shapes and designs.

"Welcome to the town circle." Darcy spun around unceremoniously in the open area. "Announcements, meetings, festivities . . . I mean almost every important event is held here. Of course, some things require a more sacred setting, but outsiders are not usually privileged with the knowledge surrounding that." She grinned mischievously.

A large, golden statue they hadn't noticed in the darkness, stood in the middle of the circle. It had the head of a wolf, but with horns and eyes cut with vertical, slit pupils like a snake, its teeth bared in a malicious grin. It had the body of some kind of ruminant, but stood on its hind legs. The hind feet were hoofed, but the front legs instead bore claws like no known beast. Its body tapered into the plated tail of a dragon, pointed and forked at the end.

Kiara jumped as her eyes landed on it. "What is that?" she asked. It reminded her far too much of the statues of the watchers to even begin to hide the disgust in her voice.

"Oh, that?" Darcy waved a hand. "That's the Beast. Think what you want of it. Personally, it terrifies me."

Kiara and Hadyn didn't know whether they should laugh or take her seriously. So their chuckles filtered out nervously.

"Well," she half sang, half sighed. "Not sure what else to say. We store stuff for said secret gatherings under there." She waved a noncommittal hand to the stage. "But it's pretty much just an overrated, over-glorified . . ." she grinned, "circle." Clapping her hands, she said, "Well, on to the next stop?"

They nodded and Darcy picked up her feet, starting off at a trot.

They didn't walk very far before they started to hear a pinging sound like metal banging on metal. If Darcy was aware of it, she wasn't fazed by it, so Kiara didn't take much heed of it.

They rounded a corner and the pinging/banging grew even louder. Kiara tracked the sound as best she could to a small hut with a wide open front. Dirty, thick smoke poured out from a hole in the roof. She strained her eyes, peering into the darkened space under the thatched roof to see a leathery-skinned man leaning over an anvil and hammering away at a piece of glowing metal. The hot coals burning in the forge illuminated his grave face.

Darcy paid him no attention, already on to her next bout of theatrics. "Oh, Hadyn! I just remembered!" she squealed. "Before we go anywhere else, I have to show you something. Come on, it's just this way." She started to go, but turned to Kiara. "But it'd probably bore you, Kiara," she squinted apologetically, "so you can just wait here."

Kiara balked, wondering if she really expected her to take her seriously. Apparently she did, but when she began to drag Hadyn away by the hand, Kiara felt only mild annoyance and even a bit of amusement. Hadyn looked back at her, eyes pleading like Darcy was some ogre, dragging him off to her lair to roast on a spit.

Kiara laughed, rolled her eyes, and washed her hands of it, knowing he'd be just fine, and *she'd* be Darcy-free for at least a little while. However, she didn't care much for Darcy's "stay put" order, and decided to explore a little on her own. The glimpse of a young man peering out from behind a tree beyond the road caught her attention, but his eyes popped open wide and he zipped out of sight as soon as he noticed her spotting him.

"What in Caverna . . ." she muttered out of habit, head cocking and feet shuffling towards where she had seen him.

"Hey." A hushed voice stopped her. "Girl."

She turned to the forge illuminated hut. The swarthy man stood in the light of the embers staring right at her. "Kiara, right?"

Looking at him sideways, she took tentative steps his way, casting one last look into the forest for the boy, but of course, he was gone. ". . . Yes."

"I'm Delsin. I'm the town's smithy." He had kind brown eyes with flecks of gold that seemed to glow just as warm as the forge. He wiped his sooty hand on his apron, a fruitless attempt to clean it, and held it out to her.

Reluctantly, Kiara took his hand. "Nice to meet you."

"Yes, nice, but also surprising."

"What do you mean?"

"I mean," the blacksmith looked left and right and he lowered his voice a bit when he said it, "that this is a happenstance that I will not ignore." He raised his eyebrows, but Kiara didn't quite follow yet. "But nice to meet you all the same." He had a kind smile, but it faded quickly. "Are you sure you want to let your friend out of your sight like that?"

Kiara's lips twitched with amusement. "Hadyn can take care of himself."

"Oh, I'm sure, but you just let him go with *her*." He said nothing else, as if his silence explained itself.

"Darcy?" Kiara pulled a face. "I'm not afraid of Darcy and neither is Hadyn."

"That's what they say. 'I'm brave enough.' But let me tell you this, you may think it as bravery, but from my experience it is only ignorance. A healthy fear of the darkness can be beneficial; don't ever mistake it as weakness. You and your friend *should* be afraid. You never know what you're going to get with Darcy, except that, like a beguiler of dark charms, she always gets her way." He shifted back into working. "You should be afraid of everyone here. This very village is a shadow. You can not trust it." He picked up a piece of red-hot metal with a set of rusty tongs and dipped it in a barrel of water. The bright iron dimmed with a sizzle. Kiara fluttered her eyes in disbelief as she noticed the color of the coals and fire in the forge.

Red.

Ruddy, rugged, red fire. And it was hot too! It was so normal, it was shocking. And yet, she supposed it only made sense, as the Dalmatia didn't produce heat the same way and could never sustain a smithy. She rubbed her bandaged fingers together. She couldn't help but think it said something about the man who worked those fires.

"Should I be afraid of you?" Kiara tested.

Delsin met her gaze with a fleeting glance, before continuing to busy himself.

"If you know all this," she pressed, "why are you here? Why don't you leave, find a new home?"

"Lower your voice!" Delsin hissed, then dropped his gaze. "It's not that simple . . . I have nowhere else to go . . . not the way I am." He glanced at his right palm where an old scar traced its line of history. Kiara would have thought it a work accident (the rest of his skin certainly not without blemishes) if not for the way he gazed so solemnly. His gloom didn't last long, his voice taking on a desperate edge and his eyes pleading with her. "But you can leave and need to before it's too late." He looked from side to side to make sure no one was near enough to hear. "If you think for one moment that you're safe here, you're lying to yourself. The Beast wanders about like a hunting predator, seeking whom he may devour, not who he may keep safe. If you believe Deorc in all his fancy diction about dying internally and eternally for the Beast, then—"

Delsin stopped when he heard footsteps approaching, but it was just Hadyn.

"Hey, glad I found you."

"Where's Darcy?" Kiara asked.

"I told her I needed to go check on you and I guess that irked her. I'm sure she'll show up soon enough."

"Figures . . . What did she want to show you anyway?"

"She showed me some kind of weapon she's making. A bow, I think she called it. I guess she likes to hunt."

"And that she does," Delsin muttered.

Hadyn looked him over for the first time.

"Um, this is Delsin," Kiara introduced, "the town's smithy. We talked while you were gone."

"Hello," he greeted. "I'm Hadyn."

"I know very well who you are," Delsin said, but shook his hand anyway. "I was watching you two last night." He paused and they stared at him. "And I've seen," he continued slowly, "that you have been caught . . . just like the rest of us." He looked very sad, but then his expression changed and maybe it was the light from the coals, but his amber eyes seemed to begin to glow and burn with a fire from his heart. "It is not too late for you. Don't let this place fool you like it did me. The darkness is alive here. The very shadows whisper lies. But you don't have to listen. You can leave and you must!"

Hadyn looked to Kiara, uncertainly.

"Look," Kiara began. "We appreciate your concern—"

"You don't believe me," Delsin said and hung his head despairingly. ". . . Nobody does."

Kiara opened her mouth to speak. "That's not—"

"There you are!" Darcy shouted from yet a ways away. She jogged the distance between them and came up beside Hadyn, somehow, even attractively winded. "Why'd you just take off on me like that?"

"I didn't. I told you, I wasn't going to just leave Kiara back here."

"Oh, right. But, as I said, I'm sure she was fine. Right, Kiara?"

"Um, yeah . . ." she muttered, still running Delsin's words through her mind. If she was honest with herself, what he said held a lot of weight and she wasn't sure if she had enough energy to carry it. "Yeah, I was fine."

"See." Darcy looked at Hadyn with playful frustration. "So, did Hadyn tell you all about how incredible I am?" She jabbed Kiara with her elbow, but Kiara just stared, unsure what she wanted her to say.

"I'm joking," Darcy said, rolling her eyes in disappointed annoyance. "We should get on with the rest of the tour. You know we have to be back for dinner. Father will most likely be having something special prepared."

"Fatten the sheep for the slaughter . . ." Delsin mumbled, bumbling about his business.

"What did you say, Delsin?" Darcy spoke with a drop of venom in each word.

"I said, have fun, your highness." He then mocked her as he bowed.

"That's what I thought." Darcy turned away from him as if he didn't exist anymore. "Now come on, you two, we have places to go, people to see. Well, not really people to see, except for me. And, I mean, come on, when I'm around, what other people do you need to see?" Darcy chuckled and led them away, an arm around each of them. "What were you doing talking to that old kook anyway? Delsin is the crazy man of the village."

Kiara craned her neck to look back at Delsin, while Darcy dragged them along, talking their ears numb. Delsin stared back, watching them go, sorrow tugging on every feature of his face.

Darcy talked about as fast as she moved her rushing feet. "So, we'll go to the mill next because it's on the way to Jaci's place, but then will stop at Jaci's because I'm hungry."

Kiara marveled at the fact that Darcy could already be hungry again, but supposed the extra dramatic flare she threw into her actions might work up an appetite.

Down the slope from them, the mill looked like an oversized cottage with a big, wooden wheel as its best friend. Paddles on the wheel dunked in and out of an energetic stream as it went round and round, churning out rickety, clunky noises, the water they carried out cascading back down in silvery threads. Peacefully set back in the jungle and away from town, Kiara liked it right away.

"So that . . . thing," Darcy gestured to the wheel, "powers the mill and the mill grinds our maize for us." Darcy squinted at it for a moment, "Yep, that's it." She turned to go back up the path.

"Wait," Kiara said, "Can we not go inside?"

"If you really want to." She made a face. "Aren't you hungry?"

Kiara waited.

"Fine," Darcy huffed.

They approached the mill, Darcy stomping as she went. She struggled with the huge barn door, so Hadyn jumped in and helped her heave it aside, revealing the bustle of one big open room, like a warehouse, with the grinding millstone in the center of all things. People traversed on catwalks and gangways above their heads. The once tranquil scene buzzed with a productive sort of excitement, everyone in sight busy with something.

Several people bustled about nearer to them, but one man had that look of being in charge. He strode straight for them, a stocky man with a sour expression, small ears, and a blunt nose.

"What are you doing here, Darcy?"

"I'm giving our new guests a tour of Tykaraijre. Chief's order." She grinned. "They wanted to see inside."

"Well, you've seen it. Not much here. Are you satisfied?" Kiara would have begged to differ, gazing at all the industry in fascination. He grunted, seeing her wonder. "Alright, I suppose you can stay. Just try not to get into trouble, hey, Darcy?" He raised a bushy brow at her and began to turn. "On second thought, it's best you didn't go farther than the entrance." With that, the grumpy man took his leave, shouting at someone named Jimmy to "Stop that nonsense!" as he walked away.

"Well, have you seen enough?" Darcy asked. "A sour, old mill boss and a boring old mill?"

"I guess," Kiara said.

Hadyn smiled at her, tilting his head. "Come on, the tour has only just started."

"Great!" Darcy clapped. "Now we can go eat!" She trotted back up the path and weaved her way through the town, on a mission for her stomach.

They came to a straw-roofed building, short in comparison to the area it covered. The smell of frying, searing, and roasting foods wafted out the glassless windows. Darcy inhaled a deep breath through her nose, delight brightening her face. Kiara grinned at her, finding ever more what a character she was. They stepped inside the dim, smoky building. In a word, it was basic, with dirt floors and rough wooden tables and chairs. Kiara found it more or less like one of Caverna's taverns, though she'd never been inside one. People sat at the tables, some already eating their meals, others carrying on calm conversations while waiting for their food.

Darcy picked a table with four chairs, sat down and Kiara took the spot next to her.

"So, I always get the peccary soup when I'm here for lunch, but you two get whatever you want." Darcy started to list different meals by their native names and explained what they were, but Kiara and Hadyn just decided to have the same as her.

Darcy left them then to apparently say hello to someone she knew across the room, and when she returned, she took the seat on the opposite side than before. Right next to Hadyn.

If you suddenly have the urge to shake your head or bury your face in the palm of your hand, you know exactly how Kiara felt, except, from where she sat, she was forced to refrain.

"Do you come here often, Darcy?" Kiara asked, if only to unclench her teeth.

She nodded. "Mostly after I've been out hunting or when-ever I just need to leave the house. You know, my father used to live in England. He told me, there are lots of places there like this, but of an unruly sort. They're called pubs or taverns and most of the time the customers end up in fist fights and bloody brawls," Darcy related with wide eyes. "Sounds quite exciting to me, but nothing like that ever happens here."

Kiara would have thought she sounded disappointed. She looked around again at the people, peacefully talking and eating their meals. None seemed capable of even raising their voices. She couldn't help but note the normalcy, the dullness. From what Bartholomew had spoken of the Kyjar, well, she just assumed to see more of that, of the buoyant life and color.

"I guess, if I'm being honest, I myself expected more . . ."

"Liveliness?" Darcy asked. "Vibrant living and rambunctious celebrations? You and me both. I hear it used to be that way. Father has much altered the people of the forest. Most praise him for 'civilizing' life here in Tykaraijre. Settling hard-won peace, father calls it. But if no longer fully living is the sacrifice of peace, I don't want any part of it . . . I never have."

A plump, kind-looking lady, wearing a food splattered apron so colorful it could have been a painting, walked up to their table with a greeting smile.

"Hello, Miss Darcy!"

"Hi, Jaci."

"I see you brought some new friends. New faces to be sure, but I already know your names. I'm Jaci and I run this place."

"Nice to meet you," Kiara said.

"You been hunting lately, Darcy?"

"Yes, ma'am!"

*Ma'am?* Kiara mouthed the word in disbelief and caught Hadyn smirking at her.

"Any luck?" Jaci asked.

"A little, but who needs luck when you're here to brighten everyone's day."

Kiara almost choked on her own spit. She wanted to clean her ears out and ask Darcy to repeat that sentence.

"Oh, you're just saying that." Jaci blushed. "Now, I know what you want, honey, but what will it be for your friends?"

"They're going to have the same."

Just then someone slid into the chair next to Kiara.

"Is this seat taken?" He looked at Kiara and then at Darcy as she rolled her eyes. "I didn't think so."

"Mr. Delsin!" Jaci shouted, a broad smile splitting her face.

"Miss Jaci!" he shouted back.

"How do you know these two?"

"Oh, didn't you know? We're good friends now."

"I don't believe you for a second. They haven't been in town long enough for you to be friends."

"I beg your pardon?" he faked offense.

Jaci just laughed, a heart-warming, belly laugh that made a person feel at ease, it's only fault, maybe lasting just a moment too long. Finally, she sighed. "You having lunch?"

"Yeah. The usual, please."

"You got it!" She waved as she left and Kiara caught the faintest scar on her right palm. Kiara imagined, along with taking orders, that she cooked too and could have easily cut herself in a kitchen accident, but the same hand in the same place. Unintentionally, her eyes darted to Delsin's hands, but they were laying placidly, one on top of the other.

As Jaci trotted back to the kitchen, Delsin said, "She's a sweet lady. Can't help but love her." Darcy actually smiled at his words and took it one step further by nodding in agreement.

Delsin then leaned over the table. "Hello, friends."

Darcy's smile dropped. "You're not my friend."

"Oh, I'm sorry, your highness, but I wasn't talking to you."

Hadyn chuckled, but Darcy silenced him with a look. Kiara kept her smile. At least someone wanted to sit next to her.

"What are you doing here, Delsin?" Darcy asked with a vile bite.

He looked at her like she was stupid. "Eating lunch. Sitting with my friends." Darcy rolled her eyes. "I know you think that wherever your royal bum sits is yours, but I have a right to be here and that's not going to change, no matter how much dislike you carry for me."

She huffed and slumped in her chair.

"So, how are you two liking the tour so far?" Delsin asked.

You would think Darcy would just stop, but she interrupted again. "How do you know it's a tour? What if we were just walking around as friends?"

"Oh, please. Deorc pass up an opportunity to show off the magnificence that is his village? He has to get the visitors intrigued and fascinated so that they wish to stay. Of course, this is in his humblest of hopes."

"You don't know anything, Delsin."

He ignored her, looked at Kiara, and raised his eyebrows questioningly.

"Uh . . . I don't know." Kiara struggled.

Her eyes shifted from him, to Darcy, to Hadyn, and then back to him, but his gaze didn't twitch. He looked at her as if to tell her that she was only talking to him, that it was safe to tell him what she really thought, and part of her wanted to, she really did, but she couldn't, not with Darcy there.

"We haven't seen much yet," she said. "The mill was very interesting."

Delsin decided to let it be. "Old Mr. Carl let you in, did he?"

"Well, we had to stay by the entrance."

"I thought as much, Mr. Carl is crusty but shrewd." He looked at Darcy, while she feigned innocence and shock.

Jaci came back with their food. "What are your plans for the rest of the day, Darcy?"

"I'm taking Hadyn and Kiara on a tour of Tykaraijre."

Delsin smirked.

"Oh! How nice!" Jaci said. "You helping too, Delsin?"

"No," Darcy spat, but Delsin rolled with it.

"It wasn't planned, but seeing what good friends we already are, I don't see why I wouldn't. No doubt, we'd have great fun."

Jaci scrunched her nose as she smiled. "Sounds like it! I'll let you all eat so that you can get on with your day."

Darcy put a palm on her face and continued to claw the skin of her cheeks as she pulled it down with a growl.

"Calm down, Darcy." Delsin had a tone one might use to talk to a pet. "There's no need to get vicious."

Chapter Eighteen

# TYKARAIJRE

**L**unch finished and out in the streets again, Kiara didn't know which was worse— loud, obnoxious Darcy or quiet, moody Darcy.

Delsin plodded along with his hands behind his back. "So where to, your highness?"

Lips tight, Darcy sighed through her nose and it didn't take a whole lot of imagination to see smoke puffing out of her nostrils. "Delsin," she fixed him with a stare, "your time with us is privileged."

"Is that so?"

"So don't test me!" she finished.

"But where *are* we going?" Hadyn was brave enough to ask.

Darcy huffed, realized who had asked the question, and then smiled again, "We're going to visit Gypsy Suze's place!"

"Um . . ." Delsin cleared his throat. "You sure that's how you want to kick off your grand tour?"

"Delsin, I'm allowing you to follow; not to give your opinions."

"Who is Gypsy Suze?" Kiara asked.

Delsin sighed. "Suze is sort of Tykaraijre's medicine . . . woman?"

"First in the village!" Darcy said proudly. "Of course, she's not nearly as powerful as Klah."

Kiara and Hadyn didn't follow.

"She talks to the spirits," Delsin explained. "And claims she can see the future."

Kiara blinked. "Really?"

"Is the tour hinging on this visit or . . ?" Hadyn trailed off.

"Well, no." Darcy pouted. "But why wouldn't you want to go?"

"I just," he wrung his hands, "I'd rather not."

Kiara watched the way he fidgeted. "Yeah, maybe we could skip that part of the tour."

"But Suze is wonderful! Not only can she see the future, she can," Darcy leaned close, "talk to the dead."

Kiara and Hadyn blinked at her.

"Darcy, can't you see?" Delsin widened his eyes. "They're clearly not interested. So can we carry on or what?"

"Fine," she fumed. "I guess we will just 'kick off' with the butchery."

"What an appropriate alternative."

"Quiet you!" Darcy spat. "Anyway, the tour started a long time ago. Before you became our dead weight."

As Darcy resumed her march, Kiara turned to Delsin. "Why are you here?"

"Look, I know it may seem I'm tagging along only to irk Darcy, but that's not the case. It's only an additional compensation." He smirked. "Hope you two don't have weak stomachs."

Kiara wondered what he meant. She didn't think she did, but today was an exception, with all her intermittent nausea. As they neared their next destination, a great stench of semi-rotting meat assaulted her nose. With a sudden heave, Kiara gagged. She thought she might do worse.

She pinched her nose. "What exactly is this place?"

"The butchery is where all the meats from the hunts go to get cut up," Darcy explained.

"Lovely."

"You sure know how to charm your guests," Delsin added.

Darcy rolled her eyes as she pushed the door open.

The irony smell of blood took over and overwhelmed. Kiara covered her mouth and nose with her sleeve to filter it, and stop the bile rising in her throat.

The room inside wasn't as unsanitary as the smell would have suggested. Chicken-sized birds hung from the ceiling by their feet with no heads to speak of or with, but simple cleanliness kept the place workable. The same could not be said of the main table in use. A white man stood behind the table in an apron covered in blood stains both old and new, working on the carcass of some sizable mammal. He held a vicious cleaver in one of his bloodied hands and kept a sharp knife close by. A rack lined with more wicked tools of butchery created the backdrop to this macabre scene.

"Hello, Richard!"

"Hey, Darcy," he waved the cleaver at her and went back to hacking into the meat. "Got something for me today?"

"No, haven't been out. Father has me taking the guests on a tour."

"Looks like you got your hands full anyways," Delsin gestured to all the hanging birds. "I'm sure their meat will be just *impeck-able*," he emphasized the second syllable.

Richard wouldn't look at Delsin directly, ignoring his joke entirely. "Yep, the hunters have been busy."

Kiara didn't dare look around the room as freely as she might have let her eyes roam the mill, but an elongated carcass running the length of the long table at the left side of the room captured her curiosity, morbid as it was. Picked clean to the bone, its skeleton lay bare and jumbled, except for its massive, dark head, the mouth open as if gasping and its big eyes looking out at her, glossy and expressionless. Kiara knew at once it was a fish, though she'd never seen one with a pair of eyes.

Seeing how she stared, Richard gestured with his cleaver, "Pirarucu." He raised his brows. "Red fish."

Kiara looked at its black head and wondered how its body must've looked. "Pirarucu . . ." she mused. "Arapaima!"

"So it's been called," Richard nodded. "It's said to be the reason why some fishermen never come back from the river. Dragon fish, some call it. It is dreadful, awful, but feeds a lot of mouths."

Kiara remembered herself tucked in her hideaway, reading of the great creatures. She gawked at the colossal carcass, bigger even than what she ever imagined.

"I wonder why then," Delsin pondered, "so many large specimens are caught. What? Bigger still are the ones that drown the hapless fishermen?"

Richard sneered, but kept his head down and chopped away. "You think you're smart, but I rarely see you outside of your smithy. There are monsters in the deep, beneath the tannin-drenched black," he hacked down hard with the cleaver, "and no one, not even you, knows the limit to their enormity. Now, if you'll excuse me," he grabbed up a grimy towel to wipe his hands and Kiara nearly gasped when she caught the scar on his right palm, "but I have work to do."

"To be sure," Delsin conceded. "All this meat will have you working around the *cluck*."

Darcy pulled in her lips to keep from laughing, but when no one else even cracked a grin, Delsin raised his brows at her. She got the hint. "Alright," she said, "Ready to move on to the next stop?" Kiara nodded a little too eagerly. "Thanks, Richard."

He didn't lift his head, but just gestured with the cleaver again. "Yeah, sure."

Back outside, Kiara gasped for breath. The air smelled as sweet as a garden compared to the rancid fumes.

"Oh, don't be so dramatic," Darcy chortled.

Kiara looked at her ". . . Funny." She couldn't get the scar out of her mind. Each of their occupations very well could have warranted such wounds, but three people with nearly the same scar?

As they left the smelly hut behind, Delsin looked to Darcy to explain the butcher's behavior, but she would have rather ignored him.

"If you won't, I will," he said.

"Be my guest."

Kiara looked at him, hoping for an explanation, but certainly not expecting one.

"Richard had a brother named James," Delsin began. "He was a fisherman, *a very good one*," he added with emphasis. "One day when he went out fishing, the others came back, but not James. The other fisherman said he was killed by the pirarucu."

"They said, the fish leapt clean out of the water!" Darcy jumped in. "Knocked him unconscious, and dragged poor James down to its lair in the depths."

Delsin's drooped lids asked her if she was done with her dramatic episode. He sighed. "Richard carried the death on his shoulders. He feels like he should have been there to protect his little brother."

"That's terrible," Hadyn said.

Delsin nodded.

"He's really nice, once you get to know him," Darcy said.

"Yes," Delsin agreed, "but he's had a temper ever since the death of his brother. And he has never liked me."

"Can't imagine why."

"Anyway, that's the story."

"And that's just what it is, isn't it?" Kiara said.

"Excuse me?" Darcy bristled, while Delsin grinned at Kiara, both surprised and impressed.

"If you haven't noticed," he said. "I don't believe a lot of things this village says as fact. Ever since it happened, I've always suspected *fowl* play." He smirked.

It took her a moment, but Kiara's mouth split in a slow grin. "Oh, I get it. Because chickens are a type of fowl."

Hadyn looked to be yet struggling to put the pieces together.

"You two don't get out much do you?" Delsin arched a brow.

Darcy fluttered her eyes. "Oh, forget the jokes. This is exactly why nobody likes you, Delsin."

"Excuse me. You know as well as I that James wasn't exactly, what Tykaraijre would call, in harmony with the village."

"Yes, but that— well that—" For once Darcy had no words, eyes almost sad.

They walked beside each other in silence for a moment.

"Jaci likes me," Delsin said.

"Jaci likes everyone." Darcy said.

"I suppose you're right on that account . . . Where to next, your majesty?"

"If you must know, our next stop is the Temple. And so help me, if I hear one more chicken pun out of you before the end of the day, I'll stuff you with feathers and use you as a pillow on my next hunting trip."

They walked along the still quiet streets. In Caverna there was always a bustle on the streets. People making their way through town on social calls, or just plain walking for the sake of running into others for the daily gossip scoop. Here it seemed that everyone was always busy with no time to aimlessly wander about the streets.

"Darcy, where is everyone?" Kiara asked.

"Well, there's not one particular place. Some are out hunting and fishing, you saw Richard at the butchery, some are at the mill. What do you mean?"

"Nothing. I was just wondering if everyone was in fact working."

"Yes, they are. Here, your occupation is practically chosen at birth. Everyone has a job and purpose in Tykaraijre. That is why there is harmony."

*Harmony* . . . Kiara thought, recalling back to the crabby mill boss and the terse hospitality (if it could be called that) of Richard, not to mention Darcy's own relationship with her parents.

"There's Gypsy Suze's house . . ." Darcy sighed wistfully as they wandered past. "You know, nobody knows where Suze is from."

Kiara followed her eyes to a lady in a draping, layered skirt. Patterned and colorful, the hem slid across the dusty porch where she swayed in a woven hanging chair. Silver streaks threaded through a head of dark curls so full it rivaled Kiara's own mane.

"Really?" Kiara asked, curiosity waking to life.

Darcy nodded. "Some believe her a stowaway from one of the trips from England, but before that? Who knows?" Darcy's eyes flared. "I've heard, she's been everywhere. And coming here, she's combined all her knowledge from around the world with what she's learned here to create something truly powerful."

Kiara watched her, pleasantly incognizant to the world around her as she puffed blue smoke from a long pipe.

"What do you think of meeting her now?" Darcy sidled closer to Kiara.

"Well . . ."

Delsin shook his head at her.

"Maybe a short chat wouldn't hurt."

Kiara used her eyes to plead with Hadyn. He tried to stand his ground, not budging an inch, but at length, huffed a sigh. "Fine."

Matching grins split both the girls' faces as they turned to approach the steps. Hadyn and Delsin followed reluctantly behind.

Eyes closed, Suze rocked and hummed a content melody to herself, bare feet poking out from under her draping skirts of deep reds and purples.

"Good afternoon, Suze." Darcy gave a little wave.

The melody caught in the woman's throat and her foot put a halting end to the swinging. She peaked open an eye, stared a moment, and gathered herself up out of the chair, decorative coins along her skirts clinking as she stepped out of the shade of the porch.

"My, my, what have we here?" A smile stretched her full lips. "Young souls, visitors from afar. You are Hadyn and Kiara, contrite travelers seeking rest, but I see have not yet found it?" Her words ended in an uncertain question. Her accent was strange, different than any they'd yet heard, layered and rich as her colorful skirts.

Kiara felt held by her round eyes, swirling pools of light and darkness, earth and flora, with some wild thing dancing inside them to keep them changing in different lights. She had a silver ring in her nose, and when she brushed her hair aside, she revealed many more piercings lining the edge of her ear.

The woman seemed to give Delsin some concern. Kiara could see it in the slant of his brows and the way he put a gentle hand on her shoulder, placing himself slightly in front of her.

"Suze, how nice to see you," he greeted. "I would have

thought you'd be busy with your daily customers."

"One thirty canceled," she said bluntly, wondering why he had interrupted her.

"Oh, what a misfortune." Delsin tried not to sound too disappointed.

"I will gladly take their place!" Darcy said.

Suze smiled at her, but then set her penetrating eyes on Hadyn. "What about the newcomers?" She slid up to him. "Such a handsome face! But what sorrows lie behind those eyes. Do I see guilt? What darkness lies in the shadows of your past, hmm?"

Hadyn stepped back, as she invaded his space, cheeks growing redder by the seconds, and not just out of embarrassment, or so it seemed to Kiara.

"No matter," Suze backed off. "If not the past you want, come to the fire. The ashes will tell your future. No charge for the visitors," she purred.

Hadyn planted his feet like a tree, growing ever more impatient.

"I can talk to the dead," she enticed. "So if you would like to speak to someone, just ask."

"Em . . . Suze?" Delsin started, "when's your next client?"

She waved him off, her dangling jewelry clinking together.

"Can the ashes read my future, Suze?" Darcy fought for even a slice of her attention.

Suze patted her on the head. "In time, love. But what about the red lass?"

Kiara bristled at the title, jerking back as she came near. But then she picked up the end of her braid and held it carefully, almost admiringly.

"Such beauty." Suze's eyes rose to her face, expression crumbling with sadness as her gaze roved across her freckled features. "Yet . . . you don't see it, do you?"

Kiara didn't know what to say. She lost herself in her eyes. It gave her the feeling of spinning around and around in the forest head raised to the thick canopy blazing with the hidden sunlight.

"Oh, but let us see . . ." Suze held to the beads of a chunky necklace she wore, eyes closed as if reading them with the tips of her rough but slender fingers. "Let us see . . ." she mumbled. "Oh, I see royalty in your veins."

Kiara sucked in a breath and Suze popped open her eyes, almost as if she was surprised she had gotten something right. "Or . . . maybe not." Her eyes darted to the others. "Maybe just a royal attitude." She smirked. "No doubt, used to getting your way, I see."

"Oh. come now, Suze!" Delsin spat. "That's got nothing to do with her future and you know it."

Suze threw him daggers. "Very well. I see . . . Oh!" She sobered, speaking without facade. "Great danger . . . Yes! If you go, but maybe even more so if you stay."

Kiara's brow scrunched. "I don't understand—"

Delsin had just about had enough. "Alright! Thank you very little, Suze, but we're on a tight schedule here. Please forgive our rude departure, but we must be going."

The fortuneteller's eyes lit with both panic and offense. "But something lies ahead!" she continued. "Very soon! Something you will not want to face alone!"

Delsin came up behind Kiara and Hadyn and began to push them down the road.

"Kiara!" Suze cried.

Her own name, said so desperately, drew her back in. She pulled away from Delsin. Suze stood where they had left her, but her eyes had turned dark, cast in a dreadful foreboding.

When she spoke, her voice was deeper, slow and deliberate. "You don't belong here."

Kiara felt frozen under her severe gaze until Hadyn came beside her and turned her away.

Delsin patted them on the backs as they rejoined him. "Don't let her worry you," he said, seeing Kiara's distant look. "She's a lunatic! Not present most the time. Lost her marbles in a caldron years ago. I'm surprised she was coherent. Did you smell what she was smoking? That woman has half a brain left and the mind to tell you everything and anything that floats through the many holes in it."

"But isn't that exactly what you told me?" Kiara asked.

"Well, it—" Delsin had to think for a moment. "That's beside the point. She doesn't know what she's saying."

"If you say so," Kiara said, but an unsettling feeling wouldn't leave her. Rubbish or not, Suze's words had brought a look into Hadyn's eyes she hated to see. And her warning to her didn't exactly make her feel at ease.

She shook the thoughts, forcing a smile. "Hadyn, remember when you snuck me into the Styx and we just barely escaped the fortuneteller? Twice? What was her name?"

A weak smile turned up his mouth at the memory. "Madam Grizella."

"Sorry it wasn't the same this time. I know you didn't want to meet her. But really, the stuff she said about you. How absurd!"

His smile evaporated; she didn't notice. "So she doesn't have a filter?" she continued to jest. "Are we supposed to applaud her for—"

"Can we just stop talking about it?" Hadyn snapped.

Kiara and Delsin turned to him, their smiles steadily fading. Kiara searched his eyes. It was no secret Suze had upset him, but Hadyn didn't just snap like that, and she had no idea what could have touched such a nerve.

"Wait! Wait up!" Darcy called, running behind them. "Why did you all leave me?"

"We didn't leave you; you didn't come with us," Delsin corrected.

"Fine, but why did you have to go like that?"

"If you cannot understand, then you are blind enough to be stumbling in the dark."

Kiara cringed, but if it hurt, Darcy didn't show it.

"Don't think I didn't know that walking past Suze's was part of your plan," he said.

Darcy shrugged with a satisfied grin. Throwing her hand above her head in a triumphant point, she announced. "*Now*, to the Temple!"

As Darcy lead on and Delsin began to follow, Kiara turned back to Hadyn, concern and questions slanting her eyes. The corners of his mouth ticked into a reassuring smile and he nodded his head for her to follow. But she didn't want to. She wanted to stay right here and make him explain himself.

Did he really not trust her?

Kiara didn't return his smile. Shaking her head, she turned to catch up with Darcy.

The Temple was almost built as finely as Deorc's mansion, just much smaller. Still, its height and presence cast a heavy shadow. Clay steps led up to dark, double doors with stained glass windows, arched and engraved just like the entrance to the mansion. Darcy pushed against one and it gave way with a groan. Dimly lit by only a few high windows, the quiet in the empty building seemed to whisper, but Kiara soon realized why. The Temple wasn't as empty as she assumed. A man knelt in front of the altar at the far side of the room, his back turned to them and his head down. His words quietly echoed off the steeply vaulted ceiling, disembodied and muddled.

Darcy strode up the middle aisle, passing by the many dark pews, when she stopped and turned around, her expression pained. "I didn't think anyone would be here," she whispered.

"Maybe we should go," Delsin suggested.

The man by the altar began to rise and didn't seem to stop, straightening until he was a towering six and a half feet tall. He turned and walked up the aisle toward them. He had a menace about him and it wasn't just the large scar on his pale face, snaking from his left ear, under his eye, and all the way to the tip of his nose. It wasn't just the scowl that turned every feature that could have been kind into something cold, that made him something to fear. There was something more. Something inside. Something hidden. Whatever it was, even Darcy seemed to grow small as he approached.

A quiver shook her voice as she greeted, "Afternoon, Mr. Sullivan."

He merely nodded his head as he passed. The door slammed behind them, making them all jolt and realize that they were holding their breath. With a collective exhale, they chuckled nervously.

"That was Edmond Sullivan," Darcy explained. "He was my father's best friend back in England."

"And now?" Kiara wondered out loud.

Darcy shrugged. "Father, doesn't really have friends . . . but if he did, I suppose . . ."

"How did he get that scar?" Kiara asked.

"I was wondering about the scowl," Hadyn said.

Darcy tried to laugh, but it sounded weak. "My father said he got both sometime back in England, but that's all he tells me."

Another carving of the beast loomed like a hulking menace over the altar, mounted high above, this incarnation hewn of dark wood, almost black in coloration. Kiara noticed how Delsin kept his head low. Maybe he didn't like to look at it either. He stayed happily at the entrance while Darcy walked them around the temple.

Up on the stage, Darcy waffled on like a real tour guide. Kiara didn't hear her much, yet too shaken from the recent meetings to take in the irrelevant information. She looked out on the pews, imagining the room filled with people, certainly expansive enough to accommodate at least half the town at once. She gazed at all the dark wood, observing how not even the golden light streaming through the high windows hardly made a dent in the gloom of the place. Even with her imagination, she couldn't picture all that many people wanting to come here. Just standing there under the dark carving of the beast made her skin crawl.

# FORSAKEN

"You know, there's more places in Tykaraijre to see?" Delsin called from the entrance. His words echoed about the room and made Kiara jump. "Haven't you wasted enough time here?"

Darcy smirked, drawing some kind of sick enjoyment from his squirminess.

"I'm ready to go," Kiara agreed, trotting down the steps of the stage.

"Yeah," Hadyn nodded.

"Alright." Darcy lolled her head to one side. "It's never been my favorite place in the village anyway."

Chapter   Nineteen

# THE ENCHANTED TRAILS

**A**s the tour drug on, Kiara's patience for everything Tykaraijre and Darcy related dwindled along with her steadily failing constitution. Maybe it was just all the walking or even the stress of escaping Caverna all catching up to her, but she felt like if she dropped down right where she stood, she might not get up again.

Delsin departed sometime in between Old Man Weever's place, who made fish hooks and lines, and the tailor's— a woman named Maira's house who had nine daughters to help her mend and make most of Tykaraijre's clothes. Though, as their surroundings started to assume that blue calm of twilight, Kiara wished she would have gone instead, longing for nothing else than to rest her weary lids and feet.

"How much more is there to the tour?" she asked. "I really don't know how much farther I can walk today."

"Oh, there's just one more place," Darcy smiled amiably, "but I can certainly walk you back to the house, if you want, and just show Hadyn instead," she beamed at him, and he smiled back awkwardly.

Suddenly, departing early didn't look all that necessary. "No. Of course not. I can make it to one last place."

"Whatever you'd like. The Enchanted Trails await." As she turned, Kiara rolled her eyes, understanding immediately why Darcy would have gladly taken her back.

Darcy led them to the edge of town, where the night already had a tight grip on the dense forest, dark except for the wide trail before them washed in blue by stone pillars topped with fire. The very same trail that had led them to the village, though this time each of the fires were already blazing, leading the way. Kiara might have taken off at a giddy run if not for her fatigue. Instead the three plodded down the path together, taking in the magic as the sounds of the forest's evening symphony filled the silence.

"Enchanted," Kiara said at length. "Don't you think that's a perfect name for them, Hadyn?"

He smiled.

"Well, that's just what I call them," Darcy said. "Father thinks it's silly."

"I like it," Kiara countered. "Very much."

Darcy leaned to see around Hadyn, smiling at her softly. Shaking out of it, she said, "This is one of my most favorite parts of the village. I never tire of walking this path. Though . . . the dark always has made me so terribly frightened," she cried, grabbing up Hadyn's hand.

Hadyn tensed and his gate stiffened like he walked on nails instead of dirt. Kiara rolled her eyes. She didn't believe her for a second. She imagined the dark would delight her. It would give her the concealment to do all the sorts of nasty things a Darcy would do.

"But somehow," Darcy continued, "I feel safer with you here, Hady."

Kiara mouthed the horrible nickname in disgust and Hadyn almost choked trying not to laugh at her. Her ears flushed with heat when she realized he had seen.

"I hope it's alright if I call you that," Darcy said.

"It's not," Kiara snapped. "He doesn't like nicknames."

"Kiara, it's alright. I—" he started to say.

"Oh, I know!" Darcy cried and Kiara couldn't fully stifle the laugh that climbed out of her throat. "They're *so* patronizing, aren't they?" she said to Hadyn.

For once Kiara was thankful for Darcy's dramatic flare as she released Hadyn's hand to further emphasize her outrage with all her limbs. "I mean do they think we're not mature or old enough to be called by our names?" She continued. "I hate it when my father calls me Darce. Is my name not short enough? I sometimes wonder, what if we were never named? What would they call us in the afterlife? Or what if we had to earn our names like some of the natives still do? Set out on a harrowing journey to find your name. I guarantee you, no one would take your name and twist it. They would respect it. So Hadyn it is. And, Kiara, if you like to be called Kiara, that's all I'll call you too."

"Thanks, Darcy," Kiara said, trying not to sound too surprised.

She nodded. "You're welcome."

Out of the corner of her eye, before she could seriously contemplate Darcy's uncharacteristic kindness, Kiara caught a glimmer through the branches. She stopped, unsure why a light would catch her eye, surrounded by light as she was. Though it wasn't just light, but red light. Red fire! moving through the forest as if held by a hand. Kiara's heart pounded, at once intrigued and a little afraid. If the person had red fire, they didn't live in Tykaraijre. And if not from the village, who were they?

"Dar—" Kiara froze to see Darcy and Hadyn still walking, now several yards ahead. ". . . cy?"

When she had stopped, they had continued on, unaware that she was no longer with them. Darcy's words drifted back to her as she waffled on about none other than hunting. Stabbed with a sudden pain through the heart, a fire threatened to spark in her chest. But Hadyn couldn't know, could he? Darcy, on the other hand, she wasn't so sure about. She wanted to stand there, make them have to come back for her. But how far would they go before he realized? She watched them abandon her, for some strange reason unable to call out to them. She wondered if she was even there anymore or if she was just a vapor watching from another realm.

Darcy cracked a joke and Hadyn turned to share his laughter with what would have been Kiara. He froze, whipping his head about in a panic. "Kiara?"

Now she felt foolish, like she had no idea what she was trying to prove.

"Back here!" she called.

His shoulders slumped and he ran for her. "What are you doing?" He laughed it off nervously.

"I . . . thought I saw something." Kiara scanned the forest for the now conveniently vanished torch.

"Like what?" Darcy asked, genuine worry also etching her face.

"I don't know . . . Maybe nothing."

Darcy narrowed her eyes. "What do you *think* you saw?"

Kiara hesitated to say. "Fire . . . Red Fire"

"Really!" Darcy's mouth gaped with a smile, eyes rounding. "Where? How much?" Her face fell. "Oh . . . but I'm not supposed to talk about it. You'll have to ask my father."

"I'm not so sure, that's a good idea," Hadyn said.

"No, he'll want to know. Don't worry."

Resuming their walk, Hadyn shook his head. "I can't believe I didn't know you had stopped. I'm so sorry."

"No. It's alright, really!" Kiara felt like the one needing to apologize, and just hoped the blue light all around them stopped her cheeks from looking so red.

"Don't do that again without saying something."

"Yeah, no more running off on us," Darcy said, elbowing her playfully.

The trails didn't end in the middle of the forest as they might've expected, but looped back around to the village, and on the way back to the mansion, they actually laughed with Darcy. Her real laugh found its way back into her throat and for a while, she became just like a friend, to both of them.

As they emerged from the woods back into the village, night had fallen quickly, but it seemed Tykaraijre was only just beginning to wake up. Many people traversed the streets, but where they might have walked soberly during the day, diligently traveling from one job to another, they now had a skip in their steps, wandering without a care. Some even danced, others carried around drums they beat to a contagious rhythm, all shouting a loud melody at the tops of their lungs. Many of the men were bare chested and shoeless. The women wore things that exposed their bellies and arms, but where there were no clothes, designs of swirling lines and geometric shapes glowed right on their skin, as bright and blue as the Dalmatia they hoisted on torches. Kiara couldn't believe her eyes. She did a double take at Darcy, to make sure she didn't glow at night too.

Darcy laughed, seeing her confusion. "It's clay," she explained, "mixed with a mineral powder. It's only reflecting; not glowing. We call it matia paint."

No less amazed, Kiara turned back to the villagers, blinking in wonder. Their bodies flashed with light, every movement bouncing the blue firelight around the crowd. She could feel the drum beat in her chest, the jumps and stomps of the people through her feet.

"What is this?" She asked breathlessly.

Darcy beamed from ear to ear, watching her people. "It's the Mboi Tata," she shouted to be heard above the ruckus. "A celebration of the night and the Dalmatia. Nobody ever knows when the next one will come. A tribe member will simply start one and it's hard not to join in."

Just then, a young man with glowing swirls all down his arms stepped forward and grabbed Kiara by the hands, pulling her into the festivities. Immediately Hadyn tensed, taking a step to intercept him, but he stopped when Kiara threw her head back laughing as the young man spun her around.

Darcy cupped her hands to her mouth. "See what I mean!" She turned to Hadyn, his arms crossed and mouth downturned. She stuck out her bottom lip, playfully mocking his pout and gave him a shove.

Someone strode by, carrying a bucket and Darcy dipped her hand inside. She held Hadyn by his arm, and with one quick swipe, ran a glob of wet matia paint down his nose, giggling wickedly. Hadyn jerked back. He could see the reflective paint on the tip of his nose. Without thinking, he tried to wipe it, but only smeared it more, making Darcy laugh even harder. Before she sobered, Hadyn grinned, taking his paint covered hand and making a sloppy streak across her face, from one cheek down across her mouth.

Kiara heard their laughter first, trying to get a look while her new friend pulled her this way and that. The tips of her ears began to burn when she caught sight of their little paint war. With some difficulty, she told the young man she had to go (to his disappointment) and stomped straight up to them, obviously clearing her throat.

"You two are a mess."

"Don't tell me you don't want to look this good?" Darcy said, striking a pose.

"Here." Hadyn stepped towards her, steading her with a hand on her shoulder.

Kiara jerked back, but instead of smearing a hand across her face, he gently brushed a thumb across her cheek bones, drawing a line under both her eyes. Kiara froze up, holding her breath. She watched his face, but he seemed focused, intent on making the lines straight. He caught her eyes a moment and abruptly stepped back. He made an oops face, seeing the incomplete, glowing handprint he left on her shirt.

"Don't look so horrified. It washes out." Darcy shoved Hadyn aside. "And . . ." she said, using her thumb to paint a crescent, half, and full moon across Kiara's forehead, ". . . there. You are inducted into the night." Her eyes flashed as she grinned at her.

Kiara couldn't help but smile back, partly from Darcy's messy face and partly from the giddiness in her chest.

"Now, come on!" Darcy said, pulling them into the crowd.

They fell in line in a lively march. The crowd thinned, stretching itself into a snaking line through the village with no specific destination. Some ran out of their homes as they passed, splattering themselves in matia paint and joining the line. Even more completely enveloped in blue than they were on the Enchanted Trails, the red flame Kiara saw in the forest was quickly washed from her mind.

So sufficiently caught up, Kiara and Hadyn hardly even knew when it all happened, when they stopped being individuals and became a part of the crowd, all one entity. They shouted along with the rest even though they had no idea what they were saying. Kiara felt a strange and pleasant loss of control, like she didn't need a reason for anything she did, nor a reason for where she was. They laughed and stomped and made noises for no reason at all. For the Mboi Tata had no reason except to let go and join the nocturnal chorus of the forest.

When they at last broke away from the crowds, stumbling onto the lesser roads to the mansion, it was like stepping out of a dream. Kiara beamed and waved to those still carrying on without them, the songs and drums fading with distance.

"Come on." Darcy smiled, shaking her head. "We're gonna be so late for dinner."

"Oh!" Kiara put a hand to her face, her mind ramming back into reality. "What about the paint?"

"Don't worry. We'll clean up first. Anyway, Father used to love the Mboi Tata."

"Used to?"

Darcy shrugged. "He hasn't joined one since I was a little girl."

"Oh." Even though Kiara had only experienced a small part of one, immediately the knowledge made her sad.

Chapter     Twenty

# DINNER AT THE BLUE MANSION

**A**t dinner that night, Kiara found out not only Darcy, but each member of the Tykara family also had a similar scar in their right palm to the ones she had already seen, all but confirming this was no odd coincidence, but at the same time giving her no real answers.

When at last they stepped into the dining room, the table was elaborately set, much more so than the breakfast they had eaten there. Even Gadferlin had a banquet of his own. Away from the table, he perched on a wooden platform, dunking his head in and out of a gold wrought chalice. His atrocious table manners sent dead beetles and moths launching this way and that in his scrupulous search for just the right insect. In between insect projectiles, he threw occasional narrow-eyed looks in Kiara's general direction, which may have well been straight into her eyes for all she cared.

Deorc and Lyra already sat at both ends of the long table. Gold candelabras tipped with blue flames provided only enough light to see.

"Welcome back!" Deorc said, a great smile on his face. "How was the tour?"

"Fine, Father."

Deorc frowned at his daughter.

"It was wonderful," Kiara said. "Darcy took us everywhere."

He smiled. "There, you see? That's the kind of enthusiasm I like to hear."

Darcy sat down without another word, but Kiara and Hadyn didn't dare sit before Deorc told them to.

"Won't you sit down?" he asked as if he would have never deprived them of doing so.

Kiara took her seat next to Darcy and Hadyn next to her.

Darcy flicked her eyes over the seating situation. "Oh, I thought . . ."

"Something wrong, Darcy?" Kiara blinked at her innocently, same as she had done the night they arrived.

From the look of her scowl, Kiara was surprised Darcy didn't just growl at her. So much for her being just like a friend.

Servants glided into the room like a choreographed performance, delicately placing steaming trays of food in front of them. They took their glasses with white gloved-hands, pouring their drinks from golden pitchers. Gadferlin gave a squawk as if he just noticed everyone else was getting something far better than his dish of insects. Kiara thought he must be very well behaved to not fly in and steal something for himself.

Kiara blinked at the sudden formality, certainly used to such banquets, but surprised all the same since Darcy had served them breakfast herself. Mentally strapping herself in, she sighed inside, not looking forward to sitting up straight and behaving in fashion through however many courses were prepared, rather wondering when this day would end.

Hadyn on the other hand, hadn't the slightest familiarity with such things, tensing and leaning away from the micromanaging hands as people he didn't even know the names of did everything for him. He had two capable hands and working legs. What were they doing? When a young girl came to pour his glass, Hadyn said, "Thank you," and took the pitcher to pour it himself.

The girl didn't say a word, hands frozen in the air. All eyes trained on Hadyn as if he had committed murder. Kiara kicked his foot under the table, a painful grin stretching her face. He scrunched his brows at her, and then found every other gaze around the room, realizing his indecorous actions all too late.

Hadyn finished and handed the pitcher back to the girl, who seemed to be trying not to giggle, cheeks growing rosy. Hadyn's own cheeks flushed red with embarrassment.

"This all looks very delicious." Kiara smiled at the Tykara family, attempting to rescue him.

Deorc, still frozen with glass half raised to his mouth, smiled at her. "Thank you. I do take great pride in the talents of our chefs," he said evenly though, noticing Kiara's impeccable manners and Hadyn's lack thereof, he at once made a distinction between the two he had not seen before.

"Kiara," he ventured, "what was your raising like?"

"Excuse me?"

"Well, I can't help but notice how competent you are with elaborate affairs like this feast," he flattered.

She forced the food to go down her throat. "Oh, my parents were very wealthy." She scrunched her nose. "Is it really that noticeable?"

"Why, it cannot be ignored! Your table manners are the finest I've seen, outside of my family's, since I left England. You are both from England, correct?"

"Wales, actually."

"Uh-huh. And what city, may I ask?"

"Aberporth," Kiara said almost instinctively.

Hadyn remained silent, certain he couldn't think half as fast.

"Ah, yes, I know that town." Deorc turned his face to Hadyn. "And, Hadyn, you were in a different social class entirely?"

Hadyn bristled at his bluntness. "You could say my family wasn't as fortunate as Kiara's, yes."

Kiara got the nagging feeling that Deorc wasn't simply a host trying to make polite conversation with his guests, but more like a suspicious man interrogating intruders. Though, how he could know they were hiding something in the first place she had no idea.

"So however did you two meet?" Deorc questioned Hadyn, knowing if Kiara had lied, she thought much too quickly for her own good. While Hadyn, in his agitation, had shown a weakness that Deorc poked at like an exposed nerve. He was playing them and Kiara felt her already poor appetite weakening at the thought of it.

Forced to remember just how strange their first meeting really was, Hadyn knew he couldn't tell Deorc that. "Oh," he shrugged, "under strange circumstances really."

"Such as?"

"I don't want to bore you."

"Oh, come now. This dinner table is in dire need of a fresh story."

Gadferlin, now finished with his insectivorous goblet, shuffled to the edge of the platform, as if he too waited with bated breath. Kiara realized why he hadn't dived onto the table earlier. A gold chain drug across the platform with every step of his little bird feet,

*Not as free as you look,* she thought, *or at least not all the time.*

Hadyn glanced at the bird as he collected his thoughts and crafted the subterfuge. "Well, you see, there was this old forest . . .

in between our two houses," Hadyn began slowly. "The Forbidden Forest. It was said to be haunted by evil spirits. But I never believed much in the legends and spent most days inside, exploring new areas."

"Brave man," Deorc said, but his eyes still held suspicion.

"I, however, had never ventured a foot into the forest," Kiara took over her part of the story, "but one day, for whatever reason gripped me, I braved the woods. You must think me quite the fool when I say, the sun was already going down and I became lost almost instantly."

"But that's when we met," Hadyn said.

"Yes, knowing the forest far better than me, Hadyn saved me from a cruel, cold night spent in the woods. He led me home." Kiara looked at him, the gratitude of every time he had saved her piled into one smile.

Hadyn's hands fidgeted on the table. "We then became fast friends and have been ever since." With a clap he wrapped up the story as abruptly as a mock spring shower.

He couldn't help but feel a pang of guilt, remembering the chill of their second meeting. They were unquestionably not friends. It felt wrong to be lying like this. Kiara felt it too, in the very pit of her stomach. But it wasn't like with Bartholomew. They'd have the whole village's questions to answer. What would they think of them? What would Deorc think of her?

"How cute." Darcy sneered.

Deorc looked busy with his own thoughts, tapping the pads of his fingers together. "So what brought you two here?"

"Adventure," Kiara said simply, still not knowing exactly what the word meant. "I'm also a bit of a naturalist. We both are."

"Great aspirations for so young of an age. I had those too. So, are either of your parents very religious?"

*Oh, when is this going to end?* Kiara's thoughts screamed, wondering why the chatter birds of the family conveniently had nothing to say.

"Um, no . . . I wouldn't say that they were," Kiara replied, cringing inside at yet another lie.

"Oh, but that's perfect!" Deorc said. "Then you wouldn't mind if I told you a little bit about our faith."

Kiara shoved a smile on her face. "Not at all."

"I'm sure you saw the magnificence that is the Beast at the town circle today and in the temple if Darcy remembered to take you."

"Yes, Father, I told you I'd take them everywhere."

Kiara and Hadyn nodded, only because they had seen it, not because they would have used the word magnificent to describe it.

"Like I told you before," Deorc continued, "he is our king and what a great and mighty king he is. One of his greatest attributes being that he wants us to live as we truly are, not grasping for a lofty title of piety, but letting our hearts move freely about our lives. We do not turn away any want or need that we may feel." Kiara didn't know if it was from her growing nausea, but his words didn't seem to make too much sense. "You see," he continued, "we ceremoniously and spiritually die internally and eternally," Kiara's stomach twisted having heard those words before, not in education, but in a warning, "so that we are not bound to rules. We are not affected by accusation, but free to be what our hearts fall into naturally every day."

"And what is that exactly?" Kiara asked, unsure if she wanted to know the answer.

Deorc smiled. "Whatever your heart wants it to be."

Hadyn wasn't having it. "What if someone's heart wanted to kill someone?"

Deorc didn't flinch. "Then we do not think less of him."

Hadyn tried to hide his outrage, but he wasn't Kiara. He didn't have it in him to pretend. "But what if my heart wants him to get punished?"

"Well, I suppose you'd have to do it yourself," Deorc almost chuckled.

"But it doesn't make any sense. What if you didn't want him punished at the same time?"

A servant girl, the same one Hadyn had taken the pitcher from, stifled a giggle where she stood in a row of standby servants.

Deorc ignored her. "Do not misunderstand my words," he skirted. "We do have laws here, merely to keep the peace, but we were only able to do so because every current member of this village agreed. Those who didn't, broke away until every heart desired peace. And now we have it in abundance."

"Help me clarify, if I don't desire the same things you desire, I get kicked out?"

Deorc smiled devilishly "More or less. There are different levels of . . . forgive my lack of a better term— banishment here in Tykaraijre. But I don't believe your heart would want to stay here in the first place. It is my sincerest and humblest of hopes," Deorc said with a light in his eyes, "that you will both *willingly* come to adore and respect our village and king as we do. Have . . . have you given it any thought?" His eyes questioned with an almost innocent expectancy, like a lonely person in need of a friend.

"Oh-I . . . Tykaraijre is wonderful, but . . ." Kiara hated to watch the way his face fell, "there is something we have to do first, before we make any decisions like that."

"Right." He smiled to hide his disappointment. "Of course."

Kiara nibbled at her food. Though it looked delicious, she simply couldn't find the stomach for it. Thankfully Lyra terminated her quiet streak before anyone could take too much of a notice. "So, did you enjoy yourself today, Darcy?"

"If you must know, Mother, my day was trampled on right from the start."

"Oh?"

"Delsin," she jammed her fork down. "He was in the smithy and that man has no respect for anyone! Nor does he have an ounce of sense in his big head. He ruined our lunch at Jaci's and invited himself on the tour!"

"Well," Kiara defused, "I wouldn't say he *ruined* it."

Lyra threw her a cold glare and then smiled pathetically at Darcy. "Oh, doesn't that man have anything better to do? I hope you didn't let it ruin your whole day. I bet the Enchanted Trails were absolutely whimsical on this cool night."

The corner of Kiara's mouth curled in a smirk as she caught Deorc roll his eyes.

"Oh, they were, Mother. Utterly romantic!"

"It's a shame Mato wasn't there."

Gadferlin gave an ear-splitting squawk and Deorc's knife scraped across his plate.

Darcy gave her mother a sideways glance as the silence fell. "Uh . . . Oh, yes! I was thinking about him the whole time. I know he would have been there, but he had to help his father with the cattle."

"I thought cattle were a diurnal species," Kiara mused.

"What?"

Kiara looked at her blankly for a second. "Oh! You know, they're active in daylight hours and sleep when the sun sleeps?"

"Oh! They are. He was just, you know, getting them in for the night."

*Right*, Kiara thought.

"Oh, and there was a Mboi Tata tonight!"

"I can see that." Deorc had an amused grin as he reached across and brushed at a spot of dried matia paint his daughter had missed.

Darcy scratched at it with little effect. "Best one in a while

I'd say," she said, looking at him hopefully.

"Yes, I thought I heard the ruckus. They better not go too late."

Darcy's smile withered and her eyes wandered to her plate. "Oh, Kiara!" She looked up. "Tell Father what you saw in the woods!" Darcy couldn't manage to fully swallow her excitement.

Kiara looked at her questioningly. The memory already felt hazy and far away and it made her head spin.

Darcy's eyes went wide and she mouthed the words, *the fire*.

Kiara gulped. "Oh, that."

"What?" he asked. "What did you see?"

"Go on," Darcy elbowed her.

"It was um . . . red fire. Out beyond the trail. I saw it for only a moment."

Deorc rubbed his chin. "You say it was in the forest beyond the Enchant—" he scoffed, "the Blue Trail?"

"Yes," Kiara confirmed.

"Strange . . . They have never scouted that area before."

"They? Who are they?"

"Spies. They must be trying to . . ." Deorc trailed off.

"Whose spies?" Kiara pulled him from his thoughts again.

"Ugh! The Kingsmen. Their leader is a mere proselyte," he raised a brow, "and not for us."

"I don't follow. Why—"

"Enough!" he snapped, but quickly checked his tone, "questions . . . If you must know, they are a riotous group of savages who insist upon waging war on our peaceful village."

"We've been enforcing peace with them for years, yet they still attack," Lyra said.

"Yes, so if you would please stop questioning, I would be obliged."

"Of course," Kiara said.

Once they finished dinner, Deorc stood and addressed them, "You may go into town if you want. I suppose you'll be leaving tomorrow . . ." his eyes wandered to the floor. "But do not go down the unlit paths."

"Because if you do," Darcy said with feigned ominosity, grabbing Kiara's shoulders, "the Mapingauri will get you."

"What's that?" Kiara asked.

Deorc ignored Darcy and continued as he went to unchain Gadferlin. "Or if you choose to stay here, feel free to roam about the house as you wish, except the lower and upper levels."

He freed Gadferlin's leg. The bird shook, ruffling his feathers, and flapped his wings twice to get up onto his master's shoulder. Deorc stroked the bird's neck with a knuckle and there was no missing the surprising love in his eyes.

"Or if—"

"Excuse me," Kiara interrupted as respectfully as she could, "but I think I'll just retire for the night. I don't feel very well."

"Oh. That's not good at all," Deorc said. "I hope you feel better by the morning."

"Thank you. I believe I will. A good night's sleep is probably all I need. Thank you again for having us here and for dinner. I'm sorry I didn't have the appetite to enjoy it more."

"It is our pleasure." Deorc said and Kiara smiled that polite smile of hers.

Hadyn had seen that look before, and from previous instances it seemed she only used it when she was holding back some kind of emotion or feeling. He caught her questioning him with a glance as if asking if he'd be okay by himself. He smiled at her, hoping she'd go and get some real rest. When she did finally go, he was left to wonder how both her and Deorc could just smooth it over like that, making it seem like there was never a single harsh word spoken between them, as if Deorc really was the perfect host and they the perfect guests.

*My, my, Princess, seems you did learn a thing or two when being taught the posh, lying ways of politics and royalty. Father would be proud.*

Kiara halted midway down the hall, wondering when she had last called herself Princess or referred to Nnyric as such . . . even in her head. Before she knew it, a wave of sadness hit her like a horrid stench. It leached her strength in one awful moment, dragging her down, ambushing with a paralyzing sting. Determined to march it off, she continued towards her room, replaying the things she would have said to Deorc, if she . . . Why didn't she just speak her mind? Did she fear that badly to offend him? One thing was certain, she had questions, like how he could have so many rules when his entire religion preached the opposite. Or the scars? Did the entire village have them? Did only a select few? What did they mean?

She thought of her dream. She had seen Deorc behind bars, tortured by things he was helpless to fight, and yet for reasons she couldn't explain, she was the one who felt trapped.

She needed to talk to Hadyn. So much had happened since they last had a moment alone. They had a lot to discuss, but all of that would have to wait till the morning.

She came to her room, walked in and closed the door, this time not waiting for a predawn visit from Gadferlin before moving the chest up against the door. A blue candle glowed persistently on the nightstand. Kiara didn't dare tussle with it again. Instead, she grabbed the leftover water in her pack and drowned the flame.

She lay on the bed in the dark, stomach churning in a riot of fears. When she remembered her reasonless happiness in the Mboi Tata line, it felt like recalling the memories of someone else and it frightened her.

Delsin had quoted Deorc word for word. It seemed they would leave in the morning, that despite Deorc's disappointments, he would kindly see them off, but an unsettled feeling deep in her gut made her wonder if they really would. She didn't listen to Delsin when she had a chance, now her fears begged the question, was it too late?

# Chapter Twenty One

# THE LIBRARY

**H**adyn squirmed in his seat to be left alone with this unpredictable family, but he didn't have the excuse that Kiara did.

"Hadyn," Deorc said.

He looked at him apprehensively, not sure what he would say next.

"Maybe our library would interest you? You strike me as a man of sense, and if you two are the naturalists that Kiara says, you will be intrigued to know we have quite the extensive selection of encyclopedias, especially on reptiles. I can show you to the room, if you'd like."

"Or maybe Darcy could," Lyra suggested.

"No, Mother," Darcy said, exasperated. She turned to Hadyn. "Sorry. I'd love to, but I have something else I have to do."

"That's okay. I understand," Hadyn said, unable to fully mask his relief.

Deorc waited at the end of the table. "Shall we?"

Hadyn nodded. At least he would be left alone there. Hopefully.

Deorc led Hadyn to a grand room, minuscule compared to the library in the bowels of Caverna, but grand all the same. A few tables and chairs for reading and research collected in the middle of the floor. Shelves rose up and up, stuffed full with books. The ceiling yawned wide open to a second level where only a balcony ran along the bookcases and two catwalks stretched to either side of the room. Great archways sectioned the room into different parts, encompassing both the upper and lower level. Exquisitely engraved corbels nestled under the balcony embellished the bookcase dividers of the lower level. While the gold chandeliers high above cast it all in a pulsing, blue glow.

A light clinking, like tiny bells or . . . coins played a miniature melody from somewhere in the room. It pulled Hadyn from his gawking. He followed the sound to a corner he had failed to notice, the one closest to them. He spotted her layered skirts first. Gypsy Suze. Hadyn's gut twisted to have to talk to her again. But he didn't really have a choice, as she turned around, book in hand and feet yet bare.

"*Bonne soirée*, chief," she purred, voice like butter, and curtsied before him.

Deorc bowed his head. "Suze. Always a pleasure."

"Thank you again for allowing me to borrow from such a great collection of knowledge."

"You're welcome. I just hope you found what you were looking for."

"Oh, I did," she said. "I found *exactly* what I was looking for." Her lips curled into a smile and Hadyn found something dangerous about it, but he couldn't help but notice Deorc seemed to like it very much.

"Excellent," Deorc said, turning to Hadyn. "I'm sure if Darcy had any say, you've already met Hadyn?"

"But, of course." She turned her eyes on him which looked quite dark and starry in the blue light. "Doing some evening reading, I see."

"Going to try to."

She bounced with a chuckle. "Yes, the sight alone of this place is distracting, is it not? But do enjoy yourself. You never know what you might find." She dipped her head to both of them. "*Lachhi tjiri rat.*"

"Good night." Deorc smiled, eyes following her all the way out. He turned his grin on Hadyn as he continued to gape at the library. "Browse at your leisure and enjoy," he said.

"Oh." Hadyn shut his mouth long enough to give a self-conscious smile, nodding. "Than-thank you."

Maintaining the confident grin of superiority, Deorc added as he left, "as Suze said, you never know what you might find."

Hadyn watched him go, shaking the shiver his words gave him. He returned his gaze to the wide room. Now free to marvel without judgment, he took a good moment before he found the legs to walk around. Everything looked so fine and rich, it demanded he take some time to stare and do nothing else.

*Kiara would have been exploring by now and would have probably already found something of interest,* he thought. Without her curiosity to chase around and try to keep out of trouble, he didn't quite know what to do. He thought he should just enjoy the break, but part of him did miss her wide-eyed wonder. Something about exploring an eerie, grand library didn't seem right without it.

Hadyn wandered to the right side of the room, right up to the bookcases, and gazed up at the shelves of dusty books. Above him was the floor of the balcony and a corbel clinging snugly in the corner where the ceiling and the post between two bookshelves met. Hadyn squinted up at it. On closer inspection, the etchings came to life in the form of swirling, knotted snakes with blue sapphires set in the wood for their eyes. At the right angle, the jewels caught the firelight and seemed to flash with a sentient glow.

Hadyn shook with a shiver, thinking of the snaking line they had joined through the village before dinner. The Mboi Tata was strange. He still couldn't shake an oddly hollow feeling it had left in his chest.

He lowered his gaze back to the shelves. He got the sense that he needed to find something he didn't even know he was searching for. But why? If he listened to Kiara, the enigmatic Tykara family and their blue village were completely harmless, if not normal . . . He wouldn't be so sure. But with a sudden feeling like eyes on the back of his neck, he didn't have the focus to scan even a single title on the shelf. His eye shifted one way and then the other as the feeling intensified. Slowly he began to look about, wondering what could make him feel so on edge. He froze. Halfway down the wall of bookshelves, a section was swung out just a crack, like a door someone forgot to shut.

"Hello?" he called, but the library remained as silent as ever.

The sight of the opening stole his breath, just a sliver into a black void the blue light of the room didn't have the strength to illuminate. Hadyn swallowed a lump of fear and felt his feet shuffle toward it, a strange pull calling him forward. He reached the place where the bookcase had left the rest of the wall and with one tap of his finger, sent it swinging the rest of the way open. It swept its way across the carpet like a grand flourish of a hand, barely making a sound save for the deep, guttural groan.

Hadyn turned to a short but steep staircase, leading up into a dim room with only vague shapes to be seen. His heartbeat quickened. Everything about it blared the words *secret room!* And yet, somehow he knew it wasn't a secret at all, knowing Deorc was much too shrewd to ever leave it open. Unless . . . he wanted him to find it. And if not Deorc . . . someone did.

Hadyn shook his head. Who? Why would he even think that? This place was messing with his mind, and he didn't like it.

Then, as he stared at the dark staircase, the same pull that had gotten him here seemed to intensify, calling him as if it knew him, telling him to go up. Hadyn brushed aside the fear that crept up on him like a sharp gust of cold wind and put one foot on the first step. As he climbed, he clenched his hands into fists, seeing no need for this ridiculous anxiety.

The summit opened up to a room not at all different from the rest of the library, more like a miniature version of it, with one small bookcase that looked like a sort of favorite with its intricately engraved shelves, and just two high-backed chairs conveniently waiting nearby. Hadyn wanted to officially dismiss the fear, say that it was all in his head, that Kiara's wild imagination was rubbing off on him, but something, like a persistent chain around his lungs, insisted on shortening his breaths. It kept him from feeling completely alone, like a sinister presence, lurking just beyond the shadows.

A chest in the corner of the room caught his eye, but one look at the bulky padlock and he didn't give it another thought. He crossed to the bookcase, wondering what types of books Deorc kept on his favorite shelf. A volume entitled, The Carved Image of the Beast, piqued his attention. He pulled it off the shelf, thumbed past the first few pages, and stopped on a page with big, bold lettering at the top that read, The Eyes.

The eyes of the Beast. Maybe his most important feature, but who are we to speculate about so great a lord.

The eyes are that of a snake's because the snake saw the world as it is from the very beginning. It saw it as a place where whatever you desire is good. The snake did not hold back the lusts of the heart and urged others to do the same.

Just as noteworthy is his ability to see in the dark. Fiery bright, the Beast's eyes don't see well in daylight, but in the darkness all is enlightened to him, and for those who follow him. A talent he achieved long ago from eating out all the eyes of those foolish enough to ignore the way of peace and indulgence.

Hadyn grimaced, wondering who could have written such macabre nonsense. But, prepared to enjoy a good chuckle over what other ridiculous things the book contained, he plopped down in one of the chairs. That's when he heard a voice. Just a breath of a sound like an unintelligible whisper.

Hadyn jumped and snapped the book shut. "Hello? Who's there?" He tried to mask the tremor in his voice and sound pleasant, but there was no answer anyway.

Then, out of the corner of his eye, he spotted a quick, jerky movement. He whipped his head toward it, but there was only the shadow of one of the high-backed chairs. He blinked a couple times, and for half a second, he thought he saw a flash of something again, something dark. Yet, when he stared, all was still.

Each breath became more shallow without his consent, his feet felt nailed to the floor. Slowly, as if he might awaken some slumbering demon, he returned the book to its place.

Eyeing the exit he made one last attempt at acting rationally. "Hello?" he called. "Anyone there?" After all, the whisper could have come from anywhere, maybe not even being a whisper at all but only the hiss of the pages moving against each other.

Then it came again, a thousand fluttering tongues for one short instance, like the rustling of dead leaves in the night. It froze the blood in his veins and sent a shiver crawling up his spine. He still couldn't make out a single word, but this time it seemed to laugh, derisively . . .

Hungrily.

Hadyn could actually feel his face drain of color.

". . . Okay," he barely breathed, scoping out his escape. He bolted from the room, down the steps, and out into the open. Careening around to the other side of the bookcase, he slammed his back into it hard, pushing with all his might until it started to swing shut. He grunted against the heavy weight, the bookcase proving itself much harder to close than it was too swing open. Finally, it closed with a resounding thud.

He panted, leaning against the old books. No more whispers, but that didn't mean he felt safe. He needed to get out of the library, and yet he could just hear Deorc's questions— *Back so soon? Did the library not interest you?* So he thought he would find a book and read it outside. Lyra had said herself, it was nice out tonight.

With everything conveniently labeled in alphabetical order, he found the E for encyclopedia section quickly enough. As Deorc had said, there were a great many books on reptiles, but strangely enough most of them were about snakes. Hadyn picked the first book he saw that wasn't specifically about snakes, a thick tome on the thermoregulation of ectotherms, and ran for the exit.

Hadyn walked down a dark hallway, trying to find his way to just about anywhere so long as it was far away from the library. He threw quick looks over his shoulder, expecting something to be stalking him.

Nothing.

He slowed his gate, trying to get a handle on his prepos-terous thoughts. Thumbing through the pages of the book, he stopped in the pale light of an open window. The night air filled his lungs and made the horrors of the library seem like a distant nightmare. No longer running for his life, he began to contemplate his choice of literature, wondering how in the world the subject of the thermoregulation of ectotherms filled a book of that thickness? He shook his head then did a double take out the window as he heard the creak of the front door.

Blue light from the foyer streaked out into the yard. Then it was gone as the door closed without a sound and a shadow stepped down from the porch and into the garden out front.

Hadyn closed the book and squinted into the dark.

*Darcy?*

After the initial shock he found the instinct to jerk away from the window in case she happened to look. He strained to hear her hushed voice and dared to look again.

"What are you up to?" he whispered.

"Come on!" he heard her hiss impatiently. "Would you come out already!"

A second figure stumbled into view, this time, out from the edges of the forest.

Darcy's laughter floated across the yard. "I got your note. What are you doing here, Mato?"

"I came to see you," the boy spoke for the first time.

"Why? You know you're not supposed to be here. It's too dangerous."

He huffed. He could have eased into it, but Darcy didn't seem in the mood for small talk. "What are you doing with that one?"

Darcy laughed again. "Hadyn?"

"Yes. I'm worried about you. He's a stranger and an outsider you know nothing about."

"Technically your whole family are outsiders."

"Not like that and you know it."

"Save your worry. Hadyn is a gentleman."

"So you say."

"What do you care anyway?"

He hesitated. "I'm your friend, Darcy, and I . . . well, I see you doing what you always do. Why do you like him? Can't you see he doesn't care about you?"

"Oh, what do you know?" She cocked her head and giggled. "And besides he's a mysterious, handsome stranger, so who cares about who cares about who?"

Mato fought hard not to laugh, wanting to stay serious, but he couldn't help it. "I know you do, Darcy," he said, bringing it back to seriousness. "Deep down, you do. One day you'll stop denying it. It didn't always used to be this way. When did our friendship stop being enough for you? Why do you search out love in those that won't give it? What, because if you can make them care about you, somehow it'll—"

"Stop!" she shouted. "No. You don't know these things. It's not like you're any different from the others. You say that you care, but you're just the same as the rest."

"You know that's not true," he said gently.

Darcy stayed quiet.

"Just be careful, dear friend. That's all I'm asking."

"Can I help you?" a voice behind Hadyn questioned.

Hadyn jumped and spun around to Deorc, one brow raised in perplexed suspicion.

"Um . . . no, sir. I was just reading." Hadyn held up his book. "It was just so pleasant out tonight, I wanted to read by a window."

"Yes, the Library can get a bit stuffy. But I'm sure another window would suffice. This is the hallway, after all. Maybe the drawing room. There are windows in there and *chairs* that you can *sit on.*" He spoke slowly, as if teaching Hadyn the concept for the first time. "Unless, there is some other reason that keeps you at this particular window?"

Hadyn furrowed his brow, as if thinking. "No . . . not that I can think of. But I will certainly try the drawing room. Thank you, sir."

"Mm."

Hadyn spun on his heels and kicked a swiftness into his walk. But with one last look over his shoulder, he saw Deorc slide his finger along the dust on the sill, then look out the window and grimace, as if what he saw out in the yard troubled him even more than the grimy window.

Thankfully, Hadyn found the drawing room empty, though he didn't really feel like reading anymore. But, if only to abate Deorc's suspicions, he sat down in a chair near a window. He stared at the thick book in his hands.

"Just start at the beginning, right?"

He opened the cover, but he soon found out that an encyclopedia is nothing like a naturalist's journal, certainly not interesting enough to keep his mind from wandering to every strange thing that happened since Kiara retired to her room. He needed to talk to her. At least they were leaving in the morning.

His lids grew sleepier with each heavy blink, whether from sheer boredom or drowsiness caused by sheer boredom, it didn't matter. But returning the book meant braving the library, something he preferred to avoid, perhaps for the rest of his life.

Just then one of the servants walked past the doorway of the drawing room.

Hadyn shot up. "Excuse me." The servant turned around, not the one he had grabbed the pitcher from at dinner, but Hadyn was sure he had been there. "Would you mind taking this book back to the library for me, please?"

The servant took the book from Hadyn without a single word or change in his expression.

"Thank you," Hadyn said, but the servant was already walking away. "Sorry about . . . Oh, never mind," he mumbled, more than ready to go to sleep and find in the morning it was all just a terrible dream.

# Chapter Twenty Two

# WHISPERS

**H**aze.

That same smoky, choking haze.

Kiara saw the prison bars and she wanted to run the other way, but her feet moved towards them without her even taking a step. She was forced to look in, and there he was, crumpled and surrendered. Deorc laboriously lifted his head, his cracked lips parting with a raspy plea. "Help me . . ."

Every fiber of her being wanted to swing open the prison bars and set him free, but (maybe not even fully there) all she could do was watch, watch as the shadows came once more and the fear ravaged his face. But this time there was another presence. A black dread fell over Kiara as it arrived. Something consumed her field of vision, something terribly dark. And in the middle of that darkness, two white, horrible eyes burned through. Their hate pierced her soul like jagged daggers.

"We always see," it seethed.

The voice infiltrated her mind and crawled under her skin, until she wanted to up and leave the miserable shell of her body behind.

Kiara sucked in a breath and found her face, smooshed in a pillow, wet with drool. The haze became a groggy fog that took some effort to shake. She tried to move, but every joint ached, even the ones in her fingers.

"Noooo," she groaned, forcing herself up.

This could not happen. She should be better after the night of rest. She *had* to be better so they could leave today and get away from this village! She shivered with a desperate sort of chill, only wanting to ball herself up deep inside the sheets and disappear until it all went away, but with the morning light delivering her a fresh headache, going back to sleep wasn't an option.

She lugged herself out of bed. She'd walk this off. Yes. Walk it off. Aches, chills, and all couldn't really affect her if she didn't acknowledge their presence. She'd give this the boot, one stubborn thought at a time, and they'd be on their way by noon at the latest.

Or so she thought . . .

With not a clue on the time, Kiara dressed herself, ignored how much time it took to do so, and peered out into the hall, quiet, save for a gentle and steady breathing. She looked down and shook her head, a warm smile on her lips. Hadyn sat against the wall, his legs sprawled out and his head slumped towards one side. It must've been terribly uncomfortable.

What was she to do? She could wake him. She *should* even be angry with him. He went directly against what she asked of him and yet . . . all she could do was smile.

Kiara stole back into her room for a half a moment, returned with a blanket, and gently arranged it over him. She supposed she should carry on after that, but part of her, almost unconsciously, wasn't done watching him yet, eyes beginning to follow each spiral of his messy curls.

A pleasant humming on its way up the hall pulled her back to reality and a sudden wave of embarrassment heated her cheeks. She turned towards the melody as if she could ignore the moment out of existence.

A young servant girl, arms laden with clean folded sheets, plodded along in her own world until she nearly bumped straight into Kiara. "Oh! Good morning, Miss Kiara!"

Kiara grinned, holding a finger to her lips.

The girl's wide eyes searched until she found Hadyn slumped on the floor. "Oh, good morning," she said again in a whisper. "What's he doing sleeping there on the floor?"

"I would ask him the same thing."

"He's a silly one, isn't he?"

Just then, Kiara realized she was the same servant girl from their dinner, the one Hadyn took the pitcher from.

"Bella," the girl introduced, seeing her recognition.

"Nice to meet you, Bella. Do you mind if I walk with you?"

"Me?" Hands full she could only register her shock with her almond-shaped, brown eyes. "I mean, of course not."

Continuing up the hall, the girl looked at her sideways. "You don't look so well. Are you feeling at all better?" No longer whispering, her high voice warbled with a constant, self-conscious tremor.

Kiara plastered on a wide smile. "A little, thank you."

"I'm glad to hear it. But you look so pale. You should eat something. What can I get you?"

"Nothing, thank you. I'm really not that hungry."

"But you've got to keep your strength up."

Kiara was beginning to regret asking to walk with her. "I'm sure you're busy with other things. How's this, you show me to the kitchen and I'll fix myself something."

"Oh, Miss, but I couldn't. You're a guest!"

Kiara sighed through her nose and checked her patience. "Please, just Kiara."

The girl fluttered her eyes with a flustered huff.

"You see, we're just the same, you and me. And if you're fine getting your own breakfast, so am I."

"Well, if that's what you want. But— and please don't mind me saying so," she said, lowering her voice to a whisper again, "but I could get in trouble."

"And why's that?"

"Well . . ." Bella squirmed. "It's the fire, miss. No one's supposed to go in there unless they have to."

"The fire?"

She nodded. "The *red* fire, miss."

"Of course," Kiara mused. "Trust me, if anyone gets in trouble, it will be me. I won't tell a soul you were involved." She scrunched her nose.

". . . Alright," Bella conceded. "Follow me."

As they walked to the kitchen, Kiara marveled at the time it took them to get there. "This place is just so big."

"I know," Bella agreed. "When I first came here, I always got lost."

"Do you–" Kiara stopped herself.

"Yes?"

"Oh, I was just wondering. Do you like it here?"

Bella made a face. "Very much. That's an odd question— Oh! I'm sorry I shouldn't have said that."

Kiara laughed. "It's alright. But you've never been . . . frightened or uncomfortable here?"

"No," she said wide-eyed, "can't say I have. Some of the other servants say the master has a temper, but he's never once raised his voice at me. But I suppose I've never given him a reason to. I like my work, and I keep to my own business."

"Of course," Kiara said. "I should have never thought otherwise."

"Since you asked though, my friend, she refuses to do anything by herself anymore because of how terrified she is of this place."

"Oh? Has she ever said why?"

"Has she ever!" Bella chuckled. "There's hardly a day she doesn't mention the whispers." She flared her eyes. "She is convinced this house is inhabited by evil spirits."

Kiara hoped the girl didn't notice the shiver she had to shake off. "Do you believe her?"

"Try to. She's my best friend. But would you?"

Before Kiara could answer, Bella pointed out the archway to the kitchen. "We're here."

"Where?" Kiara said.

Bella looked at her sideways. "The kitchen?"

"Right! Well, thank you very much."

"For what?"

"For talking to me and answering my questions."

"Oh, you're welcome. And a word of advice, stay out of Nukpana's way. Unnecessary faces in her kitchen can cause her . . . well . . ."

"Got it," Kiara said.

She watched Bella until she turned a corner, and spinning on her heels, Kiara trotted off directly away from the kitchen. She still had a determined walk to do away with whatever wanted to keep her sick and in bed. Food she didn't want to eat would only slow her down.

Eyes still closed with lingering sleep, Hadyn started to straighten with a stretch until his back seized with a shooting pain that radiated all the way up to his neck. He cringed, easing himself out of the stiffening cramps. It reminded him of falling asleep against the stone walls of cramped hiding places, cowering from monsters, but his were never the make-believe ones. And he realized with time, most of the monsters were in the hideaways with him.

He stretched again, slower this time, and had much better luck with sitting up straight. He rubbed his face, and dropped his hands onto his lap where a soft blanket had been laid. For some reason, his first thought was Kiara and it made him smile, but one look at her shut door, and he realized it could have been anyone. He assumed it must be early then, but as he wandered half lost around the mansion, he stumbled upon the Tykara family already seated at the dining room table, a quarter through breakfast.

"Hadyn!" Lyra greeted with an extra dash of cheer. "How nice of you to join us."

Deorc gave a customary smile at best. "Where is Kiara?"

"Uh. Still asleep, I think. Her door was shut."

"Oh, poor girl." His gaze wandered with worry. "She was so set on leaving. I do hope this won't impede your departure."

"Knowing Kiara, it shouldn't. But, I probably should check on her. Maybe bring her some breakfast."

"Good idea," Deorc said.

"Oh, but won't you sit down and eat with us first?" Lyra interrupted

Darcy patted the chair beside her, batting her eyes.

"Oh . . . I suppose I could."

"Wonderful!" Lyra cheered.

Hadyn took the seat offered to him. He listened as they talked. After the morning pleasantries, Darcy's mouth ran every bit as chatty as an Amazon parrot. Hadyn tried his best not to engage in much conversation with her. He did not succeed. He answered questions when Deorc and Lyra asked them, but mainly just wondered how Kiara was doing. And he took the first moment he could, to bound off to her room. Knocking on the door, he called her name. In a moment, she came to the door fully dressed, but that's where her appearance to be ready for the day ended. Paler than a sheet except for the dark circles under her red eyes, she looked half dead already.

"Oh," Hadyn blinked in surprise, "were you just about to come out?"

"I was already out this morning."

"You were? You look terrible."

Kiara frowned. "Thanks."

"Sorry, but it's the truth. You don't look good at all."

"Again, thank you."

"So does that mean you're not feeling better?"

"I feel fine. Why do you ask?"

He tilted his head. "Kiara . . ."

"Don't Kiara me. I have to be fine. We're leaving today. We have to." She pointed a finger at him. "And you know I'm right."

He eyed her warily, and blew a breath through his nose. "I brought you breakfast." He lifted a tray off a narrow table against the hall wall.

She tried to smile, but what she managed was more of a twisted grimace. "Thank you, but I'm not hungry."

"And you want to leave today? When you can't even eat?"

"Hadyn, please. We should have left yesterday. We might have been to the river by now. Look, I'm going outside. I'm sure the fresh air will make me good as new! You want to come?"

He sighed. "Sure. I'll go bring this back to the kitchen."

Hadyn took a seat next to Kiara where he found her on one of the garden benches.

"Where is everyone this morning?" She asked.

"Deorc went into the village, but he said he'd be back to see us off. If you felt up to it, of course. I think Lyra went with him. And Darcy?" He shook his head. "She wanted me to go hunting with her this morning. I told her to go ahead without me, that I didn't know anything about hunting and would probably scare off any potential kills."

"What do you mean? You're good at being quiet."

Hadyn fought a guilty grin.

"Oh, I see." She prodded his arm. "You needed an excuse. You *lied* to her."

"Hey, would you want to go hunting deep in the woods with anyone from this village, especially one who, need I even say, has no space boundary?"

Kiara laughed. "I'm only kidding you."

"Well, you seem a bit better. I guess you were right about the fresh air."

Kiara looked away, sighing a shaky breath.

"No?"

She swiped a hot tear off her cheek, resenting its abrupt appearance.

Hadyn leaned forward to see her face. "Hey, what's wrong?"

"Nothing, I-I just don't want to be here anymore!"

"Me neither. But . . . you'll get better soon, and we'll be on our way."

She sniffed. "I just thought we'd have at least reached the river by now, maybe . . . maybe even found my mom." She raised her hands. "I know now that it will take longer. I get that. But to be stuck here? If I can't walk from the door to this bench without a rest, what good is my stubborn will going to be in the wilderness of the jungle?"

"I understand."

"No. No, but you don't."

His brows bunched.

"You don't get it, Hadyn. I keep seeing this dream. It's so dark and there's these prison bars. But I'm not the one behind them."

Hadyn searched her worry-darkened face, waiting for her to continue.

"Deorc is. He's . . ." she grimaced seeing the scene as if it played before her now, "beaten and tormented. There's these shadows and a voice. 'We're watching,' it says, 'we always see.' " The dream faded from her vision and she looked at Hadyn for the first time. "Why would I dream that?"

He didn't know what to say as he watched another tear escape her eye. Hadyn knew more than most that sometimes no amount or combination of words can make sense of the horrors one's seen or experienced, so he kept his silence.

Kiara continued without an answer. "And the worst part is, I'm the one who feels caged."

Hadyn's face paled. "You don't think Deorc will let us leave."

"I *think* you were right to be wary. I don't know why or how, because Deorc, well, Deorc is . . ." she came to a loss to even complete her own sentence. "Yes, he wants us to stay, but not to force us. And even Darcy isn't all bad. And yet something's not right. Like a crooked picture frame. And I just get this feeling . . ." Her hands clenched into fists. "Like I'm stuck. Like I can't do anything good. I always pick wrong. What if there's just something in me that will always pull me to the wrong thing, to destruction? Something I was born with, that's impossible to get rid of . . . no matter how hard I try?" Her shoulders slumped. "I'm not sure if I'd know good if it grabbed me by the shoulders, looked me dead in the eyes, and proclaimed the truth to me."

Hadyn didn't know if it was the sickness talking or if she really thought that, but he didn't want to hear another word of it. "Kiara, you're gonna get better, and Deorc will manage his disappointments. He'll see us off, and we'll be on our way. Okay?" He held her gaze until she nodded. "Anyway, how could you have known to choose anything else?"

"We were warned, Hadyn."

He waited, not following.

"Delsin pulled the words right out of Deorc's mouth," she

explained. "Before he even said them to us."

His eyes shifted back and forth, remembering and realizing. "Delsin. Didn't he mention something about whispering shadows?"

Kiara scrunched her brows. "I think so. Why?"

"Well, something strange happened last night after you went to bed, something with Darcy too, but . . . well, I'll start at the beginning.

"After you left the table, Deorc showed me the library. I should really show you. You'd love it. But Gypsy Suze was there."

"Gypsy Suze?"

"Yeah, borrowing a book or something. It was odd. But after she and Deorc left, I realized there are snakes everywhere in there. Well, that doesn't really make sense if I don't tell you about— You see, there was this secret room that I'm fairly certain wasn't all that secret and this book about the beast and how his eyes are snake eyes because the snake sees life right. Then there were the whispers. They came from nowhere, saying things I couldn't understand. I . . ." He gave a weak grin. "I ran out of there so fast, but I did grab a book and what do you know, every one of them are about snakes! And then there was Darcy."

Kiara's eyes grew wider with the seconds. She had half the mind to feel his head for a fever, never had she seen him talk so fast or so much. "Hold on. Will you slow down?" she said, making him look at her. She tried to smile, but Hadyn could see he had confused her. "A secret room that wasn't secret? Whispers?"

"Kiara, it was awful. Just like a secret room, the bookcase was swung wide open, yet I knew, someone wanted me to go inside. Look, I know it sounds crazy, but it called me, Kiara, like it knew me. And while I was inside, reading the book about the beast, the whispers started, though I am almost certain I was not supposed to hear those. Nothing sounded like words, but it was like they were asking me something . . . and laughing."

Kiara shivered. "At what?"

"I don't know. It was almost like they were taunting me." Hadyn paused and turned to look at her. Her eyes weren't wide with fear or disbelief as he might have expected, but narrowed and thoughtful.

"We have to talk to that servant girl."

"Who?"

"Just this morning, Bella told me about her friend and how she heard whispers. Just like you."

Hadyn shook his head. "Who's Bella?"

Kiara stood with a rush of pounding hammers to her skull. She grimaced. "Your friend from dinner last night. Now come on."

Upon walking back into the mansion, they located Bella surprisingly fast, as she prepared to float by on her various errands.

"Bella!" Kiara called when she spotted her.

"Miss Kiara, what can I do for you?"

"I was wondering if I could speak with your friend, the one you told me about."

"Cassabree? I'm sure she could spare a minute. But I don't know if she'll talk to you. She . . . well, maybe if I tell her how nice you are." Bella eyed Hadyn, "but just you. With Cassabree, one stranger calls for one friend to be present. With two strangers . . ."

Hadyn sighed. "If this is about dinner last night, I really didn't know—"

"No," Bella giggled. "It's nothing like that. I thought it was the funniest thing. Did you see the look on Lyra's face?"

"Bella, focus." Kiara locked her gaze and cocked a brow. "What if you told her, Hadyn heard the whispers too?"

Bella blinked. Her eyes flitted to Hadyn, then back to Kiara. "Come with me."

"Just tell them what you told me, Cass."

Cassabree's worry-filled eyes told them that was exactly what she didn't want to do. Bella had found her and convinced her to sit down with them, but not necessarily to tell them everything.

"Umm . . ." She looked everywhere but at them, her hands fidgeting in her lap.

"Cass, I know what you're thinking, but you can tell them. It's okay. He won't find out. I won't let him send you to the outside."

"But they're Deorc's guests!" she hissed to her friend.

Bella sighed.

"The outside?" Kiara questioned.

"Please," Bella said, "one secret at a time," but Cassabree, head hung, didn't look like she would even tell the first one.

"I was in the library," Hadyn broke the expectant silence, "when I heard them." He made sure to give all his attention to her as he retold the story, speaking as a friend who had shared in the witnessing of some horror, though she never once held his gaze.

He laughed and shook his head as he neared the end of the

tale. "I was so scared, I was shaking and ran out of there as if my life depended on it."

Cassabree cracked a self-conscious grin. "Me too."

"Where were you when you heard them?"

She swallowed hard. "The library."

Kiara and Bella exchanged glances, while Hadyn tried to stay focused.

"In Deorc's room, just the same as you. I was dusting when they started. I couldn't understand a word of it. I thought it was some of the other servants playing a trick on me, but when I looked . . . I was all alone." Her voice cracked with emotion.

"It's okay. You don't have to say anything more," Hadyn reassured.

She steeled herself. "Look, I know that place is haunted by evil spirits." Cassabree leaned forward. "I wouldn't ever go back in there if I were you. It's horrible and dangerous. Please, tell me you won't."

Kiara shook her head. "We won't. Thank you, Cassabree. It was very brave of you to tell us this."

She smiled, just happy that someone believed her.

Out in the hall, after they left Bella and Cassabree, Kiara said, "You have to go back, Hadyn."

He stopped in his tracks. "Are you serious?"

"What? There is clearly something to this. And if we're going to stay here until I get better, I'd prefer to know just what that is."

"You just told Cassabree that we wouldn't."

"And you said, you wanted to show me the library."

"I said, should. I *should* show you the library. There is a difference."

Chapter Twenty Three

# THIS ONE DOESN'T FIT

On the way to the library Hadyn remembered to tell Kiara about Darcy and Mato.

"You say Deorc looked upset?" Kiara asked, mostly focused on trudging down the hall as fast as she could. "Like Darcy isn't even supposed to *talk* to this Mato?"

"Looked like it to me."

"Then I wonder why Lyra talked about him the way she did."

"It was probably the first name that came to her mind that would fit into her scheme. I've found that when people play games, they don't tend to think too much about consequences."

"You know, that's actually . . ." Kiara trailed off, suddenly at a loss for words as they turned and walked through the entrance to the Library.

"I know," Hadyn said. "Took me a while to stop staring too." With one quick look down the way, he found the bookcase swung wide once again. He grimaced. "I would have wandered this place all night if it weren't for, well, you know why."

"I believe it." Kiara swept her eyes over the vast room, the exquisite engraving of the corbels, the stretching catwalks running overhead, and most of all the towering bookshelves, like castle spires waiting to be climbed. The whole place begged for her to explore, to search out. And oh, if she could have. She'd have read every book on every shelf from cover to cover before she exhausted the entertainment she could procure for herself in such a place, letting her curiosity take her up every ladder and race across the suspended gangways. But alas, they came here for a purpose; not aimless wandering, however enjoyable it may be.

Very much to her credit, Kiara managed to wrench her longing heart away from the literary playground, however reluctantly, and found her eyes resting on one chilling sight. The bookcase, still eerily swung open, just like Hadyn said.

"Is that . . ?"

Hadyn took a gallon of a breath. "Yep."

"Well, come on then!"

She dashed away, before he could even tell her to be careful. Hadyn hesitated to keep up and at the bottom of the steps he stopped altogether. Kiara grinned at him, not a worry line on her face. Of course, she wasn't scared. She hadn't heard the whispers, seen the shadows move. And without the strange pull and voices, what was there to fear in a grand, awe-inspiring library?

"Come on, Hadyn." She nudged him. "It's not as though the voices did anything to you."

"No, but I didn't stick around to give them a chance either," he retorted, but resigned with a sigh, not about to let a few shadows bully him.

Up the steps in a flash, Kiara took in every square inch of the room. "It's . . . so ordinary."

"Yep, just like the rest of the library." He could almost feel the believability of his story slipping away.

"And yet . . ." Kiara paused, only moving her eyes, "I feel a strange chill, as if my eyes are not seeing what is really here."

"So you believe me?"

She cocked her head. "I never doubted you."

"Oh, I guess—"

"Hadyn, I believe you." She smiled at him and stepped further into the room, her eyes rounding when she found the dark chest. "You never told me about this!" she said, sliding down in front of it.

"I forgot." He shrugged. "After the voices, I didn't find much room in my head for other things. Anyway, it's locked."

"Oh." Her shoulders slumped in disappointment.

Even with the distraction of the chest, Kiara couldn't shake a certain trepidation, looking around as if something lurked in the deep shadows cast by the blue candles. She stood and perused the titles on the shelf. Almost every spine was regally embossed with gold lettering, some even set with tiny, glittering jewels. The titles used high, eloquent words to describe points of religion and philosophy, and incorporated strange names she'd never heard of in her life.

She spotted Hadyn out of the corner of her eye, standing in the middle of the room, just itching to leave, but still he stood by her side. It reminded her of exploring the colossal library beneath

Caverna. Always he stood by her, even when it was clear he didn't want to. She tried to look faster for his sake, and squatted down to search the lower shelves. She snickered. "Well, this one just doesn't fit, does it?"

Kiara picked a plain, little, leather-bound book off the shelf. Simple brown lettering told them its contents: The Key to Making Perfect Maize Bread.

"Maybe maize bread is Deorc's favorite?" Hadyn suggested, glancing over her shoulder.

"Yes, but Deorc himself is not going to make anything. If he loved it so much, he would give it to his chefs to study." Kiara struggled to pry open the little book, its spine protesting with a tiny squeak, as if it hadn't been read in ages. As she flipped through the brittle pages something clattered out and onto the floor. Hadyn bent to pick up whatever had fallen, while Kiara scrutinized a square, compartment-like, space gouged out of the pages. When Hadyn straightened again, he held a little brass key in his open palm. Kiara gasped and turned to the chest, not about to waste any time.

"Kiara, wait. We can't just go rifling through Deorc's things."

"No? Not like he rifled through our lives last night?"

He narrowed his eyes, contemplating. "But that's besides the point. It doesn't make it right."

"You're right . . ."

He sighed in relief.

"And you don't have to!" She snatched the key from his hand.

Before he could sputter his disbelief, she had already fit the key snugly in the padlock. With one turn, the bulky lock clunked to the ground. Hesitating only for a moment, fingers tingling over the lid, Kiara opened the chest and looked inside. Kindling and wood logs, ready for burning, filled the entire chest to the top, leaving no room for anything else.

"Firewood?" Hadyn spat. "Who puts a lock on a chest of kindling?"

"Maybe it's used to make the Dalmatia!" Kiara exclaimed.

Hadyn wasn't so easily convinced. He started to move the wood around, searching for something, anything else.

"So much for not rifling."

He paused. "It's just kindling, Kiara."

"Kindling you think is hiding something more important."

Just as he began to roll his eyes, Hadyn did find something. There, at the very bottom, he could feel the leather of an old book.

Hadyn froze as he turned to Kiara. The skin of both their arms shivering with the mystery, Kiara helped him remove enough sticks for him to carefully lift it out.

Hadyn felt a weight to it, hefting it in his hands, not in pounds, but in importance, like it was precious somehow without even showing why. It had no title, no defining marking, in a word, humble, like the bread book, but infinitely more valuable.

Kiara lifted the cover while it still lay in Hadyn's hands. Realizing it was the back, she shuffled through the pages to find certain sections marked by various names, but names that looked vaguely familiar, each their own book inside of the weighty volume.

Reading the titles as she passed them, her heart beat faster and faster. "Wait a minute." She flipped to the front and read out loud, "Genesis . . . Exodus! This is a Bible!"

Hadyn looked over the book with new eyes. "How is that possible?"

"Possible? How is it not?"

"What with Deorc's vehement hate for it, I wouldn't exactly find it probable for him to have one in his home."

"But that's why it's locked away! Even ready to be burned!" She nearly squealed the epiphany.

Out in the library, Deorc's voice floated to their ears. "Kiara? Hadyn? Are you in here?"

Kiara's blood ran cold as she froze up. "Oh, no! What do we do?"

Hadyn did the only thing he could, throwing the Bible back in the chest and jamming the lock back on. Taking his lead, Kiara put the key and its book back in its place on the shelf. She tried her best to shake the guilty tremor from her voice as she called, "Yes. In here!"

Deorc walked up the steps to find Kiara and Hadyn sitting snugly in the high-backed chairs, both reading books pertaining to the Beast.

He smiled that crooked grin, and there was no missing his honest delight. "Ah, I see you two have found my favorite room."

Kiara just gave her polite smile, as she wondered if Hadyn was right about Deorc wanting them to find this place, but not in a malignant way. Because there was that child-like look again as if he wanted to share his secret treehouse with his new friends, his smile was that pure and warm.

"I came to find you, because I wondered when you wanted to be off."

# FORSAKEN

Kiara found it hard not to let her face fall. "Oh. I'm afraid it wouldn't be good for me to leave right now. If you don't mind, I think we'll stay here until I get over whatever this is."

Deorc's face fell. "Oh, my dear girl. Are you still not feeling well?"

"Unfortunately, yes."

"Well, of course, you can stay here. I hope you know, we're more than delighted to have you. I'm more than delighted to have you."

Kiara couldn't help but feel a great warming of her heart at those words.

"But this is more serious than I thought," he said. "You really should see our doctor."

"Oh, I'm not sure—"

"In fact, I will take you there this instant. If you're up for it."

Kiara looked to Hadyn and back at Deorc. She smiled. "Of course."

# Chapter Twenty Four

# THE MEDICINE MAN

In minutes, Deorc had rushed them out of the house and into town. Kiara walked along with her eyes at a half-mast squint, any light gnawing at her nerves like little gremlins bent on making her day difficult. An irritating chittering added to her annoyances, somewhere in the forest running alongside the path that the three of them walked. Unfamiliar noises, but definitely animal, Kiara could guess. Something rustled the foliage several paces off the path. She looked to Deorc. His expression alone answered part of her question, his face washed pale and his eyes round with fear. He seemed scared spitless and he hadn't even seen the creature yet. Gadferlin also appeared on edge, huddled down on Deorc's shoulder, eyes squinted to slits.

Hadyn noticed it too. "What? Are you afraid of those squeaks?"

Deorc looked at him. "I'm not overly fond of the creature that makes those squeaks."

"What are they?" Kiara asked.

Deorc quickened his pace. "A fierce creature that can and will disembowel you in mere seconds if given the chance."

"But—"

"Please, don't ask me more."

He planned to scurry past the spot of foliage, so lively now in its rustling, when out stumbled a small mammal, slender in build with slick brown fur. It rolled about in the dirt gurgling with playful sounds. Deorc jumped back, inadvertently but most certainly putting his guests between him and the creature.

Two more scampered out of the weeds to tackle the other. They romped around each other, biting and pulling with their paws, tangling their long bodies and tails together. Something about them was familiar, and Kiara was sure she knew them, though the name of such charming animals remained elusive.

Kiara bent at the waist, watching in delight, her heart just melting at the sight of them. She almost forgot she was sick, so thoroughly captivated. She looked at Hadyn. He mirrored her smile of adoration before they both turned back to watch the little pups leap and reach, chasing a butterfly back into the brush, and away they went.

Kiara's heart drooped a little at their departure as she straightened to continue their walk. Though she quickly realized their company was one short. She and Hadyn found Deorc three paces back from them. Every muscle tensed, he stood with a clenched fist near his mouth, gnawing on a knuckle and Gadferlin balled up against his neck.

Kiara tried not to grin, but it couldn't be helped. "Everything alright?"

He cleared his throat and dropped his hand, self-consciously smoothing his white shirt. "Yes, of course. Why do you ask?"

Hadyn thought he'd have some fun then too. "Perhaps because your face is as pale as a sheet. They were only pups."

Deorc scoffed. "Yes, you can be thankful for that, but there's no doubt the mother's not far off."

His tone was serious, and they wondered if they should heed his concern, but the longer the silence, the more their smiles came creeping back.

A grin of his own cracked Deorc's lips, not above acknowledging his own cowardice. "Come on. We best keep going."

Once in town, they had left the chittering critters far behind, however, Deorc then led them on another path away from the heart of the village. Feeling safe now, Gadferlin took off, flying happily through the trees above them. And when they finally arrived at the "doctor's" house of practice, it was nothing more than a small hut with a curtain of bones for a door. Sooty, dark smoke poured from the roof and the rancid smell of rotting meat hung in the air. Secluded and set apart from the village, it had apparently not been on Darcy's list for the tour.

As they approached the hut, Kiara observed a collection of strange wooden totems set up by the house like guardians, just a bunch of logs carved into the image of bizarre creatures and monsters, not nearly as terrifying as the beast, but disconcerting all the same.

Hadyn nudged Kiara with his arm and she followed his gaze to a tree. A bloated carcass of a peccary hung from a tree branch by a rope tied around its hind feet. Lacerated in random places, sticky, dried blood oozed from the wounds and stained its fur. Kiara cringed and they exchanged horrified looks.

*That explained the smell,* she thought. *First impressions . . . not so good.*

Deorc stepped up to the bone curtain and drew it aside while Kiara struggled to see inside the dark room. She suppressed a shiver, hesitating to enter, but Deorc waited for her patiently. One look at Hadyn told her he was just as concerned if not more, but somehow that gave her comfort. At least she wouldn't be the only one on her guard.

Slowly, she walked through, trying desperately not to touch any of the bones, unsure if they were animal, human, or both.

Once her eyes adjusted to the dark, I'm quite certain she wished they hadn't. One look around that space and your skin wouldn't be able to stop crawling. Skulls stared lifelessly from the shelves with wide, empty sockets; different sized eyes consequently floating in jars filled with a thick, murky liquid. Various other ingredients for unknown recipes accompanied the many skulls, mainly other animal parts, ears; tongues; hooves; and tails; and dried and shriveled plant things. The room looked more like a witch's warehouse, where the items littering the shelves waited to be tossed into a caldron. The air hazy with a blue smoke, the sickly sweet smell hit Kiara with a new wave of nausea upon entrance.

Through the smoke she could see a man, grumbling softly and standing with his back to them. A patient lay on a table, seemingly unconscious. The man shuffled through objects on a long, cluttered table and finally turned to the patient bringing a bowl swirling with smoke close to his face.

During their stay in Tykaraijre they had met some characters to be sure, unimaginable beauty even, but this small, mumbly man looked from another world entirely. With bare feet and chest, ink markings trailed over all exposed skin. Wild, dreaded, and knotted hair stuck out from behind a black, wooden mask painted with white, contrasting features— wide rings for eyes and a gaping mouth filled with teeth all as sharp as fangs. Only his beady black eyes showed under the mask. Bits of twine held cuffs of dangling grass on his calves and forearms. Necklaces of colored beads and bones, draped around his neck.

The masked man wafted the fumes over the supine patient's mouth and nose. His mumblings grew louder as if chanting. Picking up a hollow gourd filled with beads and seeds, he shook it over the man's head. He began stomping the louder he got, his body jiggling along to the rhythmic mumbles. Tension began to mount, like a string pulled more taut by the second.

Kiara wondered if it was only because they had come in during the middle that she didn't understand, but she couldn't see how any of this would contribute to making the sick man better. But it's a strange and dark business, that of a witch doctor, and is bound to make some of the stoutest hearts uncomfortable.

The mounting tension snapped like a bow string, and his volume boomed like a thunderclap, shouting now, as if possessed by some thundering demon. The man began to drag his hands upwards from the patient's face and into the air, seemingly pulling some invisible thing from him. Over and over again, he pulled to the steady rhythm of the chant. Finally, it all ceased and he jumped back, but the patient lay as still as ever. After watching in silence for a moment, the man pushed the patient up into a sitting position. He swayed, in fact awake, but appeared drugged or something. He sat on his own and the strange man brought him a sprig of some dried plant. He spoke to him in their native language and then the patient went stumbling out of the hut.

The doctor, man, thing, then turned to the three standing by the entrance. Kiara tensed, suddenly not just the observer, but now the observed. One look into those black eyes and she knew she couldn't stay there. She knew she had seen them before.

She opened her mouth to state her concerns in the politest way possible but Deorc spoke first. "Kiara, Hadyn, this is Klah, Tykaraijre's doctor."

Klah blinked at them in silence.

"Now, Kiara here seems to have a fever of sorts and I—"

Klah held up a hand to stop him. Deorc shut his mouth and swallowed his words down hard. Klah bowed to show some respect, but somehow it seemed only mandatory to Kiara, almost endured.

Deorc calmed. "Of course, you are the doctor. You know best."

Klah gestured for her to come over to the table. The mounting fear rose up in Kiara like a black tide and she thought she would drown in it.

"Why doesn't he speak?" she stalled.

"Klah understands English as best as he can, but he has never spoken it well," Deorc explained. "Now, go on. He will know what to do with you. Klah is the only one in all the village who regularly enters the *Iwa*, the abode of the spirits. He says he has even talked to the Beast himself."

Kiara scoured her mind for another question. She turned to

Hadyn. If anything his look told her not to go, but she didn't know what else to do. What would Deorc do if she wanted to leave? She took a couple hesitant steps across the room towards Klah, already preparing and gathering things into a bowl. He brought the bowl over to the table Kiara now stood by and she examined the contents: claws, teeth, and small bits of bone.

She looked back at Deorc. "And what is he going to do with those?"

"He is searching for your illness. Apparently my diagnosis wasn't credible enough . . ." he muttered, but then pushed his offense away. "The Beast will tell him what ails you through the bones and teeth."

Kiara turned back to Klah and when he started his mumbling again, a ripping need to back away as far as she could tore at her mind. She chewed her lip nervously. Klah closed his eyes and shook the bowl a few times, making the pieces fly into the air. He shouted again, stomping his bare feet on the dirt ground, and spilled the pieces out onto the table. He fell silent, waving his hands over pieces, but Kiara still heard a voice, the voice from her dreams. *We always see . . .* the voice that came from those black eyes. Klah's black eyes.

Something bumped against her back, and she realized she had backed away, straight into Hadyn. He turned her about and grabbed up her hands shaking like leaves.

"What is wrong?" Deorc asked. "Why have you stepped away? You may hinder the connection to the *xairipi*, that is, the spirits."

Kiara didn't know what to say, how to make him understand. Her eyes flicked back and forth between him and Klah.

"If I may," began Hadyn, "and I mean no disrespect, but we're not exactly used to this sort of . . . medicine. And I think it's safe to say, as of right now, it's only upsetting her."

"I'm sorry," Kiara said, not able to fully hide the desperation in her voice, "but I don't think I'm as sick as you have assumed. I think all I really need is some more fresh air. I need not waste any more of Klah's time."

Deorc's face said he didn't fully understand, but he played the gentlemen and moved the bone curtain aside for her. "I will try to explain to Klah."

"Thank you. I think Hadyn and I will take a walk in the village now."

"Very well. I hope you enjoy yourselves. Darcy should be back soon."

*Wonderful . . .* Kiara thought, and with a polite smile she led their escape.

They fled the smoky hut, hastening away until Kiara bent over, gasping for clean air. All of a sudden her lungs and throat felt so small. Hadyn just stood by her side, not knowing if a hand on her shoulder would be more suffocating or comforting.

With one last quaking breath, she began to straighten. "Thank you," she said, "for what you said back there."

"Don't mention it. That man was the stuff of nightmares."

Kiara shivered, thinking he didn't know the half of it.

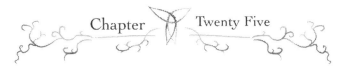

# Chapter Twenty Five

# THE MAHOGANY TREE

E ven in the village, the need to flee didn't depart from Kiara. She kept walking, feeling as though if she stopped, her fears would overtake her. She led the way, rounding a corner so quickly, they almost ran straight into—

"Delsin!" Kiara exclaimed.

"Kiara!" he shouted back, then raising an eyebrow, he lowered his voice. "Hadyn. Nice to see you two again."

He carried long metal scraps in his arms, on his way to his forge, and when they only stared like the shell-shocked victims they were, he decided to continue his haul. They followed him without hesitation.

He looked at them sideways. "Can I help you with something?"

"We just came from Klah's." Hadyn said as if to explain their behavior.

"Oh, my condolences then."

Kiara's mind was already on to other things. "Hadyn heard the whispers," she blurted, leaving Hadyn to blink at her, flabbergasted.

Delsin skidded on the dirt road. Slowly, he turned. He didn't say a word; only nodded for them to follow him. Arriving at the smithy, he led them inside and deposited the scraps onto a workbench.

He locked his gaze with Hadyn's and spoke carefully, "We are talking about *the* whispers, correct? From the shadows?"

"I think so . . ." Hadyn said hesitantly.

"You think? If you really heard them, you would be sure!"

Hadyn bunched his brows in offense.

Delsin let out a breath and softened. "Forgive me. No one but me has ever heard them. Well, I do think there was a servant girl, but she doesn't talk about it. So you can imagine how years of being called crazy and the village kook could start to take a toll on you."

"But we did talk to that servant girl," Kiara said, "and she heard them in the same exact place Hadyn did."

Delsin leaned closer. "Where did you hear them? What did they say?"

"In Deorc's library," Hadyn said and explained how he heard them and even about how the shadows seemed to move.

Delsin sat back on a stool and blew out an astonished breath. "All these years . . . So you believe me?"

They nodded.

"And that's not to say we didn't before," Kiara said. "It's just . . ."

"I understand." Delsin gave them a tired grin. "Trust me, I do."

Continuing the story, Kiara didn't waste any time. "You know, when I went to check out the room with Hadyn, we found something else too." He waited, so going out on a limb, not knowing if it would even mean anything to him or not, she spilled it. "A Bible."

Delsin burst with laughter. "Not possible."

Positive he had had his fill of crazy today, Hadyn rolled his eyes. "Look who's not believing now. We know what we saw."

"I'm sorry, but that is very hard to believe."

"We found it in a locked chest under a pile of firewood," Kiara explained.

Delsin's smirk sobered rather quickly. "Prepared for a great pyre . . ." he mused. "Deorc must have never been able to carry out the deed. I wonder why."

"It unnerves me," Kiara said. "How can he be so hateful about something he can't even destroy?"

"He's a coward," Delsin said, eyes brightening as if he just figured it out. "He knew it would be wrong and is afraid of the consequences."

"Maybe . . ." Hadyn pondered, "but I think there may be another reason that stays his hand."

"Like what? Entertain me."

Hadyn shook his head. "Not sure. Perhaps he's just half mad."

"That he is and don't you forget it."

Kiara traced the scratches on the workbench with her index finger. "It doesn't make sense. How can he be so kind, but so unstable? At times, he seems like two different people."

"At least," Delsin chortled. "Deorc has been at war for a long time, and maybe not just with the neighboring tribe, the Kingsmen."

Kiara understood, she had since her first dream of the shadowy prison. "But if he's at war, shouldn't someone come to his aid? Doesn't that mean there is still a battle to be won?"

Delsin sighed. "A nice thought. But you don't know him as well as I do."

"That's what frightens me. What if . . ." She looked up and into Delsin's eyes, her brow bunched with worry. "What if he's so mad that he won't let us go?"

"Oh, so now you want to leave?"

She had no patience for humor, and as her face stayed filled with fear, it seemed to melt his crustiness away in a moment. Compassion softened his gaze. "I'm sorry. I'm so sorry you're even in this situation." His face changed to something like a father who'd do anything to keep his children safe, his eyes shifting back and forth from Kiara to Hadyn. He saw them as different. They weren't like the rest of the village and they needed to be protected, sheltered, maybe even from themselves.

"I should have done something years ago. I can mumble my skepticism under my breath, keep my head low and tinker away in this smithy, but how will the village ever know the truth if someone doesn't act?" He shook his head, ashamed of himself. "And the fact that it has taken Deorc ensnaring two innocents is beside the point. One thing is for certain, you don't belong here."

"Neither do you," Kiara said.

He smiled, grateful that she cared. "I just might."

"But what will you do?"

"Never you worry about that. You just work on leaving. As soon as you're better, get away from this place, as far as you can, and don't look back."

As they left him that day, all Kiara could think about was the look she saw in his eyes just then and how it reminded her of the very same one she saw in her grandfather's the day he disappeared. He had been growing restless, more than usual, and looked older than he ever had. Kiara was never told the details, but the older she got, she always wondered– what if he spoke out? What if he had gotten so fed up that he had gone out and railed against the injustice of Caverna and darkness itself? What if that was his demise?

What if Delsin planned to do the same?

Kiara couldn't get rid of a painful knot in her stomach no matter how hard she thought. They couldn't just leave, but just how dangerous was it to stay? You might understand their predicament, wrestling with an uneasy premonition but having no actual proof, nothing substantial enough to sink the teeth of a decision into.

Kiara slowed, gaze distant. "Hadyn, what are we gonna do? I don't even know what to think anymore."

He turned to her desperate eyes, not shying from the question for a moment. "We're going to take it one day at a time. You're too sick to go anywhere right now and that's a fact. You said yourself, it's not all bad here. At least you have somewhere to get better. And when you do, very soon," he smiled, "we'll be on our way. Deorc himself has never given us a reason to believe he won't see us off when the time comes."

Kiara's eyes wandered thoughtfully. "I guess you're right."

"But, for now, let's just work on getting you back to a place where you can rest." Arms fumbling, he shuffled closer for perhaps a hug? He wasn't quite sure. But he was interrupted or saved by a smiling face, a face Kiara had mixed feelings about running into.

"Hi, guys!" Darcy chirped as she came skipping out of the forest and onto the path.

"Hey, Darcy," Hadyn greeted.

She trotted up with a small capybara limply slung over her shoulder. If it was any other animal, Kiara told herself she could have borne it, but having seen the gentleness of these creatures, it didn't make an ounce of sense to see its lifeless eyes, staring but no longer seeing, its life deliberately taken from it.

Darcy didn't even seem cognizant of the carcass. "You two want to go walking on the trails we walked last night."

Hadyn looked to Kiara for the decision. "Well, Kiara should really get some rest.

"Oh, then just us then," Darcy said, none too put out.

"No," Kiara piped up. "A walk sounds nice."

Hadyn scrunched his brows. "But you—"

"It's so lovely out," Kiara cut him off. "And it beats laying around the mansion. Prolonged fresh air will do me good, don't you think?"

". . . I suppose. If you say so—"

"Then it's settled."

"Good! Because I packed lunch." Darcy patted her bag.

"But um, are you going to drop . . ." Hadyn eyed the carcass, "that off somewhere first?"

Darcy followed his gaze to her shoulder. "Oh! Yeah. Uh . . . I'll just meet you there."

They didn't wait long at the trailhead. Darcy caught up with them fast enough and they began their walk.

"Hey, sorry about that," Darcy said. "I've been hunting since I could hold a bow string back," she continued. "Sometimes I forget others, well . . ."

Kiara refrained from the urge to narrow her eyes in skepticism.

"I appreciate it, Darcy," Hadyn said.

"Yeah, thanks," Kiara added.

Darcy swung her arms. "So, why the sad faces? I mean," she snorted, "besides the kill." Then it hit her. "Oh, no. Are you still not feeling well?" She smacked her forehead. "That's why you wanted to rest!"

"I'm alright," Kiara said. "I definitely didn't need to see your doctor, but your father insisted."

"Wait, Dad took you to see Klah?"

"Yeah." Kiara eyed her suspiciously.

"And you're not falling apart, scared to death? You're still in this village?" Darcy shut her mouth, sealing her lips before she could say anything more.

"In all honesty, I was terrified, but I'm okay now."

Darcy looked at her as if for the first time, and there was something Kiara hadn't seen in her eyes before. Respect? No. Not possible. A funny noise of surprise escaped Darcy's throat and she dropped her gaze. "So, do you like Tykaraijre?"

Kiara's insides grew squirmy under the pressure. "Um . . ."

"No, wait." Darcy stopped her. "You don't have to answer that question." She shook her head and fell back into what was comfortable. "Hadyn, you really should come hunting with me sometime. I mean, if you don't like that kinda stuff, that's fine, but we'd still have fun."

"Well, I don't know," was all Hadyn said.

She skipped in front of him and walked backwards. "There's a first time for everything." she said, shrugging a shoulder with a smirk.

A cry of alarm was the only warning they got before a young man stumbled out of the forest and onto the path. Darcy's eyes went wide as her heel caught and she tumbled back right over the top of him. For a moment Kiara and Hadyn could only tilt their heads in puzzlement.

Darcy moaned, but the boy was already laughing.

"Mato!" Darcy whipped her head about and shot him a look. "What do you think you're doing here?"

*So this is the infamous Mato,* Kiara thought and at once recognized him as the boy she had seen peering through the trees the day before. It was all coming together and yet she had more questions than ever.

Mato's long, black hair was pulled back, but a few loose strands hung in his eyes. He shook them away. "Oh, just taking a stroll through the forest."

Darcy shot to her feet, yanking him with her with a fistful of his shirt. "On paths you're not supposed to be caught dead on."

He chuckled. Taking a step back from her, he dusted the dirt off himself. "Oh, Darcy. You know strangers don't get your humor like I do. You'll sound crazy."

"It's not—"

He walked past her, straight to Kiara and Hadyn, before she could finish, and stuck an arm out to shake their hands. "Hi, I'm Mato. Darcy's best friend." He shrugged and raised his hands. "I don't know where that puts you, but it's not there, so . . ."

Kiara grinned in amusement. "Nice to meet you."

"Yes, so nice," Darcy butted in, cutting him a cloying smile. "Isn't he just the sweetest? But sadly he does have to go, because not only he, but his whole *family*," she said through her teeth, "will get into some unfortunate trouble if he's spotted here."

He laughed as he backed away. "Oh, Darcy, always trying to bring the laughter. I told you, they won't get it," he said, stumbling over a log behind him, but he managed to stay upright this time.

"Again, so thoughtful," Darcy simpered. "Goodbye, Mato!"

"Alright, you have fun now, you kids . . . and I'll see you later, Darcy!"

"Uh-huh. Bye." She waved. Then as he disappeared again into the bush, she sighed. "Sorry about that."

"Oh, no," Kiara grinned, "you're not about to walk away from this one without an explanation."

She huffed. "There's nothing to explain. Mato and his family live on the outside."

Kiara's amusement fell with her face.

"They don't live in the village?" Hadyn asked.

"They did . . . once, but now they're out, simple as that. And it's not easy for people to come back from the outside. But you're not even supposed to know about that."

Kiara watched her with uncertain empathy, wondering if she was actually beginning to feel sorry for the flirt. "But he *is* your best friend?" she prodded.

Darcy pushed ahead, snatched up a stray stick, and whacked a fern overhanging the path, ignoring or avoiding the question entirely. "So, Kiara," she turned back towards her, "where do you get a name like that?"

"Excuse me?"

"I mean, I've never heard it before and it's so . . . it's just so brave and fantastic. To a degree."

"Um, It's just the name my mother gave me."

"Oh, but I didn't mean anything by it. It just doesn't seem to suit you all that well."

"What's that supposed to mean?" Hadyn asked.

"Nothing. Except that she's so delicate . . . like a princess and my father said that where he used to live, there were kings and queens. The queens had names like Victoria, Caroline, and Anne. I don't know, it was just a thought."

They all fell quiet then.

"Don't you think you're a kind of princess?" Kiara asked.

"Pff! No," she answered, and it made Kiara sad, though she didn't know why, seeing she never liked anything about being a princess nor wanted to be called one.

Darcy took another swipe at an encroaching branch. "What's Europe like? Is it every bit as sophisticated and elegant as my father describes?"

"Mmm!" Kiara agreed with a nod. "Very much so." She cringed, pleading inside that Darcy wouldn't ask another question about something she knew nothing about.

"Well, tell me about it!"

Kiara's stomach wrenched a twist. "Oh, I really couldn't do it justice."

"Sure you can."

Kiara sighed. "Where to start? Well, Hadyn's family were poor farmers so there's not much to tell there." She faked snobbiness and threw him a playful grin.

Darcy laughed, but didn't quite know where to look.

"And me?" Kiara continued. "You see, I was somewhat sheltered and kept from society so I'm almost as much in the dark as you."

"But you set out on a great adventure; you couldn't have

been too sheltered."

"But that is the very reason I'm here. I rebelled and ran away." Kiara felt her insides twisting even as she lied. She hated this.

"I didn't know you ran away!" Darcy squealed, staring at her wide-eyed.

Kiara comforted herself in the half truth of it and breathed a tentative sigh of relief as Darcy all but up and eloped with the idea of running away.

"I've thought of leaving many times . . . too many times," she said, sobering. "But I don't know where I would go. The village of Tykaraijre is all I have. Darcy Tykara, stuck in her own village and that's just what she is— stuck. I've always wondered what it would be like to be brave and just leave. Get away from all . . ." she groped for a word, "this." Her ever gesticulating hands fell to her sides. "One day . . ."

"You know, It's not all the blissful dream you might have imagined," Kiara said.

"Says the girl who is so free that she probably doesn't even remember how miserable she was. You seem pretty happy to me," she remarked, her eyes straying to Hadyn. But she didn't seem too fond of the new mopey mood. She skipped to get ahead of them and with a jump she spun around. "Hey! Let's climb a tree!"

"Climb a . . ." Hadyn eyed the young mahogany Darcy had run under.

"A tree." She giggled. "Haven't you ever climbed a tree?"

"Oh, um– of course, I have."

"Well, what are we waiting for?"

He grinned following after but in a moment they both turned back to Kiara.

Darcy cocked her head. "You comin', Kiara?"

"No, that's alright. I'm afraid I'm too tired. But you go ahead."

"Okay!" she chirped, not the slightest bit miffed. "Come on, Hadyn, this is one of my favorite trees. It's like a dear friend to me."

Hadyn's eyes followed the trunk up to where the branches split and reached toward the canopy. "A dear friend . . ."

Darcy smiled. "Yeah, Father thinks it's silly."

"But Deorc seems so appreciative of nature," Kiara said.

"Sure, if you mean he appreciates those little bits he's perfected, the treasures he's procured and locked away in his own private collection." She simpered. "Father isn't one for disorder."

"I would suppose not."

Darcy's brows bunched regretfully. "He never seems to understand when I talk about how connected I feel to everything when I stand atop the roots of the forest, or how something like a tree could be an old friend." Darcy placed her hand on the rugged bark of the mahogany. "It's like one living thing, you know? With all the roots connecting in unseen places below the rich earth. And if I stand still enough, it's like I can feel the great beating heart up through my feet." She closed her eyes, wiggling her bare toes. "I know," she grinned, "I'm not so good at the standing still part, but I like to think I'm getting better."

Kiara roved her eyes over the ground and then up into the treetops as if seeing it all for the first time again. Darcy's words made so much sense, reminiscent of Kiara's own first thoughts of this wild land. Sunlight warmed the greens as it emerged from the clouds and a flock of scarlet macaws blazed overhead, like a rainbow below the canopy. The three of them smiled at each other, a kindred wonder glowing to life somewhere between them. Maybe Darcy wasn't so different from them after all.

"Come on, Hadyn," Darcy's eyes flashed, "I'll show you the way up."

As Darcy began to scale the mahogany like a young monkey, Hadyn exchanged one last wide-eyed look with Kiara, before giving in and apprehensively climbing after her. His feet slipped sufficiently before he started to find his footing. Kiara laughed with a shake of her head, but her smile dissolved like her fading energy. It looked like a blast, and here she stayed earthbound, too tired to even keep standing.

She sat down at the base of the tree. Her temples pounded with every quake of her thundering headache; Darcy's mouth, running like a swift brook, didn't exactly serve as a salve. But her voice grew quieter as she climbed higher and soon Kiara could block her out. She let her eyes close, thinking of the wild, but deeply connected jungle, its many layers of beauty and peril. She didn't know how long she sat there or if she fell asleep, but presently a kind greeting pulled her from her rest.

"Hey there," he said, with a light tap on her nose.

Kiara popped her eyes open to a very blue-eyed boy. Hadyn hung upside down from a low branch, curls springing from his head.

"I wish you could come up here. You'd love it."

"I'm sure . . ."

He went cross-eyed and a laugh bubbled inside her that felt better than any kind of medicine. Then as the laughter faded, she just stared, suddenly, almost uncomfortable. Because he stared back. She couldn't pin the reason, knowing Hadyn had never done anything to make her uncomfortable, but she supposed it was a different kind of discomfort.

Having lived in a world where literally everyone had blue eyes, they had long ceased to impress her, if they ever had at all. And though his were a deeper blue than any she'd seen, she knew it wasn't the color that made her cheeks grow warm, nor the way they glinted with playful joy, but the innocent sweetness and the way she found her trust so deeply rooted in them, the safety she found in them. For so long she swore she'd never find another she'd call friend. Cida was there before she shut up her heart, and so, was the exception, but he had found a way in, even with all her walls.

Instinctively, to break the awkward moment, Kiara planted a peck of a kiss on his nose.

Hadyn's eyes went wide and he seemed to stop breathing before he fell the few feet he hung above the ground. Kiara's mind shut down, melting into a burning, white void.

"Oh my goodness! Hadyn, are you alright?" Darcy yelled as she hopped her descent down the tree.

Darcy's shouts broke her from her thoughts. "I'm so sorry!" Kiara cried.

"It's okay," he said, rubbing the back of his neck. His cheeks flared bright red and Kiara figured her whole face was with the burning she felt.

"No, it's not. I—"

"Kiara, I'm alright."

Darcy jumped down from the tree. "Whoa, are you hurt?"

"Yes— No, I'm fine."

"You're sure?"

Hadyn chuckled. "Yes, Darcy. It wasn't that high of a fall."

"Phew! Well, that's good." She placed a hand on her hip. "Either of you hungry? I'm thinking lunch."

"Sounds good to me," Kiara was all too quick to answer, for once thankful for Darcy's brutish appetite.

Cheeks still blazing red, Hadyn gave a tight nod of his head. "It's a plan."

Chapter      Twenty Six

# A DESPERATE PLEA

**D**uring lunch, Kiara kept her mouth at a convenient state of fullness so she didn't have to talk, forcing herself to eat even with a fresh stomachache slapped on top of her previous nausea. Darcy, with her antics, kept them entertained well enough on her own anyway.

On their way back through the village, the day had already warmed to a weighty sort of heat, as if anticipating the sort of commotion waiting for them in town. It started as a far off murmuring, but walking in a slumped fatigue, Kiara stood straight as a board as she began to make out the sound of shouts and cries from the town circle, one man's voice somehow managing to stand above the babble. Hadyn and Kiara whipped questioning faces to Darcy.

"Don't look at me!" she said, and they each quickened their pace toward the ruckus.

At the town circle an angry crowd had gathered spewing belligerent accusations. Spotting the object of such unrest, Kiara felt her stomach drop. On the stage, bending down to the people stood one man, desperately trying to be heard. Delsin . . .

"Looks like someone had an adverse opinion," Darcy said.

Kiara wanted to rip out a chunk of her perfect hair, at the sound of her unconcerned tone, but Darcy's face told a different story, frozen in shock, maybe even horror.

"We have to help him!" Kiara shouted above the noise.

"Delsin?"

"Yes, they're going to kill him!"

"Kill? Come now, don't be so dramatic."

Kiara huffed, beginning to lose her patience. For Darcy, of all people, to tell her that . . .

"I'm serious!" Darcy yelled. "Delsin is on his way to getting himself locked in a cell or worse! You remember what I said about Mato and his family? How do you think they got there?" She shoved a hand at the commotion. "Do you really want to join him?" Darcy turned to the stage, face twisting with an inner struggle. "He's a fool."

"A brave fool," came an accent like many distant spices all mixed into one jar. Gypsy Suze had come up on their left. Her hazel eyes, locked on Delsin, swirled with both anger and sorrow.

Kiara didn't have the mental strength to question what she meant or what she was even doing there. Stuck in place because she could do nothing, she turned to listen to Delsin. Desperation leaked from his tone like a river that could be stopped up no longer.

"You're all believing lies!" he shouted, his emotions bursting at the seams. "This entire village was built upon lies!"

"Shut your mouth!" the crowd yelled. "What do you care?"

"Are you even listening? I wouldn't be here if I didn't care! I'm sorry . . ." he hung his head, "that I never tried sooner. But I'm here now, so, please . . . just listen!"

The crowd simmered to an inconstant murmur.

"Thank you." He caught his breath and slipped down from the stage to stand level to them. The crowd stepped back making space for him.

"I know well the very things we have all built our new lives on, some of you even grew up on, but it is only a shadow that you trust, a trick of something blocking out the real light. It's a trap that has ensnared us all, but it's not too late to get out of. The only thing for you here is danger and darkness, not some prosperous afterlife. The Beast will devour you the very moment he can!"

"Lies!" One violent man screamed, and the crowd erupted once more.

Delsin's face twisted as hope left him. "No!" he cried. "Deorc has fed you lies for too many years. Please! Listen to the truth now before it is too late!"

"What makes you think you have the truth and we don't? My truth is true to me!"

"Yeah!" A few jeered in agreement.

Their collective volume, fueled by a monstrous hate, far exceeded what he could overcome and his desperate pleas were lost in the tumult.

"This is because of us," Hadyn said, watching with a stony gaze.

Kiara glanced at Darcy, but she seemed too distracted to hear. "But I never wanted this," she said quietly, barely holding back her tears. "I wanted him to save himself, to get out of here."

"I know. Still, we have to do something." Hadyn stared into the crowd a moment more and said, "Stay here."

"No! I'm coming with you!" She ran after him.

The crowd was a raging sea and they plunged straight in, weaving through wave after wave of faces so full of hate until they finally pushed their way to the front. Delsin caught sight of them. For him, the crowd might as well have fallen away. A sad sort of smile twitched on his face, but it darkened to such concern and fear.

"You have to get away from this place!" he shouted just as two large men came up from behind and clamped their mitts down on his arms. Delsin whipped his head between them. "There is no need for this. I have caused no violence!"

The men only tightened their grips and without explanation started to drag him away.

Delsin struggled against them, but gave up before he could waste another moment. Turning his attention back to Kiara and Hadyn, he cried, "Don't believe the lies! I know you can make it out of this! Make it out!"

Kiara didn't understand. Everything was happening so fast, so loud. She started to follow. "No!" she shouted. "They can't do this!"

Hadyn held her back, and Delsin seemed satisfied to know at least she would be kept out of danger.

Through the crowd and her tears, Kiara saw a dark, wild-haired man; tufts of it stuck out behind his masked face painted with a white, wicked grin. Gypsy Suze was there too, standing tall with a dreadful beauty about her. Her eyes held a dangerous fire, but for what? Kiara's head swam with the chaos. Suze stood by Klah or maybe was kept there, Kiara realized, seeing his talons wrapped around her slender arm.

The guards hauled Delsin off, while the shaman watched, black eyes staring out like light-devouring pits as he waited silently and peacefully. Then she lost sight of them as the crowd enveloped the gap like hungry vultures to a scrap, rushing to parade Delsin out of the village.

Sitting on the ground in the stage's shadow with her back against its wall, Kiara wanted to weep, every ounce of the fault weighing on her, pulling her toward the ground, but her eyes were dry, staring aimlessly out of her skull at nothing at all. A hollow void that had started in her stomach, continued to grow, threatening to overtake her.

The crowds had gone and all that remained in the quiet clearing were the echoes of Delsin's pleas. Hadyn paced back and forth across the colored bricks, thinking far too much.

"What will they do to him?" he asked.

"You really need to let this go." Sitting on the stage, relaxed and detached, Darcy leaned back on one hand and examined the fingernails on the other. "There's nothing you can do. Unless, like I said before, you also want to get taken away for who knows how long," she said, throwing her hands in the air.

Hadyn looked at her. "Maybe I do. How can you be silent?"

"Easy. I'm safe silent. Isn't that reason enough?"

"Safe from what? You seriously think your father would banish his own daughter?"

"There are punishments worse than banishment and Father is not the only authority with power in Tykaraijre." She narrowed her eyes. "Besides, Delsin got what he deserved."

"Deserved?" Hadyn repeated, a dangerously unstable timbre creeping into his tone. He took deliberate steps, striding up to the stage, but Kiara rose to her feet, placing herself in between them. Her eyes drooped with dreadful exhaustion.

"I need to lie down," she said.

Hadyn relented, but Darcy grinned as if his threatening her only made him that much more attractive. "Come on," she heaved herself off the stage, "let's go back to the house."

They walked along the dirt path, Kiara's feet both dragging and stomping. Though they left the town circle behind, Kiara could not rid herself of the fear and desperation in Delsin's eyes, or the image of them carrying him away while that awful creature of a man watched over it all like some dark lord. In the thick of it, her thoughts had been too scattered, but now the questions filtered in like late, unwelcome guests.

"Klah was there," she blurted. "I saw him."

Darcy scrunched her face. "At the town circle?"

"Yes. He must have been the one to call for the guards. But how would he know?"

"Exactly. He wouldn't. Klah rarely leaves his hut."

"But I saw him," Kiara insisted.

"You're unwell," Darcy said, "and you were scared. You just thought you saw him."

"Excuse me? I'm not delirious—"

"Look," Darcy stopped and spun on her heels, "I don't care

what you saw, but it wasn't Klah. You–" the slightest hint of fear flickered in her fierce eyes, "you need to be more careful about what you say."

Darcy turned to keep walking, but Kiara only grew more confused. "I know what I saw . . ." she mumbled to herself.

Hadyn was no help. He merely shrugged when she looked at him and nodded for her to keep up.

# Chapter Twenty Seven

# OF MONSTERS AND THEIR PAIN

**F**or the remainder of the day, Kiara rested in a miserable solitude, her mental and physical strength wrung out by maligning, unforgiving hands. She rose for dinner only to avoid alarming anyone who would have any mind to bring her back to Klah.

At the dinner table she let others carry on the conversations. Frankly, she didn't feel like eating or talking . . . or thinking, for that matter. She listened absentmindedly, half waiting for whatever chaos happened today to be brought up, but at the same time never expecting it for a second.

"How was your hunting trip this morning?" Lyra asked.

Darcy stopped chewing for a second, looking up at her mom, eyes full of suspicion. "You want to know?"

"Of course."

Darcy brightened and took it as her chance to romp into a lively tale she seemed to have just been itching to tell.

Deorc smiled as he listened and Kiara watched him. She tried to imagine herself sitting at dinner with her own father and letting her tongue run as freely about her adventures in the Forbiddens or something she enjoyed, but she knew he'd never be smiling. Not like that.

She wondered how Deorc could seem so harmless and kind at times and why she felt so much fear here at other times. Though she did notice, beneath the smiles and attentiveness, he seemed a bit agitated, eyes never once settling restfully, hands at a constant fidget of some sort. Did he know about what happened today? Course he did. This was his village, right? So why not say anything?

"Father, may I be excused?" Kiara hardly heard Darcy ask.

"Yes, of course, Darcy."

"Come on, Hadyn, you're excused too."

That she heard.

Hadyn stood and looked at Kiara, waiting for Darcy to invite her.

"So, Kiara," Lyra began in her signature, dripping tone. "Darcy told me you ran away?"

Darcy bounced on her heels in the doorway. "Come on, Hadyn!"

Hadyn walked over to Darcy, throwing looks back at Kiara the whole way.

Kiara pulled her gaze off them and turned to Lyra. "Yes. That's right."

"Is it? You know it reminded me a bit of myself when she told me that. I used to be quite the reckless soul, I mean . . ."

Deorc caught Kiara's gaze, rolling his eyes in a show of annoyance and she couldn't help a smirk tugging at her lips, honored that, in Darcy's absence, he'd find a friend in her to suffer together through his wife's rambles.

Lyra's words soon became a mumble of sounds as Kiara's mind wandered to Hadyn and Darcy. What could that little minx be up to? She picked at her food (the majority of it still on her plate) while she waited for Lyra to be done talking. Finally, when her tale of unnecessary lengthiness came to its end, Kiara spoke up before anything could prompt act two. "Thank you for dinner. I think I'll go see what Hadyn and Darcy are up to."

"Oh," Lyra seemed crestfallen, shocked that she wasn't begging for more stories.

Deorc beamed at her more than grateful for the interruption. "By all means. Enjoy yourself!"

Going out the way they had, Kiara had half the mind to go to her room and sleep until morning, but she found them soon enough, sitting on the steps of the porch, and the ensuing sights froze her solid, suddenly unsure if she should believe her eyes, or pass it off as a hallucination of the fever setting in. Kiara found herself outside the door, but apparently they hadn't noticed it open or close. She was a ghost, unable to speak or move, punished to watch.

Darcy leaned closer to him  "Don't you just want to kiss me?" she giggled.

*Of course not, you little snake!* Kiara's thoughts screamed. She wanted to run at her, push her from the steps. But why? Well, because she was Darcy, right? Because she wasn't right for him, not in the slightest . . . right? But like the apparition she felt like, Kiara continued to float there unnoticed.

Before he could answer, Darcy leaned even closer, lips

inches from his, but Hadyn pulled away from her. Then, putting gentle hands on her shoulders, he pushed her back to arms length. "Sorry, Darcy, but no, I don't."

He shifted away and stared out into the yard, his posture stiff with awkward tension, as Kiara herself (she noted with some concern) all but slumped in relief.

"Well, why not?" Darcy laughed, shoving him playfully, but there was a hurt whine to her voice she couldn't hide. "What's so wrong with me?"

"Nothing. You're beautiful and funny, but, Darcy . . ." He didn't want to be harsh or even say anything at all, but she didn't really give him a choice. "I don't even know you," he stated as gently as possible. "You don't know me. Why would you even look for something like that in someone you don't know? I heard you say how trouble just finds you, but I think you know you seek it out."

Her brow scrunched and he sighed. "Look, all I'm trying to say is, you don't have to live your life like this. Love is not in the places you're looking."

At first she just blinked at him as if it meant more to her than if he had done otherwise. A tear trickled down her cheek. She quickly wiped it away and looked at her wet hand, stunned. "You made me cry." She let out a breath of a laugh and looked down. "No one can make me cry." Anger sparked to life in her eyes. "What about Kiara?" She looked back up, all playfulness and flirtation lost in her dark eyes.

"Kiara? What about her?"

"Oh, come on!"

"What do you . . . I mean, why would you—"

Kiara felt a warmth flush her cheeks out of nowhere as he stuttered. She touched a hand to her face, questioning her own racing heart.

"Yes?" Darcy pressed.

"It would never work. She's the pr—"

"She's the what, Hadyn?"

"I mean, she's my . . . well, she's my best friend."

Kiara's heart melted in her chest, a soft smile blossoming on her face.

"Well, what then?" Darcy asked. "Don't you have any hope that I'll be better one day?"

"I never said I didn't."

"Oh, but you said enough, didn't you?" Darcy turned her face and there Kiara stood, her back against the door

Darcy shot to her feet, nearly bursting into flames. "What is this! Some kind of demented joke?"

Hadyn craned his neck. "Kiara? What are you doing there?"

"Oh, don't play stupid." Darcy shook her head, her lips thinning. "You two think you're so much better than me. That's fine! You really think I care?" Hair whipping behind her, she ran for the road.

"Darcy!" Hadyn stood. "That's not what I think at all!" he called, but she was gone and had closed her ears to his words.

He collapsed back on the steps, hanging his head and Kiara came around to his side. "How long have you been there?" he asked.

"Long enough to know this isn't your fault."

His shoulders collapsed with a heavy sigh.

"Hadyn, you did the best you could."

"Did I?"

Deorc stepped out the door, concern painted on his face. "I heard raised voices. Is something wrong? Where's Darcy?"

Hadyn popped back to his feet. "I'm sorry, sir. I have greatly upset your daughter."

His face paled. "What did you do?"

"It's more something I said, but I'll try to go find her."

"Oh no, there's no need for that," he said, adjusting his jacket. "I'm sure it was a minor offense. Darcy is very dramatic and takes enjoyment in making things seem bigger than they are. She'll be back soon. Trust me, she's fine."

"I mean no disrespect sir, but I don't agree that she's fine. She was nearly in tears when she left."

"Like I said," Deorc sharpened his words so they cut like a blade, "she makes things seem worse than they are. Remember, boy, you have known her for two days, I've known her, her whole life." He fixed him with a warning look. "Now, my wife and I are leaving for the night as is most of the town. Perhaps you'll want to come to these sorts of things one day, too. Darcy may come to this meeting, but her spirit does what it wants. You are welcome to wait for her here, but I ask you not to search for her. And I will only warn you once more, under no circumstances should you wander the unlit paths." He cocked a brow. "Do you understand?"

Hadyn locked his gaze with Deorc's for a moment, before begrudgingly conceding through clenched teeth. "Yes."

"Good," he said and turning to Kiara his gaze softened significantly. "Try to get some rest, dear. You look exhausted."

Kiara nodded. "I'll try."

After Deorc and Lyra left, Hadyn sat on the porch steps as the moisture in the air cooled with the deepening blue night. His elbows on his knees, he propped his heavy head in his hands and stared out at nothing. Kiara sat at his side, but not near as close as Darcy had placed herself. The silence between them lasted so long, time didn't seem to move the same way. Only the steady fall of the darkness and the blooming glow of the blue mansion marked its passing.

Kiara didn't know what to say or how to snap him out of it. She reached out and put a hand on his shoulder. He looked at her and she tried to smile.

"It's going to be alright," she said. "You didn't do anything wrong. I don't know what's eating at you."

Hadyn stood, leaving her comforting hand. "Please, I don't want to talk about it."

Kiara tried to hide the sting. "Okay," she said.

He smiled then, but Kiara had seen his real smile too many times to be fooled by this counterfeit. "Let's go inside," he said. "You look cold."

Kiara dropped her hands from around her arms. "Sure. We could read some books from the library?"

"Yeah, okay," he agreed, holding the door for her. "But I won't stay in the library to read them."

After choosing a few books, they promptly left the library to read in a less nightmarish space (if you could call it reading.) Kiara flicked her eyes back and forth across the room, from Hadyn and then back down at her book as he fidgeted and squirmed. When she thought about it, she realized he hadn't turned a single page in the last fifteen minutes. She eyed him over the spine of her book, contemplating if she should comment, then brought her gaze back to the page, sweeping it for her last spot.

"Aaah!" Hadyn snapped his book closed, making Kiara jolt in her chair. "I can't concentrate!"

"*You?*" She chuckled.

"All I can think about is what happened earlier," he continued. "She's out there, waiting for someone to find her. Deorc won't. He couldn't care less! Which makes her all the worse."

Kiara set her book aside. "I feel badly for her too, I really do, but you need to let this go, Hadyn. What makes you think she wants to be found?"

"Let it go?" he stood up to pace the room. "She's all alone, hurting, angry with me—"

"Not for any good reason," Kiara cut in. "Why do you think this is your fault?"

"I don't. But I can't help but think she's going to do something reckless."

"Because you think it's your fault. And what about Delsin? Did you just forget about him? I don't know about you, but I feel like we have bigger problems."

Hadyn sighed and mentally exited the conversation.

Kiara hated the frustrations that rose up inside her, but she also couldn't stand that he felt this way, unable to reconcile his concerns or even his logic.

Just then the front door creaked and slammed shut. Hadyn and Kiara spun around, watching the doorway of the room in silence. It was Darcy. They could hear the residual anger in the stomping of her gate. As she passed the room, she froze, sensing their presence and pivoted to face them. Her hazy eyes and puffy features gave away the evidence of past weeping, but her expression was now cold, her gaze hardened as a stone, wholly untouchable.

"What?" she spat. "Were you waiting for me or something?"

Hadyn spoke first. "Darcy, I'm sorry. I—"

Darcy cut him off with a roll of her eyes and a fearfully cold laugh. "For what? It isn't as if you have caused any great deal of pain I haven't felt before. Please, no apologies. I don't want your pity." She stood as a viper ready to strike, her dark eyes piercing with horrible beauty. "You know, I wasn't blabbing just to talk when I said I hated nicknames." They waited in silence for her to continue. "You see, it's not just a petty annoyance." She inhaled to throw more power behind her voice. "Because, for every Darce, there comes Monster, Wretch, Brat," she shrugged with a terrible smile, "Nothing."

The name nearly knocked the wind out of Kiara and for a fleeting moment, she felt Darcy's pain as her very own.

"And Mother is the worst of all," she continued. "You probably just think she's the sweetest, but it's all just a mind game that I gave up on trying to win long ago. She loves me alright. She loves me to be her doll that she can manipulate into the most perfect form she can. She wants a princess. Don't ask me why she decides to be so sickly sweet at times. I assure you it's for her gain; not mine."

"Darcy . . ." Kiara felt tears welling in her eyes. "I don't expect you to believe me, but I do understand."

Darcy laughed bitterly.

"Like I said, you won't believe me."

"No! Don't try to pretend you know what I suffer every day. You do not know . . . you don't know what I am." She paused. "But, please, I don't want your sympathy, because none of it matters anymore. I have embraced what I am. The titles can't hurt me if I accept them."

Kiara tried to check her anger, but it rose with every move Darcy made to separate herself. It was a selfish, self-pitying act, and trying to comfort her as she was, it only made Kiara sick.

"So that's it? You've got it all figured out?" she narrowed her eyes. "Or at least pretend you do. You don't have a clue. You act like no one can hurt you now, but I see through you." She softened. "Because I've done just the same. You're desperately searching for love in those who hurt you . . . Like me, you just want someone to help you understand why life is so painful."

"Quiet!" Darcy shouted tears leaking from her eyes. "Call me whatever you like, but do not presume to know me!"

A painful quiet followed, until Hadyn gently spoke up. "And Mato?"

Darcy's eyes flared. "What about Mato?"

"He's your best friend, isn't he? I've heard him say similar things . . . 'dear friend.' "

Darcy dropped her jaw. "How do you—" Her expression melted into smug contempt. "You know what? You two are sick. I'm sorry Father ever welcomed you into Tykaraijre. Why don't you both try minding your own business for a change?" She spun around, whipping her hair, and stomped out of the room.

"Darcy, wait!" Hadyn cried.

"No! I won't listen to you anymore!"

Hadyn's shoulders slumped with a sigh, as she slipped out of his grasp again.

"I feel her pain," Kiara said, "I really do, but she said it herself, she doesn't want our sympathy. She's just one of those girls who thinks she's the only one with problems and heartache."

Hadyn cringed. "Kiara."

"What? It's the truth."

"Even so. Really? Now?"

Kiara huffed. "Why do you feel like you need to protect her? Didn't you hear her? She doesn't need nor want us to care," she reminded him, as if he hadn't heard her the first time.

Hadyn looked away, anger and frustrations tightening his expression.

"Can you at least agree this isn't your fault?"

"By whose judgment?"

"Mine. Can't you trust that?"

When he didn't answer, she realized what she had been fearing for a while now, but so far had only wanted to ignore. He *couldn't* trust it because he didn't trust her."

"Why don't you trust me?" He refused to look at her, and as her heart tore a crack, she could only whisper her next sentence. "I trust *you*."

"Yeah, well, maybe you shouldn't!" At last he looked at her, but with the steely cold in his eyes, she preferred the former. There was a wall there. In those deep pools of trust she would have once willingly lost herself in, she saw only bars, suddenly shut out on the outside.

Tears filled her eyes, and he softened in a heartbeat. "I'm just saying, what does trust ever really get you, except heartache and disappointments?"

She shook her head. "You're wrong. It's more than that."

He waited expectantly.

"It's-it's hard to explain." She faltered until she lashed out. "But if you haven't realized that yet, I'm afraid you never will!"

That stung, she could see it on his face, but she was tired, done with the conversation. She shook her head in disbelief of how unreachable he had become, and turned away to the open window. The cool, evening breeze brushed the hair off her face. Night up here, reminded her of every hour down in Caverna, but it wasn't all bad because here night by definition was just that, temporary, different and separate from day, not the uninterrupted sameness that she used to know. Night in Caverna didn't have any sounds or smells save for the ever present must, but here the wind carried in a sweetness that only a cooling rainforest could bring, and as the diurnal animals all sauntered off to burrows or roosts high up in the trees and the sounds of the night came alive, a peace rested in the air.

Kiara stood there pondering into the darkness. She didn't want to think about anyone right now, not Hadyn and certainly not Darcy. How had things degraded so quickly from the warmth and relief she felt when he said she was his best friend. And now this? It threatened the very integrity of their friendship.

She drank in a healthy dose of the night air. She had only

begun to focus solely on letting that nocturnal peace settle into her heart when an icy chill froze her blood like an assassin sneaking up from behind. A strange sound rode the breeze, a moaning or chanting of a thousand voices accompanied by the rising and falling of a pounding drum beat, a sort of foreboding or sad melody. It crept through the forest with an eerie lurk and seemed to rob the peace right out of the night, replacing it with a fear its victims would fight to understand.

Hadyn came to the window visibly less angry.

Kiara jumped. "Do you hear that?"

"Yeah . . . What did Deorc say was happening tonight?"

"The town was having a meeting of sorts."

He listened a moment more, the voices running chills down both their spines. "Strange sorts, I'd say. Maybe . . . we could look for Delsin. If there's a chance he's still in the village, we have to take it. He'll know what's going on."

"Oh, so you're concerned about Delsin now?"

Hadyn's brows bunched in confusion. "I thought you wanted me to be."

She huffed. "I wanted you to be concerned because you care, Hadyn; not because I want you to be."

"I do. I care."

She crossed her arms, cooking him up a look of judgmental skepticism when a clattering from a neighboring room made them both whirl around. They exchanged a wary glance. With the distant, lamenting moans outside and the otherwise crushing silence inside, the sound did more than just put them on edge.

"Darcy?" Hadyn called with a quiver in his voice. But there was no answer, just another clank and unbearable silence.

"Ga-Gadferlin?" Kiara squeaked.

"Come on." Hadyn grabbed her wrist.

"W-where are we going?"

"Anywhere but here."

# Chapter Twenty Eight

# A FORGE LONG COLD

Hadyn led the way out of the mansion and into the yard where things were, at least, less confining. The voices had only grown in volume and intensity. Somewhere out there in the dark, beyond the blue glow of the house, people had gathered, Tykaraijre had gathered. But why?

"What do you think they could be doing?" Kiara asked.

"I don't know, but something tells me it can't be good. It reminds me too much of Caverna's ritual meetings." He paused, watching her curious expression as she squinted out past the light. "You want to go check it out, don't you?"

"I didn't say that."

Hadyn raised a brow.

She sighed. "Fine. Yes, I want to go *'check it out.'* Don't you? I mean, it might explain all the strangeness we've experienced."

He smirked. "Yes, Kiara, I do."

"You know you could benefit from just a *little* more curiosi— Oh . . ." she blinked, "then what are we arguing about?"

"Not a thing." He swept a hand for her to continue when he froze momentarily. "Except . . . maybe we should try to find Delsin first, see what he knows."

"Do you really think he could still be in the village?"

Hadyn shrugged.

"You're right," she nodded. "It's worth it to check. But," Kiara's shoulders fell, "we're forgetting one thing."

"What's that?"

"We don't know where he lives."

"Right . . ." His eyes wandered, then he brightened. "We could check the smithy for any clues to where he is. And who knows, maybe he'll be there."

# FORSAKEN

Another scuttle from inside the mansion had them both whipping their heads to the door. Perhaps it was just one of the servants, but for once, Kiara wasn't the least bit curious to find out.

"Good enough for me," she blurted.

Save for the distant cries on the night air, the village proved more reticent even than usual. They found it a ghost town. Blue lanterns lit up the dirt roads with a ghastly glow, the buildings and houses seemingly abandoned, just like when they had first arrived.

Kiara could hear her own heartbeat like a drum in her ears. Feeling exposed in the silence, they made their footfalls as quiet as possible, carefully avoiding dead leaves and twigs. They did their best to recall the way to the smithy, and when the thatched roof of the humble building came into view, Kiara felt her heart give a sudden tug at the reins in her chest.

"Delsin!" she cried out, bursting into a run.

"Kiara, wait!" came Hadyn's urgent whisper and a jerk to her arm pulled her to a stop.

Hadyn scanned the area with wary eyes. "There's no one here," he said at last.

Kiara pulled herself from his grasp and ran the rest of the way to the smithy. Desperation rising, she entered through the wide open front, stepping into the empty space, and it was like watching him be taken all over again. Instead of the blazing heat that had filled the space before, she felt only loss. Cold light from the Dalmatia outside glinted on bits of metal here and there, tools, unfinished projects . . . otherwise shadows consumed all else.

The crunch of Hadyn's feet behind her cut through the silence.

"The forge is long cold . . ." Was all she could say, one hand laid on the sleeping iron of the anvil. She turned around to face him. They both knew what it meant.

Hadyn's eyes slanted in sorrow as he held her shattered gaze, but he knew he had no words to make this right. A shadowed presence pricked the hairs at the back of his neck as he watched Kiara's eyes morph from sadness to round fear. She gasped as a figure moved in front of the blue light of the doorway.

"That is because he is not here."

Hadyn whirled around to face the smooth voice. Gypsy Suze stood in the entrance, both dark curls and bare arms outlined in blue as if she glowed faintly.

"Kiara, get back." Hadyn waved her away, never taking his eyes off Suze.

"Please. Listen to me," she said, accent still as tangled as a strangler fig, but maybe less hollow than one. "As I said, he is not here, and you will not find him anywhere else in the village."

"You were there!" Kiara stepped up beside Hadyn, emotions getting the better of her. "You know where they took him? You know what they did to him?" she screamed.

Suze flinched. "If you want, I will show you." A weighty gravity pulled at her features. There seemed to be a veil lifted, as if she had been playing a part and had only just stepped down from the stage.

Hadyn's feet remained planted as if for a fight. "Why?"

"My reasons are my own. I will only guide you if you leave them as such."

Kiara's head spun. Gypsy Suze's entire role in Tykaraijre, her very existence was an enigma. Good or ill, ever since she had met her, neither impression could win out. She was there when they took Delsin away, standing right next to Klah, and yet . . . she had never looked like she wanted it. Whatever the past, she stood here now, an urgency swirling in her eyes and Kiara got the feeling they didn't have the convenience of time to waste deciding who they could trust.

"Show us," she said at last.

Hadyn glanced between the two of them uncertainly.

Suze nodded. "This way. Come with me."

Following the clinking skirts of the barefoot woman, they kept in stride while Suze led them through the deserted streets of Tykaraijre. The crying voices only grew louder as they walked until a great multitude indeed could be distinctly heard. Clearly Suze knew where she was going. The woman didn't voice another word and she didn't look behind her, guiding them on with a haste to her steps.

Kiara watched the ghost town as if actual spirits might emerge from the quiet homes. In the shadows of one of the larger houses Kiara thought she saw a tall figure. Almost completely one with the darkness, it shifted and caused the slightest variation in the black mass living comfortably at the house's side. She wondered if her eyes were playing tricks on her. Then Suze froze.

"No," she breathed.

The figure moved again. Kiara's heart skipped in her chest. Hadyn saw it too.

"Run!" Gypsy Suze cried.

Without another glance at the shadow, each of them shot off as fast as their legs would carry them. Pursuing footsteps beat the dirt behind them. A rabid panic pumped through Kiara's chest giving speed to her legs, but all at once the footsteps faded, peeling off in a different direction for no apparent reason. Still, Suze bade them to press on. They didn't rest until they arrived at the thick of the forest's edge. Kiara panted, irrationally out of breath. She doubled over, trying desperately to find the oxygen she needed to keep running. Hadyn stood alert, watching for the figure from the village. He looked down at her. "Are you alright?"

Kiara raised a hand. "I . . . just need to catch my breath."

"Take however long you need. I think it's gone. Whatever that was."

"*Whomever*," Suze corrected. She stood stoic and watchful, eyes scanning. "Be thankful you do not know him."

A path before them wound into the jungle, but the last lantern in sight was several paces behind them. Hadyn could feel more than see the heavy darkness laid out on the trail, seemingly crawling out to breach the border of the light. The longer he stared the stronger the sensation of being swallowed up became.

"The Unlit Paths . . ." Hadyn said.

The persistent chants came from within the forest, haunting the woods and forewarned path. Recovering, Kiara straightened and found the intimidating sight with her own eyes. They hadn't given it much thought, mostly because neither had any desire to wander the village alone, but now, faced with this mystery, every warning Deorc had slid them in passing bore down on them with a weight they didn't have before.

"This is where I leave you," the gypsy's words pulled their attention back, turning their heads, mouths dry from fear.

"Why are you doing this?" Kiara asked.

The Dalmatia reflected in Suze's starry eyes like a sunken galaxy washed in blue and the shadows sharpened her strong features. "Things are not always as they seem." A knowingness winked in her expression. "If anything, I do it for you. For Delsin's time . . . I fear, has already run out."

Kiara shook her head. "What are you saying?""

"Only that, I would ask you to come with me now, but I know you won't. At least, if you do this," she swept a hand to the Unlit Path, "it may lift enough shadows for you to see." And it was with those words that she left them, bowing her head and taking her leave.

Kiara turned back to the path. Suze's words were a riddle,

but she herself refused to believe it was too late for Delsin. To her, there was only one path besides retreat, and as terrified as they both were, she could tell Hadyn was just as prepared to not waste another moment.

Together they took the first step, hands finding each other's unknowingly, and plunged into the darkness.

# Chapter Twenty Nine

# THE UNLIT PATHS

T hey wandered blindly along the path, stumbling over stumps and roots, every noise exploding their nerves into a frenzied fire, and every step taking them closer to the mournful voices.

A cry pierced the night and Kiara jumped, barely stifling a frightened squeak. Hadyn squeezed her hand. She didn't know if it was just him reminding her he was there or if the scream had made him tense too. The cry ripped through the black woods again, a pathetic moaning or crying out, almost human in nature, but drawn out and guttural, tortured and altogether wrong.

Kiara's throat constricted. She could feel each struggled breath scraping its way in and out of her lungs. Unwelcome pictures of the horrible creature playing possum in a ditch somewhere, manipulating the curiosity of its prey, flooded her mind and she had nothing but vague shapes of black to replace it. A new fear froze her blood as she realized they were heading toward the unknown creature, both its cries and the human cries growing louder with every step closer to the gathered crowd.

As they crept along little lights would appear, some far away and some nearby, inquiring eyes, reflecting the minuscule moonbeams that had managed to find their way to this rare, sparse understory. Each set stared at them a moment before blinking away as fast as they came.

"They're watching us," Kiara whispered. "What are they?"

"Let's just hope we don't have to find out," he replied, giving her hand another squeeze.

They were close now. They could almost feel the low beats of the drum vibrating up through their feet. Several paces down the path, a blue glow emanated from behind a rise on their left. Turning to each other, their noses nearly brushed, but they could finally see the vaguest definitions of each other's faces and jerked back at the sight, dropping each other's hands for good measure.

"It's the Dalmatia," Kiara whispered and they turned off the path to climb the short rise.

At the top, they lay flat on their bellies. The edge dropped down only about five feet into a wide clearing awash with blue and governed sparsely by only one species of tree. After such rampant and unorganized growth Kiara had seen in every other part of the forest, this space, this garden, seemed almost tended to. Yet, why leave this one species and so many of them, unless the very soil itself was cursed and the trees were the keepers of such grounds, the only candidate with the means to push through and establish a grip on life.

*mmoooAAAAAMMM!*

Having almost forgotten about it, the shrill cry from before sent Kiara's heart beating nearly out of her chest. The cry was so loud, it had to be nearly on top of them now.

The branches above them shook and the black shape of a sizable bird swooped down into the inexplicable clearing, carving an arc over what looked to be the whole town gathered together. The bird circled a great pit, its feathers catching a soft blue glow pulsing from its depths. Flapping up to a raised platform, finally, it lighted down on the shoulder of a man speaking down to the congregation. The distance obscured his features and the light did them no favors, but they didn't need to see his face. Kiara recognized the proud voice as Deorc's and he had the masked figure of Klah right at his side. The shaman led the gathering in a chant that sounded increasingly mournful the longer it went.

"I hate that bird," Kiara said, hunkering down to listen.

"This man is guilty of which the punishment was chosen long ago!" Even as Deorc spoke, the sad song carried on. "We gather because though he has done unholy acts, we will try to make his death a sacred one in hopes that we may please the Beast, and he may yet allow him passage to the afterlife." As he let his words rest with the respect they supposedly deserved, Kiara's mind raced with the implications, still too shocked to acknowledge what she already knew.

"Bring forth the transgressor!" Deorc shouted.

The crowd parted and kicked forward a shaking man, bound at the wrists and mouth gagged.

"Delsin!" Kiara cried out, and Hadyn immediately cupped a hand over her mouth. She shook away, eyes flashing. Hadyn pointed to the edges of the crowd below, a decent drop below, but not so very far from them. Begrudgingly, she submitted to silence.

The crowd pushed Delsin out from themselves as if they couldn't bear to touch him any longer, lest they be infected with his sin. He crashed to his knees, a crumpled form, head bowed in despair. Kiara wondered how anything she had seen him do could merit this kind of treatment, loath to accept the terrible wrong they meant to do to him.

The song took a chilling twist. The drum beat faster and the voices, no longer sorrowful as before, lashed eager tongues and gnashed their teeth, their bestial blood lust manifesting into a frenzy. Deorc raised a hand ever so slightly and, at his command, two guards marched out of the crowd and heaved Delsin up, each carrying one arm, his legs dangling lifelessly behind him. He had no will left. Kiara's heart cracked painfully to see it. She wanted to shout out, run down into the clearing and demand they stop this madness being passed as justice. But she could only watch helplessly, unable even to turn away, hoping against hope that it wasn't what it looked like.

The guards drug him to the pit, holding his face over the edge. At the sight of whatever lay below, life (or maybe just reflexive fear) seemed to jolt back into his surrendered limbs. The glow from the pit illuminated the horror in his eyes. He struggled against the two big men and screamed against the gag that muffled his pleas for mercy.

Kiara watched in agony through blurring eyes, when a sudden calm came over him, like a breaking of an ocean storm. Ceasing his struggle, Delsin raised his eyes, continuing to plead, but not with anyone in sight.

Deorc withheld further commands, watching as the guards held Delsin over the blue pit. Delsin closed his eyes, sweat and tears dripping off his nose. Kiara wanted to scream at him to fight, just as he had told them. She wished she could beg him not to give in, but he seemed strangely resigned to his fate. Deorc's hands shot above his head and all the drums and voices fell silent at once, like a snuffed out candle.

Kiara and Hadyn held their breath. Their stomachs dropped as Deorc, with a flick of his wrists, sent Delson to his death. The guards tossed him in the pit. Blue flames leaped up and out, roaring to life with malicious pleasure. Kiara turned her face into Hadyn's shoulder with a restrained cry. Hadyn wouldn't deny it; he felt the horrible pang just as deep as her, but the burning anger washing over him like some black tide wouldn't let him turn away. He watched with fury flickering in his eyes as the crowd seemed to jump and cheer for joy. The music had started up again, the drums beat wildly with glee as the village sang a horrifying praise to their dark lord. Then a procession of strangers started to file out of the crowd one by one, familiar riots of color worn by people they didn't know.

"Kiara, look," he whispered.

She reluctantly lifted her head and followed to where he pointed.

"It's the feather outfits we found under the stage!" he said.

Six shapes covered in vibrant feathers jumped in a choreographed dance around the flames. Each had a mask painted with a different grotesque face. The dancers along with some of the rest of the tribe wore the festive matia paint that they had the night of the Mboi Tata. The paint flashed and glowed just as incredibly as it did that night, but now it only made Kiara's stomach turn.

"What is this?" Kiara cried. "Who celebrates a death like this? Even for a criminal?"

"I don't think they see it like that. With the way Deorc was speaking, I think they truly believe this was the best thing for Delsin . . . sacred even."

Kiara wouldn't have it, turning away. "I don't want to see anymore!"

But Deorc pulled her attention back, somehow shouting above the ruckus with significant power. "My friends! Fellow followers of the Beast! Come, let us now turn from endings and move onto beginnings— the final test and initiation of the newest members of the Village Guard!"

A loud shout went up from the crowd, just as a towering man strode up to Deorc and walked along with him. Kiara recognized him from the gruesome scar running across nearly half his scowling face.

"Scathe . . ." she whispered. "It was him. It had to be him."

"What are you saying?" Hadyn asked.

"Back in the village, it must have been him that was chasing us."

Hadyn turned his eyes back to the man. "So what's he up to now?"

Edmond Scathe pulled his "friend" into confidence, passing some form of information. Deorc gave him a solemn, somewhat impatient nod before continuing to lead the village over to a strip of rocks all glowing with an ambient blue light. To Kiara's horror a line had already formed at one end of the strip, composed of a few big men, barefoot and fidgeting. At the other end, Klah waited with a patient hunger for the champions.

# FORSAKEN

"Fire walking . . ." Kiara whispered in horror, her wide eyes flicking across the scene in disbelief. "Back in Caverna, some in the palace used to say that anyone who wanted an important job close to the king or protecting the city would have to undergo the test of a Fire Walk to prove their bravery and strength. But instead of walking across as quickly as they can, the slower they go and the more they endure is what reveals their potential." She shook her head. "I always thought of it as a myth. How can anyone actually walk on fire let alone hot coals?"

"You mean they're going to walk across that?" Hadyn asked.

Kiara just stared as the first hapless soul took his initial step. Kiara grimaced seeing the pain on his face, but he swallowed down any scream or cry of agony, even a whimper meaning immediate failure. They were told that any pain was better than a life as a coward, but as he walked only a few steps, sweat pouring down his face, his face said he had begun to question that logic.

"I can't watch this." Kiara stood backing away from the edge. "I won't! I want to leave. Run so far– as far as we can. He's a madman! A madman!" she shot a finger at where Deorc had stood, but found herself pointing to empty air. She searched the clearing. "Where did he go?"

Hadyn scanned the area. "I'm not sure."

Kiara shook her head, heading back into the shadowed forest. "We have to get out of here," she said. "Delsin was not a criminal. He killed him because he couldn't control him anymore!" At the sound of her own words, the shock finally had the time to hit her and she halted in place, feeling like she had smacked headlong into a tree. She was frozen, stuck in place, with no foreseeable way to escape the horror. Like a caged animal, her heart raced, but she shied away from the bars instead of fighting them. "How could I be so foolish? I blatantly refused to read the signs." Tears leaked from her eyes as her expression filled with anguish. "I just wanted so badly for all of this to be good."

Hadyn raised calm, disarming hands. "Hey, so did I. But right now, the best we can do is stay calm," he said, his even tone unwavering.

"Stay calm?" Kiara's brows arched dangerously. Stay calm? He just killed him! He killed him!" she kept crying, teetering near the edge of what sanity she had left.

Hadyn's face paled and his eyes grew distant. It started to sink in, and he could feel his hard fought composure coming unglued. He placed a hand on her shoulder. "We're gonna get away from here," he assured her as well as himself. "Far away." He might have pulled her closer, but they both froze, breath caught in their throats as that voice, slick as oil, crept out of the darkness.

"Is that so?"

They whipped their heads about to find him.

"Don't you know?" Deorc continued, still nowhere in sight. "No one leaves this village unless I permit it."

"You can't keep us here against our will," Kiara said, still searching for him.

"And I wouldn't dream of it," he said, and you could almost hear the smile drop from his face, "but you two have seen far too much." His tone shifted then, not so much his voice but the timbre, still smooth, yet vicious now too, somehow ensnaring as if it was everywhere at once. "Foolish little lambs to travel in the dark and on the paths so severely warned of they did embark. Don't you know, little lambs, that there are hungry wolves in this wood? And hungry wolves don't give mercy even when they should."

Hadyn spun around trying to pinpoint Deorc's position and keep Kiara behind him at the same time. "Show yourself, you coward!" Hadyn's voice cracked, betraying any attempts at sounding fierce. "I'm done with you trying to make us fear you!"

Deorc laughed with derisive mockery. It echoed around them and made one feel so small. "Oh, but, little lamb, I'm not trying . . . I am succeeding!" And suddenly he was right behind them. Before Hadyn could turn, Kiara screamed as she was ripped away and pulled into the thick brush.

"Kiara!" Hadyn screamed, but his charge was jerked to a stop as a hand grabbed the collar of his shirt. Before he could struggle, a crack to the back of his head rendered him unconscious with one strong blow.

# Chapter Thirty

# IMPRISONED

C Langing . . .

Clanging so loud, it seemed inside his head. Hadyn grimaced as he pushed himself off a stone floor, squinting painfully at his surroundings. The dim blue light didn't allow for much sight, but he knew well enough what the inside of a prison cell looked like. His head ached and pounded with every ring of the persistent clanging. His hand went instinctively to the source of the pain, a sizable lump at the back of his head flaring with rage at the touch. A chain followed his hand when he held it to his head and rattled on the stone floor as he lowered it again. He followed it from the cold manacles on his wrists to where it ended, held fast to a metal ring in the floor. The more he woke up, the more he just wanted to fade back into oblivion.

An acrid smell of dried blood and human waste accosted his senses, making his eyes water. He half coughed, half gagged on it as he continued his observations.

"Kiara?" his voice rasped.

A fine dust in the stifling air stuck to the sweat on his face and further decreased the already poor conditions of visibility, but on closer inspection, Hadyn could see that only the wall to his back was made of stone and the other three were metal bars. Two other cells lay on either side of his and an open hallway ran parallel to the stone wall.

The steady clanking continued, having never stopped for more than a second, actually growing louder with every sounding. Finally a bald, sweaty man with a scowl that could boil water and a bulk of weight that had felt the effects of gravity for far too long stepped into view on the other side of the bars. He carried with him a fat stick that he ran along the prison bars, banging each one as he lumbered up the hall. He locked his horrible glare on Hadyn as he walked past. Hadyn shivered even in the rancid heat as he listened to the clangs fade away. In the ringing silence that followed, his mind at last began to properly clear. He thought he detected the sound of soft weeping.

"Kiara?" he said quietly and edged closer to the cell on his right. There, on the other side of the bars, was the crumpled form of a girl hugging her knees and burying her face. Chains fastened her wrists just as his. Her wild red locks fell as a veil about her, concealing her tears.

"Kiara," he said again, but she didn't answer.

Hadyn reached through the bars for her hand. Without raising her head, she grabbed it and held fast, not willing to let go until the tears stopped.

One by one, the meager lights of the prison snuffed out, the darkness pulled like a veil behind a second figure walking past the cells. Far up the hall now, the lamp dampener's feet tapped out an uneven rhythm on stone steps. Kiara flinched at a concussive slam and blue turned to black as the last remnant of light was cut off, sentencing them to a long and dreadful, black night.

In the enveloping darkness Hadyn and Kiara sat against the bars separating their cells. Not a word passed between them. But while they kept their silence, they soon learned they weren't alone. Almost immediately after the lights went out, evidence of others in the prison began to rattle off the walls. Most awaited their deaths, their last days lived out in a dark confinement. Low moans of pain from wounds, or hunger, or simply their own depression limped about the prison hold.

Kiara tried to edge closer to Hadyn, but the bars restricted her. Unlike Hadyn, Kiara shivered with painful chills as the fever took a greater hold. To Hadyn her hand felt unreasonably warm and he knew that something was desperately wrong when she shook and trembled.

Kiara felt her soul compress, flattening like a sheet of paper, blank with white surrender. She was certain she had escaped one kingdom of darkness only to die in another stronghold. She continued to cry softly, her eyes leaky like an ill-thatched roof. But it was in that crushing darkness, where she felt things couldn't be more horrible, that she astonished even herself and reached. She reached for those lofty melodies, the ones higher than any circumstance. There in that acrid black space, she began to softly hum.

The lullaby Hadyn had once played came to her memory and she sang each note with ease. Every other sound ceased. Not a cough or wheezy rasp could be heard. However many souls confined held their breath to hear the simple melody. Kiara sang to comfort herself, but in turn the song spread peace throughout the entire prison hold. The ears that it fell on heard her as an angel of light, never having had the privilege to listen to something so sweet. The prisoners allowed her to sing on without complaint, knowing that this could very well be their one chance to hear something so perfect, at least in this life. Hadyn too would have thought an angel had stepped into the darkness to sing the shadows away, but he recognized the tune and more so the sweet voice. Closing his eyes, he listened as the song defied the darkness with feeble strength.

At length, Kiara drifted much like a tetherless raft into uneasy sleep, the lullaby just not working quite the same when sung by herself. She often awoke confused and bewildered, ever prolonging the long dark, but then she'd hear the steady rhythm of Hadyn's breathing somewhere nearby and find the strength to calm. Still, even when her heartbeat settled, the struggle to sleep proved arduous at best. The inescapable black trapped every horrible thought in and locked out the good.

She squeezed her eyes shut, pretending that it was only for that reason that she couldn't see and that if she opened them, light would stream in through open windows where bird song tumbled in on the fresh morning air.

Shuffling feet pulled Kiara from her light sleep. Someone limped down the hall, lighting lamps on the way, by the sounds of it, dragging a foot or two. The shadow of a slight form came to the lantern outside Kiara's cell. He struggled to reach it, unable to stretch quite like another might. Eventually coaxing it to life, the cold light illuminated his soft features. Kiara couldn't do much else but stare. Just a boy . . . no older than ten. A deep loneliness etched his face, his left arm hung limp at his side, and the shadows cast on his hollow cheeks made him look dreadfully underfed.

The young prison hand preferred to keep his head down when passing the cells, never eager to meet the eyes inside that could hold such horrible threats, but when he saw Kiara, he muddled through his own moment of shock and limped closer to the bars. They stared, both pitying each other and oblivious to the empathy drenching their eyes. The boy swallowed hard and blinked at her as if what he saw made so little sense. He opened his mouth like he meant to speak, but one loud shout from one of the prison guards, and he turned mechanically away, eyes slanted in fear.

"Oi! What are you doing, Slacker!" The guard was on him in minutes, the bald one from the night before. "Ow many times do I gotta tell you not to dawdle? You little whelp!"

A firm smack sent the boy to the ground. He curled up on the floor and whimpered softly.

"Get up!" The guard kicked him. "And get back to work!"

Kiara winced as the skinny boy peeled himself off the ground and limped off with a twisted, crippled foot, not daring to look at her again.

Hadyn sucked in a breath and squinted as he looked around in a foggy daze. He saw both the anger and sorrow in Kiara's watery eyes.

"Kiara?" he asked. "Kiara, what's wrong?"

"The boy," she whispered. "He looked so sad . . . and the guard just threw him and kicked him like some beast he could abuse when it didn't do what he wanted."

Still waking up, the information came in a little befuddled, but looking at her now, all Hadyn could see was a nasty laceration above her brow crusted over with dried blood.

"What did they do to you?" he said, reaching out to touch her face.

"Nothing." She drew away and searched the wounded area with her hand. She flinched in pain, but shook her head. "It's just a scratch. I didn't even know it was there. They didn't do anything to me. I probably just hit my head, stumbling in here." She huffed and fluttered her eyes. "Did you hear what I said about the boy?"

"Yes, but I'm confused. Why is there a boy in the prison?"

"You expect me to know?" she snapped, anger flashing in her eyes.

A great wave of fatigue crashed over her irritation and she rested her head back on the wall with a sigh. Her mind swam in chaos, like she was a door and someone had popped one of her hinges out of socket, yes, just one, so she hung crookedly between the sane and insane.

"Kiara . . ." Hadyn trailed off, thinking he understood what she felt, but having no words to say so.

"How did this happen?" Her words carried no strength, barely even audible. Last night could have been a nightmare, one of the worst, but a nightmare, all the same. Yet here she sat, the Dalmatia had been lit once again and she was too awake to deny the reality of it. Delsin was gone, devoured by blue, and they were trapped, imprisoned in a blue dungeon.

Kiara sat with her eyes closed until she heard the sound of

the crippled boy's shuffling feet. He limped past their cell, neither glancing to the left or the right as he walked out of sight again.

Kiara slumped in disappointment, only for him to reappear not two minutes after, on his way to the other end of the hall again. With his good arm, he held a tray of several bowls tight to his chest to stable it. It was drudging work, as he did this two more times, distributing the bowls to each of the prisoners. Kiara began to get an idea of the length of the hall and just how many prisoners were kept here, when the boy finally came to Hadyn's cell. He pushed a bowl (of what can only be described as brown slop) through an opening at the bottom of the bars.

Hadyn grabbed the bowl. "Thanks, kid."

The boy blinked at him, confusion and surprise lighting his face. He shifted his gaze to Kiara, piecing together that these two unlikely prisoners knew each other. He nodded, mouth barely lifting in a smile, but, as if his oppressors could smell idle nature, he turned away, eager to avoid their castigating.

Knowing he'd have to come back at least one more time, Kiara hastily searched her mind for some combination of words she could say to him. When he returned, he carried only two bowls of slop and a basin of warm, clean water. Instead of sliding it under the bars, he set the tray on the ground, fishing a ring of keys out of the pocket of his tunic, much too big for his boney frame, and unlocked the door. Carefully picking up the tray, he kicked the door with his foot so it swung wide and stepped inside. He didn't bother to lock the cell, seeing Kiara was chained anyway, and shuffled over to her with the tray.

The child was filthy, grime streaking his face and dark hair, soft and straight, but sticking out in every which direction. He handed Kiara her complimentary breakfast and pulled a rag out of the water. He worked silently in his shuffling way as he wrung the rag out and scooted closer to her. Kiara stiffened, pulling away, but he quietly persisted, gently dabbing at the wound on her brow. Kiara sat still as he cleaned the blood off her forehead, his round, hazel eyes fully intent on the cut. His skin was ashen where it should have been a healthy brown, but those eyes shown as vivid as the forest, dark greens interspersed through the browns and gold, like young woodland nymphs playing in the dirt.

"I heard an angel's song last night." The boy had a tremble to his soft voice, but sad as it was, it seemed to suit him. "Was it you?"

Kiara winced as the water stung in the cut and managed a nod.

"You an angel?" He paused and looked her in the eyes for the first time since his hiding.

Kiara smiled and shook her head. "Nothing like."

He sighed, returning his attention to the cut. "Yeah. I knew it was prob'ly stupid. Why would an angel ever be in a prison? And I doubt one would ever talk to the likes of me."

He turned away, setting the rag and bowl aside to scoop up his own helping of slop. Putting a spoonful in his mouth, he twisted his lips and squinted his eyes. "Never get used to it."

Kiara set her bowl aside, not feeling brave enough to try it yet. "Is it okay for you to be here? I don't want you to get in trouble again."

"It's my breakfast break, one of the only times I'm allowed to 'dawdle' without . . . well, I guess you know." He shivered ever so slightly. "The name's Skipper."

"I'm Kiara," she answered.

"And you?" He looked through the bars.

Hadyn looked the kid over thoughtfully. "Hadyn."

"I know you two ain't done nothing bad." Skipper fiddled his spoon around in the bowl.

"What do you mean?" Hadyn asked.

"Some people that's put in here," he shrugged, "there's just somefin different 'bout their eyes." He looked up for a fleeting moment. "Like you."

Kiara watched him painfully. Here he was telling them they didn't belong here, when that's the only thing she could think about him since she first saw him.

"Skipper," she said. "That's an interesting name."

"Yeah, ya' fink so? I don't consider it a real name since I don't got any parents who's gave it to me."

Kiara fell silent as her change of subject backfired.

"The folks that found me said they only called me it 'cause I skipped a good life that I should've had," he explained, "when really I should've been skipping the world of pain I call my life.

"Mbyja says that my parents left me to die because I was crippled. Nobody wants a crippled boy who can't do no chores, and hunt, and stuff, she says."

"Who's M-Mbyja?" Kiara struggled with the foreign name, "and why does she think she can talk to you like that?" Kiara asked.

Skipper's look asked her if she was serious. "She's the cook. She made your delicious breakfast." He snickered, then continued. "Why does anybody fink they can do the awful things they do? They don't care." He answered his own question. "Maybe they's twist it in their head to make it look fine, but I tell ya', most just don't care who they hurt. This world is cold, and dark, and full of voracious wolves. That's what Deorc always says."

At the mention of his name, Kiara felt her heart sink just a little deeper in the mire.

"A man came to talk in the town circle once," Skipper said. "He yelled a whole lot, but me finks he just had somefin important to say. He talked about one God over all, and that He has this great love for everyone . . . He said we's don't have to follow the Beast no more, that God wanted to give us all eternal life and keep us safe. A lot of good that did him. Not nobody knows what became of 'em." He flicked a spoonful of slop at the already grimy wall, listlessly watching it slide like a southbound slug. "If there is a God . . . I know He hates me, just like everyone else does."

In that moment every wound in Kiara's heart ripped open painfully and a new one rent just for him. Her hand went to reach out for him, unsanctioned, unthought, but the grating of her chain startled her into an awkward retreat.

Skipper saw what she meant to do and immediately changed the subject. "Why not eat your breakfast?" he asked, mischief sparkling behind his eyes.

Kiara contemplated trying the slop. Somewhere in the midst of her nausea she had to be hungry, right? But needing and wanting to eat were extremely different things, especially when considering this colorless breakfast, which (as she raised it to her nose) she realized even smelled funny. At length, she plunged a bite into her mouth, having absolutely no control over how her face contorted, simply focused on not retching as she swallowed it down.

For the first time a smile burst across Skipper's young face. He tried so hard to stifle his giggles, not wanting anyone to hear, but it takes a stone cold heart to successfully contain laughter like that. High pitch squeaks escaped, between lips splitting with mirth. He laughed so hard, Hadyn and even Kiara (after a good shiver ran a lap or two down her spine) found themselves laughing too.

Tears sprang to Skipper's eyes before it subsided, and for a moment he was neither crippled nor worthy of pity, at least not defined by those things, but simply a young boy, giggling for sheer silliness' sake.

"Oh! I ain't seen a prisoner's first try of Mbyja's cooking for a long time!" He slapped his knee and wiped his eyes. "Aren't you gonna try, Hadyn?"

Hadyn tilted the bowl, the slop all remaining as one solid form as it slid to the side, leaving a slimy substance behind. He blinked with wide eyes at the breakfast. "Umm . . . no thanks. I'm actually not that hungry."

Skipper shrugged, clearly disappointed. "I should go. Don't want another hiding."

He struggled to his feet, gathering up his things.

"Skipper," Kiara said, and he turned back to her. "You said that everyone hates you, but I already know I don't. I don't hate you."

Skipper smiled. "Good. 'Cause I don't hate you either." Then he went limping back up the hall.

Hadyn watched Kiara shake her head in amusement, glad to see her smiling, but already wondering how long it would last.

As the morning grew old, the prison started to brighten until the Dalmatia lanterns actually became obsolete. The dungeon they would have thought no less horrible than a cavern, had to at least be partially above ground. A weak light slanted in from overhead and across the way. High up on the wall, boxes of light lined the length of the prison hall. Hadyn stood and turned to find the one in his cell, a rectangular opening to the outside, coating the dusty air in daylight. He hopped up and down to try to see out, but couldn't catch a glimpse of much of anything. Even though they remained far out of reach and only a very small child could crawl through, they were barred, just like the rest of their cells, and cast a very prison-like shadow on the ground.

"Yep!" A wheezy voice laughed. "You won't be gettin' out troo dere."

Hadyn turned to the abutting cell. In the dingy light, he could make out the shapes of others in their cells and more importantly the incomplete grin of his neighbor. There seemed to be not much left of the man but a bag of old skin and bones. Nimbus whips of unkempt hair swayed this way and that as he shook his head in amusement, but like most of the people of the rainforest, he had not a hair on his chin. He rocked back and forth just slightly, a constant shake in his gnarled hands which clutched a necklace-like string of seeds.

"No?" Hadyn asked. "I thought I just might squeeze through."

The old man laughed again, leathery skin wrinkling up around his eyes.

"I'm Hadyn."

"Ygary," he said. "You're gonna learn fast. There's no gettin out of this trap, even for one as spry as you."

Hadyn's eyes wandered about the space. "I suppose not," he said.

Ygary didn't seem to hear, quietly counting his beads of seeds under his breath.

Hadyn sighed, "What have we gotten ourselves into, Kiara?"

But Kiara answered only with a soft huff, already sound asleep again, lying on the thin, tatty mat the cells offered as beds.

He smiled softly, but there was no real power in it. He only hoped she found even a smidgen of comfort and rest in sleep.

Chapter Thirty One

# AN UNLIKELY VISITOR
# AND A CROOKED DEAL

**P**ast the town circle, down a path on the outskirts of the village, a war waged on. In Deorc's own kingdom, in an upper level room where even Darcy wasn't permitted at times, a fray was starting to take shape.

"Why are you doing this? You know they've done nothing wrong!"

"Oh, but they have." Deorc leaned back in his chair behind his desk, an almost amused smile on his face. "They went on the unlit paths," he stated simply and held up a finger, "*which* I quite *vehemently* told them not to do."

Darcy had her hands on the desk, leaning forward, fighting to keep his attention. "Vehemently," she scoffed. "You merely warned them a *couple* times. You didn't even tell them why."

"The key, Darcy, is as you said, I told them a couple times. Now, I know it's hard for you to grasp the concept because you need to be told something just one hundred times before the information sinks into your head, but a couple times *should* suffice for a warning."

Darcy blew over his offense with eyes as daggers to his soul, unwilling to let him see how much it hurt. The sticks that he used to beat her with only stoked her fire, only fueled her discovery of the real root of his actions.

"You don't care about the unlit paths." She grinned with the revelation. "Sure it irks you that someone didn't listen to you, but that's not it. They saw what you did to Delsin, and they were going to leave, weren't they?" Darcy laughed at her own cleverness. But when he didn't answer, her eyes turned sharp once more. "Weren't they?"

Calmly considering her from behind his desk, he preserved a resolute smile. "That's enough, Darce."

She rolled her eyes. "You're sick, you know that? And don't call me that."

"Darcy, I know you think you like Hadyn, but it's not a reason to challenge my judgment."

More angry laughter bubbled out of her before he could finish. "No." She scowled. "This is not about Hadyn. This isn't about Kiara. It's about you and you know it. Are you gonna lock up everyone who disagrees with you?"

Deorc just raised an eyebrow.

"Are you gonna lock me up?"

"No."

"Why?"

"Because I need you. I need you to be my good daughter who shows the village another reason why I'm fit to lead. And because . . . I love you." His eyes and smile softened. "Darcy, we're a family and our actions reflect on each other."

Her walls remained as thick as ever. "So, what if I don't?"

Deorc sighed. "Don't what?"

"Continue to be your good daughter."

He laughed derisively. "You know you already do that."

"Well, fine. I'll get worse. I'll . . . I'll run away!"

"Darcy, what has brought this on?"

She ignored him. "Release them, or I will."

"And I will, once they've pledged themselves to the beast."

She looked away. "Yeah, and take the journey they won't come back from?"

"Not alive they won't. They must die internally and—"

"Yeah, yeah, yeah. Or else they'll just die, die, right?"

"Darcy, you have overstepped your bounds."

"Pfft! My bounds . . ." she mocked, spinning on her heels and stomping out of the room.

Deorc sighed. "I have the mind to punish you, young lady!"

"Uh-huh," Darcy called, letting her feet speak for her as she thundered down the steps.

Hadyn watched the shadow of the bars inch across the floor of the cell, diagonally crawling, lethargically moving, unnoticeable unless he looked away for some time. The shape of the six bars stretched the prison cell like some pack of demented inchworms.

*Boredom . . .* he thought and puffed a laugh, remembering times when he had thought he was bored. Looking back, even their time spent living in the Forbiddens felt free comparatively. And if it were true, if he had really experienced boredom in his life, this was something else entirely.

Kiara lay on the mat resting again, but he knew she wasn't sleeping. She lay too still. Whenever she drifted into sleep, it was never long before the black tide of her nightmares rose above her head and she was drowning in them.

Each time he'd try to wait it out, hoping she would struggle into some peace, but each time the agony became too much to bear, as he watched her stir and jolt restlessly, listening to her sad whimpering. Then he would reach through the bars and pull her out, only for her to wake, frantically searching the prison as if for the demons of her dreams. Only when she found his eyes and steadied her gaze on their surety did she calm, lids drooping to a dark exhaustion, somehow continually more heavy than the last.

As the day wore on, Hadyn lost even the shadow to watch, the sun now directly overhead.

Whenever Kiara sat up they would talk together to pass the time, both secretly wondering what would become of them here; both never mentioning their lack of hope for freedom

Then, as the light faded, the grey prison became even more colorless until the call to light the lanterns came again. Skipper shuffled down the way, coaxing each blue flame to life, with only a wave and small smile to give them. Then he began the slow job of bringing the second and last meal of the day to each of the cells. He did this with more fear than anything as the big guard, the same one with the fowl look, patrolled the halls like a hungry bear. He lumbered up to their cells and stopped with a horrible, brown grin.

"Well, if it ain't the two we was just talking about. We're taking bets, you know."

Kiara and Hadyn kept their questions to themselves.

"About how long you'll last, of course!" he bellowed.

"What does he mean?" Kiara whispered.

A wicked laugh started to gurgle deep in his throat, but he choked to a stop. "Hmm. Seems you have a visitor," he said and slogged away.

Hadyn sat up straighter as a hooded figure padded up the prison corridor, sneaking paranoid looks over a shoulder every two steps. While the stranger stole yet another glance, Skipper came limping back with a tray full of empty bowls from that morning's breakfast. Eyes rounding, he saw the figure coming, but he couldn't move fast enough to do anything about it. They collided with a smack. The bowls flew in every which direction, clattering against the prison bars and the ground. Skipper fell backward and the stranger bent down immediately, gathering the bowls back on the boy's tray.

"Sorry, kid. I didn't see you there," a familiar voice said as she handed him another bowl.

Skipper reached out to take it with a hesitant hand.

"You alright?"

He swallowed hard and nodded, struggling to get up and leave. He knew exactly who she was, and the Tykara family had never meant good things. He didn't want to get in trouble because of her.

She helped him to his feet. "I guess I better watch where I'm going."

"Yes, ma'am— I mean, it wasn't your fault."

She chuckled. "Not yours either."

Skipper calmed a bit and then he seemed to stare at her so intently.

Hadyn's chains grated on the ground as he shuffled closer to the bars. "Darcy?"

She forgot Skipper and his mess and turned to the bars. Crouching low, she removed the hood, the lantern dimly illuminating her dark features.

"What are you doing here?"

"Hi, Hadyn."

Kiara didn't budge. "Come to revel?"

"Of course not."

She crossed her arms where she sat. "Oh, would you get off it? Don't act like you haven't got it in you."

"I don't believe this." Darcy blinked away her anger, chewing on her tongue. "I come down here, to a place where I should never have to set foot, behind my father's back, knowing if he knew, he'd kill me, I just show up, that's it, and you can't get over yourself?"

Kiara gave a loud huff and struggled to get up, "Why I—"

"Kiara, please!" Hadyn begged. "Don't waste your energy."

She leaned back. "You're right, Hadyn. She is a waste of energy."

Hadyn's eyes fell shut. "That is not what I meant."

Darcy pushed herself to her feet. "You know, I'm sorry I ever came. Clearly you'd rather I hadn't." She whipped her hair as she turned to go.

"Darcy, wait." Hadyn said, taking hold of the bars.

With a sigh she turned around only because he asked.

"You came here for a reason."

"Yeah, a reason that doesn't seem so important anymore." She huffed. "Honestly, I just came to say . . . I'm sorry . . . for everything that's happened. My father plans to offer you a deal soon, he's probably on his way here now." Her eyes flashed with desperation. "But you can't listen to him. I don't know what else you can do, but please don't agree to his terms. They're not what they seem and you don't . . . belong here. You don't deserve this." She said through gritted teeth.

"It's alright," he said. "We'll be fine."

"I tried to talk to him, really, I did, but he refuses to come to his senses."

Kiara didn't believe her for a second, and frankly she had heard enough of their whispers between the bars. "Gee, thanks for the effort," she mumbled.

Darcy threw her hands in the air. "You're unbelievable," she said, standing again. "Goodbye, Hadyn."

"Darcy," he said.

She stood in the hall with her back to them.

". . . thank you."

She turned her head to the side and he could just see her grief ridden profile, and then she was gone, back up the tunnel.

Hadyn turned slowly, eyes wide and mouth agape. "Why did you do that?"

"Don't, Hadyn." Kiara closed her eyes in indifference. "Don't you turn on me."

"Turn on you? Kiara, what are you talking about? I wouldn't do that. I couldn't."

Looking at him now she cocked her head. "I wouldn't be sure. You care for her too much. She has beguiled you just as Delsin said she does."

"She did nothing wrong."

"Not now. But, Hadyn, she's been playing with both our minds this whole time. How can you trust a word that comes out of her mouth? *I'm* the one you can trust. *I'm* your friend!" Face red, her tear-choked words poured out until she fell back against the wall exhausted.

He considered her painfully. "And I'm yours." He shuffled closer to the bars separating their cells. "Nothing could make me forget that."

Kiara felt the floor drop out beneath her heart. She wasn't angry anymore, she didn't know if she ever was. All she felt now was despair. "Why did this have to happen?"

Hadyn followed Skipper with his eyes as he limped past with two more plates of prison dinners. "I don't know . . . I don't know why any of this had to happen. It makes me feel like I've never had a single answer to any of the questions I've ever asked. It's all so upside down. Like even if we tried to climb out of this pit, we'd only end up falling further down. But we can't just give up either. There's nothing in it."

"What is there to do, *but* give up?" she asked.

"Keep fighting," he looked at her and gave a reassuring blink, "till we can't." Then his smile turned rather wry. "Too bad you can't just break me out this time."

Kiara smirked. "Too bad."

No matter how well she felt during the day, Kiara's fever seemed to come back with a vengeance in the evening, and in her delirious fatigue, her head had managed to droop into a light sleep even before Skipper had finished distributing meals. But a gentle hand on her shoulder was pulling her out of it before she slipped too deep.

"Kiara," she heard her name. "Kiara, wake up."

Through the grogginess in her mind she was vaguely aware of a great procession moving up the prison hall. Oh, wait . . . it was just Deorc, Gadferlin perched proudly on his shoulder and two personal bodyguards in tow, ready to challenge anyone who dared look upon his magnificence.

With a raise of his hand, Deorc bade the guards to stand back, stepped into the blue glow, and offered his crooked grin. "Hello, little lambs." On his shoulder, Gadferlin glared with eyes narrowed to wicked slits.

They sat silently at the back of their cells, Kiara still too discombobulated, and Hadyn glaring out from the shadows with a dangerous fire in his eyes.

"Oh, come now," he simpered. "There is no reason why we can't still be civil."

Hadyn remained unflinching, making no attempt to hide his anger.

Deorc shifted uncomfortably, but it did not shake him. "You can't honestly think that this is what I want," he balked, "that it doesn't pain me to have to do this to you. To both of you. But it is the people. You have to understand, you are transgressors and for me to show favoritism to outsiders would set the whole village awry."

Hadyn looked away in disgust, unwilling to listen to another word.

"Well," he straightened his waistcoat, "I see no apologies are necessary, not where they wouldn't be accepted anyway. So I'll cut to the matter at hand, shall I? I have found a solution to our problem."

Hadyn gave him a skeptical glance.

Seeing he had his attention back, Deorc grinned. "Ah. See? I knew you were a man of sense. So, a way to make this all right. In alignment with my heart's desire, I will release you *if* you come before me and the village with your wrong doings, seeking for-giveness. Then, to show your respect and loyalty, you will pledge yourselves to the beast."

"And if we don't?" Hadyn said. "Will you just get rid of us as you did Delsin?"

Deorc snickered softly. "I highly doubt it will come to that. Besides, Delsin's end was not—"

"Murder," Hadyn corrected. "Delsin's murder. Call it what it is."

Deorc collected himself. "It was not on some capricious whim, but rather long overdue. Furthermore, it's simple really, what you have to do. There would be no reason for you not to."

"No," Hadyn said.

Deorc's smile fell. "I don't think you understand. I do not idly fraternize myself with prisoners. You would be wise not to treat this as dross. I could be your last chance."

"How?" came Kiara's weak voice. "How do we do it?"

Hadyn faced her, eyes shocked and pleading sorrowfully. "Kiara, no," he whispered.

Deorc's smile came creeping back. "How indeed. First, pledge yourselves in blood, six drops to be exact, then on taking a last journey as your old selves to die internally and eternally, you will return, changed forever."

When neither said a word, his smile drooped again.

"No," Hadyn repeated.

"Fool!" He cuffed the bars with the flesh of his palm as his anger flared, but he snuffed it out with a sigh.

Gadferlin peered about the prison, his yellow eyes now wide. Kiara realized all at once that he only squinted out of un-certainty and fear of new surroundings or individuals, an untrusting look, not an attempt to intimidate. For a moment she thought maybe she had judged the bird too harshly.

"I also came to tell you," Deorc searched Kiara's tired eyes and he seemed to shrink back to a normal man, the man she had almost trusted, "I'm sure I could work something out with the village so that Kiara could stay in the mansion, as she is unwell. At least for a time. Maybe while you both came to your senses."

"No, I stay with Hadyn."

Hadyn began to protest, "Kiara, no. You—"

"No," she said, holding his gaze with an unshakable resolve. "If we can't both go, then neither of us do."

"I'm afraid that would be just to much to ask of—"

"Then I stay."

Deorc sighed, less out of remaining composure and more from disappointment. "Your loss. Fear not, I will be back, but for now . . ." he tipped his head, flashed a winsome grin, and began to walk up the hall.

Just then, Skipper came limping on his way with another couple of dinners. When Deorc's gaze fell on him, he became very small and shied to the side to avoid another collision, but Deorc's look wasn't angry or sinister. It was nothing. All emotions locked away, maybe yet trying to contain his frustrations.

Skipper came past their cells.

"Hi, Skipper," Kiara whispered.

He returned her smile, and after he shuffled by, Hadyn broke the silence first. "Why did you do that?"

Kiara didn't look at him. She knew what he meant. "Hadyn," she groaned.

"Please, Kiara, don't be angry. I'm asking you as your friend."

She looked at him, heart breaking and eyes filling with tears, but she wouldn't cry. "I– He said it could be our last chance and I just . . . I'm scared."

"So am I. But you can't listen to him. Darcy tried to warn us. Deorc just wants more people under his control. That's it. I don't know about you, but I've been owned for too much of my life to willingly hand my soul over to another, real or imaginary."

"What if we can't afford to think like that?"

"We have to."

She searched his eyes for any hint of conjured up, fabricated strength, instead found what she always found, that quiet surety, and not an ounce of it counterfeit.

"We have to keep fighting," he continued. "If the Creator that people talk about, that our *friends* talk about is real, He won't leave us here."

"How can you be so sure?"

Hadyn didn't know how to answer.

"How can you look at me and say that when we watched Him leave everyone in Caverna for lifetimes? No one saved us, Hadyn. We saved ourselves."

"Did we though? Look at where we are." His eyes fell shut when Kiara looked away. "I'm sorry." He wrung his hands. "But don't you ever wonder if there was light even there. That maybe He never left, but was there too."

"What do you mean?"

"It's like what we talked about with Cida, the people that said they believed in the one true God."

"Anybody can say that about their god," Kiara said.

"Yeah, but this was different. Something you just know. You know?"

She looked at him sadly for a moment. "Yeah."

"We know that Madressavilla's friend believed in God. What if, like we said, people like him hid their faith, but also kept it alive through the years. Then, no matter how trapped they were, at least they knew they'd be free one day."

Again Kiara searched his face, this time trying to understand what made his hope so strong. "You're just saying that to make me feel better."

He fought a grin. "Of course I am, but I'm not making it up either." Hadyn thought to himself for a moment. "I guess . . . I guess part of me has to believe it. If not, everyone who ever lived there, my mom and Viviana, they lived and died in darkness. And I wonder if at least now they're free . . . I have to.

Kiara didn't say a word, only nodding in agreement.

"Don't give up, Kiara. There's nothing in it."

Skipper served them their dinner and came to sit with them as he had done before. The three of them ate together huddled close to the bars between the two cells, sharing a few hushed giggles before Skipper had to leave again.

But as the guards made their rounds snuffing out the lights, so did the lumbering giant with the mean mug, banging his stick along the bars with a dreadful, tolling rhythm, ringing out their comfortless lullaby before shutting them in the darkness for another cruel night.

# Chapter Thirty Two

# ALLERGIES AND A BIRTHDAY IN PRISON

T he morning broke grey and depressive. But then Skipper came around with breakfast. In accordance with what had already become an unspoken routine, he plopped down in Kiara's cell, a smile on his young face. Kiara smiled back, but hers held a great deal of questions. Ever since Kiara tried the prison food for the first time, Skipper had smiled often enough, but this one shined with particular brilliance, almost begging for someone to ask why.

When they only stared, he gave a quick jump of his eyebrows. "It's my birfday!"

Kiara's smile dropped with a painful pang of sadness. No child should have to grow up in a prison, let alone spend a single birthday in one.

Hadyn's face settled in a mix of that same sadness and brave joy. "Happy Birthday, Skipper!"

Skipper giggled, delighted that someone was happy to celebrate him. "Eleven years old." He puffed out his chest. "Practically a man! And, look, I even lost anover toof!" He flashed an open mouth grin and stuck his tongue in the gap left by his top left cuspid.

"Practically?" Hadyn balked. "You old fool!"

Skipper reached through the bars and slugged him. "What does that make you?"

Kiara laughed softly and finally the heavy shadows lifted a shade. "Happy Birthday, Skipper."

"Thanks. You know the masters are decent enough to give me less work on my birthday, so I'll get my chores done early and come back."

"Sounds like a plan."

"Anyway, how's prison life treating ya'?"

Hadyn's words caught in his throat and Kiara scrunched her

face.

"Just kidding. I hate that you're here."

Kiara smiled. "Hey, it's not your burden to carry."

"I can't help it. You's don't belong here."

"What about Ygary over there?" she asked. "He doesn't seem to fit either."

"Yeah, Ygary," Hadyn called. "What are you in here for anyway?"

Ygary jumped where he huddled over his string of seeds. "Who, me?"

"Yes, you. What'd you do to get yourself in here?"

Ygary's wide eyes wandered. ". . . I ton't rightly remember," he said, then his lips split into that patchy grin, and he wheezed with a chuckle.

Skipper bent his head to the side. "S'pose there's a few of you who don't deserve to be here. I just wish I could help."

"You are," Kiara said.

Skipper looked at her expectantly.

"Your being a friend is the most I could ever ask for."

His shoulders slumped. "No, I mean really do somefing."

"Skipper, you are."

"You mean it?"

"Without a doubt."

A beaming grin spread across his face. "You mean, even if I could free ya', just being your friend is better?"

They laughed at him.

"I don't think anyone but Deorc can let us out, kid," Hadyn said.

Skipper looked down and scrunched up his mouth. "I heard him trying to cut you a deal. Why don't ya' take it?"

"It's not that simple," Kiara said.

"Why?" Skipper cried, but then stopped himself. "Sorry. Now I'll just say I understand, even thoughs I don't."

"It's alright," Kiara said. "We just have something we need to do, and if we agree to Deorc's terms, we may be able to leave this prison, but we will never be free from him."

"Oh . . . I *do* understand," Skipper said. "least . . . I'm not in one of these cells, but I'm no more free than a caged bird."

Kiara watched him with great pain in her eyes, but as his brows scrunched and his face twitched, he seemed to only see the red wave of his anger crashing over everything.

"I wish I was stronger," he said through clenched teeth. "I'd show them. Let them know how it feels to be beaten into the ground with fists and words, lock 'em in cages till they lose their will to survive, give 'em all the pain they's given me, that they's given you."

"You don't mean that," Hadyn said gently. "You know how it feels and you wouldn't wish it on another, not a soul."

Skipper sighed. "You're right." He looked up from his hands and saw the mortification on Kiara's face. "Sorry. I haven't been learned the ways of gentle talk."

Her expression softened.

"I just like to talk brave sometimes."

"Skipper, listen," Hadyn said. "Bravery is many things, but using your power to bully and seek vengeance isn't one of them. Courage, true courage, really shows when you stand up to the voracious wolves, not only for yourself, but also for others, even when you *know* you're weaker than them. And sometimes it has to wait for the right time. Don't make the same mistakes I have. Bravery isn't the same thing as rash anger."

Skipper gazed at him with a new found respect. Then he picked up the chain to Kiara's manacles. "I wish you didn't have to wear these . . . but I'd get in trouble if I unlocked them."

Kiara smiled in appreciation of his thoughtfulness. "They're not all that bad." She slid her fingers over the cold metal. "When you're around, I hardly even remember they're there."

A smile spread across his face only to be robbed from him.

"SKIPPER!" A voice boomed.

His face paled and he gathered up the tray and bowls.

"Hey," Kiara said, "we'll see you soon."

Just a shadow of the smile flickered back to his face before he shut the cell door and limped away.

Darcy walked in the front door of the mansion, unbrushed hair tangled up in the string of her bow slung across her back. She went out before dawn for an early hunt with no luck at all. Normally that didn't bother her much. Even a fruitless trip still offered a walk in the forest, just her, solitude, and the birds; trees to climb and think in; and tracks to follow even if they didn't lead anywhere. She had been hunting for too long to know one takes the good days and the empty days as they come. Today being the exception. Today, bad luck hunting was only a burn to accompany her bruises.

She slammed the door and threw her pack on the floor. She turned her nose up the stairs. If he was awake, he'd be in his study.

This was all because of him, the fact that her favorite activity could become an irritant, the ever present agitation in every minute of her days, the sleepless nights . . . Whenever she thought about him, a burning anger consumed her, but with that anger also came confusion, a confusion she hated. Darcy had always taken pride in her control over her thoughts and decisions, but now she had these feelings she couldn't seem to put a simple harness on and she didn't know why. Her father had always made her mad, so why did she care now?

After her time up in the boughs of a young wimba tree, watching the forest breathe and wake, she started to get an idea—for once it wasn't about her.

Darcy herself was used to it, she could bear it if needed, but these outsiders feeling the brunt of his madness stirred something in her she didn't quite understand. Even as part of her writhed in hate for them, she knew Kiara and Hadyn didn't deserve any of this. Her father wanted to control them, just like he wanted to control her and everyone else for that matter.

Darcy took the spiral staircase one determined step at a time and strode to the door of his study with neither a plan nor an argument. She just had to talk to him. She had to try again. Coming to the door, she almost threw it open without a knock when from inside the room, she heard the hint of soft, angry sniffs.

Darcy cracked open the door one degree at a time. Deorc stood at his desk with his back to her, but Gadferlin, his talons curled around his perching tree, gave a loud squawk of alarm. Deorc put his hands to his face, and spun around.

"Darcy. You're up early."

"I was hunting," she said flatly. "Were you . . ." she narrowed her eyes, "Were you just *crying*?"

"What?" He reared his head back. "That's preposterous. Have you ever seen me cry?"

"No," her wide eyes emphasized her astonishment.

"So why would you now?"

"You tell me."

"I was not crying. You know I have allergies at this time of year."

"You have allergies at every time of year, Father. You're allergic to the jungle, but you never sound like that."

"They're much worse at this time and . . ." he looked back down at the papers on his desk. "I wasn't crying. I'm trying to work out what to do with one of the newer recruits to the high guards. The rest can't stand him and are . . . making threats."

Darcy cocked a brow. "Why not the usual?"

Deorc turned away from her and rubbed his forehead. "And what is that, Darcy?"

"Get rid of him,"

He gave an exasperated sigh. "What do you want?"

"I came to talk to you," she said, stepping further into the room.

"About?" He glanced at her.

She answered with a raise of her other eyebrow.

"No. We've discussed this. You have no place in the conversation. In fact, I'm on my way to see them now."

"But—"

Deorc strode past her, and Darcy felt her cheeks begin to burn. "You know, the saddest part about this is you actually believe you're doing nothing wrong!" she screamed, and to her surprise, it gave him pause. In the doorway, she watched his shoulders collapse with a sigh.

"Darcy—" he sucked in a breath as if to cut himself off.

"Father?" she sassed.

Deorc turned around and took two steps toward her. He reached out a hand to her face, but with the way she watched the gesture, he dropped it back to his side. His eyes wandered before settling on her. "As leader, sometimes I have to make tough decisions. Sometimes they don't make sense, and until they do, they might look wrong."

"But that's not true," she cried, almost pleading. "You don't have to do this."

"If there is another way . . . I don't know how to find it."

Darcy sharpened the intentionality in her gaze. "Let. Them. Go."

"How can I?" He smiled sadly. "When I don't even know how to let you go?"

Darcy had no words, no way to answer a question she wouldn't have expected in a million years.

"I'm aware that I can be harsh with you. And that I've done things . . ." he trailed off and Darcy tried not to look as confused as she felt, "that I wish I hadn't." Shaking his head, Deorc continued, speaking even gentler, "But, Darcy, you are my daughter. And I hope you know, I *do* love you."

Darcy blinked at him. She wanted to believe he was just trying to manipulate her, playing on her emotions just to get her to forget about all the horrible things he was doing. She wished for it desperately, for that would be easier to face than whatever this was now. His eyes, so sincere, so urgent to make her know this, confused her more than anything he had ever said to her before.

Quickly, before any tears could well in her eyes, Darcy pursed her lips into a smile and nodded.

Deorc returned her smile. "Good," he barely whispered and, reaching out, he brushed a thumb across her cheek. "That's good."

Turning then, he went out from the room, clopping down the steps, leaving Darcy standing there watching an empty doorway.

Darcy blinked the tears away in an angry struggle. She felt like she had just woken up from a dream, but one she still fought to figure out whether it was real or fiction. She heard the door swing shut and went to the window to see him stomping down the path. Gritting her teeth, she pounded her fist on the window sill and turned away.

Deorc found his way to Kiara and Hadyn's cells well after breakfast when he came to give his offer for the second time, asking the same thing as before, still pleasant and cordial, but to his chagrin, also receiving the same answer.

At his inevitable departure, Kiara felt the pit in her stomach grow, expanding like a black hole prepared to swallow her from the inside. Another opportunity to get out of this prison and its manacles had come and gone. She let it go by and she couldn't move past the certain kind of depression that it brought. It rotted inside her, only fleeting momentarily when Skipper's smiling face came back around a little past mid-afternoon, carrying a tray of three earthen mugs and a flat, wooden box.

"Sorry I took so long." Skipper distributed their mugs, wispy with hearty steam.

"What's this?" Kiara asked, expecting tea but finding a thick brown liquid.

"Shhh!" Skipper hushed and eyed them both. "Listen. I never gave you a Xocolatle. Ya' hear?"

"Xocolatle?"

Skipper's eyes bulged. "Quiet! Or I'll have to get the whole prison a mug."

Kiara and Hadyn shrugged and brought the contraband to their lips. Kiara reared back sputtering on the bitter spice.

Skipper burst with laughter. "Oh, no. Mbyja's sludge is one thing, but you can't tell me you don't like this. Try another sip. You'll get used to it."

Hesitantly, she did as he asked. The spice tickled her throat and made her eyes want to spring a leak, but there was something to be admired about the unique flavor, twisting her cheek muscles at first, but then sliding smoothly down the throat and warming her up from the inside.

"I like it," Hadyn said.

Kiara made another face. "What's the . . ." she couldn't find the words.

"Chili peppa's," Skipper said, "and cocoa. Who don't like cocoa?"

*Peppers* . . . Kiara thought. *That explains things*. "No. I do. I do like it. It's just . . . very different."

Skipper snickered, shaking his head as he pulled the board-like box out from under the tray, revealing its face marked with a square section and a triangular expansion, both carved with perpendicular and diagonal lines to make the spaces.

"This is my favorite game. It's called—"

"Backlobash!" Kiara gasped.

Skipper frowned. "No . . ?"

"Oh," her shoulders dropped, "well, maybe it's something similar. I grew up playing a strategy game with a board quite like this, minus the triangle. It's my favorite!"

"Really?" Skipper beamed. "I can never find anyone who wants to play with me."

Kiara gave a weak laugh. "Well, you now you have two."

Skipper looked at Hadyn with expectant, wide eyes and Hadyn nodded.

Kiara covered her mouth and whispered to Skipper, "Though I can't say he's very good." She smiled at him, knowing he heard every word.

Skipper giggled and pulled a sack from his pocket, scattering the pieces on the floor, one black stone and fourteen white.

"This one's called Adugo," he explained. "One person plays as the black jaguar, unça, and the other plays as the cacharro, the white doggies." He grinned rubbing his hands together. "Oh, this is going to be such fun! We can take turns. Whoever didn't play the last game takes the loser's place!"

"Sure," Kiara said.

"Of course you'd agree to those terms," Hadyn said, and Kiara stuck her tongue out at him.

Skipper began to set up the stones. "So, Kiara, you and me?"

She smirked. "You sure?"

Skipper bunched his brows with uncertainty.

"Yeah," Hadyn said, "I don't think you know what you're getting yourself into."

"Back where we used to live," Kiara grinned, "I was unbeatable. There is untamed, hidden power here."

Skipper caught on to their teasing. He looked back and forth between them. "I accept the challenge."

Skipper taught them the rules, but other than the set up and strangely uneven odds, the gameplay was not so very different from Backlobash and Kiara caught on quick.

Skipper took his favorite side of the cacharro and the two surged into war, seemingly matched in a battle of wits. As is the case with such a game, if the players are especially competitive and evenly matched, the matches can last for hours even. Likewise, with a deplorable excess in both, the match found itself dragging before Kiara deftly scanned the board and secured her fifth and last cacharro, exacting her victory.

Skipper gaped at the board. "Incredible! You are more than just talk. A worthy opponent for sure."

"Thank you." Kiara bowed where she sat.

She played Hadyn next. Skipper whispered secret advice to him now and again, trying to help him without letting Kiara in on their plans. He put up a fight, however futilely, and in the end, lost much quicker than Skipper.

By now the whole prison was invested, Skipper relaying every move with all the skill and enthusiasm of a sportscaster. He'd announce a winner and various cheers and boos would erupt until the warden silenced them once again and they'd return to waiting at the edge of their bars with bated breath. Hadyn certainly played the least, not that he cared much, rather enjoying all the more to watch how much happiness it brought Kiara and Skipper to play.

Dinner was served by a different prison hand, a lanky young man with a glum look.

"Nice to see ya' servin' me for a change, eh, Kwat?" Skipper asked.

The man gave him a wry grin and shoved the trays under the bars.

Skipper shoveled a bite into his mouth and made a face. "Aw! Ya' know I don't like my paçoca so dry."

Kwat narrowed his eyes. "It's paçoca. It's supposed to be dry."

Skipper shrugged and Kiara tried not to giggle.

"Take it up with Mbyja." He moved on serving Hadyn and Ygary next.

Hadyn shuffled to the bars to grab his tray, but presently was busy watching his cell neighbor hastily grab up his portion of nuts and seeds and steal them off to a corner with glee.

"Aren't you gonna eat those?" He asked.

"Oh, Ygary don't eat nuts," Skipper explained. "He makes things out of 'em. But don't tell the warden. He'll say it's a 'waste o' provisions.'"

The three stared as Ygary proceeded to count his newest additions.

"Not a word," Hadyn agreed.

They continued to play, even scrounging up something for Backlobash on the stone floor. They took a note from Ygary and used their nuts and seed as the unique pieces.

The joy they created in that dark, fetid prison that night glowed with a persistent defiance against everything horrible in each of their lives. Skipper was positively giddy, having never had such nice friends to spend his birthday with. For Kiara and Hadyn the day felt a bit like Caverna, with the stone walls and all, but a good day in Caverna, a day they didn't mind remembering, one that made them think of all their friends they stayed alive for.

They tried their best to keep their voices down, but times come when laughter can't be stopped, and to attempt to stop it only causes more uncontrollable noise. The majority of the noise came from Skipper, his giggle as sweet as spring rain. Contagious and bubbly, it always made them want to laugh right along with him

"This is the best birthday I've ever had!" Skipper said, after beating Hadyn once again.

Kiara smiled. "I wish it could be different for you, Skipper."

"It's not always so bad." He made his first move on the board. "Sometimes I'm called the cat," he popped his eyebrows, "and I get to catch the mice."

They smiled uncertainly at him.

"It's actually fun!"

"Whatever you say, Cat," Hadyn teased.

"No, really!" Skipper giggled. "And even though I got a limp and stuff, I'm the only one who can catch 'em. I tumble 'n roll, chasing them all over the place. It certainly beats scrubbing the scum from the floors." He shivered. "Your move."

They played and talked until guards came to snuff out the lights and a cranky voice scratched out Skipper's name like a curse.

A fear Kiara hadn't seen all day washed his face of color for a moment. "I have to go." He packed up their trays and the Adugo board, but as he got to his feet, he regained his smile and said to both of them, "I'll *always* remember this day as a very good day. The best actually."

Hadyn smiled and Kiara said, "So will I, Skipper."

The lantern light washed his cheshire grin in blue before he left and went limping up the hall, clutching his board game close to his chest.

# Chapter Thirty Three

# FORKED TONGUE

The days began to run together like a thick sludge, sliding by in a stench of slime, Kiara's condition only continuing to fail. She scrounged up enough strength whenever Skipper came by and they continued regular rounds of Adugo and Backlobash on his breaks, putting to use the new rules and speed rounds she and Hadyn had made up during their time living in the Forbiddens.

Skipper had also taken to special antics at meal time, striding back and forth as he served the meals with all manner of foolishness, making the whole prison laugh. One day he'd decide he was a great lord, strutting so elegantly, you'd forget he had a limp, eyes closed in royal majesty. The next he might as well have up and joined a traveling circus, balancing the dinner tray on his head. It wobbled dangerously, bowls trembling, until crashing to the floor. Kiara tried to hold back her giggles as his cheeks flushed bright red and he began to pick up his mess, which wasn't much at all due to the "breakfast's" consistency of mixed cement. But when Skipper left, Kiara's smiles would fall and the world would cave in once again. She spent her days in and out of fevered delirium, stomach churning like a violent storm and head a painful minefield of confusion and fear.

Hadyn watched her nervously as she shivered and trembled despite the relatively warm temperatures of the prison. Every day that passed added another mountain of worry to his weary mind, her condition sometimes stable, though inexplicably never bettering. Quiet mumbles and whimpers slipped from her mouth as the nightmares attacked, never letting her fully rest. He had given up on pulling her out of them, fearing she needed the rest too desperately. Still, it took everything in him to not wake her every time she jolted or cried.

When she was awake, he'd ask her each time if she wanted

to talk about it. Sometimes she would, talking through the horrors and being better for it. But it didn't stop them from coming.

Deorc came at exactly the same time every morning, always as decent as ever, but evidence of his patience running out began to show. A subtle rage was growing harder for him to swallow back down like a monster on a leash, and every refusal they gave him only fed it, made it stronger, until the beast was in danger of becoming the master. Likewise, Kiara only found it harder to remember exactly why they even fought. She'd have given in by now if not for Hadyn by her side, his gentle encouragements constant reminders that giving up would gain absolutely nothing. But even he (though he tried not to show it) had a hard time making sense of it all, as time continued to pass and they remained stuck.

The truest hope believes and stands firm without an expiration, but as Kiara steadily worsened and he worried about how much longer she could last here, he realized that even his hope had its limits. The very things he had developed that hope to overcome gained a hold over him once again— anger and confusion (both things he had stuffed away in a corner and never wanted to see again) snuck into their old places of power, becoming more constant companions than they had been in a long time.

Confusion muddled his head, making him question everything he once told Kiara as truth. If he had been right in thinking they should fight, why did it feel so wrong? He didn't feel valiant or brave. He didn't even feel like fighting.

*God must be so far away,* he thought, rationalizing that if He was as kind as people said, clearly He couldn't see them, busy with other things. Or maybe this was a punishment. But why Kiara? Was it his fault that she was stuck here?

Anger told him he didn't like the God that this prison had led him to see. Just like the souls He would one day turn away, He left them in this prison because he wanted to, maybe not seeing the benefits of setting them free, or maybe not finding them worth the effort.

He crossed his arms and his chains drug across the stone. He couldn't move anywhere without that grating, raking sound. The sound of imprisonment, locked down by heavy chains, cutting into their wrists, taunting them with just enough links to walk about their cells, but never to leave, even if the cell door *was* open.

"Hangin' in there, Kiara?" Skipper asked, when he brought around their breakfast, by now very much aware of Kiara's failing health.

"Just." Kiara gave him a smile she saved especially for him.

"You oughta to get out of here. You . . ." Words failed him. "I'm afraid . . . you could die here."

"Nonsense." She tried to be brave for him. "Don't you worry about that."

"Don't worry? You keep getting worse!"

"I know . . ." her hopelessness leaked through her mask. Faking a smile, she said, "That's not a pleasant thing to talk about. It's not like the Skipper I know to want to talk about such things. You always know how to make a bad situation better."

Skipper looked down. "Not today."

"Sure you do, Skip," Hadyn countered, the nickname having fallen into place sometime after his birthday.

*I thought you didn't like nicknames,* Kiara had said and Hadyn answered, *Okay so I like some, just not most,* which got a smile from her that he seldom saw of late.

"Tell us one of your fantastic stories."

"Yeah!" Kiara forced down a mouthful of sludge. "I always enjoy that."

"But I can't!" He cried. "I don't have any more stories!"

"Well, I don't mind if you tell one again."

"What's the point?" He hung his head. "They's all lies anyway."

"What?"

"I make 'em up, okay? Not a lick of 'em is true."

Kiara's smile sobered. It wasn't like they believed he had really been chased by a jaguar while out digging for tubers for Mbyja's stew or hung from his toes by monkeys, but his frustrated honesty still broke her heart.

"I hardly leave this prison." Skipper sniffed and swiped a tear off his dirty face.

A voice bellowed his name, and Skipper had to swallow down his tears and emotions, popping to his feet.

"Hey," Kiara called softly, "I don't care if they're made up. Your stories make me smile. You make me smile, okay, Skip?"

His lips trembled with fragile joy and he nodded before locking the door yet again.

Kiara had a tangled up sort of ache in her heart. So much heartbreak, the world, colorful as it was, was ripe with it, Bartholomew said it himself. And leaving Caverna did nothing to escape it.

She barely noticed Ygary beckoning Hadyn over to the other side of his cell and handing him something through the bars.

"For Kiara?" she heard Hadyn ask and saw Ygary nod vigorously.

Hadyn came back with a sample of the fine craftsmanship of their neighbor, a seed and nut shell necklace, draping through his fingers. "Ygary says this one's for you."

Kiara looked at the simple necklace, feeling both honored and unworthy. Just past Hadyn she could see Ygary clutching the bars, big eyes twinkling with expectation. Reaching out, she took the gift and slid it over her filthy curls, possibly feeling more royal than she ever had.

"Thank you," she said and Ygary flew to his feet dancing around his prison cell.

Kiara sat back against the wall, finding it hard to maintain her smile. She wasn't helping him or Skipper while she rotted in this cell, not one bit, just another thing making her question why they were even fighting. It did no one (including themselves) any good and after waking up from yet another ghastly dream that afternoon, whatever bit of the tunnel walls she yet struggled to hold up, finally fell, burying her in the rubble.

"Hey, it's just another dream," Hadyn reassured, reaching through the bars and taking her hand in his. "I'm here."

She held limply to him, staring straight ahead, positively numb. There was no strength left in her hands.

"Do you want to talk about it?" he asked.

She bit her lip, expression twisting in anguish, and shook her head. A single tear slipped down her cheek before she finally spoke.

"I can't do this anymore." She turned to him, letting her words hang there for a moment, adding to the stench-filled air. "I don't know what you think we're fighting for. Hadyn, the whole reason we're here is because we're trying to get to my mother. We're never going to get to her while we're trapped here. Why? Why are you holding on to what's not there?"

Now *he* stared ahead, lips drawn in silence.

Kiara slipped her hand free and crossed her arms, sitting back against the wall. "Well, I can't. And I can't have you looking at me like I've given up."

Finally, he faced her, his eyes staring out from his dirty face, glossy and empty. "I know."

"You-you do?"

"Yes."

She held his gaze, again shocked he agreed with her, for once, unsure if she wanted him to. What she found in his eyes shook her core even more than his words. Because for the first time, she found nothing. That constant, unwavering hope, the fiery surety, the even stability . . . all evaporated without a trace.

Her feelings wriggled themselves into countless knots. She was certain something would change now, as was desperately needed, and at the same time she felt sick inside. Hadyn, who had been the rock, the unwavering one, now broken, defeated.

Her eyes welled and stung as she whispered, "So what do we do?"

Hadyn dropped his gaze, unable to look in her sad eyes. "Tell him . . . tell him that we'll do it."

Kiara knew that when Deorc came the next day, she would have a different answer for him, but that didn't make her feel any better, somehow finding new, maybe unending depths to this pit she didn't know if she could ever climb back out of.

Per routine, ever since his second visit at least, he walked his crooked grin up to the bars a little before noon. Hadyn tried to stir Kiara awake when he saw him coming, a task steadily increasing in its difficulty.

Deorc strode down the corridor alone. Posture neat as ever, he pivoted to face their cells. "Hello, little lambs."

"Deorc, she needs help," Hadyn pleaded

He turned his mouth down in thought. "Hhmm, I'm almost certain that all the citizens of Tykaraijre and guests, for that matter, have full access to all manner of medicines and remedies," he fixed him with a dark gaze and sneered, "but not prisoners."

Hadyn sighed and scowled at the stone floor. The vines in his neck bulged and his fists grew ever tighter.

"Of course, you can change that with one simple decision."

"About that . . ." he began, but with the way Deorc's eyes lit up, Hadyn didn't know if he could go through with it. "We . . ."

Defeated.

The word didn't bring anger but the worst feeling Hadyn had ever felt, a horrible dragging down of his soul and shrinking of himself.

Deorc leaned closer. "Yes?"

"We—"

"No," Kiara said, pulling herself out of a dream, for once not a hint of terror coursing through her blood. She struggled to remember much at all, except those kind blue eyes, Bartholomew's eyes. She couldn't recall a word he said, only the love. Such a great love.

In the dream she was enveloped in it, like bathing in warm, bright light.

"I won't," she finished firmly.

Deorc closed his eyes and let out a measured breath. "You are trying me."

"Jesus loves me. He loves you."

His eyes flashed back open, rage blazing within.

"He loves us all. And all He wants is for us to love him back," Kiara continued, a strength rising up in her she couldn't have dreamed of conjuring on her own. She tried to speak as Bartholomew had, trying to remember what he wanted them to know. "He will not leave us here. Because He doesn't do that. He never ever leaves and He doesn't forsake."

"You wretched girl!" Deorc finally exploded.

Kiara jumped and fell silent, scared half to death.

"Do not speak to me about the Christ or His Heavenly Father." He glared at them a moment as he reeled in his temper. "Do you really believe that you could ever be loved or are capable of loving? You see, Kiara, that is the glory of the Beast. He loves what we truly are. Maybe not us ourselves, but he loves our deeds. Our deeds that come from the truest parts of us. We are born to be evil. Why fight it? The Beast beckons us, invites us to do the things that please us. Why try to become something you're not? When that something is so hard to attain, why grasp for it? Where is the reward in being 'good?' There is something much better and far, far easier to attain. But you only need to close your eyes, for it is already inside of you."

"Quiet!" The cry burst from her. "I won't believe you!" Then she added meekly, looking with such horrible sorrow on the man she once had thought of as kind. "I couldn't see it before. I don't know why. But your eyes are just like my father's. At times the darkness didn't seem so deep, and yet, I have also seen them in the head of a snake. Nothing but lies comes from the forked tongue behind those lips."

"Oh, but, little lamb," his mouth twisted into a smile, "I would never tell you an untruth. You see, I may not want you to see the Light, but rather want to give you a sort of *enlightenment* so that you may see in the dark. Your soul is black as well as mine." He grabbed onto the bars of her cell. "You are pathetic and weak in the state that you are, thinking you must be saved. Rubbish! Save yourself, before you have to realize no one else will! Let your anger grow and you'll gain your strength. You see, we are not unalike, you and I. Living in shadows, believing we're as weak as everyone makes us feel, but it doesn't have to be this way. You can give in to the anger and hate I know you have."

Kiara retreated inwards, drawing her knees up to her chest. He frowned down on her. "Perhaps not. Maybe you're just as hopeless and wretched as you appear."

"Enough!" Hadyn screamed. "Is there no end to your madness?"

Deorc smiled as he turned to him. "And you. Your hands are as dirty as *any* of the souls in this prison. Are they not?"

Kiara watched helplessly as Hadyn's protective fire doused and his eyes dropped to the ground.

"I don't know what it is, but you are something. A thief maybe?" Deorc paused, reading him like a scrap paper note. "No. It could be so, but the guilt in your eyes tells me that there is also something else. Something much more . . . glaring." He smiled devilishly. "My, if I didn't know any better, I'd bet the claim of Tykaraijre it was murder."

Hadyn's head fell lower.

Deorc clicked his tongue. "So very young to already have blood on your hands." His face slanted with counterfeit sorrow.

Kiara didn't believe him, she couldn't. "Hadyn?" she could barely say.

He managed to look at her, his eyes brimming with tears.

"What is he saying?"

"I didn't kill anybody!" He shouted, making her jump.

"And I almost trust that," Deorc frowned. "But believe me, Kiara, he is capable of it."

"No. Hadyn wouldn't do something like that."

"Oh!" He chuckled madly. "You really are pathetic, aren't you? Everybody has a dark side, Kiara, even you. Face it or sooner than later you will be made to. You sicken me, both of you. Even if there was a God who loved, do you really think he would love *you?* Someday you'll realize it, maybe the same day you finally face up with the rancorous truth that you can never do anything good."

As Kiara looked up at him, he could see he had struck a chord. "Oh. Or maybe you already have. You already understand the extent to your inadequacy. Well, let me tell you now, you will never be enough. No matter how hard you try. No matter how many times you fall to your knees in bitter shame. No matter how much good you scrounge the abysmal floor of life for yourself to accomplish. It will. Never. Be. ENOUGH!" His voice broke and it was a shadow of a shout, if at all, much more like a cry, a whimper of a lost child tossed into the dark in deliberate hate. His eyes had grown misty, but whatever emotion had broken loose, he shook away in an instant.

Kiara's lower lip began to tremble. She buried her face, trying to hide the tears.

Deorc backed away from the bars, still not quite the same man. "I just hope that when you come to, you remember to thank me."

"Will you just stop?" Hadyn begged. "Leave her alone." Deorc gave a snort, but Hadyn held his glare, knife for knife. "Leave."

Finally, he obliged, this departure devoid of the flashing grins and bows.

Kiara couldn't stop the tears. They flooded out like a storm. Hadn't she done the right thing? Why was she repaid this way? With hate. She didn't feel *any* love right now. In fact, it wasn't difficult for her to believe that love didn't exist. Deorc's words had echoed her confusions and fears too closely. Had she really believed she could be loved or had she just faked it like everything else, just believing what she was told because she didn't know any better?

Hot tears of anger and pain streamed down her face. She was right back in that pit, shivering alone and defenseless. Physically she had walked so far from the only person who could put her there, and yet she could hear his words as if he whispered them in her ear.

*Nothing . . .*

*You are nothing.*

At his departure, Deorc took with him whatever pride or fight she had left, leaving her in that pit with only her fears and hate. She knew this place well, its stench, its chill. All she had to do was curl up in a ball as it welcomed her like a lost pup, gathering her up in boney, cold fingers.

Hadyn hated to watch her crumble. He wanted to wrap his arms around her, at least then they'd be in the pit together, but unpermitting bars lay between them in more ways than one, almost certain she wouldn't accept the gesture.

He was dirty. Somehow she had made him forget that . . . for a time. But his stains showed plain as the grime on his hands and face. He didn't blame her if she was afraid of him. Yet, he couldn't just sit by, he had to at least try to convince she wasn't alone.

"Kiara, I'm sorry." He reached his hand through the bars to take hers, but she drew away. Even though it matched his every expectation, it still felt like a knife.

"Why is He leaving us here?" she sobbed into her arms.

Hadyn couldn't answer. It all felt like his fault. He was the one who had led her to trust in something that he couldn't even think about anymore without feeling overwhelming anger.

A loud boom shook the heavens and rolled across the sky. A moment later, the soft pitter-patter of rain began a steady rhythm. Kiara hardly noticed over the sound of her own tears, but Hadyn stood to try and see out the window. Water droplets fell in sheets past the bars.

"Kiara, look," Hadyn said quietly, and she lifted her head, "the sky's crying too."

The memory of their conversation in the Forbiddens made her want to smile through her tears, but she only cried harder. Those were simpler moments when conversations started just for the sake of talking. Nonsense turned into deep, ruminative contemplations as easy as breathing. And she had called it boredom.

Hadyn's face fell as he watched her rebury her tears, crawling deeper into that pit, her shoulders shaking violently. No longer able to hold his own tears back, he sat back against the stone and let them fall. An unbearable helplessness weighed on him, threatening to crush him. He was reminded of times when he was too young, too small to fight back, and even though he had grown up, he still felt small.

The rain poured harder and began to drip down the side of the wall from the window, trickling onto his back. Hadyn looked up and sighed. Soon he'd be sitting in a puddle. He reluctantly shuffled further away from the window and Kiara. Her heart-wrenching, sorrow-drenched sobs continued as steady as the rain.

Hadyn hated Deorc for making her feel this way. He hated himself for not protecting her from his words. He couldn't believe the damage Deorc had caused. In minutes he had broken her down to pieces as easily as glass, and he didn't even lay a finger on her. And unless he was going to lie to himself, Hadyn had to acknowledge *his* own shattered pieces, scattered about his very own pit. Hadn't he been the one telling her to fight? Now all he wanted to do was give in.

As Kiara tears only continued without an end, Hadyn's didn't last long, burning up in a searing anger he hadn't felt in so long. And he hated it.

# Chapter Thirty Four

# THE ONLY THING I HAVE LEFT

A new moon over the rainforest proved to be even darker than night. If not for the sounds and scents in the night air, the dreaded black might as well have been Caverna's miles thick, stone walls, trapping Kiara in, suffocating her.

The rope binding her cut painfully into the blistered scars already gouged into her wrists by the manacles. It pulled her along, running into the dark ahead. She followed blindly, like a lamb led to slaughter.

That morning, they almost expected Deorc not to show, but his madness wouldn't allow for even one lapse in persistency, all too thrilled to finally hear the glorious news of their acquiescence. Ever since then, Kiara couldn't shake a now commonplace, sickening feeling. It started in the pit of her stomach and then moved out from there, successfully numbing every nerve in her body.

In the distance, that all too familiar, azure light filtered through the forest. Her heartbeat quickened in a flash. What once intrigued her, had become a source of such horrible dread. Fronds and branches crawled out of the darkness the closer she treaded, reflecting the faint glows.

Kiara wondered if Hadyn was near . . . if she even wanted him to be, but his name wouldn't come to her mouth if she tried, her throat tight with fear.

They had taken him first. No words, no explanations. They just came, unlocked his chains, forced him to his feet, and drug him out of the prison. Kiara herself said nothing when he left. She watched until her isolation was complete. Before long, they came to take her too. Feet stumbling, she didn't fight or struggle, only following where the strangers led her.

The rope on her wrists went unexpectedly slack. Kiara

paused briefly, hesitantly stepping into that inexplicable clearing, empty now save for the few scattered trees, all the same species, like sacred tenders of the waste ground. She only had to close her eyes to imagine the crowds once gathered here, all celebrating something she had struggled to wash from her mind, but now a haze blanketed the memory. What were they celebrating? A death? A pang in her heart told her it was more than that, but the fog remained stubborn.

She took tentative steps over the bare ground, and stood directionless before the inferno of the encompassing pit, the blue flames placid now despite their size. They licked the air like serpents' tongues, sampling for their prey, the deceitful fire that led her here, the same fire that destroyed the only truly kind person in Tykaraijre. She shivered from a violent cold before its heatless light. Her knees trembled and she felt weak enough to collapse.

She knew this was wrong, she always had. She wanted nothing more than to escape this, but her weakness had eaten up her fight. In her frailty, she saw no other choice.

Struggling to find the strength to lift her head, she thought she caught sight of open sky above. The pollution from the fire's light poisoned the view. Squinting, she was determined to see past the blue haze. Pin pricks of light, not quite as strong as a glow, seemed more like specks of chalk on a blackboard dotting the expanse. But they had to be stars. She needed to believe this.

A tear slipped down her cheek as she thought of the distant light, just a memory of the hope she used to have.

Pounding drums sent a new shockwave of fear through her senses, hidden drums yet inside the edge of the forest. Something leaped out from behind the fire, shaped like a man, but horribly hunched and gaunt, his body painted with the design of a skeleton. The bones glowed with the unique property of the matia paint against his dark skin. Feathers stuck up wildly from his head as he jumped about like a possessed animal. His sunken eyes, paired with a smile grotesquely exaggerated by the reflective paint, locked her in a hungry leer.

Fear pumped Kiara's limbs with a dose of energy and she tried to make a run for it, but a jerking stop pinned her back to the ground. Her wrists screamed with searing pain, the ropes digging a new depth in her cuts. She flicked her eyes across the ground, following the rope to where it ended in a knot on one of the sturdier trees. She pulled and fought against her bonds, only causing herself more pain. All the while the wicked bone creature leapt ever closer. She whimpered in a panic, scrambling like a deer with two broken legs, and finally just curled into a ball. But as he came nearly close enough to touch her, the skeleton man hopped back as quickly as he approached. Paint flashing, he made his way around the pit again. It was just a dance . . .

Kiara sat up straighter, shaking terribly all over when, performing his signature move, Deorc appeared out of nowhere at all.

"Ah, Kiara. What is this? Have you finally come to your senses?"

She stared at him from her place on the ground.

He frowned. "You choose silence. It does you no good." With a snap of his fingers, figures jumped into the clearing. "Get her bonds, bring her closer."

They created a ring around the edge of the tree line, and started a bouncing dance, complete with its own hungry chant. Some had drums, beating on them with a malice-filled passion. One of them stepped out from the chain or, rather, was kicked out. He stumbled forward, then straightened as he came toward her. He grabbed her ropes as he was told, but he didn't seem like the rest. He raised his eyes from the ground to her face. Dolefully sad, something in them told of a gentle kindness the others lacked.

He shook his head slowly, deliberately, but Kiara only stared back in confusion. Was he actually asking her not to do this? When she said nothing, he heaved a sigh and led her toward the pit, leaving her there with Deorc and rejoining the line.

Kiara watched him meld with the others and turned to Deorc, his head and hands raised, his eyes closed. Klah had come to his side, staring straight forward maskless.

Finally, Deorc dropped his arms and the chanting ceased in an instant.

His mouth curled into a grin. "Kiara," he said, but it almost sounded as if there was another speaking with him, imbuing his voice with amplitude and power. Kiara looked at Klah, but his lips remained sealed. Other voice was thin and grating, with underlying malice that could boil blood and turn it to ice at the same time.

"You have come to pledge yourself to the Beast," he blathered on. "You have come before the great flames to die as the rest of us have, internally and eternally." Deorc came closer now and spoke much more like himself. "Kiara, you once asked me how the Dalmatia is made. Now, as you are becoming one of us, I will tell you. Three ingredients of six— six feathers of the hyacinth macaw, six drops of blood, and six oaths to the Beast. But the blood must be replaced every now and then."

# FORSAKEN

Klah came and grabbed her bound wrists.

Kiara struggled, eyes growing wide, but Deorc only continued evenly. "You see, the fire needs to feed. We must find new flesh for the flames to devour, to satiate their hunger. Your internal death is perfect for this. Fresh meat for our Beast."

Klah pulled her closer to the fire, drawing an ornate dagger from his belt, the blade cruelly jagged and the hilt ending in the hideous mug of the Beast. Kiara pulled against him, eyes flaring with panic.

"Please," Deorc's eyes struggled with some form of empathy as if he fought to fully reconcile himself to this, "don't struggle. You'll only make it worse for yourself."

Kiara looked at him with disbelief. Was he really pretending as if he cared?

Klah drug her along and the flames closest to her, seemed to take the form of vague hands right before her eyes. Klah let go and Deorc jumped a step back as the flames leapt out and seized her wrists in an unshakable vice. Kiara screamed in pain from the ice cold burn.

Taking up the dagger, the shaman sliced a cut into the flesh of Kiara's right palm. She yelped and pulled away to no avail. Deorc turned away as Klah forced her hand into a fist. Kiara watched in such agonizing pain as five drops of blood dripped into the pit. One by one they went, but the last hung on, clinging to the side of her palm like it would rust there. However, gravity proved more immediately inevitable than evaporation or any other work of physics. Giving into the pull, the drop fell away, finishing that which should have never begun.

All went dark. Not a light remained save for the coals in the pit. Kiara's breath came unsteady and fast like a rabbit with nowhere to run.

Out of the dark came an unnerving whisper. "You are now the Beast's . . ."

Ghostly, satisfied chuckles rolled about the clearing, but grew quieter with time, as if departing. Kiara crashed to her knees. Her bitter tears dripping off her cheeks glowed blue in the feeble light cast from the embers.

"What have I done?" she whispered.

She had lived most of her life with some form of loneliness, cried herself to sleep because of the violence of the ache, but never in years had she felt so unmitigatedly alone. No arms could hold her dirty, soulless husk now.

Empty.

There was nothing left but a shell. Like a conch, each spiral led her to even more cramped darkness and a weary heaviness that wouldn't let her get up.

She wondered if she'd be left here to die. It was just so quiet. Had they really all left?

Noises in the woods made her flinch. Branches and sticks cracked in the wake of someone's urgent flight through the forest and into the clearing. "Kiara! Kiara, where are you?"

She tried to yell, but only squeaked. He found her anyway, crumpled on the ground.

Hadyn rushed to her side. "Oh no, please . . . Come on, Kiara, get up."

She collapsed against him shivering worrisomely.

"Why don't you just leave me?" Her voice was so thin, he barely heard her.

"No . . ." He shook his head, tears stinging his eyes. "No, Kiara, I won't do that."

She lay limp in his arms, because she had no strength to do otherwise. "I would . . . I'm dying anyway."

"No, come on! Don't talk like that! We have to get out of here; I hardly got away with my life. They'll be coming soon." He bit his cheek as she didn't make a word of reply. "Hey, you're going to be okay. We just have to get you out of here, Kiara. We're going to finish this together, we're going to find your mom." His voice broke as he pulled her closer, unsure if she even remained conscious enough to hear him. "Please don't give up . . . There's nothing in it. I'm not going to leave you."

"Trying to skip out on the rest of the deal, are you?" A voice ghosted out of the forest. Deorc came striding back to them with a blue lantern and backup in toe. He walked up to them and shined the light on Haydn's face. "You will finish your part."

Seeing that Kiara couldn't walk, Hadyn picked her up. "Finish? Can't you see she's dying!" Angry tears leaked from his eyes. "Won't you do something!" he pleaded.

Deorc's eyes flashed with some kind of twisted anguish as he considered her limp body, almost shocked, as if he actually hadn't noticed the extent of what she had endured.

He blinked as if fighting his own vision. "That was not part of our agreement."

Hadyn just stared at him as he watched the man convince himself back into apathy.

"You will sleep in the prison tonight and in the morning, fulfill your debt." Deorc called to those he had brought with him.

"Bring them back to the village and lock them up."

Hadyn carried Kiara back under the watchful eyes of their silent escorts. When they arrived at the prison hold, he gently let her down on the thin mat that they called a bed.

Just in time for the nightly tolling of the prison bars, the warden strode up the hall with his fat stick. The concussive rhythm pulled Kiara halfway out of her sleep and she saw Hadyn turning to go to his cell. Reaching out, she grabbed his right hand, the one that took the gouge, still just barely bleeding. Her eyes filled with tears and found his. He tried to smile and be brave for her, but she knew he felt that emptiness, that shriveled husk of an identity.

She thought she wanted this. She had forced her way, fighting with every fiber, to get this, this thing she assumed she knew. She had thought herself trapped back in Caverna, even owned, but now she realized, she had not begun to know what imprisonment meant, what it felt like to be enchained.

But captivity comes in many different forms, not one more horrible than another, and shackles only really lock when the prisoner succumbs to their chains, when they define themselves as kept, whether by another or their own vices. It doesn't take much to cage a bird that has lost the will to be free. And yet, as captivity entraps its fetters on countless wrists in so many different ways, there remains only one version of true liberty, one way to its freedom.

Finally, Kiara let go and rolled onto her side. Back in their respective cells, two unmerciful bangs of the doors, and one last toll as the guard finished his rounds announced them captives once more.

The morning brought fresh throbbing pain to the inflamed lining of her skull as Kiara awoke to the desperate sound of Hadyn pleading with Deorc.

"She's too weak. Just let me go alone. Why does it have to be both of us?"

"I fear you will never understand the true ways of the beast," Deorc replied, "ignorant fool that you are."

Hadyn's chains drug across the ground as he turned away with a bitter huff. "No. You don't have a reason, except that you enjoy watching others suffer." He narrowed his eyes. "What ever happened to you?"

Deorc stared at him in silence, doing his best to remain expressionless, but registering the slightest twinge of pain. Hadyn had hit a nerve. Surprised it was even possible, Hadyn stared at him in a way he never had. He had seen that look leaking through too many times now, to not notice the tortured parts Deorc kept caged. For the first time, he looked at him like a victim. For the first time, he looked on him with pity.

"What . . . *did* happen to you?"

Deorc swallowed and it looked difficult. But he must have swallowed down his emotions too, regaining his stolid state of detached superiority as quickly as he could. "I will not trifle myself with you." He opened both their cell doors. "Now. Finish our deal."

One of the guards unlocked his manacles and they clattered to the ground. Hadyn rubbed his raw wrists. Whatever pity had grown up inside, boiled alive in a raging anger simmering beneath the surface. His hands clenched into fists and he slowly raised his eyes from his scars to the man now leering at him from a safe distance. A dangerous fire smoldered in Hadyn's gaze. He stepped out of the cell, never breaking his glare. Deorc's smile melted and his foot slipped backward.

Hadyn couldn't be sure what he would have done, if not for the many guards keeping watch. Everything looked so warped, like he could hurt him and Hadyn himself wouldn't feel an ounce of remorse. His ears burned with the temptation of knocking him to the ground, guards as witnesses or not. But one thing saved him— simply the fact he had more important things to worry about. With some difficulty, he let it go. Walking into Kiara's cell, he bent down and shook her shoulder. "Hey," he said, "it's time to go."

"I'm awake," she mumbled.

Hadyn helped her to her feet.

"I can stand on my own," Kiara huffed.

Hadyn obliged, letting her try. Her legs trembled dangerously, her stubbornness almost planting her face down on the floor, but Hadyn caught her just in time.

"Whoa, you're okay," he reassured. "Here, put your arm around me."

Her head swam in a spinning sea, pounding with every turn. She could hear her heartbeat in her ears. Kiara squeezed her eyes shut as she caught her breath. "I'm ready," she said. "Let's go."

Hadyn helped her up the stairs and out of the bunker-like prison. With her free hand Kiara shielded her eyes. The light cut like daggers to the back of her brain. For a moment, she could only see white. She could only feel white, white hot pain. Her stomach lurched.

"Hold on." She let go of Hadyn, crouched behind the nearest

tree, and emptied what little food she still tried to sustain herself with.

Hadyn winced and went to help her back up. "You alright?"

She swallowed with a gasp and gave him only one look for her answer.

"Right . . . Let's just take it slow. We have all day to get there."

Four native men, barrel-chested and built with the strength to keep people in line, walked with them. They didn't offer them any help, only there to ensure Hadyn and Kiara didn't act on any bright ideas. Their sentries, one at each corner, led them through the village to a thin path cutting its way through the jungle.

On their way through Tykaraijre, they had seemed to accumulate quite the crowd, each one gathered to see Hadyn and Kiara off on their last step in becoming wholly devoted to the beast.

Dead quiet, the only sound they made came from their shuffling feet. Kiara caught glances from them between the guards. Some actually sported delighted grins, while others almost looked to have pity in their eyes. Each face, though different, heralded dark presage of the things awaiting them.

Kiara leaned close to Hadyn. "What are we walking into?"

"I don't know." he said, also noticing the murky soup of expressions.

She bit her lip. "That's what worries me."

Before their guards pushed them into the jungle, Kiara caught one last look, perhaps more conflicted than all the rest combined. Darcy looked like she wanted to be happy to be rid of them, but the grin couldn't quite take full possession of her face. Her expression changed, further softening with pain. Kiara realized that past her smug exterior, there was a heart in agonizing turmoil, like the crocodile that cries tears as it rips its prey in two.

She shuddered as the forest walled them in. "What are we walking into?"

# Chapter Thirty Five

# RIGHT BACK AT THE BEGINNING

Wherever they were going, Kiara couldn't recall much of the trek. Trees, sights and sounds slinked by in a green fog. She couldn't walk without Hadyn's help, feeling as though she drifted in and out of consciousness. The buzz of insect wings sounded like they were inside her head. Patches of black constantly formed and disappeared in her vision. She didn't even notice Hadyn's anxious glances at her every few seconds.

A darkness grew in the understory as heavy clouds rolled in and as they covered the sun, so the birds fell silent.

"Where are you taking us?" Hadyn finally broke the wordless quiet.

The guards didn't flinch, their gazes trained ahead of them. Hadyn eyed them up one by one, realizing he had never heard a word out of any of them. He wondered if they could even talk if they wanted to. He imagined the guards of the village lining up to have their tongues cut out for some sort of sick initiation, further numbing them to pain and feelings. He shivered and tried to shake the thought out of his mind.

Kiara's feet stumbled with fatigue. She tried to speak up, but her mouth and throat had dried to a useless desert.

"We have to stop," Hadyn said, not even expecting them to slow. "She needs to rest." To his surprise, one of the men turned to him, seemingly prepared to listen. "Please."

The guard gestured for the others to take a break. Hadyn watched the others scowl at the guard, prepared to scalp him alive, but they complied anyway.

Hadyn lowered Kiara to the ground, propping her up against a tree along the path. She drew her arms around herself, shivering. He looked at her pale face and dark puffy lids. Heaving a sigh, he slid down next to her.

Hadyn held his head in his hands, such uncontrollable anger twitching beneath the surface, begging to be released on all those seemingly blind to their own madness. Could they really not see that she was dying? Had they any hearts, or had those been cut out too? It was bad enough with Deorc, but what reason did these men have not to let them go? His hands clenched to fists and even with his eyes shut, he saw the fire of his rage.

A gentle tap on his arm and Hadyn lifted his head, blinking at the tan-skinned hand near his face. The guard, the same one who had called for the rest, squatted before them, offering his own water skin. Hadyn nudged Kiara and her eyes fluttered open to the kind face before her. A weak smile graced her face, and she accepted the water.

The red anger faded to nothing in an instant and suddenly things weren't so black and white. The men had orders and to disobey them meant consequences— consequences that weren't theirs to pay.

"Thank you," Hadyn said.

The guard nodded and stepped back in line with the others.

Hadyn shook his head. "I wish we had just run when we had a chance, run from all this." He ground his teeth. "I hate what being here has brought out in me! . . . It's like I'm right back at the be-ginning."

The water brought Kiara some relief and a little strength back to her voice. "And what's that?" she croaked, "the be-ginning?"

For a moment he kept silent chucking twigs he picked off the ground. She waited.

"Didn't you hear Deorc?" He sighed. "The same blood of the man who led his wife and little girl to their deaths is in my veins. The same rage clenches my hands into fists in an instant."

"But you're not—"

"No, Kiara . . . you don't know. It was years ago." He paused, blinking away the hot tears stinging his eyes. "I should have told you."

"Hey, it's—"

"No! You should know what I've done . . . what I *am*."

Again she waited.

"I was twelve maybe. On my way back to the orphanage after a gem delivery for the clansmen and there was this other boy, bigger than me, older than me, but still just a boy. He had cornered a girl in one of Terminal Avenue's alleys. Probably just wanted whatever little argents she had on her. I could have just let it be, people get robbed on Terminal Avenue all the time, but he wouldn't let her be, calling her things, pulling at her hair, making some sick game out of it.

"I don't know why, but I just couldn't, I couldn't look away. I called out to him, told him to leave her alone. He ignored me, so I tried again, but it was already too late for me. The sort of anger, the violence that had risen up, had already taken its hold on me. And that's when he came at me.

"I guess I was scared," he shrugged, "but not nearly enough. My rage was stronger than anything he had.

"I attacked him . . ." He bit his lip as his emotions threatened to drown him. "I can still hear her voice in my head, crying, 'Stop! Stop! You'll kill him!' " Hadyn's own voice broke. "But I wouldn't . . . I didn't want to. Kiara, I would've killed him if it weren't for the girl running and screaming for the guards. And when they came and I was pulled away, I saw what I had done. I saw the face of the girl I thought I was protecting. Horrified. Disgusted. I saw the beaten body that had once been an arrogant boy. And I saw my hands for what they were. Bloodied. Violent weapons. Not to be trusted. *I* was not to be trusted." He shoved back the sadness with an angry sniff. "The orphanage had a harsh way of punishing boys with what they called 'devils inside them.' I was sentenced to a week in the black room. A place of solitude, darkness and meager food rations. Each day felt like an eternity, but I had a lot of time to think. I thought about almost everything. My mind wouldn't let me be . . ." He stared off, recalling those black days. "I had never been one to ask others for help, but in there, I learned to rely on myself even more. That . . . *That* is why I don't bother with trust. In the end people will always take care of themselves first, you might as well do the same.

"I felt like a monster in that place, sentenced to a dark cage, but it's okay because in that same cage, I learned I'm not the monster, I'm not sure if anyone is. But in there, for the first time, I became well acquainted with the one living inside me. Just like my father. I learned pretty fast, I'd never be rid of it. I just have to keep it caged. I can't let it out, can't let myself become like him. So I strengthened the bars with thicker metal everyday, ensuring its captivity.

"In that room, with only myself to talk to, I decided to never choose violence again."

Kiara didn't have the strength to say all the things that she wanted to, her heart bleeding with a storm of feelings, so she just laid her head on his shoulder.

Hadyn stiffened for a moment, surprised at the selfless gesture. He expected her to move away if she had the strength, look at him with the disgust he deserved. Instead, not only did she stay, she understood.

He felt every single one of his expectations with all their bottled up fears release themselves in one sigh. He knew in his heart, deserving of it or not, this was what a real friend looked like. After all his worry, she didn't care about what he had done before, it didn't change the way she thought about him, and the power in that sent his mind spinning, wondering with fragile hope if this was what real love felt like.

Without warning, the only guard to yet acknowledge them on a human level, pulled them both straight to their feet. He nodded to them.

Time for rest was over. They had to keep moving.

Just when Kiara thought they were getting close, their tiresome trudge proved longer still. She couldn't be certain of exactly how far they had walked, but stumbling and tripping over her own feet, it felt like an eternity to her.

At last, their guards halted, standing rigid at their four corners. Hadyn stumbled to a stop in the middle and searched each of their stony faces.

Kiara hardly knew they had stopped. She thought she heard the splashing of a lively stream, but could hardly even raise her eyes.

As Hadyn watched, each guard stretched out a muscular arm in unison, pointing ahead to a natural entrance in a craggy, moss-covered rock face. Hadyn followed it up from where it jutted abruptly from the ground all the way to the top. Backlit by a breach in the canopy, even with the overcast skies, the contrast of menacing shadow and burning grey made him shield his eyes. He lowered his gaze back down to the cave entrance where an even deeper shadow lay, twisted and agape like a mouth crying in pain. Hadyn drew a breath. He knew their guards meant for them to enter.

A stream bubbled out from the entrance, but it flowed white and milky and had a sour stench about it. Again, the same guard as always, set himself apart from the others. With a surprising flair of animation, he pointed to the water, then his mouth, and shook his head vigorously.

"Got it," Hadyn nodded, "don't drink the water."

The man smiled, satisfied he understood. But, as if remembering his place, he rejoined the others and swung his tree branch of an arm out to the cave entrance.

Hadyn eyed the entrance with no small amount of concern.

He turned back to the guard, but he only gave him a slow nod, though not like the others might have done. There was a certain reassurance in it, as much as if he actually said, *go on. It will be alright.*

Could he trust him? As he mentioned before, he had reasons why he didn't prefer to. But he didn't really have an option, did he?

Hadyn steeled his nerves, drinking in a measured breath, and began to lead Kiara to the cave.

All at once, Kiara caught sight of the dark entrance and a fear as old as her life on earth knifed through her veins. Her muscles stiffened and her heart pounded. "No! No, I'm not going in there." Her lip trembled as she whimpered. "They can't make me go back!"

"Hey, It's okay! It's not the same as before," Hadyn reassured. She squeezed her eyes shut and wriggled to get away, but he made her look at him. "This isn't Caverna, we get to come back out again. We don't have to stay."

She focused her fear-rounded, bloodshot eyes on his steady ones. "How can you be sure?"

"Because I'm here and I'm not gonna let you die in a cave. We're going in there and we're coming back out again."

She nodded and he shifted her arm back around his neck to better help her walk.

A single tear slipped down her nose as they passed under the shadow of the towering rock. "How did it come to this . . ." she whispered. To her knowledge, no one heard her above the rush of the milky stream, not even Hadyn, but someone did hear and He wept right along with her.

Thunder cracked the sky and the rocks answered with their own shout, the earth itself seeming to cry with indignation as if knowing the turmoil that strides about its surface sometimes so barefaced and even proud; knowing it was made for goodness, not heartache. The heaven's cracked again, the voice of the Maker mourning along with the made.

A storm was rolling in.

# Chapter Thirty Six

# THE LAIR OF BAHRAM

They sloshed into the stream as they entered, damp stone walls closing them in. The close smells, the echoes of their own breaths, felt terribly familiar, a shadow, a hazy haunting of all their years living in darkness.

Only a few paces into the cavern, the main passage turned away from the water, leading deeper underground. A rotting stench greeted them with a sting to both their eyes and noses. Kiara fought a violent urge to throw up a second time.

*One step at a time,* she told herself. *Just breathe . . . but not too deep.*

The light only dimmed the further they walked, and though they left it behind, it felt like the other way around— the light abandoning them to shadows once more. Ahead the passage yawned with a wide black mouth.

"How are we supposed to see?" Kiara whispered. "Where are we going—" Her words died with a squeak as deep, guttural laughter clawed its way up the hall, followed by a scraping of stone against stone. "Hadyn . . . there's something down here."

He didn't know how to answer, so he just held her closer.

"New fleshhh," came the barely intelligible words.

They waited, their feet glued to the ground by terror alone. A large, hunched form emerged from around a bend in the tunnel, dragging a stone club. As it lumbered toward them, Kiara and Hadyn primed their limbs to run, but apparently it knew their intentions before they had the sense to carry them out.

"Do not run," it grumbled as if gravel churned in its throat. "I'm here to guide you to your final step."

Hadyn didn't care what it said, if it came any closer he would run. But he had a feeling the sloth-like movements could be cast off like a bad habit if necessary. As if it knew its limits, it shuffled to a stop and slowly lifted its head. A scarred face obscured by long, stringy, black locks stared past them with eyes that appeared white from the damage that had been done to them.

"You're a man . . ." Kiara said, shaking from both fear and fascination.

He lulled his head to one side. "Perhaps I was once."

Though, yes, his hulking form looked more bear than human, draped in a large skin cloak, his words made her sad.

"Are you the Beast?" Kiara dared to ask and jumped as he roared with laughter.

Even as he gurgled that horrible laugh, he began marking the wall of the tunnel with the more pointed end of his club. They had failed to notice until now, the countless marks suffocating the stone, and now two more were added. Two more souls.

"No," he finally answered. "My name is Bahram. A beast?" He paused, "I've been called worse. But believe me, if you had met the Beast down here . . . you would wish for someone as merciful as me."

Kiara shivered.

"Come," he smirked, "you must now take your last step."

"What does that mean?" Hadyn snapped, any remaining patience long gone. "What could there possibly be left to do."

Bahram didn't answer. He turned to lead them down the tunnel he had come from, talking to himself in low whispers. ". . . and I saw a beast rise up out of the sea, having seven heads and ten horns, and upon his horns ten crowns, and upon his heads names of blasphemy . . .

"Then I saw a second beast, coming out of the earth. It had two horns like a lamb, but it spoke like a dragon. And he caused all, both small and great, rich and poor, free and bond, to receive the mark in their right hand or in their foreheads."

The image of it made Kiara's skin crawl, his baritone voice manifesting the dread of the scene his words painted. She looked down at her palm and the crusted gouge, a gory reminder of the previous night's horrors. Bahram's words only made her further realize what exactly she had done. They told themselves it was their only way out, but something about it felt so final, so trapping.

Torches on the wall lit the way further in, blue, flickering torches, and the eye-watering, noisome smell they noticed upon entering only grew in intensity. They passed many tunnels before Bahram stopped at one veering to the left. He grabbed a blue-topped torch off the wall and handed it to Hadyn. "This is where you must continue alone. You will know when it is finished."

Hadyn squinted down the dark tunnel wondering why it wasn't already lit. "Wait," he said. "Know when what is finished?" Answered only by silence, Hadyn peeled his eyes away from the unlit tunnel.

Bahram was gone.

"Hey!" He shouted. "Know when what is finished?"

Instead of silence, this time his own echoes replied.

"Hadyn," Kiara spoke up, "I'm frightened. I don't want to do this."

He gulped down his fear and considered the unlit passage once again. "Me either . . ."

Holding the torch high with one arm and holding her close with the other, Hadyn walked them inside. The same acrid smell as before, but ten times stronger hit them like a dizzying punch to the jaw. It slinked its way out of the passage and they could only imagine they'd meet the source of such putrid death at the very end.

Well inside, they could hear distant, erie laughter echoing up the tunnels. Bahram's laughter. Kiara's eyes wandered about the tunnel as big and alert as they'd been in days. Snot-thick slime covered every inch of the ceiling, hanging down in goopy strings.

"Ugh! What is this stuff?" Hadyn reached up to touch it and screamed out. "It burns! Kiara don't touch the slime."

She shied away from the milky strands even further than before, but Hadyn's touch had set off a chain reaction. Like a sprung trap, globs started to fall off at random. Kiara yelped in pain under the poison rain. Hadyn ran down the passage, pulling her along with him as the bacteria burned into their skin.

Two more steps.

A glimpse of horrible death.

Scattered and rotting corpses, all piled on top of one another.

Then all went dark.

The torch had gone out, but not with a sizzling douse, just slowly dimming as if the life had been strangled out of it, and suddenly it was hard to breathe. Panicking, they ran faster. Kiara collapsed first. Hadyn tried to keep her up, gasping for air, where there was none. He fought to keep consciousness, but it felt like someone had a vice on his lungs, like he was drowning in perfectly dry air.

He could feel Kiara's shirt and maybe her hair, still in his clenched fist. He held onto her. He held onto her with all he had left.

"Please, God . . ." The words tried to pass his lips, but maybe they were more just in his head.

The last thing he remembered was falling and hitting his

skull against the tunnel wall.

You're probably wondering how much more Hadyn and Kiara can endure or even if they'll have the opportunity to endure more. But it's hard to say how they would get out of this one.

A patch of bad air is as damning as any prison, shackles on your lungs rather than wrists, and without reaching oxygen fast, they'll never breathe the free air again.

I know that sometimes all we want to hear is that the bad is over, or better yet, it never has to come. But sometimes shadows fall without warning and darkness comes inevitably. In our hearts we hold onto the light that's above the clouds, wishing for a brighter day, hoping for the winds of change to blow the overcast day away. But most of the time, storm clouds stay longer than welcome, and night never ends when we want it to.

The events of this tale have battered and bruised our young protagonists, and I'm sorry, but I never said this would be a happy story. Truth is, most aren't. But every *good* story has a turning point. Every *good* story sticks with you and makes you feel something that you'll remember throughout your days, something that helps you through the storms and dark nights of your own life.

So maybe there is hope for Kiara and Hadyn. Hope for their dawn to break and for sunshine to spill onto their gardens that have now received enough rain to grow.

*Because the darkness is passing away, and the true light is already shining.*
*—1 John 2:8*

If you enjoyed this story, please consider writing a review on the sight of your choice! It's one of the greatest forms of support you could give me as a self-published author and it would make my day!

If you'd like to join the crew here on the S.S. Hideaway, what are you waiting for? Hop aboard! We'd love to have you, mate!

My website: elliemaureen.com

# Acknowledgments

Before I say anything else, I want to thank everyone who has supported me in any way during this journey. Whether you bought Forbidden and read it, or reviewed it, or even just gave me some kind words of genuine encouragement. I may not have hundreds of people backing me up, reminding me my stories are worth reading, but I have you. And your support (in whatever form) means more than you will ever know.

Also, apologies are in order, dear reader. I know this last cliffhanger was a brutal one. Sorry.

Thank you to my amazing family, my rock, my safe shore away from the chaos of this world, my home no matter where we are.

Thank you to my editor, Pam, for getting through all my lengthy sentences.

And all glory and praise to my Savior, Jesus Christ. The true gift giver of these stories, my strength, and my only reason to press on. My only reason that I *can* press on.

Without Him I am no more than unqualified, but with Him I can do all things.

# ABOUT THE AUTHOR

Hi! I'm Ellie Maureen, a Christian, YA and MG fiction author with a voracious affinity for just about every genre. I started writing at sixteen years old and never stopped. I live in Minnesota with my family and feisty kitty cat. Besides being an avid storyteller, I'm a violinist, artist, and naturalist, at my happiest when I'm out in God's natural world, especially when that involves climbing to high elevations or getting soaked in some form of water adventure.

## Find me aboard the S.S. Hideaway

elliemaureen.com

## Or follow me on Instagram!

@ellie__maureen

If you liked Forbidden consider lending a huge hand of support and writing a review!

Made in the USA
Columbia, SC
17 October 2022

69550303R00186